THE DIDYMUS CONTINGENCY

"Jeremy Robinson's novel, *The Didymus Contingency,* blends the cutting-edge science of Crichton with the religious mystery of the Left Behind series to create his own unique and bold thriller. It's a fast paced page turner like no other. Not to be missed!" **-- James Rollins, international bestselling author of *Black Order* and *Map of Bones***

"[A] thrilling and fast-paced "what if?" scenario." **– MidWest Book Review**

"What surprised me, with [Robinson's] take on the possibility of two 21st century men meeting Jesus, was the utter lack of predictability... He offers a new perspective on ripping apart the time-space continuum I am shocked no one has ever considered before now." **-- Round Table Reviews**

"[A] rollicking adventure... The story opens explosively and is laced with suspense and humor. Robinson writes quite well and is an up-and-coming author to watch... we'll hear, read, and see a great deal more from him in the future." **-- Christian Book Previews**

"...Wonderfully executed. This is a traditional thriller (think Crichton) with a focus on the penultimate Christian event (do *not* think LEFT BEHIND.) ...DIDYMUS will have you reading until you hit the final page. ...It is a super page-turner and a thought-provoker." **-- POD-DY MOUTH**

"...action filled, page turning journey through time. ...a well written, thought provoking piece of science fiction, which is also at times both touching and humorous." **-- TMC Reviews**

"...surprisingly thought-provoking and exciting.... ...a fast-paced, intense thriller in which the very essence of the time-space continuum is at risk." **-- clubreading.com**

"The twisting plotline raced ahead of my expectations and ventured in directions I had never considered. To anyone who likes action, drama, and comedy, coupled with cleverly laid out plotlines and fast-paced adventure, read this book!" **– G-Mag**

OTHER BOOKS BY JEREMY ROBINSON

FICTION

THE DIDYMUS CONTINGENCY

NON-FICTION

THE SCREENPLAY WORKBOOK

POD PEOPLE
BEATING THE PRINT ON DEMAND STIGMA

RAISING THE PAST

By

JEREMY ROBINSON

Cover design by Jeremy Robinson

BREAKNECK BOOKS
PUBLISHING COMPANY

Published by Breakneck Books (USA)
www.breakneckbooks.com

First printing, July 2006

Printed in the United States of America.

Visit Jeremy Robinson on the World Wide Web at:
www.jeremyrobinsononline.com.

For Solomon

ACKNOWLEDGEMENTS

I would like to thank the following folks, without whom I would be lost.

Before this novel saw the light of day, it was read by numerous people whose critiques and editing helped shape what it is today. They are: Hilaree Robinson, Roger Brodeur, Frank Robinson, Lauren Rossini, Frank Ferris and Karen Cooper.

Special thanks to Charity Heller Hogge at Mighty Pen Editing for swooping in and editing the book four months after it was first released. Your diligence and hard work have vastly improved the book.

Stan (AOE) and Liz Tremblay, Sarah Valeri, Brian (AOE) Dombroski, Tom Mungovan, Aaron and Stasia Brodeur and Kathy Crisp, your encouragement, prayers and friendship are always needed and welcome.

As seems to be an ongoing theme, I am honored to have had the advice of author James Rollins who was yet again kind enough to supply the blurb gracing the cover of this book. He is a phenomenal author and a great inspiration to me.

I would also like to thank the entire Robinson family (Mom, Dad, Josh, Ana, Eli, Matt, Sandi and Cole), the Brodeur family (Cathie, Rog, Jason, Katie, Alex, Aaron and Stasia), and all the Vincent families (who are too numerous to list individually) for their unceasing support and encouragement. Special thanks to my uncle, Mark Vincent, who won a contest to have his name included as a character in this book. While the character is nothing like you, I hope you enjoy your fate.

And what would I be without my wife, Hilaree? Not much of anything is my guess. I owe you so much. I hope this book makes you proud of the sacrifices you've made so I could write it. My feisty daughter, Aquila, you never cease to amaze me and continue to inspire me. And little Solomon, who has just been born and is already making us smile, you are more amazing than any story I could concoct. I love you all dearly.

"The only way God could impose peace on the world would be to robot-ize our wills and rob every human being of the power of choice. He has not chosen to do that. He has given every person a free will."
 – **John Haggai**

"And the Lord God commanded the man, 'You are free to eat from any tree in the garden; but you must not eat from the tree of knowledge of good and evil, for when you eat of it you will surely die.'"
 – **Genesis 2: 16-17 (NIV)**

"Free will, as I see it now, is an illusion, dangled in front of our noses like a carrot before a donkey. We desire it all our lives; we fight wars for it. But the will of every human being is influenced by outside forces whose motivation is selfish in nature. Free will, true free will, is as extinct as the dinosaurs."
 – **Dr. Eddy Moore - Paleontologist**

PROLOGUE

HAPHNEE

Haphnee's tongue recoiled as her mouth filled with blood. She had bit her lip with shivering teeth and popped her flesh open like cooked sausage. When she inspected the damaged area with her tongue, she was glad that the same cold shredding her skin also kept her from feeling the wound's pain.

Three layers of hand-cut fur wrapped and bound to Haphnee's body did little to speed her travel through the three foot wash of snow or stop the winter chill from cracking her leathery face. She spit blood from her mouth, staining the white snow, and pushed forward. She was spurred onward by the knowledge that her people, who had only just emerged from a life of scrounging in the wilderness, might soon face a future predetermined by others "more cunning than the smartest man and more powerful than even the mighty mammoth."

Haphnee's mind drifted to the past as she recalled the man who had originally spoken those words.

Fifteen years had passed since Haphnee met the strange visitors from another land. It was a day she remembered well . . .

HAPHNEE LAY resting on a moss-covered boulder after a long after-
noon of picking wild berries, when three men approached. In years past,
men from other tribes had tried taking her, claiming her for their own.
The first man to try escaped with a few scrapes and bruises, but the next
more persistent man lost his life. Since then, she hadn't trouble from
neighboring tribesmen. But these men were different. They hadn't
avoided her because of her reputation as a fierce and skillful warrior—it
was for her reputation that they sought her out.

The men stood taller than most and nearly two feet taller than Haphnee. But they weren't just tall; they were straight, like trees. Their arms
were long and covered in fine hair, like that of a baby. How can these
men survive the winters? she had wondered. And their clothing was
odd—it rested flat against their bodies and was thin, devoid of fur, not
suitable for even the warmest day.

But what stood out to Haphnee most was their faces—wide
eyes, pale skin, trim beards. All three smiled with bright white teeth, like
she had never seen before. They stopped ten feet from her and waited,
neither moving nor talking.

Haphnee drew her saber-jaw.

"Fear not, good woman," said the tallest man. "We are from a far
away tribe called the Aeros. My name is Artuke."

Haphnee squinted at the men. Most tribes couldn't speak the language
of neighboring tribes, but these men, whom she had never seen before,
could speak her language with the fluidity of her kinsmen. She eyed the
three men. The short one would go easiest, Haphnee thought. The thick
one would be slow and could be caught off guard before the entrails of
the first hit the ground, and the tallest one, Artuke . . . she'd just wound
him and let him limp home to show the others of his tribe that Haphnee
of the Jetush was not available.

She waited for their attack, but it never came. Artuke took a step forward and Haphnee raised her saber-jaw. But then he just sat on a rock
and motioned for his comrades to do the same. "Haphnee, we are not
here to harm you," Artuke said with a grin.

"How do you know my name?" she asked.

"We know many things."

"What do you want?"

"Your help."

During her twenty-eight years of life, Haphnee had given birth to five children, migrated thousands of miles, and battled every size and shape of animal, but never once had a man asked for her help. "No."

"There is a grave danger to your people, whom we know you love," Artuke said then paused as Haphnee tightened her grip on the saber-jaw and focused her eyes on his throat.

"Haphnee, it is apparent you do not consider the three of us a threat to you, even alone. Why would you consider us a threat to your entire people?"

After standing in silence for a moment, Haphnee let her muscles relax. She sat on a rock across from the three men and crossed her thick arms. "Tell me."

"There is a tribe like ours—"

Haphnee squinted again.

". . . only in that they come from a faraway land," Artuke said. "In every other respect they are the antithesis to our peace-loving people."

Haphnee relaxed again and Artuke continued. "We have given them the name 'Ferox,' as we do not know much more about them other than they spread death and destruction wherever they go."

"Let them come," said Haphnee. "They have yet to face the warriors of Jetush."

"They do not attack out in the open; if they did, even you would not survive. They are more cunning than the smartest member of your tribe and even more powerful than the mighty mammoth. Your people would not be aware that these men even arrived. They will join your tribe and lead it to destruction. They are the corruptors of worlds. They—"

"Your tribe fell to them."

Artuke seemed pleased by the statement. "You are truly wise, Haphnee. Indeed, the Ferox came to our land and brought our proud people to the brink of ruin. But we discovered their deception and purged the beasts in time."

"And now you are warning others," Haphnee said.

Artuke nodded.

"I don't believe you."

Artuke motioned to the thick man, who pulled an object from behind his back. Haphnee became nervous, shifting on her rock; but if there was any truth to these strange men's story, she was determined to learn it.

Artuke took the object and opened it up like a skin sack, but it was unlike any skin she had seen before.

Then he showed her. It looked like an egg . . . like a large, grey, bird's egg, but oblong, not as rounded. *Click!* The object popped open and flashed red fire at her. Haphnee drew her saber jaw and prepared for a fight. It never came. The men of the Aeros tribe smiled and held the object out to her.

"On the ground," Haphnee said, nodding toward the forest floor.

Artuke bowed, placed the smooth object on the ground then backed away.

After a few tense moments, Haphnee took the object in her hands. Its surface was cool to the touch. It was hard, the hardest thing she had ever felt, but it was also very light. She thought it would make an excellent grinding stone. A light, like a small red sun, flashed at her as she inspected it, sure a flame must be burning inside.

The light flashed blue, causing Haphnee to drop the object to the ground and leap back. What happened next she would never forget. It was enough to change the way she thought about her world, her people, her future.

That was the day Haphnee dedicated her life to the Aeros's cause. She waited and watched for the signs they told her about—the signs of the Ferox.

She had to wait only a year.

Leaders emerged, skilled at rallying the people to a common cause. The Ferox influence was so subtle that none of the tribesmen in any tribe noticed their culture being swayed.

But Haphnee did.

Tribes squabbled and small numbers of men died, but then alliances were born and soon huge bands of warriors from both sides of the river were slaughtering each other for land that they had shared without malice for generations—and all the while, tribes grew larger, stronger, more advanced. One could not walk through the forest without the constant threat of attack or stumbling upon a field of dead bodies.

Still the Ferox influence spread, as tribe after tribe fell into line and into service. Men grew smarter, but their advances destroyed rather than improved, and even beasts of burden were used as mobile weapons. With all the death, Haphnee wasn't sure there would be enough tribesmen left to continue fighting, but the Ferox tribes grew. They advanced at a staggering rate and had soon changed the way the world had been.

After fifteen years of observation, making certain it was in fact the Ferox's influence her people, Haphnee realized time to act had arrived. It was her duty to call back the Aeros, who promised to return and remove the Ferox. She knew the trials she would face on her quest would be the hardest of her life.

She was now, at forty-three, one of the oldest among her people, not even considered strong enough to join the hunt. It had been ten years since a man tried to take her to a neighboring tribe, and her reputation had long since diminished. Her people saw her as an undesirable old woman with nothing to offer. How wrong they were. If only they knew their lives, the lives of all people, were now in her hands.

In the dark of night, Haphnee packed what she could, stealing furs from two of the other women, and headed north through the woods. Seven days later, she found herself in a desolate land—the frozen hills, where her people never ventured.

A SECOND gush of blood from Haphnee's ruptured lip brought her back to the present. She spit the blood out and looked over her shoulder, following a thick twine cord up to a looming shadow. She stopped and waited for the shadow to emerge through the fog of falling snow, which fell constantly in this evil, frigid land.

Why the Aeros had put their—what had they called it?—beacon, in such a foreboding land was beyond her. Perhaps the Ferox weren't inclined to cold temperatures; or maybe so no other men might stumble upon it, take it for an evil god, and destroy it. She knew they must have had a good reason, but just then she wished it was someone else who had to make this journey.

The wooly mammoth stepped forward and emerged from the blanket of snow, its thick brown hair matted and wet. The creature stopped in front of its master and shook the snow from its head. Haphnee gasped and ducked as the beast's ten foot tusks whooshed over her head.

"Teechoo, watch yourself," Haphnee said through the thick hide wrapped over her face, as she shot an annoyed glance at the mammoth's broad head.

But Teechoo wasn't watching what he was doing because he couldn't see at all. It was Haphnee's touch on his trunk that allowed him to sense her.

Haphnee saw that Teechoo's eyes had frozen shut. She felt her own tears form and solidify with the thought that her companion, who had been her friend since childhood, was going to die for his loyalty to her. Why had she dragged him along?

Haphnee wrapped her arms around Teechoo's trunk and squeezed it tight as she was fond of doing when they wrestled. But the trunk that had so often wrapped around her waist and lifted her into the air remained limp.

"I am sorry, old friend."

Haphnee began to sob as she felt Teechoo's body sway. Haphnee would have cursed at the never-ending storm if she had the energy, but she feared her end would come soon as well. Her people, her poor people, would be coddled like infants by the Ferox, eager to learn the new ways of doing things. Teechoo groaned and fell to his side like a cut tree, pounding a massive depression in the snow.

Haphnee ducked under the prodigious tusk and trudged toward Teechoo's belly. She leaned against it and listened.

Nothing.

The rush of air sucked into his massive lungs stopped. The thump of his gigantic heart was silent. Haphnee gripped Teechoo's fur and sobbed.

She knew what she had to do to survive. It was the only chance she would have to save her people, to save the entire world that the Aeros had shown to her on the fateful day in the woods. Haphnee drew her bone blade and placed it against Teechoo's thick hide.

A sudden shift in the breeze caught Haphnee's attention. She spun around and readied her weapon. Nothing was there. The wind shifted again, from above. Haphnee looked up and saw an object floating twenty feet above her. It looked just as the Aeros had described it, dark as the night sky and as round as the moon. The Aeros had told Haphnee there was only one thing she could do if she saw this object—hide.

The work went fast, cutting with her blade. As she slipped inside her carved-out crevice she began to feel warmer, but she knew now that the storm wouldn't let up for some time, if ever. But she had no choice. A haze of gleaming white snow was the last thing Haphnee saw before closing the thick layer of Teechoo's still-warm hide over her body.

EXPEDITION

1

DISCOVERY

Brian Norwood ran for his life. The ice behind his feet crumbled and fell away as he neared the safety of thick permafrost. He looked back. The fissure was at his heels, opening like a monstrous jaw. Norwood screamed and cursed himself. If only he had been less eager, this whole mess could have been avoided.

That morning, Norwood had rolled out of his cot and roused his hired crew. Six o'clock was an early start, and the crew would have grumbled if they weren't being paid so much. Norwood paid top dollar and he expected top performance from his team, even if they were working on four hours' sleep. They could sleep when the expedition was over.

Of course, this was just a preliminary expedition and Norwood wasn't accustomed to joining the grunt crew—not one of them held a PhD—but the potential of this discovery seemed so promising, so glorious, that Norwood had to see it himself before funding a full expedition. The site was first discovered when an Inuit whaling group had seen a pair of tusks jutting from a wall of permafrost during the summer, when the ice was low. When Norwood had heard their story, he paid for their silence and began plotting the excavation. He had chosen to return during the early winter, when the sun still graced the sky but the ice was more solid and could support a full-size camp. He was now rethinking that expectation.

The plan was to set off a few small explosions, softening the ice enough to allow the team to chisel the rest of the way. All Norwood wanted was a peek, a brief glimpse to confirm the Inuit's claims; then he would call in the troops, his team of experts, to dig out the rest.

A fully intact mammoth in the Canadian north was a groundbreaking discovery for two reasons. First, it was in Canada. Most mammoth carcasses were found in Siberia. Red tape from the Russians and travel concerns slowed most expeditions to a crawl and if anything was ever found, it had to remain in Russia. Canada was much more receptive to American science teams and usually happy to assist. Second, if he found what he was after, cloning a mammoth would soon become a reality. Its location in Canada made moving the mammoth body to his patented Freeze Lab in Los Angeles a snap. Once there, it could be dissected and analyzed for viable DNA. It would be a relatively simple task and provide the means to the realization of all his dreams: fame, academic prestige, money, and respect.

Norwood felt his foot fall through the ice. Had he been in better shape he may have outrun the spreading crack, but the love handles that had emerged over the past few years slowed him down. Norwood's dim hazel eyes grew wide as he felt himself falling backwards. The crew was yelling to him, but he couldn't make out the words. All he heard was the crack of ice and the pulse of blood rushing through his head. Most people would have thought about the freezing water below, or the dagger-like shards of ice falling around him, but Norwood thought of his father.

You never achieved anything! he heard his father saying over and over. *You took everything I gave you and spent it on foolish trips to various hells on Earth. You screwed over your sister. You gave up the family business. You wasted everything I taught you, and for what?* Norwood was sure this was how he would enter the gates of hell. What better torture could the devil conjure for him?

Norwood braced for the freezing impact that would suck the air from his lungs, chill his body to the core, and sap his remaining energy. He found little comfort in the fact that death would come quickly.

Whack! Norwood hit a surface, but the plunging cold he expected to envelope his body never came. Other than a burning pain in his left side, he was alive.

Norwood looked up through the new crevice and saw only a darkening blue sky. The light was faint at the bottom, but he could make out the smooth walls on either side. Smooth walls? Norwood leaned in, inspecting the wall, but couldn't discern anything more. A sound like a bubbling brook caught his attention. It was water—running water—he could hear it trickling down the wall. Ten below zero, and the ice was melting.

"Dr. Norwood! Are you all right?" a man shouted from above.

Looking up, Norwood saw Ron, one of the men he had hired in Montreal, leaning over the edge of the crevice, peering down. "I'm here. I'm okay," Norwood said.

"Dr. Norwood, thank God. You're alive," Ron said with a wave of relief that Norwood knew was due more to the fact that he was still alive to sign their checks than any personal concern. "Should we throw you a rope?"

Norwood hesitated, his mouth wide open to speak. He sat on the icy floor, his hands, bum, and feet all touching. A rush of liquid, a centimeter deep, pulled his eyes to the floor. It pooled around him, soaking into his clothing. The walls appeared to be melting at an incredible rate. What could cause such rapid melting? The dynamite would cause some at the source of the explosion, but this was a constant and sustained melting—there had to be a cause.

"Dr. Norwood, a rope?"

Norwood had forgotten all about the fall, about the pain in his ribs and the setting sun. "No . . . a flashlight. Get me a flashlight."

"What? The sun is going down, sir. I think—"

"Ron, do I pay you to think?" Norwood said with sudden seriousness. "No, I don't. That's my job. Now get me a damn flashlight!"

Ron disappeared over the edge without another word. He returned in thirty seconds with a flashlight and rope. Ron tied the rope to the flashlight and lowered them toward Norwood. As the flashlight came low, Norwood took hold of it and untied it. He then gave the rope a tug. It was secure on the other end. "Are you okay?" Ron asked again. "Let me know when you want to come out. We'll pull you up."

Norwood gave a silent thumbs-up to Ron then turned toward the closest wall of ice. The flashlight blinked on and lit the crevice in bright blue. Norwood squinted as his eyes adjusted to the bright, reflected light. Ice was normally a dull surface which absorbed more light than it reflected, but this ice was different. Norwood could see that a constant stream of water was trickling down the entirety of the wall. He pointed the beam of light forward at knee level and saw steam rising from the crevice floor. Norwood bent down to one knee, dipping it in the three inch deep pool of water that had already gathered and removed a glove.

Warm water rippled over his hand as Norwood submerged it. He stifled the sudden urge to pee and scrambled to his feet. What in God's name was going on? Norwood's brilliant mind hurried through several theories for what could be causing the strange phenomenon, and none of them were pleasant. Geothermal activity could be the culprit, but that was unlikely; there hadn't been any activity here for a hundred thousand years. Perhaps what the Inuit had seen was a derelict submarine . . . a nuclear submarine. Radiation could be melting the ice. Norwood walked away from the melting ice wall with one hand stretched out for the rope and the other pointing the flashlight on the steaming pool of water that splashed beneath his feet.

The ice floor had become slick, polished by the warm water. Norwood slipped like he had stepped on a bar of soap in a porcelain tub and careened backwards. As his hand reached out, Norwood felt the rope passing between his fingers. He squeezed his fingers hard around the rope and slammed to a stop against the wall. The flashlight fell to the ice floor. A momentary crashing and splashing of noise echoed as Norwood righted himself on the slick floor.

With the rope secure in one hand, Norwood leaned down to pick up the flashlight. He bent over, stopped, and listened. Silence.

Silence.

Norwood picked up the flashlight and pointed it toward the ice wall.

It was no longer melting, but had refrozen as smooth and as clear as a pane of glass. But it wasn't the ice or the melting of ice that now held his attention.

A ruddy shadow fifteen feet tall loomed behind the ice wall. Norwood imagined that the shape could be anything—a submarine, a frozen whale, or a SUV for that matter—but what separated this from any other theory were the two tusks that now lay exposed, jutting ten feet from the wall like thick, curved flagpoles.

Norwood's grip on the rope loosened and he slid to the quickly re-freezing floor with his back to the wall. He grinned and stared unblinking for thirty seconds.

"Dr. Norwood?" Ron said from above with a tinge genuine of concern in his voice.

Norwood looked up and saw Ron's head hanging over the edge, no doubt still concerned about the welfare of his benefactor. His fears were misguided of course; money wasn't going to be a problem. Norwood looked back to the frozen mammoth encased in an icy tomb and laughed.

2

EDDY

A swirling cloud of terra cotta dust billowed behind a faded red Jeep as it sped down a dirt road in the middle of nowhere. The bright sun glimmered off the windshield, free to shine at full strength in the cloudless Arizona sky. The posted speed limit was forty miles per hour, but having not seen another soul for forty-five minutes, Eve Bailey felt no compunction to remove her foot from the gas pedal.

Eve's long blonde hair was pulled and whipped by the wind as she twisted the steering wheel back and forth, dodging lizards, avoiding potholes, and just plain having fun. She cleared a hill and saw the road stretching out before her, a straight line drawn out across the desert, disappearing into the horizon. Eve smiled and the muscles of her right leg tensed as she shoved the gas to the floor. Her head jerked back from the sudden increase in speed and she laughed out loud.

The trip to Eddy's should have taken two hours, but she was cutting that time in half.

Eddy.

Her thoughts drifted and her foot eased up on the gas pedal. She hadn't seen Eddy Moore in two years. She remembered when she first met him on a dig site. He was finishing his PhD in paleontology and she had just started hers in paleobotany; at the dig site as interns, they were equals. They had swiftly become friends, inseparable, able to trust each other with life and limb, but to Eve's continual frustration, not love.

Eddy always seemed to be so wrapped up in his work, even back when she was in her prime: young, stunning, and very, very available. She once changed in front of Eddy, expressing, "I trust you not to peek," when in truth, she wanted him to peek. But he was true to his word and kept his head turned away the entire time. Eve had finally given up trying to seduce Eddy and decided to keep their tight friendship just that: friendship.

They'd worked together for five years on various projects and were very successful—a Diplodocus in Montana, a Paralititanin (the second of its kind ever found) in Egypt, a ground breaking Giant Foosa dig in Madagascar, and the T-Rex . . . They had put together a team of professionals that had become more like family, available to work on any project that suited their fancy. They were the best at what they did and no one had a better track record. They were fast. They were reliable. They were no more.

Two years had passed since Eddy had left. The remaining members of the team stayed together, working on projects around the world, but without Eddy their spirit was broken. They grew sloppy and slow and their reputation suffered. They were like a well honed body with only half a brain.

Eve snapped out of her daze and slowed the Jeep to a stop. A hundred feet off the road was a beige adobe home surrounded by cacti and red rock formations—an oasis hiding from the world. Eve looked at herself in the mirror, hair twisted and tangled, face covered with dust. Eve grinned. She wasn't the perky young woman Eddy had once known, but she was far from hard on the eyes, and she knew Eddy of all people would appreciate her current physical state. The few times he had complimented her on her appearance weren't when she was wearing makeup or tight clothes, but rather when she was working, coated in sediment, covered in scrapes and sweat. If Eddy was attracted to women at all, it was when they were dirty.

Eve plucked a twig from her hair and pulled into the sandy driveway at the side of the small ranch house. She cut the engine and stepped out of the Jeep, adjusting her beige shorts. After working her way across the winding path of stones that led to the front door, Eve rang the doorbell and waited. Nothing. She looked through the window for movement and saw nothing but books and empty beer cans. She knocked on the solid wood door.

Maybe he wasn't home.

Pressing on, Eve headed back to the driveway and stopped by her Jeep, listening. A light rhythmic sound tapped through the air. She recognized the pulse. Eyes squinting with suspicion, Eve headed toward the back of the home, following the barren driveway that wrapped around the back of the house.

As Eve rounded the rear corner of the home, the full sound of the music struck her; recognition was instantaneous: "Love Her Madly" by the Doors. Jim Morrison at his best, Eve thought.

The music came from an old radio propped up on a shelf next to a red convertible 1969 Mustang. The hood was open and Eddy was leaning inside. Eve took him in. Worn out, oil stained blue jeans and a dirty white T-shirt. If not for the piercing intelligence emanating through his brown eyes, he would have made a convincing run-of-the-mill mechanic.

Eddy grunted as he pulled on a tight bolt with a wrench, a very old wrench from the looks of it. His shoulder muscles twitched and his back flexed. Eve raised her eyebrows. Eddy was still in shape . . . that was good.

"You know, a good torque wrench would take care of that," Eve said as though this was just another casual meeting of friends, like she stopped by every day.

Eddy froze and the slightest smile crept onto his face, but he remained hovering over the engine, pulling on the bolt. "Just trying to work on a car from the past with a tool from the past."

"An honest experience?"

"An honest attempt."

Eve leaned against the wall of the garage, which was more like an old shack. "At least that hasn't changed about you."

Eddy stopped pulling. He stood up straight and looked Eve in the eyes for the first time. "What has changed about me?"

Eve's breath escaped her. His eyes were still captivating, squeezing her chest. He looked as though he hadn't shaved in weeks and was covered with dirt and grime, but that didn't matter in the slightest. She'd missed

her closest friend and did all she could to resist throwing herself in his
arms and squeezing him tight. For now, she'd play it cool.

"Look around you," Eve said. "Take your pick."

Eddy looked at his house: caramel colored, adobe . . . boring. "What?
You don't like my house?"

He knew she didn't. Hell, she knew he didn't like it, either.

"You've gone from exploring the past to hiding from it," Eve said.
"This isn't you."

Eve had always been honest with Eddy, about most things, anyway,
and he had apparently forgotten that. His face flattened. "It is now."

Eddy twisted a knob on the radio, silencing Jim.

"I didn't come all they way out here to argue with you, Eddy."

Eddy dropped the heavy wrench into a toolbox. "That's nice of you."

Eve twisted her foot in the dirt. She wasn't sure how this was going to
go over. "I came to offer you a job."

Eddy paused. He looked hurt. Was he hurt?

"Two years. It's been two years, and the only reason you've come out
here is to offer me a job." Eddy sighed and looked at the ground.
"You're wasting your time."

What was this? Of all the possible scenarios that Eve had played out
in her head, of all the variable futures that existed, this is one she hadn't
considered. Eddy, the machine, was acting like a teenager who'd just
been crushed by a girl. This wasn't the way she expected things to play
out at all; this was far better!

After wiping off his hands on a cloth that was easily as dirty as he,
Eddy walked past Eve and went straight for the house. Eve snapped out
of her astonishment and gave chase.

"The rest of us didn't quit. We're still together. Kevin, Steve, Paul, all
the guys are still on the team." Eve tried to soften him with memories of
his old friends. It didn't seem to have any impact at all.

"The rest of you didn't have a reason to quit."

That was true. Eve never blamed him for what happened, but she
didn't blame him for leaving, either. But enough time had passed.

"Just hear me out," Eve said as she followed Eddy through the back
door of the house and into the kitchen.

The kitchen was that of a bachelor: too obsessed with work, girls, and
video games to bother with dishes. In fact, there wasn't a real utensil in

the entire place. Paper plates, plastic utensils, and beer cans were strewn about the kitchen amid bags of chips and microwave meals. Not exactly health food, but it didn't seem to show on Eddy.

Eddy opened the fridge, took out two Sam Adams, and tossed one to Eve, who caught it and popped the top in an instant. She knew the one thing that had always impressed Eddy was that she could keep up with any man in a drinking contest. On certain digs when progress was slow, she did just that.

Eve took a long swig of the golden brew and wiped her mouth. "It's a mammoth."

Eddy paused, beer half way to his lips. His right eyebrow rose high on his forehead. She had him. She knew Eddy was technically the average paleontologist, skilled in excavating dinosaur bones from any environment Earth could conjure, but his passion was in recent extinctions: sabertooth tigers, the giant fossa, giant sloths, giant short faced bears, and most important—the mammoth.

"It's a complete specimen," Eve stated. "Complete in *every* way."

Eddy's eye twitched. "Where?"

"The Canadian arctic. A tiny unnamed island at the northern tip of the Queen Elizabeth Islands. We've already sent an advance crew to break through the ice. I'm putting together the second crew for raising and research."

"And you want me to lead?"

"I was hoping."

"You know I can't."

"We need you. You're still the best."

Eddy ran his fingers through his wavy black hair. "Not any more. Not after what happened."

This plan of attack wasn't going to do anything but make Eddy mad. Eve had to distract him. Only one thing would work.

"Brian thinks we'll find viable DNA."

A statement like that might normally elicit responses about how incredible a discovery viable mammoth DNA would be, the advances in science, the cloning of an extinct creature, visions of Jurassic Park. But for Eddy, the focus was on the first word in Eve's statement.

Eddy scowled. "Brian Norwood is on the team now?"

"Not on the team. Funding the team."

"You took a job from him?"

"It is a fully intact mammoth, and he's paying. A lot."

"Yeah, but—"

"We both know he'll eventually raise the mammoth and exploit it the way he always does. The only way to do anything about that it is to be on site." Eve took a swig. He knew she was right.

"Does he know you're coming to me?"

"Not a clue."

Eddy smiled.

"He's already on site, supervising the prep-team. If you don't come, I'm afraid he'll be running the dig, which we both know wouldn't be good . . . or safe."

Eddy took a drink, swished it between his cheeks like mouthwash, and swallowed it with a quick gulp. He rolled his neck around and looked at the ceiling, his thoughts turning to the past.

EDDY HAD met Eve on a dig when both were still interns. They had spent the summer digging up a tyrannosaur in the Badlands of South Dakota but had paid little attention to the big beast. They had become close friends, but the constant company of other interns and scientists kept their relationship formal. Eddy had been frustrated by the dig, the dinosaur, and every person within ten square miles that kept him from Eve. But then the summer was over and a surprise test was sprung on the group of interns. All their credit for three months of torturous work hung on this one pivotal piece of paper. Eddy scrolled over the paper, glanced at the ten questions, and panicked. He knew the answers to six or seven; the rest eluded him. He wouldn't be getting an A+, but he'd pass . . . he thought. He asked Dr. Ludlum, the professor who masterminded the sneak attack how many correct answers were passing.

Ludlum leaned over from his perch up on the rock and looked down at Eddy, peering over his glasses. "Now, Edward. These are elementary questions that you should know if you were paying even the slightest amount of attention during the last three months. If you get any answers wrong it means you were spending your time here getting a tan, or worse, chasing after girls. I intend to weed out the weak this year and set an example for future students. This is not a summer vacation. This is work."

Eddy smiled casually. "Just wondering." He walked away as his heart began to pound wildly beneath his ribcage. He had spent a fortune and gone into serious debt to pay his own way through his long stretch of education and now, because of one class, he might fail. He'd have to start again . . . or give up. Eddy made up his mind right then to do the only thing he knew could save him—he cheated.

Eddy sat on a rock above an average student; not the best and brightest, that would have been suspicious. But if Dr. Ludlum was correct and these answers were that easy, any student, save him, should do the trick. Eddy wore his sunglasses so no one could see where his eyes were and peered over Richard Sidmore's shoulder, copying the answers as quick as he could. Richard stood and walked away before Eddy could finish. He was one answer away from the end! Eddy read the final question while he held his breath. Then a smile came to his face and he laughed. He knew the answer.

Eddy passed Dr. Ludlum's test but had let Eve distract him so badly that he almost screwed up his career by failing one lousy test. After a long night of tossing and turning, Eddy decided that he couldn't allow himself to become that distracted again. He knew he wanted to work in the field, to lead expeditions into dangerous territories, but if he allowed his attention to wander, next time Richard Sidmore might not be there to save him. His friendship with Eve had remained strong, but it had never gone any further, no matter how strong his feelings might have grown.

EDDY SNAPPED back to the present, a forlorn look on his face, and said, "We take no risks, no shortcuts. We do things my way or no way at all."

Eve closed her eyes, relieved by his answer. She was smiling, but also dealing with other emotions brought up by his affirmative answer. There were a million things she wanted to say and not one of them had to do with the job, but two kept repeating in her mind like a scratched CD: I miss you. I love you.

"You won't regret it," Eve said.

"You might."

Eddy looked at his watch, then toward the front windows, viewable through the living room.

"You expecting somebody?" Eve asked.

"Well, let's just say you could have picked a better time to stop by."

Eve's brilliant mind flashed through a number of scenarios, as it was prone to do, and froze on one of them. A woman was coming and Eddy didn't want them to meet! She had to know. She did her best to sound innocent of anything more than dull curiosity. "Who's coming?"

"Contrary to your initial assessment, I wasn't working on the Mustang for fun. I was trying to get it running at a speed higher than fifty miles per hour."

Eve's forehead wrinkled. "Why?"

"To run."

"Run? Run from who?"

Eddy nodded toward the living room window facing the road. "From them."

Eve hurried into the living room and peered out the dust covered window. She saw a pickup truck from which four very large hicks dressed in overalls and T-shirts poured out. "It took you two whole years to piss off the locals? I think that's a record."

Eddy stood next to Eve and looked at the four ominous men, who were now retrieving shotguns from the truck bed. "I think you're right," Eddy said.

Eve didn't seem concerned by the men. They'd escaped worse situations.

"Who are they?" Eve asked.

"They were giving two friends of mine some trouble, physicist types from LightTech labs, so naturally I lent a hand and aided their escape."

Eve gave Eddy a questioning glance.

Eddy smiled. "They got into a fight at a local dive. Tom's a fighter, but David didn't stand a chance. I tackled two of them and . . . and then I slashed their tires."

Eve stood back from the window. "Leave it to you to get into a brawl with a bunch of pig farmers and two physicists."

"Gotta fill the time somehow." Eddy smiled. "How do you want to do this?"

Eve sighed. "I'll distract them. You get my Jeep."

Eddy smiled wide, enjoying himself. "That's my girl."

Eve's stomach churned at his words. She watched him head out the back door. What spell did that man have on her?

Muffled voices outside regained her attention. The four large men were headed toward the door, holding their shotguns high. Eve took a deep breath, pulled her tight white T-shirt up and tied it in a knot below her breasts, accentuating her curves. She tugged at her shorts, lowering them and flaunting her taut, toned belly. She felt like a cross between a teenage tramp and a southern hussy, but she knew it would get the job done.

The front door flung open and Eve stood in the doorway, leaning with one arm up and the other resting on her exposed hipbone. The four men froze. "Now what are four strong men like ya'll doing way out here?"

Silence. Maybe she'd killed them with more stimulation than their minds received in a good decade. She moved forward and noticed that all four men's eyes were locked on her breasts. It seemed the only women these men saw were their moms and the gals in *Hustler*.

She heard the engine of her Jeep roar to life at the side of the house. The four men turned toward the noise and raised their weapons. They seemed to have one-track minds. She'd have to keep them on her. Eve yawned loudly, stretching her arms in the air and pushing her chest out. The men's attention snapped back to her. One of them dropped his shotgun along with his jaw. He didn't attempt to pick up either.

The Jeep surged out from the side of the house and careened over two cacti as Eddy steered the vehicle into the front yard, on a collision course with the four assailants. He nearly crashed into the house when he saw Eve stretching her shapely body but managed to avoid the house and stay on course.

Fat men wearing overalls never moved so fast. They sprawled to the ground to avoid being struck by the Jeep. Eddy skidded to a stop in front of Eve and popped open the passenger's side door. "Your limousine has arrived, Miss Spears."

Eve climbed in and said, "This stays between you and me."

"Of course."

"Promise?"

"You know you can trust me."

Eve smiled, leaned over, and kissed Eddy on the cheek. His eyes closed and he leaned toward her lips. He accepted her kiss! True, it was only on the cheek, but it was a kiss nonetheless. Eve wasn't sure if it was because of the excitement of the moment, the fact that they hadn't seen each other in two years or the other, more frightening option . . . but there wasn't time to ask.

Eddy hit the gas and spun the wheels of the Jeep, spewing piles of dirt and sand onto the four men, who rolled on the ground like wallowing swine. They were on the road and miles away in two minutes. Safe from harm . . . better than that, they were together again. Eve didn't care about the dig anymore. The mammoth was insignificant. The money was pointless. Even if the entire expedition failed, she already had what she wanted—Eddy. Now she just had to figure out a way to hold on to him permanently.

3

RELATIONS

The frigid Canadian air bit at Eddy's skin and clung to his nostrils.

"It's freezing!" Eddy said through chattering teeth.

Eve stifled a laugh. "All that Arizona sunshine must have thinned your blood."

Eddy smirked and looked up at the large hanger bay before him. It loomed in the snow, a massive metal structure with a curved roof, like half of a monstrous can of coffee emerging from the Earth. The structure alone impressed Eddy. The size told him two things: First, there was a lot of equipment inside, and that was always a good thing. Second, Norwood was at least spending a lot of money on this little project, which meant it would get done right. And that's just the way Eddy liked it.

Eddy turned around and looked toward the horizon, white and cold as far as the eye could see—an empty stretch of the Canadian north just three miles south of Cambridge Bay. The blanket of snow was brilliant, and Eddy found himself squinting even through his sunglasses. It was beautiful, the way the sun played off the gleaming snow and the blue sky looked as though you could touch it. But it looked cold, too. And cold meant danger. Danger meant death. And Eddy wouldn't accept that again. It would destroy him.

"Listen," Eddy said, making sure Eve was looking him in the eyes, which she was—intently. "Before we head out, I want extra everything. Fuel. First aid. Food. Everything. Have Steve get as much as he thinks we'll need, then double it."

"Already taken care of."

Eddy bit his lip. Was she trying to ease his nerves or telling the truth?

"Last time I was unprepared."

Eve walked to a small box next to the hanger doors, opened it, and began punching in numbers. After hitting the final button, Eve closed the box and stood back. "Eddy, I promise, this time . . ."

The large doors clunked as they unlocked and began sliding opening with a loud whirring sound.

". . . we're prepared for anything," Eve finished.

Eyes wide, Eddy stared into the hanger. Norwood wasn't spending a lot of money, he was spending a fortune. When Eve told him he was paying the work crew fifty thousand dollars a piece, he did his best not to choke. That was more than Eddy made in a year, a good year. When she told him that the research team would be getting one hundred fifty thousand, he did choke, and she had to give him a smack on the back to dislodge his pizza.

But this . . . this was more than Eddy expected, even with the generous stipend. A large airplane, a C-130 Hercules turboprop, sat at the center of the hanger. First built in 1954, the beast was an enormous, four prop transport plane, used to move heavy equipment and personnel but rarely scientific expeditions—not the ones Eddy had been on, anyway. It was in near-new condition with red stripes down both sides and a large, maroon maple leaf on the tail. It was beautiful, and more than that, could fly in even the worst weather.

Eddy's eyes darted around the room and took in the rest of the equipment. There were four Sno-Cats that looked like a cross between tractors and UFOs—powerful beasts with four tank tread-like appendages, capable of speeding through deep snow. These Cats had been modified to carry extra crew and equipment. They were large, square, and covered with thick windows. A logo was painted on everything: *Norwood Expeditions*. Norwood had gone commercial. Interesting.

A fleet of snowmobiles, maybe twenty, was lined up at the side of the room, every one connected to a trailer on skis. They would be hauling a veritable city with them. Eddy smiled. This was going to be more like vacation than a dig.

Eddy stepped into the hanger, still impressed, when shouting voices struck his ears. Eddy gave Eve a questioning glance. She shrugged.

Eddy headed for the commotion. He rounded a Sno-Cat, letting his hand drift across its solid treads, smelling the oil that kept its parts friction-free. Three people stood arguing in front of him. Two of them he knew. The other was a stranger. Eve stood next Eddy, crossed her arms, and waited. Eddy guessed she wanted to see how he would handle the situation. She stood to the side and motioned with her hand for Eddy to have at it.

The stranger, a fiery woman with smooth brown skin and deep brown eyes, fumed at the two men. In appearance she was Japanese, but her accent gave her away. Southern California. Great, Eddy thought, who hired the valley girl?

"This stuff is on rental, you idiots! Break it and your ass is grass!" the woman spouted.

"Technically, that would be 'asses' are grass. Plural." That was Steve. Long, wavy, red hair hung half way down his back. When hair bands went out of style, Steve managed to hang on to his mop. His face was covered in sporadic patches of unshaven stubble. He thought that if he waited long enough, it might start to grow in other areas. He was an incessant jokester but knew how to get the best equipment and get it cheap. He made keeping the team together more affordable and usually made sure they traveled in style. His presence on site wasn't always in high demand, but he insisted on coming along, just in case. Eddy believed he really came along to hit on any cute college interns that might happen to join the crew.

"Yeah, lady, cut us some slack. We ain't slaves, you know." That would be Paul: Italian to the bone and with more hair on his fingers than on his head. He and Steve were chums from their first meeting, when they argued over which character from *The Matrix* trilogy was more attractive: Trinity or Neo. It ended with a slew of homosexual accusations and they'd been the best of friends since. Paul was an equipment specialist. If Steve could buy it or rent it, Paul could drive it. They generally fixed equipment as a team, though Paul would say he did all the work. They kept the team mobile and connected to the world, but they weren't always the most careful pair.

Eddy cleared his throat. The group stopped shouting and looked at Eddy. The valley girl just looked annoyed that another insolent man had barged into the argument, but Steve and Paul looked stunned.

Paul's jaw dropped. "Ed—Eddy?"

Steve's eyes lit up. He grabbed Eddy and hugged him tight. "Eddy! My man!"

Eddy laughed and picked Steve up off the ground, thrilled to see his old friends. Eddy separated from Steve and gave Paul a strong handshake.

Steve looked at Eve, smiling. "And here I doubted you. I really didn't think you'd get him back."

"Woman's touch," Eve said.

"I bet," replied Steve, elbowing Eddy in the ribs. "So what'd she do to get you back, eh? A little nookie nookie? C'mon, you can share it with old Steve-O."

"Another word and old Steve-O's gonna be old dead Steve-O," Eve said with a stern look that revealed she meant business.

Steve leaned in to Eddy. "We'll talk later," he whispered.

"Man, am I glad to see you here," Paul said, his New York accent still as thick as ever. "This whole thing was going to hell."

Eddy looked confused. "How so? Everything looks great to me. You two have outdone yourselves this time."

"Don't get me wrong. The equipment is primo; the best we've ever had. But there are a few, ah, problems with certain crew members."

The Californian woman huffed. "I'm right here, you imbecile."

Paul motioned to the woman. "You see, boss? She never shuts up."

The woman's eyebrows launched to the top of her forehead. She stormed toward Eddy and stopped a foot from his face. "So you're the big man in charge now?"

"Um, yes. Eddy Moore." Eddy extended his hand.

She glanced at his hand with a wrinkle in her nose. Eddy noticed the blue eye shadow above her eyes. Not quite drag queen, but close enough. The look was accentuated by her pink, tight fitting ski suit. Eddy could see she was a girl used to getting her way.

"Mind telling these two monkeys to stay away from my equipment? My crew will load it on the plane themselves."

Eddy's face contorted with confusion. "Your crew?"

The valley girl's shoulders dropped and she shook her head. "Idiots," she whispered to herself, loud enough to make sure everyone heard. She spun on her heels and walked away, grumbling to herself.

"And that was . . .?" Eddy asked to no one in particular.

"Nicole Lu," Steve said. "Major hottie, big time bitch."

"She's leading a film team that's documenting the dig," Eve added.

Eddy turned to Eve, surprised by the new information.

Eve smiled. "It was Brian's idea."

☼   ☼   ☼   ☼   ☼

SURROUNDED BY notebooks, charts, and laptop computers, which were busy downloading data via a satellite link, Eddy felt a mingling of various emotions. This was what he loved to do. It was his truest calling, and no one, absolutely no one, knew more about the past (as far as extinct species were concerned) than Eddy. He felt right at home planning routes, emergency contingencies, digging strategies; but did he deserve to be here—to have all these people under his control, under his watch? He wasn't sure.

He pressed his feelings aside as he was used to doing and focused on the multiple tasks at hand. To his right was a stack of personnel profiles. He could mix and match his crew to the last person, making sure that personal differences and squabbling was kept to a minimum. On his other side, a laptop displayed the latest satellite information on temperature, ice thickness, and surface stability. Eddy was plotting the safest route and safest seating arrangements simultaneously. He had learned that they often went hand and hand. Personal differences sometimes got in the way of decision making, even at critical times. Of course, he also liked people to hash out their differences before anything important came up. It was why he put Steve, Paul, and Nicole in the same Sno-Cat . For twenty hours.

Being so wrapped up in his work, Eddy failed to notice someone approach from behind. He flinched when the hands grasped his shoulders but relaxed when they began squeezing, massaging. He didn't look back to see who it was. He didn't have to. Eve.

He slouched back in the seat and let Eve continue the backrub without another word between them. It was five minutes before Eve broke the silence.

"So how's it coming?" Eve asked.

"All right, I suppose. I'm not convinced we're ready. Weather looks erratic and portions of the ice are unusually thin for this time of year."

"We have more survival, research, and excavation gear than ten teams would need. I think we're ready for anything Mother Nature throws at us."

Eddy paused with his response while Eve dug at a knot in his back. Eddy grunted.

"It's not always Mother Nature you have to worry about."

Eve stopped rubbing Eddy's back, pushed a laptop aside, and sat on the desk, facing him. "Have you ever seen an excavated mammoth before?"

Eddy leaned back in his chair, relaxed from the back rub. "Unfortunately, only skeletons."

"Well, I have. It was mangled beyond recognition. But I touched its hair, smelled its skin, and saw what it ate for lunch the day it died. Eddy, nothing compares to it. To study a near perfect specimen would be like bringing the past back to life. Then again, if Brian can—"

Eddy stiffened at the mention of Norwood's name. He felt all the knots undone in his back begin to return. "And you had me so relaxed."

Eve sighed and rolled her eyes. "Sorry, Eddy, but you're going to have to work with him on this. Better get used to the idea."

Kevin Dent, a man with a bright smile and messy hair, leaned into the room. "Greetings, Earthlings. We're all set for the final prep."

Kevin's mind was sharp and his personality loving, but he was frail and easily insulted. He had a PhD in paleontology like Eddy, but Kevin specialized in cryptozoology—the study of theoretical species. His guidance had been unparalleled in their search for the giant fossa, the largest and most savage mammalian predator the island of Madagascar had even seen, and on average projects he provided another brilliant mind to the team. For a man who left two kids, a wife, and a dog behind, he was always the cheeriest member of the team. His unwavering devotion to comic books and all things science fiction earned him a nickname.

"Buck? Is that you?" Eddy asked as he hopped to his feet, face brimming with happiness.

"Eddy!" Kevin rushed across the room and the two shook hands, after which Eddy took Kevin by the shoulder and squeezed him. They were like brothers. They all were. A big family of some of the best minds on Earth.

"How are the kids?" Eddy asked.

Kevin pulled out his wallet and showed Eddy a family photo of Kevin, his wife, and their two kids, a boy and a girl. "Salina's half way through her first year of high school, and Peter's a junior in high school now. Captain of the soccer team."

"Think he'll want to join an expedition with his old man soon?" Eddy asked.

"I doubt it. Kid has soccer in his blood. I played soccer for ten years, but he's got a golden touch. I think he'll go pro."

"That's great," Eddy said. "That's great. Is everyone in the prep room?"

Back to business.

"Yup, good to go . . . though tensions are high. It'd be better if we get there sooner than later."

Eddy shook his head. "This is going to be a long trip."

☼　　☼　　☼　　☼　　☼

EDDY STOOD in the warm glow of the three thousand dollar projector, which was shooting an aerial view of the Canadian arctic onto a large, white screen. The makeshift meeting room had been created using dividers, which provided a visual barrier but little else.

Steve and Paul sat at the back of the room, feet up on chairs and offering the occasional nonsensical comment—pointless, but always getting a laugh. Technically, they had no say in the choices to be made, but when it came to equipment, their word was equal to God's. If they found problems with the issues brought up at this final meeting, logistically speaking, they had the final say.

Eve and Kevin sat silently, listening to Eddy speak and occasionally jotting down notes. If something happened to Eddy, one of them would be in charge, and they had to absorb every particle of information and insight Eddy might offer. It was the safe thing to do, the responsible thing to do . . . that's why Eddy insisted they do it.

Nicole stayed silent for the most part, whispering occasional instructions to the camera crew who moved around the room, filming every movement Eddy made and every word he spoke. Nicole had become thrilled by him. His presence on camera was incredible and his voice demanded attention. Eddy's command of the expedition meant that ratings would double in the female demographic from age sixteen all the way up to sixty. That was a lot of women.

Eddy eyed the camera with an annoyed glance as he advanced to the next image. A graphic display appeared, showing a route from Base Camp Alpha in the Canadian Nunavut Territory, marked by a red dot, to the northern tip of one of the smaller chunks of land in the Queen Elizabeth Island group. The words "Mammoth Dig Site" blinked over the end of the graphic.

Eddy turned away from the camera. "We'll land at Base Camp Alpha and spend the night with Sam and Mary. From there I've mapped out a safer route which minimizes time spent on the frozen ocean and maximizes time spent on land. First order of business once we're on site is to secure and reinforce the labs and living quarters."

Kevin squirmed in his seat. "Uh, Eddy, you realize this will put us two days behind schedule?"

"The thought occurred to me." Eddy paused and caught his breath. They weren't going to like this. "That's why we're going to drive through the night and work double shifts for the next two days. While one team drives, the other sleeps. It will cut our drive time on the ice in half."

Steve grunted in protest, but otherwise no one voiced any objection.

"I know it doesn't sit well with any of you, and it won't with the rest of the crew. But you asked me here for a reason. I get things done, and I get them done right. We'll be safer and with any luck, we'll get to the dig site early. Rest up on the plane and save your energy. If we make good time, you can all rest before we start digging. Any questions?"

Eddy looked around the room.

Steve's hand went up.

"Let me rephrase," Eddy said. "Any intelligent questions?"

Steve's hand went down.

Nicole's hand went up.

"Yes?" Eddy said with a glint of suspicion in his eyes.

"Well," Nicole said, "I was hoping you could fill us in on the details of the dig. What we're going to see. The history of the mammoth. Things like that."

Eddy cleared his throat while a nervous smile turned the corners of his lips toward the ceiling. "Don't documentaries hire narrators for things like that?"

"Not this time. Besides, people feel more educated when they hear it from the lips of the man in charge. That would be you." Nicole motioned for the camera crews to focus their attention on Eddy. "Whenever you're ready."

Eddy sat on the corner of the table holding the computer projector and ran his fingers through his already rumpled hair and let out a long breath. "*Mammuthus Primigenius,* or 'woolly mammoth,' as it's widely known, roamed the Earth during the last ice age of the late Pleistocene epoch, about nine thousand years ago . . . though I believe there may have been living mammoths up until about five thousand, maybe even four thousand years ago, in more remote regions, of course, which would have brought them into the early Holocene epoch. Some believe that the mammoth may have even still walked the plains of high north while Jesus was walking on water. They stood around nine feet tall, though some grew as tall as fifteen feet. Their hair was dense and ranged from a ruddy brown coloration to pitch black. They had two long, curved ivory tusks that were sometimes almost as long as the mammoth's entire body. The tusks were probably used for foraging in the snow and for bouts of inter-species dominance. Their bodies were massive, between three and four tons, built similar to modern elephants—tusks, a long proboscis, or trunk, and strong musculature—with the exception of a fatty hump at the base of its skull." Eddy looked at Nicole. "How's that?"

"You mentioned some mammoths may have lived longer in remote regions. Why's that?" Nicole asked.

"It's no secret that the Earth's fauna and mega-fauna are going extinct on a global scale of one species every thirty seconds, faster than the mass extinction of the dinosaurs, which was caused by an asteroid impact. The current mass extinction, which will wipe out half of the planet's biodiversity in the next one hundred years, got its slow start ten thousand years ago with early man. The few species that are surviving are either adapting to the civilized world, like raccoons, skunks, pigeons, and the like, or are so remote that we have yet to destroy their habitat . . . or have yet to even discover their existence."

"So man is to blame for the extinction of the mammoth?" Nicole inquired.

"Disease and climatic warming played their parts, but like other animals, the mammoth would have adapted. Man simply finished the job nature started before the species could rebound."

"And what was mammoth habitat? Where did they live?"

Eddy sighed, eager for the interrogation to end. "Cave drawings of the mammoth have been found in Spain and France, but we believe they originated from Africa. They migrated across Siberia and into Alaska, where remains have been discovered. They then migrated south into the mainland of North America, the same route that early man took out of Africa."

"So," Nicole said, chewing on a pen, "if this mammoth is raised intact . . . and is cloned . . ."

"It will be the first species wiped out by mankind and brought back to life. If we can do it successfully with a ten thousand year old mammoth, we can bring back other species brought to extinction, given access to DNA samples. Our success on this expedition is not only a scientific curiosity. It could mark the beginning of the end of the largest mass extinction in sixty-five million years."

Nicole clapped her hands together and stood with a bright smile. "That was perfect! Thank you!"

Eddy nodded and turned to the crew, who had been watching in silent amusement. "This is it, people. A fully intact mammoth is waiting out there for us," Eddy said as he stood tall with confidence.

The cameras zoomed in on Eddy's face.

"Let's go raise the past."

4

EN ROUTE

Screams of anguish, like a horde of dying hyenas, tore through the enclosed cabin of the C-130 Hercules turboprop. Steve leaned over Kevin's shoulders, eyes wide at the swath of blood and gore laid out before them. Kevin pulled the trigger three more times and with each a single shot of his Electronic Pulse Sniper Rifle was fired, finding its mark in the forehead of another alien. The beasts shrieked as death came, while globules of brain matter sprayed across the ground. The alien bodies slumped to the ground, wriggled for a moment then disappeared from existence.

"Look out!" Steve shouted. "There's one more!"

Kevin glided the mouse the left. "I see him."

The creature came into the crosshairs of the sniper rifle. Kevin steadied himself, finger twitching over the left mouse button. Before he could push the button and pull the trigger, his on-screen character grunted with pain.

"What the—"

Kevin's fingers sprang to action. He turned his character and faced a large alien creature with huge fangs and dual laser pistols. The alien opened fire as Kevin ran backwards towards a virtual cliff.

Steve was in a near panic as he watched the action unfold. "You're dead, man! No way out!"

Kevin continued back and jumped. His character began to fall over the edge of the cliff but before disappearing over the precipice, Kevin fired two quick shots with his sniper rifle, killing the two remaining opponents. It all happened faster than Steve could register. The screen changed to an image of Kevin's character, a marine with Kevin's face grafted to the model, floating in mid air. An announcer boomed from the speakers, "You're the winner!"

Steve leaned back in his chair. "How'd you do that?"

Kevin smiled, eyes wide and very aware. "Nerves of steel, my friend."

Steve reached over, grabbed Kevin's chubby belly, and shook it. "More like nerves of pudge."

"Insulation from the cold," Kevin said. "If we got stuck out in the arctic, who do you think would live the longest?"

Steve wasn't one for long debates with scientists on subjects that had no bearing on reality. He rolled his eyes. "Whatever."

The computer screen flashed and gave warning that a new match had begun. Kevin resumed playing. Steve returned to watching the virtual gore-fest. "What's going on now?"

"CTF," Kevin said.

"CT-what?"

"Capture the flag."

"Who are all those other guys? Why don't you shoot them?"

The screen displayed a group of humans, all armed to the teeth and dressed in blue. "That's my team. We have to capture the other team's flag."

Kevin turned his character away from the advancing group and took an alternate route through a tunnel in the lower parts of the level. He encountered zero resistance.

"Some team," Steve observed. "Where are you going?"

A smile stretched across Kevin's face. He smelled victory. "Oldest trick in the book. If you were defending the base, who would you consider more of a threat: little old me or the fully armed squad? They're the decoys, I'm the hero."

"Risky move," Eddy said as he leaned over Kevin's free shoulder.

Kevin's character came up behind the red team's base, while sounds and flashes from a battle at the front of the base revealed that Kevin's path was clear. Kevin maneuvered through the base, heading for a red flag. "Now all I have to do is grab this flag, run back the way I came, and we're home—whoa!"

A red player emerged and opened fire. Kevin's fingers clacked against the keyboard as he returned fire. The two were locked in mortal combat, but Kevin quickly gained the upper hand; that was, until the C-130 lurched up and bounced to the side, sending Kevin's character into a dizzying spin. The red player finished him off. "Damn!" Kevin muttered.

Kevin leaned into the plane's aisle and shouted toward the cockpit, which was only ten feet away, "You think you could fly above this crap?"

The cockpit curtain slid aside and Paul leaned out. "You think you can do better, get your ass up here."

Eddy and Steve laughed at Kevin, who they knew had just received an uncommon defeat in the virtual world in which he reigned supreme. Even his own son couldn't keep up. Kevin shook his head and continued playing, eager to exact his revenge on the red player who dared kill him.

Eddy stood and wandered away from the excitement of the game. He looked back and surveyed the thirty additional crew members who were comprised of heavy laborers and Nicole's additional film crew. They looked tired, but he knew they would work hard for the money Norwood was paying. He took his seat next to Eve, who was sound asleep. Eddy looked at her closed eyes which fluttered with sleep, then her long legs, crossed elegantly. She was one of his oldest and truest friends. Her golden hair hung over her face, tickling her nose which she scrunched during sleep. Eddy eased the hair from her face and tucked it behind her ear. His hand lingered, letting her smooth hair slide between his fingers.

Eddy sighed, sat back in his seat and closed his eyes. He was asleep next to Eve in ten seconds.

Across the aisle, Nicole peeked at Eddy, looking past the latest addition of *Documentary Maker*. She put the magazine down and motioned to Mark Vincent, her camera man.

Mark saw the look in Nicole's eyes and knew to be quiet. He scurried over to Nicole and she spoke in a hushed voice. "You see those two?" she asked, pointing at Eddy and Eve.

Mark nodded.

"You ever see them alone, I want you to be there. Got it?"

Mark nodded.

"Even if they're in a sealed tent, I want you to find a shot through. Something's gonna break between those two, and I want you to get it on film. The best angle for any of these boring science things is to find a little humanity among the crew and exploit it—turn them into celebrities. Are we clear?"

Mark nodded again.

"Good. Now shut up and go sit down."

☼   ☼   ☼   ☼   ☼

A SERIES of metal buildings protruded from the solid white expanse of snow, like a fortress in the desert; five buildings in all: Base Camp Alpha. The buildings were well-maintained, as several expeditions came through every year; some thrill seekers, some naturalists and some, like those hired by Brian Norwood, seeking the ultimate scientific prize.

But Sam and Mary, the caretakers and owners of Base Camp Alpha, were wary of this new crew coming in with all the fancy equipment, all the hoopla. Others had come with high tech gizmos, lots of cash, and had marched off onto the frozen tundra. Some never came back. It was the way things were up there, at the top of the world, where everything nature had to offer meant death to a man: the unforgiving ice, the frigid sea, even the wildlife. In the dead of winter when food was scarce, killer whales and polar bears would devour a man without blinking an eye. Sam was fond of saying to new adventurers in search of a thrill, "This ain't no place to be losing your wits, and if you had any wits about ya, ya'll wouldn't be here."

Of course no one ever listened, but when they came back dead or not at all, Sam's conscience was as clean as his crew-cut grey hair. Sam spent the morning clearing off the runway for the massive C-130, which was just now touching down. "More food for the bears," Sam said to Mary.

She shook her head, keeping her bright blue eyes on the landing behemoth. "Damn fools, coming out here this time of year."

Mary put a pipe to her chapped lips, took a long drag, and held it in, letting the smoke warm her lungs. She'd been married to Sam since he escaped Texas and found her living with a tribe of Inuit, hunting whales out of umiaks at the end of winter when the ice was splitting and floating free. They'd fallen in love and called the barren tundra their home ever since. That was thirty years ago and while age had set into their faces, their bodies were still strong and agile. This year would mark their thirtieth whale hunt together.

The pair stood still as a breeze kicked up by the C-130 whipped snow across their faces. As the red striped plane slowed to a stop, they headed forward to give the damned fool leading the group a piece of their collective mind.

The back of the C-130 opened up and a wide ramp descended to the landing strip pavement. A man strode out of the plane's rear dressed in a flashy orange jacket, the kind that made people stand out to potential rescuers, and to polar bears. His head was covered with a tight woven winter cap, and his eyes were hidden by stylish, reflective sunglasses. His face seemed familiar, but with the man's eyes covered and the bitter cold causing Sam's eyes to water, it was impossible to discern his identity.

Sam leaned over to Mary as the man approached, smiling wide. "Ten to one says they're all dead by tommora night."

Mary nudged him to hush up.

"Sam, Mary, good to see you," the man said happily.

Mary squinted her wrinkled eyes and let some smoke out of her nose as she took the man in. "We know you?"

The man said nothing. Just stood there looking confused.

Sam slowly reached into his coat pocket, so the man wouldn't become aware of it. He placed his hand on an old Smith & Wesson revolver and slid his finger around the trigger.

The man's smile faded.

Sam pulled the revolver from his pocket and brought it up toward the man. But the man was fast. In a flash, the man had brought his hand around, grabbed the barrel of the gun and twisted it just so, pulling it free from Sam's hand and turning it around on the pair. Sam smiled wide at the gun in the man's hand; they knew of only one man who had reflexes that fast.

Sam moved toward the man, past the gun, knowing it would never be fired. "Eddy!"

Eddy pulled his sunglasses up to revealing smiling eyes and hugged Sam like he was hugging his father. In times past, that's what Sam had been to him: a father, and Mary his mother. Mary placed her cracked lips against Eddy's check and squeezed him tight.

Eddy stood back, beaming. "So, what are my odds now?"

Sam chuckled. "Ten and two, maybe."

"Actually," Eddy said, "I think they might be even better."

A roar from the plane caught their attention and the first in a long line of Sno-Cats barreled out of the C-130, followed by a steady stream of snow-mobiles.

"You come into some money?" Mary asked.

"Something like that," Eddy said, not explaining any further.

Sam patted Eddy on the shoulder. "So what happened to you, my boy? Last we heard you were in South America, then, nothing. We don't hear from you in two years, and now you show up with an army at your beck and call. What'd you do, son, save some rich guy's kid or something?"

Eddy's smile faded. "Actually . . . something much worse."

Eddy walked passed Sam and Mary and headed for a large building two hundred feet off the landing strip. They watched him leave without another word. They could read Eddy like a dirty magazine in the hands of a teenager. Eddy had changed, and not for the better, by their estimations.

☼   ☼   ☼   ☼   ☼

TEARS ROLLED down Steve's face as he writhed on the bare, wooden floor, laughing. Stories of the old days always got him laughing, especially when it was he and Paul doing the telling. The stories always included appropriate embellishment and wit.

The group was seated around a long dinner table that Mary had made twenty years ago. They were eating a veritable feast, the best Sam and Mary could scrounge up. Had they known it was Eddy coming, they would have flown in wine, not that anyone minded the beer. Eve, Kevin, Sam, and Mary listened with smiles on their faces, remembering the exploits of a younger Eddy. At the end of the table Eddy sat listening, face burning with embarrassment.

Two film crews—a camera man and a boom mike operator—circled like vultures, panning from side to side, focusing on one speaker, then the next, capturing the action like a two-camera sitcom crew. Nicole half listened to the stories, half whispered orders. She hadn't touched her food; whale meat and arctic hare weren't on her menu. The stories of old adventures were a nice touch . . . but she was waiting for the opportunity to dig deeper. The way things were going, she knew she wouldn't have to wait long.

Paul held his hand up, motioning for his captive audience to remain silent as he finished chewing. "So then Eddy says to the guy, 'Hey man, I'm from L.A.'"

Steve chirped in. "Which isn't really true."

Paul continued, ". . . and the guy suddenly thinks Eddy must be packing or something and takes off."

"He's got balls of steel, man," Steve said. "Eddy's fearless."

Nicole couldn't wait any longer and decided it was time to lead the conversation. "You're not from L.A.?" she asked Eddy.

Steve answered. "He grew up in the valley! I lived in tougher neighborhoods than Eddy, and I'm from New Hampshire!"

"All right," Eddy said. "Time to give it a rest, Steve. How about we talk about Buck Rogers instead."

"Buck Rogers?" Nicole said. "Isn't that an old TV show or something?"

"It my nickname," Kevin said with pride.

"Kev's a space cadet," Steve said. "A wanna-be super hero."

"These Cretans think that intelligent people can't enjoy the pleasure of space adventures and super heroes," Kevin said as though he were giving a lecture on the topic.

Steve laughed. "And super chicks with giant hooters. Let's talk about Eddy again; he's more interesting than Buck."

Nicole had learned to loathe Steve, with his messy hair and loud mouth, but now she had to thank the man. He was keeping this conversation right on track.

"I'd prefer we didn't," Eddy said, and a serious tone emerged in his voice.

Steve didn't hear it. "C'mon, man. We have so many cool stories about—"

"I'm not that person any more."

The table went silent. Everyone knew when to stop pushing.

Nicole did not.

"Um, why not?"

Every head turned to Nicole, amazed that she had asked the question. The heads craned back to Eddy, waiting to see if there was going to be an answer. Eddy stared at the table, at the hard lines of the wood, remembering the past.

5

THE PAST

The air was thick with moisture. And with moist, clean air, came very wet bodies. Eddy rarely sweated, but here, in the jungles of Venezuela, he was soaked like a man who had just played a vigorous game of dunking for apples. Eddy cut a swath of brush aside with a fast swipe of his machete then wiped the sweat from his forehead with his soaked sleeve.

Eddy stepped through the newly carved jungle and on to a clear path leading north. It was perfect. They had been at the dig site for only two weeks, working day and night to uncover the remains of a giant sloth which had been preserved in a rare underground cavern. They had excavated the cavern; segmented, labeled, and wrapped the bones with meticulous care; and were now trekking through the sauna-like jungle in search of their pick-up zone. Helicopters would be flown in to a clearing in the jungle and the crew would be carted out with a great scientific find, a still-perfect record, and with time to kill on the beach before heading home to the States.

But when a river rose too high and obliterated their original path, Eddy was determined to make the LZ on time. He began cutting into the jungle, following his compass, and led the team forward with little argument. It was only when they reached the clear path that someone spoke in protest.

"Eddy," Brian said, "I think this is a bad idea."

Eddy looked back, past Brian, past Eve, to Jim and Kat, a married couple who had joined them for the adventure of a dig and the filling of their scientifically-inclined minds. Kat had curly, long black hair and scribbled notes in a drawing pad everywhere they went. Eddy suspected she wanted to be a writer. Jim was a computer programmer specializing in Linux, fingers smooth from working a keyboard all day, but rugged and adventurous nonetheless. A scar across his check from a run-in with an African lioness gave testimony to that. "Jim, Kat, why don't you scout ahead. See where this leads."

Eddy knew that Jim and Kat loved to be given responsibilities. It made them feel like a real part of the team. But he couldn't let them go off by themselves, no matter how resourceful they had proved to be in the jungle. "Harry, go with them."

Harry moved past Eve and Brian to head north on the path with Jim and Kat. Harry's muscles were tight and his skin was thick; he was the kind of man whose charcoal eyes some would work hard to avoid in a bar. He had been on every jungle expedition Eddy ever mounted. While he wasn't a scientist, he knew the jungle, understood its sounds, its mood. Harry had never been to Venezuela before, but they counted on him to keep them alive, which was why they allowed him to carry his specially made AK-47.

"Did you hear me?" Brian asked, stepping in front of Eddy so he had no choice but to acknowledge him.

"Norwood," Eddy said, "I'd appreciate it if you'd—"

"If you're going to call me by my last name, please put the word, 'doctor' before 'Norwood.' I've earned that much. But this isn't a novel, and we're not at a university, so call me by my first name."

No man on Earth knew how to push Eddy's buttons harder and quicker. Eddy made it an exercise in patience. "Sorry, Brian . . . What did you have on your mind?"

"This path is too clear," Brian explained. "It's been used recently and frequently. We should head back into the jungle before anyone sees us."

Eddy watched as Jim, Kat, and Harry followed the path to the right, out of sight. They had just crawled through five miles of thick, wet jungle full of mosquitoes and other blood craving pests. Morale was down and Eddy had no intention of backtracking. "Not a chance."

Brian looked up at the lush emerald canopy hanging above the path, obscuring their view of the sky. "Eddy, what kind of people use a path in the middle of the Venezuelan rain forest with an overhead canopy so thick that if anyone came looking for them in a plane or helicopter, it would just look like more jungle?"

Eve stepped forward, her eyes weary and legs covered with crimson bug bites. She put her hand on Eddy's shoulder. "He could be right."

Maybe it was fatigue. Maybe it was pure stupidity. Eddy hadn't decided yet, but he didn't hear his crew's warnings. "It's a footpath," Eddy said. "If it were used by drug runners, it would have to be wide enough for vehicles. Drug runners don't carry a thousand pounds of cocaine on their backs."

Paul exited the jungle and headed south on the path for about ten feet. He knelt down and stared at the mud. He motioned to Steve, who joined him on the path.

"Eddy, this is stupid! Even for you! We need to get off this path!" Brian was fuming now.

"Hey, Eddy." Paul's voice went unheard.

Eddy was about to fail his exercise in patience. "You're a rich geneticist, *Dr. Norwood*, and that's all you are. I suggest you leave the decision making to me."

"Eddy." Paul put as much authority into his voice as he could. Still no response.

"Damnit, Eddy! Take your head out of your ass and—"

"Hey!" Paul shouted as he stepped between Eddy and Brian. It was uncommon for Paul to show anger. He had Eddy's full attention. "Eddy, come check this out."

Paul led Eddy to the patch of mud he and Steve had been inspecting. Steve was still bent down. He met Eddy's eyes as he crouched over the spot. "We got several sets of tire tracks here, man."

Eddy looked at the mud. Several tracks were thin and shallow, others were deep.

Paul crouched next to Eddy. "The thin tracks are probably from dirt bikes, not heavy enough to dig in deep. But these other tracks, in sets of two . . . could be from a loaded trailer . . . a heavy trailer."

Eddy looked Paul in the eyes, "Give it to me straight."

"Eddy, I think Brian's right. This is a drug trail."

Steve stood up. "And from the depth of these tracks, they're hauling some huge loads of cocaine."

Eddy looked down the path where he had sent Harry, Jim, and Kat. He started walking. "The rest of you get back into the jungle. Walk three hundred yards in, stay low, and wait for me to get back."

Brian looked relieved and headed into the jungle first. Everyone else followed. Eve waited at the jungle's edge, watching Eddy walk north on the path, quickening his pace with every step. He was worried. That made her worried.

☼   ☼   ☼   ☼   ☼

EDDY WAS already running before the first gunshot shattered the air, sending a flock of red-fan parrots into the air. He recognized the sound of the weapon: Harry's AK. Not good.

The following shots that rang through the jungle bounced off the trees and told Eddy it wasn't an animal at all. They were under attack. Eddy felt his feet burning beneath him, blisters tearing, but he continued forward and rounded a bend which led to a steep incline. Why had they gone so far ahead?

Eddy bounded down the incline, leaping roots and rocks on his way down. The gunfire was closer now, almost deafening, just around the bend. Eddy burst out from the path and into a clearing. Twenty feet ahead of him, huddled behind an over turned table, were Harry, Kat, and Jim . . . but something was wrong.

Harry was holding his AK-47, his eyes wide. Eddy knew he had fired the weapon. Next to Harry, Jim was sitting—no—he was rocking back and forth like he was trying to console a baby. Only Jim wasn't holding a baby, he was holding Kat. A bullet wound in her neck pumped warm blood over Jim's hand as he held it tight over the wound in a futile attempt to slow the bleeding.

Eddy's eyes widened and he took in the rest of the dire scene. It was a large camp, five buildings in all, one of them very long, with massive trees planted throughout, growing tall and covering the entire area under a canopy of thick foliage. Brian had been right. At the far end of the camp, Eddy saw some men dressed in jungle fatigues dragging away two bodies. Harry had been a good shot.

Harry pointed his weapon at Eddy and almost pulled the trigger. "Take Jim and get back to the others!" Harry said with desperation. "I'll slow them down."

Eddy wanted to object, but this was why they kept Harry around. They had known conflict might one day find them and that a quick escape facilitated by Harry's wailing guns might be necessary. But Kat was already dead . . . Kat was dead! Eddy's mind spun and he froze, as dazed as Jim was, rocking on the ground like a child on a swing.

Unfortunately, the drug runners were prepared for unwelcome intruders and had no qualms about killing to protect their secrets. A grenade hit the ground between Eddy and the others. If not for Harry sounding the alarm, Eddy would have died with the rest of them. "Grenade!"

Eddy looked down and saw the green object bounce once then stop in the mud. His eyes widened as his body spun and ran without having to think. Eddy rounded a thick tree and was knocked off his feet by the explosion.

Ringing filled Eddy's ears, but he was alive and unharmed. He stood and looked back around the tree, searching for the others. The smell hit him first, burnt chemicals mixed with flesh. He saw the overturned table Harry had been hiding behind, shattered and stained red. He didn't see how Jim and Kat could have moved. They were dead, both of them.

But Harry was quick on his feet. He was the first to see the grenade hit. Surely, Harry— An object landed at Eddy's feet. He glanced down and prepared to run from a second grenade, but he remained locked in place, staring at his feet. Harry's dark eyes starred back up at him, his head detached from the rest of his body.

Eddy had seen several heads removed from bodies, but they belonged to creatures dead for thousands or millions of years. He'd never seen a human head torn from its body and deposited at his feet. The sight locked his muscles. He was an unmoving statue.

A bullet shattered the tree next to him, bringing him back to the reality of the jungle. Eddy turned, found his footing, and sprinted back up the steep incline without looking back.

☼   ☼   ☼   ☼   ☼

HEART POUNDING, lungs burning, Eddy reached the top of the incline and gasped for air. He was a fit man to be sure, but after seeing three people—three friends—murdered, he found moving at all to be near impossible, like running through molasses in a twisted nightmare.

The shouts behind him grew louder, mixed with the shrieks of the white faced saki monkeys shaking the branches above, which were agitated by the noise of the attack. He couldn't see the men pursuing him yet, but he knew when they caught him, they would kill him. Normally, the thought might spur a man on, give him renewed energy, but not this time. Tears filled Eddy's eyes, blurring his path.

His cool demeanor had vanished in the face of death. True, he had looked death in the face a hundred times, but death had never looked back before. Now he had seen death's true gaze and was captured by it, gave in to it, accepted the inevitable.

Luckily for Eddy, not everyone had the same reaction. Some accepted it. Some feared it. And others ran from it like the dickens. Jim appeared on the path, wounded but running at full speed. He ran into Eddy and shoved him aside like a football player breaking for a touchdown. Eddy fell forward into the jungle, tumbling down a slight hill and coming to rest against the trunk of a massive, smooth-barked cuipo tree. His eyes snapped open just in time to see a bullet tear through Jim's leg, sending him to the ground. Jim rose and continued forward, struggling on his hands and knees with the effort of a man who longed to live.

Eddy felt a change in his heart and mind. A fire grew in his chest as he saw Jim clamor forward, desperate. Eddy felt his legs again. His arms became his own once more.

A second shot tore through the air and struck Jim in the back. Jim slumped forward, still reaching out with his hand. Even as death took him, Jim managed one last push toward freedom. Then he stopped moving.

Eddy sucked in deep and held his breath. Four men charged up the path. Their leader, a tan, handsome man wearing a red bandana, kicked Jim's dead body and scanned the area with his eyes. Eddy ducked down and remained hidden until the men turned around and left.

Boom! Boom! Boom!

The sound of cannons firing filled Eddy's head, but it wasn't from another attack, it was from the pounding of his blood surging through his veins, spurred forward by his body's adrenaline. His mind was cried out for revenge.

The four men didn't have time to react. Eddy bounded out of the jungle like a predatory cat, shoving the nearest man down the steep incline and stealing his automatic rifle. Eddy brought the rifle around like a baseball bat and smashed the back of a second man's head. The man slumped to his knees, bloodied before his head hit the ground.

Eddy spun, raised the weapon, and pulled the trigger. Eight shots exploded out of the weapon, throwing Eddy back and ripping through the body of a third man. Eddy twisted toward the man in the red bandana and pulled the trigger. Nothing happened. He pulled it again. Still nothing.

The man in the red bandana laughed.

Eddy ran forward, holding the rifle back, preparing to smash the man's brains in. The man was quick and had a handgun pointed at Eddy's face before he could swing. Eddy stopped, slid through the mud, and fell back on his hands. He crawled away from the man.

The man pointed his gun at Eddy's head and looked into Eddy's eyes, smiling, the whole time smiling. "I can see you are a true warrior," the man said. "I cannot bring myself to kill one such as you. You'll be much more useful alive."

Eddy saw that the man had no intention of killing him.

Why?

"But first, a parting gift to remind you of me."

The man moved his weapon to the right and pulled the trigger. Eddy screamed as a bullet tore through his shoulder. When Eddy looked back up, the man was gone as though he had never existed.

Eddy screamed as a hand grabbed his good shoulder and squeezed. He looked up into Eve's eyes. She was saying something, shouting, but Eddy couldn't hear a thing. His world went black.

☼   ☼   ☼   ☼   ☼

EDDY SAT back in his chair, face unmoving save a slight quiver on his lips. He'd just finished telling the story. "That was two and half years ago."

Silence.

Nicole was stunned. Eddy had just revealed his deep dark past in front of the cameras. Every word was captured for mass market consumption! Nicole had never worked harder to hide a smile.

Eddy stood from his seat, staring at Nicole with a fury few had ever seen in the man's eyes. "The person I was died with Harry, Jim, and Kat. Don't bring it up again."

Eddy stood and walked off without looking back. No one protested. No one moved.

Nicole leaned over to Mark, the nearest cameraman. "Please tell me you got all that."

"Every word."

"Perfect."

6

LEAVING BASE CAMP

Arctic wind bit Eddy's bare arms. He stood alone against the cold, dressed only in cargo pants and a white T-shirt. He gazed out at the milky expanse laid out before him in striking contrast to the azure sky above. For days to come it would be all he would see, save the crew and equipment they were bringing along; his world was about to be plunged into a landscape of high contrast. Light and dark, life and death; they were constantly vying for superiority of the Arctic, with little gray area to spare.

There were no drug runners in the Arctic. A policeman friend once told him that all the bad guys went inside at night during the winter in Chicago. It made for boring night shifts, but it was true; criminals, like most people, didn't like the cold. It kept them in at night and entirely out of the Arctic.

Eddy was relearning to enjoy the cold. Here in his T-shirt, without a winter cap or cup of brandy to keep him warm, Eddy felt colder than he had in years. Submitting himself to this self-induced torture was his way of preparing for the future. He believed that what he felt now was the coldest he'd get on this expedition. Everything from here on out would seem warm to him . . . That and his numbing toes kept his mind from wandering too far.

Crunching snow told Eddy someone was approaching. The sweet smell of peach perfume told him it was Eve.

"Everyone all set to go?" he asked.

Eve stopped next to Eddy and looked out to the horizon. "We're ready as soon as you're done thickening your blood."

"Few more minutes."

Eve glanced at Eddy, his eyes still glued to the view. She looked at his skin. It was red from the cold. She could see that it stung, that when he was done here it would continue stinging hours later.

"Why are you doing this?" Eve said.

"Preparing for the cold."

"You can put on a coat for that."

Eddy turned to Eve. "Not my body. My mind."

"You're telling me that you've been standing here picturing a warm turkey dinner, warming yourself psychosomatically? From the looks of your skin, it's not working."

Eddy looked at his skin, its tan color drained and replaced by a light pink. "Not a very flattering color, is it?"

"Don't change the subject."

Eddy bent down and picked up a handful of powdery snow. He began forming it into a ball in his bare hands. "We're prepared for anything we can conceive. But I want to be prepared, at least mentally, for everything we can't think of. I've been working through the most unlikely scenarios. I learned that from you, you know. Earthquakes. Polar shifts. Catastrophic type stuff. Basically anything that involves the crew dying and me having to watch."

Eve shifted, unsure how to respond. She didn't have to.

"In every scenario I come to the same conclusion." Eddy looked Eve in the eyes. "I couldn't handle it. I'd crack. I'd be useless."

Eve's gaze dropped to the snow. "That's not true."

"Death never frightened me before. It's had a stranglehold on me for two years, waiting for the right moment to squeeze again. I'm sure of it."

"Eddy . . ."

"Eve, promise me. If I lose it out there, if I put someone in danger, promise you'll take over and get everyone off the ice."

Eve was surprised. It wasn't what she was expecting. "Eddy, I'm no good at leading. I—"

"You got us out of the rain forest, out of Venezuela. I don't trust myself, and Norwood has too much invested to make responsible decisions.
If things fall apart, the torch goes to you."

Eve didn't like this one bit. It wasn't like Eddy to admit defeat before
the challenge was even known. Maybe he really wasn't ready to come
back. "Fine," Eve said. "But that's not going to happen." She spun
around and bounded away. "Hurry up with your self-loathing. The rest of
us are ready to go."

It was a rare event for Eve to lace a statement with so much hostility.
He felt her concern and anger at his show of weakness. It brought
warmth to his heart and strength to his bones. The renewed sense of reality broke through the frozen chains of the past and Eddy realized that
frostbite would claim his toes soon if he didn't head back inside.

He gave one last glance at the icy world into which they would soon
plunge and chased after Eve, holding his shivering arms and looking forward to reclaiming the soul of the man he used to be. He knew Eve
would be the key to his undoing or his rebirth.

☼   ☼   ☼   ☼   ☼

A ROAR like that of an angry dragon split the frozen air as the fleet of
Sno-Cats and snowmobiles launched out over the niveous abyss, which
lay just beneath the thick ice crust.

Eddy, Eve, and Kevin rode in the lead Cat. Eddy sat behind the steering wheel with a slight grin on his face. Eve sat on the passenger's side
and Kevin was in the back, alone except for the stack of comic books in
which he was already engrossed. Eddy looked over to Eve, who returned
his smile. "This is it," she said.

Eddy picked up his CB and spoke into it, knowing every crew member would be able to hear his voice. "Okay, people. Let's keep the pace
steady and on track."

THE SOUR-FACED trio of Paul, Steve, and Nicole listened to Eddy from
their shared Sno-Cat. They could all guess why Eddy had clumped them
together for the long journey, but they were determined not to let his
meddling work; Paul and Steve wouldn't ever become friends, or even
casual acquaintances, with Nicole. At least they all agreed on that.

Eddy's voice continued over the radio: "We don't have time for sight-seeing. Only stop if there is an emergency."

Paul glared at the radio as he squeezed the steering wheel. He looked across the cab to Steve who read his mind, smirked, and looked back at Nicole. "Emergencies don't include broken nails, gum in your hair, or dirt in your eye."

Nicole feigned a smile, which was quickly replaced by a grimace, then covered up by a middle finger thrust into Steve's face.

Steve laughed. "Ooh, feisty!"

Steve picked up the CB and spoke into it. "Eddy, my man, you need to relax, and I have just the thing for it."

Steve dug through a black backpack at his feet and pulled out a home-made CD labeled "Steve's Master Mix." He put the CD into the Cat's customized CD player and turned up the volume. For a few moments everything was silent. Steve pushed the CB button down and held it to the speaker. He counted in his mind, bobbing his head to music only he could hear.

With a burst of speed, Steve began banging his head up and down as the rhythm of Metalica's "Enter Sandman" blared from the radio.

Nicole covered her ears and screamed for the volume to be turned down, but her voice wasn't loud enough to be heard over the wailing guitar and thumping double bass.

EVE JUMPED as the sounds of heavy metal fury blasted from their CB system. She fumbled for the volume and turned it down, but the music didn't fade. Steve's feed blared through every CB system in the fleet of vehicles.

With a burst of speed, a Sno-Cat sped up next to Eddy's side and matched their speed. Steve leaned out of the open window, releasing a fresh shriek of music. "Hey, Eddy!"

Eddy looked at Steve, a smile creeping onto his face.

Steve began to thrash his head around to the music, his hair bouncing in the wind. Steve was in heaven. "Whoo hooo!"

Eddy burst out laughing. It was the first time he'd laughed since Eve picked him up in Arizona. She hoped it wouldn't be the last.

☼   ☼   ☼   ☼   ☼

STEVE REENTERED the cab of his Sno-Cat, shivering from the cold, and rolled up the window. Elated from his musical tirade, Steve turned down the volume and spun towards Nicole with a smile. "So, Nicole, why are you filming all this? Didn't someone make a documentary like this a few years ago?"

His question was honest and without trickery. Even Paul was surprised by his friendly demeanor.

Nicole stammered, looking for words beyond "go to hell." "Umm, well . . . how many documentaries have you seen on lions in Africa?"

"Uh huh, good point. But what makes this different from other documentaries? What makes your vision unique? C'mon, wow me."

Steve was transformed. Was it the thrill of finally getting underway? Could his childish teasing all been a show, like hazing? Maybe a test to see how she'd handle abrasive personalities? She couldn't decide, but she didn't want the Steve she'd met a few days ago to return, so she answered his questions without sarcasm.

"The last time this was done," Nicole said, "it was kind of anticlimactic. The mammoth was raised, but it sat on an airstrip for months. The original ratings were good, but interest disappeared and nothing ever came of it. What could have been one of the highest rating documentaries was really just a dull precursor to the one I'm going to make about this expedition."

"Okay, but what makes your film different? If you go on TV and say, 'Hey, we're showing another dead, hairy elephant being pulled out of the ice,' everyone who saw the first documentary is gonna say, 'Blah, who needs it?' Right?" Steve turned to Paul. "Am I right?"

Paul nodded and kept on driving.

Nicole was eager to respond. "Actually, you're right on the money. But I've got two reasons why people will want to watch my documentary over any other show on TV, network, cable, Japanese crossover hit, or otherwise."

Steve just waited for the answer with his eyebrows perched high on his forehead.

"First, the human element. In other documentaries, most of the action is focused on science, how the ice is chopped away, how heavy the mammoth is, you know, boring stuff like that. The first hour of my documentary is going to focus on the human side of things."

Steve was curious. "Human side?"

"You."

"Me?"

"Don't flatter yourself. Not just you personally. The entire crew. How you interact. How relationships pan out and how tensions are dealt with. Like Eddy putting the three of us in one Sno-Cat."

"I noticed you didn't complain much about that," Steve said as he tilted his head in thought.

"While I wasn't thrilled with the idea of being cooped up with two Neander . . ."—Nicole stopped, afraid to break the peace—". . . with you two, I knew it would make for good TV, so I went along with it."

Paul finally spoke his mind, "Okay, so you've got a good angle on an old idea. But how're you gonna carry it out? You got, like, four camera crews—and they're back there." Paul motioned behind them with his thumb. "It's not like you can film all of us, all the time."

"Actually," Nicole said, her lips spreading into a smile, "it's just like that."

Paul and Steve turned their full attention to Nicole, waiting for an explanation.

Nicole sat up straight. "There are four cameras mounted in each Sno-Cat and one on every snowmobile. Every word we say on the road is being recorded for posterity."

Nicole pointed to four corners of the interior cabin where small vents were placed. "There are cameras there and there. In every corner."

"Oh, shit," Steve blurted, then slapped a hand over his mouth and looked at the small camera Nicole had pointed out. "Sorry about that, sorry, you guys can edit that out, right? I don't want my mom to see it."

Paul looked at the camera closest to him and gave a little wave. "So you got the human angle. Cool. But you said you had two reasons why people would want to watch. Aside from Steve's physical humor and my stunning good looks, what's to keep people from changing the channel to a *Golden Girls* rerun?"

"Yeah," Steve added, "cause that Blanche can be kinda hot after downing a few."

Paul laughed and Nicole rolled her eyes.

"If you must know," Nicole said, "Dr. Norwood told me you'd be thawing the mammoth and extracting its sperm, or eggs, depending on if it's a male or female, before it was transported. Millions of people will tune in to see whether we find viable, clonable DNA. Even if we don't, people will still watch, just on the chance. That is, if no one spills the beans before the show airs. But—"

Nicole noticed the stunned expressions staring back at her. Paul even let the Cat drift to the side a little.

"What?"

Steve's face was more serious than Nicole had ever seen it. She wondered what kind of trouble she had just caused and was upset at herself for not thinking of whatever it was earlier.

"What? Tell me?"

"I'm no scientist, but I've been around these guys long enough to know that testing for DNA is a delicate procedure. That kind of thing is normally done is a sterile lab or something. I don't think Brian told anyone else his plans."

"Is that a big deal?"

Paul laughed out loud. "It'd be like trying to develop your film in a room full of holes. One mistake and the film is ruined for good. Defrosting a hunk of meat that old is risky because it will decompose rapidly. In a controlled setting, decomposition is minimal, but out here, in the environment, anything can go wrong. They could lose any viable DNA they find."

"I'm impressed," Nicole said, surprised by Paul's clear explanation of the problem at hand.

"I read *Popular Science*," Paul said as he put his eyes back to the non-existent road.

Nicole turned to Steve. "So what does all this mean?"

Steve looked forward, eying the Sno-Cat in front of them which contained Eddy, Eve, and Kevin: the three people he knew would react badly to this new information. "This means," Steve said as he faced Nicole, "things are going to get ugly."

Nicole smiled. Now Steve understood why.

"Which means your ratings might go through the roof."

An ominous cloud settled over the group, knowing things were going to get rough, physically and mentally in the days to come. The rest of the trip was spent dispensing casual small talk about the weather, sports, and family issues. Steve was surprised that he and Nicole shared so much in common. Who would have guessed that the valley girl who couldn't tell a story without saying, "She was all," and "he was all," would enjoy watching bone crunching hockey games; not to mention her favorite team was the Boston Bruins.

But Steve knew what some perceived as friendly interest might also be professional courtesy, especially while trapped with that person for more than a day. He knew they were all keeping a purposeful distance.

NICOLE'S VIEW was much the same. She didn't know if she would one day have to manipulate a situation involving Steve and Paul so that it played more dramatically in front of the camera, and she never could bring herself to mess with the mind of a friend. She made sure to keep the relationships professional.

PAUL WAS just uninterested. He knew Marie waited for him at home with a steaming bowl of fettuccini in a smooth alfredo sauce with mushrooms, grilled chicken, and sautéed onions. Paul missed his wife's cooking almost as much as he missed his Harley. Of course, these modified Cats would do in a pinch.

AND STEVE knew his interest in Nicole would never go beyond intense physical attraction. He could only stand her vivid viridian eyes for a moment at a time. Her straight, charcoal hair looked soft and she held herself with so much confidence it drove him wild; if only she wasn't so annoying when she spoke about anything important. True, on matters of frivolity they were a perfect match, but when it came to the stuff that mattered, she was as dim-witted as a frog on a wet highway. But Steve could get over that. He had with women before. One way or another, Steve was determined to roll over one morning and discover Nicole sleeping in bed next to him.

You're a fool, Steve. She's out of your league . . .

Steve's inner voice was squelched by a novel thought. It took hold and dug in roots. If the opportunity even presented itself as an option, it might just work. It was a risky move, and Steve might have to exaggerate the danger, but if the situation ever arose, Steve would be prepared to save Nicole's life. He knew that the farther north they traveled, the more opportunity his little plan might have to reach fruition.

7

THE DIG SITE

Brian Norwood was a mix of emotions as he wrung his hands together, staring out over the ice, as a group of small dots on the horizon grew nearer. He had been keeping tabs on the crew's progress. They weren't following the predetermined route, but the new route seemed like a safer choice. He was further surprised that the fleet never stopped for a rest. They moved at a steady pace, and even with the greater distance, arrived four hours early. Eddy was a sharp man and a slave driver.

When he first heard that Eve had hired Eddy, he was furious and even considered delaying the dig. But he decided to forget old grudges for the sake of the future; Eddy Moore was the best man for the job. No one had more experience. No one had more skill at raising ancient beasts from their resting places. But Brian also knew Eddy went by the book, more now than ever, to be sure.

While Norwood funded the dig with his own resources and a fat check from the Exploration Channel, once a team leader was hired, that man took charge and Brian became a geneticist. He played a dual role as benefactor and crew member, but his clout disappeared once the crew set to work. For safety reasons, there could only be one leader. Conflicting orders could cause calamity and slow progress, neither of which Brian wanted.

The line of Sno-Cats came to a stop outside of the dig site, which was a mass of high tech tents built out of honeycombed stainless steel framing and thick Mylar skins. At the center of the site was the area where Brian had first plummeted to the icy floor covered in warm water. The massive tusks still protruded from the wall, but that was all that would be seen of the ancient creature until it was removed from the ice and thawed out.

It occurred to Brian that Eddy might have found out about his plans to defrost the giant onsite. His stomach turned. A conflict with Eddy was best avoided, especially this early in the game. But officially, once the mammoth was free of the ice, Eddy's job was done. Then Brian could go about the thawing procedures and test for viable DNA, all in front of the cameras that would make him famous and thicken his already thick wallet.

The door of the nearest Sno-Cat was flung open and smacked against the hard metal side of the vehicle. Eddy hopped out, surveyed the area and locked his sights on Norwood.

Brian knew in that instant that Eddy was aware of Brian's plans and was about to voice his opinion. Brian sighed and put on his game face as Eddy approached. A second door was flung open and a woman, whom he recognized as Nicole Lu from the Exploration Channel, hopped out while shouting orders at her film crew, who chased after Eddy to capture the unfolding confrontation.

Knowing millions of people might hear their every word, Brian made an attempt at civility. "Dr. Moore. Eddy, how good to see you again."

Eddy must have been aware of the cameras, too. "Brian! Been a long time, buddy!"

He was putting on a show, Brian thought, and his suspicions were confirmed when Eddy gave him a hug.

"If you think I'm going to let you thaw the mammoth out here, you're insane," Eddy whispered through gritted teeth, then patted Brian hard on the back.

Eddy let go and began to walk away. Brian wouldn't let it end so soon and decided that Eddy being camera shy might work to his advantage.

"Have you become an expert on how to extract DNA while you were away, Eddy?"

Eddy stopped and turned around.

Two camera crews whirled to each side, one on Eddy, the other on Brian. Eddy glanced at the camera, then back to Brian. "Thawing a mammoth in an unstable environment is not only risky, it's moronic."

"Well, I'm glad you've expressed how you feel, no matter how ill-founded your ideas might be, but I'm afraid you have no choice in the matter."

Eddy smiled. "You know I do."

Brian returned the smile. "You should have read the fine print. Once the mammoth has been raised, team leadership reverts to a crewmember of my choosing. In this case, me."

Eddy clenched his fists.

"Frankly, I'm surprised by your lack of adventure. If this mammoth were a giant sloth in Venezuela, things would certainly be different."

Eddy held a fixed gaze on Brian. "There's no time to argue about this, Brian. It's too risky and you know it, better than anyone else here."

"Ah, too risky," Brian said with a sharp tinge of sarcasm stabbing his every word. "I see. So it's acceptable to take risks with the lives of your crew, but not with the recovered specimen. Is that it?"

Eddy's body became rigid. He was hyper aware of the cameras around him. He knew that his very reputation could be diminished on a global scale by what he said and did next. "I'm not giving you a choice," Eddy said plainly.

Brian was outraged at being dismissed so quickly. Eddy was walking away, but this wasn't how it was going to end, not on international television. Brian grabbed Eddy by the shoulder and yanked him around. "Now you listen to me! You—Omph!"

Eddy decided that the millions of viewers would probably want to knock Brian out, too. And he didn't want to disappoint. Eddy slugged Brian in the head, pulling his punch slightly. He wanted to knock the man over, not give him a concussion.

Brian fell to the ice and slid a few feet from the force. He was stunned. Eddy hit him! He looked up and saw Eddy storming away toward the dig site. He felt a lump growing on the side of his head.

Kevin and Eve ran over and knelt down next to Brian.

"You shouldn't have brought up Venezuela."

Brian nodded. "I know."

Eve took a handful of ice and held it against Brian's growing lump. He was jolted by the cold, but remained still, knowing it would stop the swelling.

"He's a different man now, Brian," Eve said. "You would do well to stay out of his way, especially when it comes to taking risks. That's not who he is anymore."

"Could have fooled me," Brian said. "He took a risk when he decided to smash my brains out."

Kevin chuckled.

Brian looked at him. "What?"

"If Eddy really wanted to hurt you, he could have. He pulled his punch. And you're lucky he did. I've seen what happens when he doesn't."

A twinkle of fear appeared in Brian's eyes. "What happens?"

Kevin smiled. "Let's just say it would have been a while before you remembered how to use an electron microscope again." Kevin slopped a second handful of ice onto Brian's head. "And all the ice in the world wouldn't do you any good."

Nicole let out a giggle as she stood next to the camera man who had recorded every word. Everyone turned to her, annoyed. "Sorry," she said. "You guys are just making this too easy."

☼   ☼   ☼   ☼   ☼

DAYS PASSED and work progressed steadily. Inch by agonizing inch, a solid cube of ice and permafrost was chiseled out of the ice and propped up onto wooden boards so that several chains could be wrapped around and underneath. The crew had taken up their roles and quarreling was at a minimum. This allowed for great progress, but made for a dull documentary. Nicole grew impatient. She needed some turmoil, some personal disagreement or physical catastrophe.

Nicole called Mark, her cameraman, into her tent for a meeting of the minds during which she would fill his mind with her ideas. Mark sat by the tent's entrance, listening for approaching footsteps as though they were shipmates planning a mutiny. The analogy wasn't too far from the truth.

"I'll see what I can stir up emotionally between the crew, starting with Eve. A little romance never hurts . . . and a broken heart is even better." Nicole smiled. There was so much potential for things to go wrong out here. "But we need some physical drama, some kind of close call to up the stakes. Nothing too dangerous, we don't want to get anyone killed, but . . . you understand?"

Mark nodded. "I think so."

"I suppose that's the best I can expect out of a cameraman."

Mark let out an annoyed sigh. "You're right. I was hired to be a cameraman, not a saboteur."

A single eyebrow shot up on Nicole's face. Mark was getting a spine—too much time with these roughneck scientists.

"You do this for me," Nicole said, "and I'll put in a good word for you back at the network. They might not make you an instant director, but it should help."

This seemed to appease Mark somewhat. "No joke?"

"I swear."

Mark pursed his lips as he mulled the issue over. "Okay."

"Perfect. You won't regret it. They're planning on lifting the mammoth out of the ice tomorrow. Plenty of opportunities for something to go wrong. Understand?"

"I just hope I don't get anyone killed."

Nicole's grin faded.

"Try not to."

Mark unzipped the tent and slid out. He walked through the maze of orange tents toward the center of the camp where a large crane was being rigged to a series of thick metal wires wrapped around a gigantic ice cube. Steve stood at the edge watching the work progress and sucking on a cigarette.

Trying his hardest to feign casual interest, Mark stood next to Steve and looked up at the wires. "You guys are lifting that thing straight out of there?"

"Yup," Steve said as though in another world.

"What happens if one of the wires break?"

"They can't break. They're braided Liquidmetal cables. Super strong. I should know. I bought them. And the weight is distributed evenly, so each cable holds only a fraction of the weight it's capable of handling."

Steve took a drag from his cigarette and gave a sideways glance at Mark, who had never seemed all that interested in anything other than his camera before.

"Liquidmetal?"

"It's the superhero of metals. Titanium and steel pale in comparison to this beauty. Of course it costs a small fortune, but we don't want Babar here to fall and break open on the ice."

Mark's face twisted with confusion. "Babar?"

"You know, the kid's book. The little elephant? Forget it. The point is, nothing can break these cables."

"Nothing?"

"Well, every superhero has a weakness," Steve said.

Mark waited with a wrinkled forehead and butterflies doing flip flops in his belly.

"They don't deal too well with heat," Steve explained. "Normal metal gets malleable somewhere around 2,100 degrees. Liquidmetal gets all loosey goosey around 750, just slightly hotter than your average oven on broil. Of course, the likelihood of that happening out here is about the same as me getting lucky with your boss."

That got a laugh out of Mark. "She's colder than the ice," Mark said, trying to put Steve at ease over his line of questioning. "Hypothetically speaking, what if one broke?"

"Why?"

Steve's bold affront caught Mark off-guard. Was he suspicious?

"Uh, I need to know how far away I should set up my equipment. I don't want to be near that thing tomorrow if it falls."

"And you wouldn't want to be. Thirty tons of ice, permafrost, and mammoth landing on top of you wouldn't feel all that dandy . . . but to answer your question, Eddy has so many chains strapped to this thing that half of them could break away and the rest could still hold the weight without breaking a sweat. Not that chains sweat, but you know what I mean."

"Right . . . okay, then. Thanks."

Mark started to walk away.

"No problemo," Steve said, adding under his breath, "nimrod."

Mark's hands grew sweaty underneath his gray cotton gloves. The worst thing he'd done in his life was sneak into the girl's locker room and hide in a stall so he could watch them change their clothes. But even then he was so scared that he just sat on the toilet without peeking once.

After entering his tent and zipping the entrance closed behind him, Mark slumped onto his sleeping bag and rubbed his temples. He was going to go to hell for this.

☼　☼　☼　☼　☼

AFTER A long day of setting up the electron microscope and computer analysis system which was supposed to make her life simpler, but really just confounded her, Eve was tired. The work was nothing compared to the dawn-til-dusk hours she put in on her father's farm during the summers of her youth, shoveling manure and bailing hay, but then again, she wasn't sixteen anymore, either. For a moment her mind replayed scenes from the farm—the willow tree out front, the sweet, earthy smell of the stream across the dirt road, and the stars at night, endless and beautiful. At least in the Arctic, where the electric glow of civilization could only be found in their flashlights, laptops, and lanterns, that old night sky was once again keeping her company. A stiff breeze brought her out of her mind's eye and reminded her of the Arctic's main drawback—it was damn cold.

She sat on a case of supplies, watching Eddy finish securing the ice encased mammoth. She shook her head and grunted. Here she was, one of the most well respected female paleobotanists in the world, reduced to a man watching teenager. She was hopeless. Eddy hadn't paid much attention to her once work was underway, which was typical and expected, but not appreciated. He didn't have to profess his undying love, or even a small crush; Eve just wanted to be acknowledged. Eddy was chummy with Steve, Paul, Kevin, and occasionally even Brian.

"Personally, I don't know what you see in him, but if I were you, I wouldn't just sit on the sidelines and do nothing."

Eve looked up, her trance broken. Nicole stood next to her.

Eve tried her best at a convincing laugh. "What are you talking about?"

Nicole sat down on an overturned crate across from Eve. "You can't play dumb with me. I'm trained to see through people's protective shields. I've seen the way you look at him."

Eve shifted, averting her eyes from Nicole's.

"I'm the only other woman here," Nicole said. "If you can't talk to me, who can you talk to?"

Eve smiled. "Good point. This off the record?"

"You see a camera?"

Eve glanced from side to side. No cameras. No film crew.

"So, are you two an item?"

Eve guffawed, no pretending this time.

"I'll take that as a no; were you ever?"

"We've had a few close calls over the years. Work just always seems to come between us."

"You mean he puts it between you."

"I suppose you could say that."

Nicole leaned forward. "And that doesn't tell you something?"

"Should it?"

Nicole rolled her eyes. "I can translate the body language of a man who's just walked into a bar as easily as putting on lipstick. If he wants sex, beer, or to spill his guts, I know before he reaches his seat. They're all open books to me."

"And what does Eddy's book tell you?"

"Eddy's book is very short and in bold print. The man is head over heels for you."

Eve relaxed and snickered. "I think you need reading glasses."

"Eve. Honey. We're the only two women here. The only two. That means all these testosterone-filled boys are either looking at you, or at me."

"Ugh, please don't make me think about that. Some of these guys are like brothers."

"Horny brothers."

Eve laughed and leaned back, relaxing more. Nicole had a sense of humor after all.

Nicole continued. "My point is, I make a note when a man looks at me. His attraction might come in useful in the future."

Eve raised her eyebrows. "And . . .?"

"And Eddy hasn't taken a double take at me once. Even when I pretended to drop my pen and bent over in front of him. He didn't take a second glance. Frankly, I was a bit offended, but now I understand why. He's only got eyes for you."

Nicole's testimony began to sink in and take hold of Eve's mind. "You're serious?"

"Completely. Have you talked to him honestly about how you feel?"

"No."

"No time like the present. What do you have to lose?"

Face contorting with obvious thought, Eve chewed on what Nicole had said. If she was right and Eddy reciprocated, she'd be breaking ground ten years old. But if not . . . if not, nothing. She didn't have him fully now. If he rejected her, she'd just go on living as she had been, only she'd feel able to consider other men. Which, for some reason, she hadn't before. Better make a move, Eve thought, before my feelings for him become fossilized versions of what once was—cold, hard and dead.

Eve stood up. "Can't lose something you don't have."

"Exactly!"

Eve looked at Eddy and headed straight for him like a heat seeking missile. She had never felt so determined to tell him the truth; once and for all, to spill it all out.

NICOLE OPENED her jacket and removed a small digital camcorder which had recorded everything through the space between her coat buttons. She pointed the camera at Eve and focused. But video wouldn't be enough alone. After setting the camcorder down, aimed at Eve, Nicole reached into her pocket and took out a small device which she unfolded into a miniature satellite dish-shaped listening device, which she plugged into the camcorder. She held the listening device out like a gun and pointed it at Eve. She would record every word and twenty-four frames a second of Eve's stunning success and the beginning of a romance, or Eve's crushing defeat and broken heart. Both were gold.

HEART THUMPING in her chest, Eve walked up behind Eddy, who was yanking on one of the Liquidmetal cables, as though a pull from his arm could test the material's strength. But Eve knew it made him feel better. Eddy turned at her approach.

"Steve, can we take another—oh, I thought you were Steve."

"A man can dream."

Good idea, Eve, she scolded herself. Sarcasm will win him over. Stupid.

"What?"

"Nothing. Everything all set for tomorrow?"

"As ready as we're gonna be."

"Great, great. Hey, can I talk to you for a minute?"

"This better not be about Brian."

"No, not about Brian."

"Good, is there a problem with your equipment? Your microscope didn't break again?"

"No, my equipment's fine." Not that you would ever know.

"Then it will have to wait. I'm kind of busy."

Eve's shoulders dropped. Just like that, she was dismissed. "When are you not?" She walked away without another word.

EDDY WENT back to tugging on cables but froze as his mind replayed what had just happened. "Damn it," Eddy said under his breath. He turned and watched Eve walk away. He took a deep breath, shook his head, and went back to testing the cables, though not with the same enthusiasm as before.

NICOLE WRAPPED up her equipment, careful not to draw Eve's attention as she stormed back to her tent. It didn't play out how she had hoped, but it was a start. Eddy hadn't turned her down directly, because Eve never spit it out. She loved him, and by the way he watched her leave, she was sure Eddy felt the same. If only she could get them to hash it out . . . preferably out in the open. They'd given her silver, but she still longed for gold.

8

THE DESERT WASP

Ryan Dombroski had suffered a barrage of insulting nicknames growing up. Dumbo. Dumb boy skiing. His favorite was Dumbbraboy. But the years of name calling and black eyes that came with his last name gave him the desire and willpower to stand up to the world's biggest bullies. He'd joined the CIA straight out of law school and excelled at Special Ops assignments. He soon longed for more and rather than hunting down and teaching a lesson to Evan Fontneau, his grade school nemesis, he had leapt at the opportunity to train as one of the CIA's elite assassins. With an IQ of 181, he was one of the smartest men on the planet. With a knife, he was one of the most dangerous.

His current assignment was typical: get in, kill the bad guy, and get out again. And if he couldn't get out again, get killed so no one could ask him questions. His mark was Sheik Abdul Bin Sherrif. The man had come out of nowhere. He had just appeared from the desert with an army of men at his disposal. The CIA discovered that Sherrif, the Desert Wasp, was hatching a scheme to overthrow the government of Pakistan in a bloody coup, after which Sherrif would be named king of a new monarchy.

A power change in Pakistan would destabilize the Middle East, and with a radical Islamist like Sherrif calling the shots, it wouldn't be long before World War III erupted. Simulations predicted that Pakistan under Sherrif's rule would attack India within one year. Sherrif, being a warrior and not the type to accept defeat, would most likely strike out first with Pakistan's growing nuclear arsenal. India would become a graveyard and Sherrif would turn his attention to other neighbors. Afghanistan, Iraq, Iran, and Saudi Arabia would all fall in line behind Pakistan and the world would be drawn into conflict.

So Dombroski had been called in. Someone high up had enough faith in his abilities to believe that one man could change the future. He'd spent a month searching for Sherrif's palace; once it was found, like an oasis in the sands of the desert, it took him a single night to work his way into the servant's quarters and through the ventilation system. He now had a front row seat in the air conditioning duct that ran directly into the sheik's office.

Dombroski stared at Sherrif with steel grey eyes. Looking down at the sheik, dressed in a spotless white robe and a red turban, Dombroski realized he could end it all right here, with one shot. But the CIA wanted intel first.

Would the coup go on without Sherrif? Who was second in command? Who funded the sheik's campaign?

The office was decorated with solid gold candelabras, large paintings of Arab warriors, and flowing silk curtains. The Sheik's oak desk shined with the glow of a recent polish. On the floor was a hand woven rug depicting Mohammed killing the infidels—a persuasive means to achieve conversion. This man was a fundamentalist. The sheik would say that he believed in true Islam, while most present-day Muslims believed in a watered down, politically correct version of the great prophet's teachings. Based on what he had studied of Islam, Dombroski agreed, but would have added that wasn't a good enough reason to proclaim Jihad on the entire world. Not even Mohammed had been that brazen. Of course, it wouldn't be long before Sherrif would see his plans of a worldwide conversion to Islam through terror spilled out on the rug, along with his guts.

After twenty minutes of watching the sheik eat fruit carried in by women dressed in black *abayaa* which covered them from head to toe, masking every inch of their skin like black apparitions, Dombroski had seen enough. Intel or not, this might be the only chance he would get to end this man's life.

Inching forward, Dombroski gripped his knife and prepared to smash open the vent, slide out like a viper, and slash the sheik's throat before he could scream for help. The telephone rang, causing Dombroski to become rigid, like he'd just looked into the cold stare of Medusa. It seemed the sheik would live a few minutes more.

Sherrif answered the phone in Arabic, which Dombroski spoke fluently: "Hello? Ah, my friend, it has been too long. How's the Cuban weather treating you?"

Cuba?

Dombroski pressed against the vent, listening intently.

"Good, good. These people are weak and easily bent toward our will. The time is coming for us to end our long-lived game."

The man on the other end spoke and the sheik snorted. "Ha! You're right, of course. It's been only two years since my time in South America, but I do miss the seclusion provided by the jungle. Tell me, Reginn, to what do I owe the pleasure of your call?"

What kind of name is Reginn? Dombroski wondered. What the hell is going on here?

The sheik had apparently spent some time in South America, which explained why his sudden appearance in Pakistan was so unusual. And now he was talking with an old friend in Cuba, of all places.

Can the planned coup be one the beginning of a much larger plot? Dombroski's instinct told him it was.

Sherrif swiveled to the side in his chair as he listened to the voice on the other end, allowing Dombroski a view of his dark face and inky, sunken eyes. The sheik's eyes narrowed. "This is interesting, to be sure, but we've tracked several expeditions such as the one you have described to me, and each without discovering the beacon.

"These people pose no threat to us. Really, I'm surprised you—" The sheik's face fell flat. "They're in the Canadian Arctic? Are you sure?"

As Sherrif listened to the man on the other end, he leaned back in his chair, opened a drawer and pushed a single button.

What is going on here? Dombroski thought furiously.

"Yes, of course. Have Hoder keep track of them. I want to be alerted right away if they uncover anything of interest. If they do, I'll handle the situation personally."

Like hell you will.

This was Dombroski's moment of opportunity. Sherrif was distracted and the room was otherwise unoccupied . . .

Boom! The double doors at the front of the lavish office burst open and two men dressed in black, wearing white turbans, and carrying automatic weapons stepped into the office. Sherrif didn't seem in the least bit surprised. He waved them over to his desk.

The two men stopped in front of his desk and one of them spoke. "Marutas, you called?"

Marutas? Was that a name? If it was an Arabic word, Dombroski didn't recognize it.

The hair's on Dombroski's neck shot up. He knew this was all wrong. Dombroski quickly sheathed his knife and drew his Glock 9mm semi automatic pistol. He figured he could squeeze off three shots into each man, two to the chest, one to the head just to be sure, and still have time to sever the sheik's jugular before he reached the door. Of course, getting out of the palace alive would be a trick, but he'd survived worse.

"Call me here as soon as you know something," the sheik said into the phone then glanced toward the vent.

Dombroski pulled the trigger on his Glock six times in two seconds, pausing for a half second to aim at the other guard. After smashing through the vent and sliding out onto the floor, Dombroski was already on his feet inside the office when the second guard's body hit the floor, staining the rug with his blood.

Dombroski ignored the ringing in his ears caused by firing his gun in such an enclosed area and raised the Glock toward Sherrif's head. But the sheik was merely amused. He chuckled.

"You find this humorous?" Dombroski asked in perfect Arabic.

"Actually, yes," the sheik replied in flawless English.

"You speak English?"

"Who doesn't? But I also speak Japanese, Chinese, Spanish, Latin, Greek . . ."

The sheik was stalling. There was most likely a small army on its way to the office. Dombroski circled to the door, keeping his weapon trained on Sherrif's head, and shoved a gold-plated chair under the doorknobs of the dual doors, sealing the room, at least temporarily.

"Now you've gone and locked yourself in," Sherrif said with a toothy grin.

Ignoring the comment, Dombroski moved on to business. "Who were you speaking to on the phone?"

"Castro, of course."

"Fidel Castro?"

"His brother, Defense Minister Raul Castro. Fidel's time is . . . limited."

"And why would you give me this information so freely?"

"I have no secrets to hide from a dead man."

The sheik made the comment so coolly, with such self-assurance, that it gave Dombroski pause. What did Sherrif know that he didn't?

"It's really a shame to have to kill you, Special Agent Dombroski."

He knows me?

"Of course the CIA has always been part of our plan, but you, I'm afraid, are just a little too smart. It was only a matter of time before you put two and two together. If you weren't so busy gallivanting around the world putting bullets in people's heads, you might have already figured out the truth."

Dombroski began to sweat. This was a setup from the beginning. To kill him. But why? What was he going to figure out? His eyes darted back and forth, there was no one else present and the sheik was unarmed. There hadn't been a single knock on the door. They were completely alone. How were they going to kill him?

Sherrif stood up. "It's a shame, really. You've always been one of my favorite killers."

Dombroski grinned. "You're stalling for time, and I've just decided your time is up."

Three shots echoed through the room as Dombroski unloaded his remaining bullets at the sheik's head. When the sound faded, Dombroski dropped his weapon and took a step back, forehead glistening with perspiration. What he had just witnessed was not only amazing, it was impossible. Sherrif had dodged the first two bullets by diving and rolling across the floor in one swift movement. The third bullet clipped Sherrif's shoulder.

The sheik stood still, looking at the wound in his shoulder which began to bleed . . . purple. His white robe became wet with lilac-colored liquid, which he rubbed with his index finger. "Shocking, isn't it?" Sherrif said as Dombroski stared at the blood covered finger.

"What . . .what are you?"

Sherrif grinned widely. He reveled in every second of this. "I, whelp, am your master. I have always been, and always will be!"

As Dombroski faced the sheik, he felt the man's evil emanate throughout the room. He didn't care what color blood Sherrif had; he was bleeding, and that meant he could be killed.

With a speed perfected through years of training, Dombroski spun around, kicking low and clipping the sheik's feet, knocking him off balance. He continued his spin, using the momentum to plant his foot on Sherrif's chest. Sherrif was knocked backward and rolled over the desk.

When the sheik stood from the floor, his eyes were wide as though he had just overdosed on speed. His teeth were bared like an animal. "Yes! Yes! Fight for your life!"

Sherrif bounded over the desk and lunged into the air. Dombroski dove to the side, rolled to his feet and drew his six inch blade. Running forward without pause, he slashed his knife through the air four times in quick succession, missing the sheik's body but shredding his robe.

Sherrif threw a single, lighting-fast blow that cracked three of Dombroski's ribs and sent him back into the corner of the desk.

With a leap, Sherrif crossed the gap in seconds, landing on top of Dombroski and cracking two more ribs.

The pain only made Dombroski angrier. He swung in high, going for a killer slash across the sheik's throat, but Sherrif moved like a cat and caught his hand . . . with his mouth! He screamed in pain and dropped the knife as Sherrif bit down like a crocodile.

Dombroski reached out in desperation and his hand found something solid, metal—a candlestick. He swung up as hard as he could and introduced the candlestick to Sherrif's temple.

Sherrif grunted and stepped back, momentarily stunned.

Momentarily.

Sherrif grabbed him by the shoulder and flung him across the room with a growl. He slid across the floor and slammed into a wall. He was dazed and dizzy, barely aware that Sherrif was stalking toward him.

On all fours.

The sound of tearing clothes filled the room, followed by a heavy breathing so thick that the confused Dombroski knew it came from a pair of lungs larger than a human's, larger than a gorilla's. His mind began to make sense of the world again and as his vision cleared his eyes grew wide. For the first time since hearing the sheik's telephone conversation, everything made perfect sense. It was the last thing he thought before he felt his belly torn open with a single slash, spilling warm rolls of intestine onto the floor.

9

THE MAMMOTH

Wondering how he got into this mess was no longer a question in Mark Vincent's mind. Several other nagging questions had taken hold: What possible motivation could there be for him to become a saboteur? What would happen if he got caught? Was he really so desperate? Would someone be killed as a result of his tinkering? Mark prayed to God that he wouldn't cause too much damage. Not that God listened to a man like him.

It was pitch black and the entire camp was asleep, catching a few good winks before the next day when they would pull the mammoth out of its frosty grave. It was also freezing—thirty below. Mark held his shaking hand as steady as he could and lit the small propane torch. He wasn't sure how hot those things got, but the blue flame shooting out of the front assured him it was hot enough . . . 750 degrees was all he needed. Was that Celsius or Fahrenheit? He couldn't remember, or maybe that Steve guy never said.

Mark held the bright azure flame against a portion of cable that was hidden by a crossing of two other Liquidmetal wires. The cable held strong, but after five seconds turned bright orange. The cable began to stretch out and thin. If this went as he hoped, the cable would snap during the mammoth's assent, giving everyone a shock and giving a TV audience another reason to sit through another block of Sunny D and George Foreman Grill commercials. Of course, only one cable would break and no one would be in any real danger . . . he hoped. Mark looked at the cable. It had gone from being the diameter of a silver dollar to that of a nickel.

Not too thin! *Not too thin!*

With the intention of making this look like an accident, Mark knew that if the cable were to break now and not while the mammoth was being hefted out of the permafrost, the gig would be up. A witch hunt would commence and he was sure it would end at his tent's entrance. Mark yanked the torch away and extinguished the flame. Just in time.

A pair of boots scrunching through the thick snow gave Mark just enough warning to duck behind one of the giant crane's treads. He peeked up over the tread and saw a body hovering by the Liquidmetal cables. It was Dr. Norwood.

Mark had been a journalist before moving to the world of documentary films, and he knew a story when he saw one. Nicole made her crew carry around cameras wherever they went, even to the bathroom—just in case. It seemed her insistence was about to pay off. Mark removed the camcorder from his jacket, switched it on and directed it to Norwood's position, leaving the side viewfinder closed so as to not light up his position. Mark switched on the camera's digital night-vision and zoomed in.

NORWOOD RUBBED his arms, trying to warm himself in the frigid air. He coughed and searched the area for prying eyes. He found none and was sure no one could hear his coughing over the loud hum of the generators which kept the ultra-modern camp warm and electrified.

Having prepared for this moment for a month, his hands moved quickly. He popped open a small grey case which contained four blobs of what looked like silly putty, each the size of a marble. From his pocket he produced a small battery powered drill. He reached inside his jacket and pulled out a drill bit, which he snapped into place on the drill.

Confidence overwhelmed Norwood and erased any doubts he had about the possible consequences of what he was attempting. After he first found the mammoth in the ice and witnessed the spectacular melting phenomenon, he had done some tests and discovered that the ice melted when exposed to seismic energy, initially created by his single stick of dynamite. Of course, what he planned now would be a much smaller series of blasts, but the results, by his calculations, should be much more lucrative.

Naturally he would deny any knowledge about the four small rumbles from within the frozen block of ice which would start the block melting. Norwood knew that if he placed the explosives a certain distance apart and set them off at just the right time, the effect would have the ice thawed in minutes. The frigid air of the arctic would instantly refreeze any portions of the flesh that might become exposed, then the future Pulitzer Prize-winning and very rich Dr. Norwood would collect his DNA sample and clone a perfect mammoth—the first geneticist to return an extinct species killed off by the hands of man to life. This was no Jurassic Park and he was no John Hammond; he'd be a hero.

It was true that Norwood still had no idea why seismic energy caused this particular chunk of ice to melt rapidly. It could be some type of new element that heated with seismic activity—perhaps something from deep within the Earth, spat out thousands of years ago by a volcano that had been melted away during the last ice age. And if it turned out to be such a thing, he would only be all the more famous for it. Then what would his father have to say? He knew he'd never be able to tell anyone how he came to retrieve his DNA so fast. He never did reveal his knowledge of the rapid melting ice discovered at the same instant as the mammoth tusks. If he had, he knew the Canadian government would take over the site quicker the he could say, "Get me a beer, eh?" It'd be a warm day in the Arctic before he ever let *that* happen.

Norwood drilled four holes into the ice at different locations. He then eased grey balls of plastic explosives, each containing a small detonator and radio receiver, into the four holes. He covered the tiny cavities with snow, packed up his equipment, and headed back to his tent.

MARK WASN'T sure what he had just seen, but he knew it was something Dr. Norwood didn't want anyone else to see. Of course Mark had seen it, and if something went wrong, other than Mark's own sabotage, everyone on Earth would see what Norwood had done. He'd be praised by the network and made a hero among documentary makers. Life was good and Mark was now sure it could only get better.

☼　☼　☼　☼　☼

THE EAGER crew was awake and moving with the sun, which would only be in the sky for a few hours each day at this time of year. People were in place and ready to make history. A kind of levity had settled over the crew, knowing that this would be their moment of triumph, another successful excavation. Even Eddy had lightened his rigid exterior, but not enough to overlook Nicole Lu setting up a camera in a "no walk" zone. No walk zones were an easy concept: in the areas marked by orange cones, don't walk. Eddy sighed. It seemed Nicole either couldn't read the signs or had ignored them altogether.

Eddy stood next to Nicole with his arms crossed, which were covered from the cold air by only a long sleeved, grey thermal top. She paid no attention to him and went about preparing her camera.

Eddy cleared his throat. "Ahem."

Nicole spun around. "Oh hi, Eddy, Dr. Moore. Everything all set for the big moment?"

Nicole gestured and her voice had a higher pitch than usual. Eddy knew in an instant that Nicole had read, understood, and ignored the no walk zone signs. "And what do you think you're doing?" Eddy asked with a raised eyebrow.

"Just setting up another camera. This angle will be great, capturing the bottom of the ice as it passes ominously above." Nicole moved her hands over her head, following the imaginary line of the ice block as it would pass overhead.

"Well you got the ominous part right, but you won't be filming it from here . . . or could you not read the signs?"

"I can read the signs," Nicole returned, mocking Eddy's voice. "Sorry, sorry. I just get passionate about my work, you know?"

"Look, it's a matter of safety. The mammoth is going to pass right over this area. If something were to go wrong and someone were underneath, well, let's just say I wouldn't want to be the person shoveling your remains out of the snow with a shovel."

"Okay, that was sufficiently gross. Thank you for the image."

Eddy smiled.

Nicole continued, "But thanks, really. I didn't realize you were so concerned about my safety . . ." Nicole gave Eddy an alluring look. Maybe she was wrong about him and Eve.

"Actually I'm more concerned about the mammoth. If it fell on you and your equipment, it could be more damaged than it might be falling on the flat ice."

Nicole's seductive gaze disappeared. "Well, don't be. My camera's mobile. I can move it in seconds if I have to. If that thing falls, it's got to snap through like forty of those cables, right? I'm sure I can move fast enough. Please?"

Eddy took a deep breath and closed his eyes for a moment.

Nicole persisted, putting as much sweetness into her voice as she could muster. She knew it was a powerful tool, having gained her numerous free coffees, video rentals, and photo developing. "*Pleeease.*"

"You'll move at the first sign that anything is remotely wrong?"

"Yes."

"And if I tell you to move for any reason, even if you don't understand it, you'll head for the hills?"

"I promise."

Eddy turned away from Nicole and made a circular gesture with his hand. "Okay, start the crane!"

Nicole had been the last obstacle to take care of before they started pulling the mammoth free from the ice. Eddy glanced at Nicole. "Better start your camera."

"Oh!" Nicole rushed to her camera, peeked through the viewfinder, and started recording. Nicole looked up to see Eddy sneaking away. "Where are you going?"

Eddy smirked. "Only a fool would stand underneath a thirty ton block of ice."

Nicole smiled. Was he joking or serious?

A loud scraping noise rumbled from the cube of ice, now surrounded by a maze of Liquidmetal cables, as they snapped tight from the crane's pull. Slowly, inch by inch, the block rose from the permafrost. After thirty seconds, the gigantic tusks of the mammoth appeared, rising up from below. After two minutes, the entire block hovered in the air like a floating ice cube with tusks.

Focusing on the massive cube, Nicole was oblivious to the world. She was right about her position; it was an incredible view. Cast in the shadow of the frozen block, Nicole continued to follow it with her lens. A voice squawked in her ear. "Hey boss." It was Mark speaking through her headset, which allowed her to stay in communication with her crew. "Doesn't look like it's gonna work out. Sorry about that."

BRIAN WATCHED as the block passed over Nicole Lu. His face was wide with a grin and he almost laughed with giddiness. After the block cleared the documentary team, Brian would detonate the small explosives using a cheap radio transmitter, which would begin the series of small rumbles and accelerated melting of the ice. No one would be hurt and he would get a head start on his research.

NORWOOD DIDN'T know was that one of the Liquidmetal cables was already weakened, or that Nicole Lu was about to use her radio headset, which used the same wavelength as Norwood's detonation transmitter.

Nicole pushed the button on her headset and spoke into the mike. "Don't worry about it, Mark. This is impressive enough without something going wrong."

Nicole was so focused on her work, adjusting the lens and zooming out as the block hung directly above, that she failed to hear the four dull pops above her head. Even as drops of water began to trickle all around her, her subconscious thought nothing of it; a rain storm, perhaps. It wasn't until the Liquidmetal cables above her head began to glow orange that she became aware that something wasn't right.

Standing back from her viewfinder, Nicole became aware of three things: water was everywhere, pouring off the block above her, the Liquidmetal cables were glowing even brighter and radiating heat, stretching out slowly, and a sea of voices were screaming her name. One of the voices was louder than the rest: Eddy. "Get your ass out of there, damnit!"

Nicole reached for her camera but before she could grab it and run, a loud twang filled her ears as one of the Liquidmetal cables snapped at the top of the cube, most likely from Mark's handiwork. The cable swung around beneath the cube and slashed across Nicole's leg, ripping open her stylish yellow winter pants and slicing her thigh.

Several sensations hit Nicole at the same time. The cut in her leg burned with pain, and she screamed. But the pain of her wound was replaced by a sudden rush of cold as she tumbled to the snow, now reduced to a puddle of slush. She planted her hands and kicked with her feet, trying to find a foot hold and escape with her life.

Nicole glanced up and saw the giant ice cube sagging down towards her, still ten feet above her head. The Liquidmetal cables were stretching out, the situation growing more tenuous. She was sure they would snap any second. Through the melting ice, Nicole could see the brown fur of the mammoth begin to appear. *Amazing.* She looked at her camera. It was still recording. If she survived this mess, it would be some of the best footage she'd ever recorded.

Determined not to die beneath the bulk of an extinct animal, Nicole dug her foot through the slush and found purchase on the frozen ice below. She pushed up, grunting as her leg protested and turned for her camera. The first cable broke, not snapping, but simply sliding apart. One after another, the cables gave way and the mammoth continued its steady descent.

Nicole scooped up her camera when she felt a tickle on the back of her neck. She turned around and found herself gazing into a tuft of rusty hair. Her eyes widened, wandered down the creature's still-frozen back, and saw only five slender cables remaining. This was it. She was going to be crushed to death.

An object moving like Superman flashed through Nicole's vision and she felt an impact like a car crashing at fifty miles per hour. She felt an immense pressure all around her, found breathing to be near impossible. She was trapped beneath the mammoth!

A second crash like an explosion shook the ice beneath Nicole. She realized that it must have been the mammoth falling to the ice . . . but what, then, was on top of her? The load on Nicole's chest and head lightened and she was able to suck in a breath of air. She opened her eyes and looked into the smiling face of Steve.

Steve had risked his life to save her?

"You okay?" Steve asked as he pushed his hair back over his head.

"Yeah . . . yeah, I'm fine." Nicole was stunned. She sat up and saw her camera lying next to her, shattered into bits against a hard chunk of ice. "Ugh! You idiot! You broke my camera!"

"What was I supposed to do?" Steve was infuriated. "It was you or the camera!"

Eddy ran and slid to a stop next to Steve. "Oh, my-"

"Don't worry." Steve said as he brushed the snow from his jacket. "We're both alive and little miss prissy still needs an attitude adjustment."

Steve failed to notice that Eddy's comment wasn't directed toward him at all. It was just beyond him, where the mammoth, now freed from its frozen tomb, lay on the ice. The rest of the crew gathered behind Eddy and stared at the exposed mammoth as Steve and Nicole continued bickering.

"You haven't seen attitude yet, buddy! Just wait till you see how bad a little creative editing can make people look! Millions of people will believe whatever I tell them about you."

Steve laughed sarcastically, growing irate, "Oh, it's *on*, Miss Muffet. You think I can't have it arranged so that you have to walk back to civilization?"

Nicole gasped. "You wouldn't da—"

Eddy's strong hand grabbed Nicole's head and turned it toward the exposed mammoth. She jumped back and screamed.

Steve looked toward the mammoth and his eyes grew wide. The beast was fully exposed, 100 percent intact. Its tawny fur was thick and matted down from the melted ice. The creature's eyes were large and dark, like the moon during a solar eclipse. Its ivory tusks looked to be even longer now that they were fully exposed to the light of day.

But something was wrong with this mammoth. Steve was no biologist, but he could tell its stomach bulged strangely. Perhaps its ribs were broken when it died. Steve leaned forward and noticed a slit across the belly. That was even odder, Steve thought as he leaned in closer, ignoring Eddy's warning. "Steve, hold on, something's-"

It happened so fast that Steve couldn't fully register what he had seen. He jumped back with a scream any schoolgirl would be proud of and hid behind Eddy. He saw Eddy's dropped jaw above him and looked forward, to the object that had burst from the mammoth's belly. It . . . it was a human, a person, wrapped in furs and frozen solid!

Eve slid past the crowd of stunned onlookers and knelt by the frozen body, which clutched an object wrapped in fur to its chest. Eve studied the face. "It's a woman," she said.

Eddy stepped over Steve and knelt down next to the body. Without being asked, Eve gave Eddy her initial assessment. "This is unheard of, to find human and mammoth remains together at the same site proves so many theories that I don't even know where to start. First of all, this creature was domesticated. Ancient peoples must have not only hunted mammoths for food, but raised them as beast of burden. Meaning we've severely underestimated the ice age cultures of North America." Eve was brimming with excitement. "This is more than we ever dreamed of finding!"

Brian crouched next to Eddy, rubbing his hands together. "My God, we're going to be rich." Brian looked at Eddy's face and saw his squinting eyes staring at the frozen woman. "What is it? What's wrong?"

"A few things," Eddy began. "First, what the hell happened here? Why did the ice melt, and what heated the cables so much that they snapped?"

Brian felt a twist in his stomach. "Eddy, this isn't the time to play Sherlock Holmes. The mammoth is exposed! We should get to work."

Eddy glanced at Brian with a serious expression. "You don't think something's wrong here? Of course, it is very convenient for you, isn't it?"

"What?"

"The mammoth is thawed and you can get your DNA sample."

Eddy turned back to the woman, his face wrinkling with thought. Brian could see there was more on Eddy's mind than his conspiracy theory, and he wanted Eddy's train of thought to head in the other direction. "What do you see?"

"She's holding something," Eddy said as he reached out with his hand.

"Don't touch it!" Eve shouted. "We need to take her to the lab."

Eddy held his bare hand just above the furry object, clutched to the ancient woman's chest. "I'm not going to touch her."

Eve craned her head towards Eddy's hand, which he moved back and forth over the object. "Then what's wrong?"

Eddy met Eve's eyes, his face scrunched in deep thought. "She's warm."

10

ACTIVATION

After transporting the body of the woman to an examination tent, Eddy, Eve, and Kevin set to work discovering what ancient secrets the woman might be hiding. Brian disappeared with the mammoth, set up a massive, reinforced tent around the carcass, then set to work retrieving his DNA sample.

Eddy leaned against one of the two titanium tent support poles which ran from five feet below the ice to eight feet above, creating an expansive space in which to work. The outer layer of the triple thick Mylar was stretched over a dome shaped titanium frame. Designed to stand up to a blizzard of extreme proportions, the research tent resembled a flimsy yellow igloo, but was built like a tank. "How's it coming?" Eddy asked.

Eve had inspected every inch of the woman's body and hadn't done more than remove hair samples. She was a meticulous researcher and it sometimes caused those working with her to grow impatient. Eve held a finger up to Eddy as she had done so many times before. It was beginning to irritate him, but he knew the message: one more minute . . . or maybe half an hour, but you better not interrupt me again! All that with one index finger.

"At least think out loud," Eddy said.

"I'll think out loud for her," Kevin said as he looked the woman over. "Maybe ten thousand years old . . . Not quite *Homo sapien* . . . Huh."

Eddy watched as Kevin inspected the woman's head. "What?"

Kevin held his index finger up to Eddy, who sighed at the sight of it.

Eve made a quick note on her portable computer tablet, which translated her chicken scratch handwriting into legible text, then smacked down a quick period. "Done!" she said. "Were you two talking to me?"

"No, no." Eddy said. "We were just discussing how one would go about knocking out one of these fine cavewomen and dragging her back to one's cave, assuming that's how things were done back then."

"I highly doubt it," Eve stated. "This woman could have easily fended off the both of you. Her muscles are toned, especially for a woman in her forties, which was elderly by ancient terms, when the life expectancy was late thirties at best."

"Though we shouldn't be judging her in human terms," Kevin said as he stood up straight, moving away from the ancient woman.

"Why's that?" Eve asked with raised eyebrows.

Kevin gave a slight smirk. "She's not human."

"What?" Eddy almost tripped backward.

"Well, technically speaking, she's not *Homo sapien* . . . or any other kind of known hominid species. She's something new." Kevin crossed his arms, smile widening. "A new link in the evolutionary chain."

"Are . . . are you sure?" Eve asked with a questioning look.

"I'm a cryptozoologist. I study new species of animal. Man is an animal. New species of hominid fall under my umbrella. Yes, I'm sure."

"No need to get all red in the face, Kev," Eve said with a smile. "I just wanted you to be sure."

Kevin made a visible attempt to relax. "Well, I am."

Eve turned back to the woman lying on the examining table. "I find it intriguing, how well she's been preserved. Her skin isn't cracked and there's no decomposition, which is extremely odd, considering the warmth of her tomb—which is odd in itself. I'm interested to see what Brian has found about the state of the mammoth. If it is as well-preserved as this woman, we should have all the DNA we need, and then some." Eve smiled wide and looked into Eddy's eyes. "We did it."

Eddy smiled in return, but only for a moment. The chain of events that began with the melting of the cables, the fall and thawing of the mammoth, and the appearance of a perfectly preserved cavewoman had put Eddy on a razor edge that had yet to be dulled. "Any theories as to how this woman came to be inside a mammoth, or what preserved her so well?"

Eve shrugged. "Not a clue."

Eddy looked at Kevin. "What about the melting cables or rapid thawing?"

"We'll have to talk to Steve and Paul about the cables. As for the thawing trick, I've never seen anything like it. That was straight out of *Star Trek,* if you ask me."

Eddy rolled his head on his neck and stood over the cavewoman, starring down into her hard, brown eyes. "What are you hiding?" Eddy's eyes wandered down to the object, clutched in the woman's hands, bound in furs. Eddy reached for it.

"Eddy . . ." Eve's voice was cautious.

"The object this woman is holding could be the key to everything we don't know." Eddy placed his hand on the fur and took hold.

"It could be a bundle of food, or even an infant. Exposing them to . . ."

Eddy pulled back the fur, cutting Eve off mid-sentence. She loathed being interrupted, but this time she didn't seem to mind. A glint of silver showed from inside the wrappings, like a swath of brushed metal.

Kevin stood next to Eddy, his mouth wide. "Did the ancient North Americans know how to work metals?"

"Impossible," Eve said.

Eddy took a second piece of fur in his fingers and prepared to pull it back.

"Do it." Eve said.

Eddy eased the white fur away from the object. After a few inches, the furs loosened and fell away, revealing the top half of a pill-shaped metallic object. Eddy's face screwed with confusion. "This isn't right! Someone's been playing us for fools from the very beginning." Eddy's voice became loud with anger.

"How do you mean?" Eve asked.

Eddy ran his fingers through his hair several times. "This entire site is compromised. Either the mammoth was a fake, planted in the ice for us to discover, or it was raised at a previous time, modified and reinserted into the ice."

"Who would do that?" Kevin asked.

"Someone who wanted a success at all costs. There's a lot of fame and fortune wrapped up in this expedition."

"Brian?" Eve asked.

Eddy nodded. "He's at the top of a very short list."

Kevin shook his head slowly. "No . . . Brian's success is determined by the retrieval of viable DNA. If this is a fake, he's screwed."

"Unless he fakes the DNA, using a modified string of elephant DNA," Eve added.

Eddy paced. "But he'd eventually be found out and sued for all he's worth. He's greedy but not stupid."

"What about Nicole?" Eve asked.

Eddy's eyebrows dipped down low over his eyes. "She has the motivation and probably would have no compunction about manipulating us, but I doubt she has the resources available . . . and the Exploration Channel has a good reputation. They wouldn't air something that had been proven to be a fraud."

Kevin walked around the woman, taking in the object from all sides. His voice was silent, but his brain was firing electrons like bolts of lightning from a midsummer thunderstorm in Miami.

"Unless no one was left to object to her claims and all the evidence was lost," Eve said.

Eddy smiled. "Murder the entire crew and bury the evidence? Intriguing but impossible."

"There is another option," Kevin said, "but it's going to take a little faith on your parts. What if this isn't a fake?"

Eddy and Eve stared at Kevin, unsure if he was joking or serious.

"What if this object is proof of Atlantis or some other scientifically advanced ancient civilization?"

He was serious.

"What if this object fell from space? Or better yet, what if—"

"Okay, Buck," Eddy said. "I see where you're going. I'm pretty sure we can rule out little green men. This object is the handiwork of modern man. The only questions we need to answer are *who* and *why*."

Eddy looked at the object and placed his hand over it, feeling warmth emanating from its silver skin. "For now, I want as few people near this as possible. Whatever is making this thing heat up might cause health issues in humans."

"Radiation?"

"Could be. We'll treat it—" A shift in movement caught Eddy's eye.

Eve saw the slight rotation of the object beneath Eddy's hand, too. "Did you touch it?"

Eddy pulled his hand away. "No." His voice was a mixture of surprise and defensiveness.

The three of them eyed the object, leaning in closer, watching for the slightest movement. When it came, they could have been twenty feet away and still have seen it clearly. The object popped open and elongated by three inches to reveal a round portion of what looked like glass. The glassy area turned bright red. The device began to slide out of the frozen women's grip, sliding toward the edge of the table. It fell from the woman's body and Eddy instinctively reached out and snatched it from the air. As Eddy lifted the object up, he turned it so he was gazing into the hypnotic red light.

"Eddy, put it down," Eve insisted, but she went unheard.

In an instant, the red light shot out and scanned across Eddy's eyes, too fast for anyone but Eddy to register. It came like a flood, rushing into his mind—vast stores of information moving so fast that Eddy couldn't catch a single byte of knowledge. Then, in the same second it began, it suddenly stopped and the mass of garbled info disappeared into the recesses of Eddy's mind, behind a door not even he had the key to unlock.

Eddy stumbled backward and held his head with one hand while he clung to the object with the other. Tripping over a tent support, Eddy began to fall backwards but was caught by Kevin's arms. "Whoa! I got you."

After helping Eddy to his feet, Kevin took the object from Eddy's hands and placed it on the research table, next to the body of the ancient woman.

"What happened?" Eve asked.

Eddy rubbed his head and groaned. "It was . . . I saw . . . too much to understand. I don't know what it was."

"Looked like a seizure to me; a very short one, but I think that object might have caused your brain to short-circuit. After it turned red, your eyes glazed over and you stumbled backwards. I think we should quarantine that thing and get you back to civilization for a medical exam."

"I feel fine," Eddy said as his strength returned. "It was like a wave of energy passed through me. Like a magnetic force."

Kevin eyed the metallic cylinder. "Guys, its still doing something."

All eyes turned to the object as it closed.

"A third possibility just entered my mind," Kevin said. "What if this thing is some kind of a weapon?"

☼   ☼   ☼   ☼   ☼

HIGH ABOVE the Earth, where the continents are reduced to smears of brown and green, the ocean glows blue, and the currents of wind can be observed by the swirling of cloud formations, a lone, dark orb spun. Clutched for thousands of years in Earth's orbit, the object blinked to life. A red light began to blink on the otherwise smooth surface.

The object's spinning slowed, then stopped as though by its own will. The continents of Earth passed by beneath: Europe and Siberia, Alaska, and Canada, revealing a frigid, frozen north. With a burst of tremendous speed created by unseen forces, the black orb rocketed toward the frozen Canadian North.

Passing through the upper layers of the atmosphere like a bullet through Jell-O, the sphere burst into the open blue sky of the arctic on a collision course with the ice below. As the orb descended toward the white expanse, an inconsistency could be seen. Small objects pocked the surface, moving back and forth—the crew of the mammoth dig hard at work.

Arcing its path over the site, the orb shot down toward the ice at five hundred miles per hour and stopped with a sudden jerk two feet above the ice, a half mile from the mammoth dig site. Just as it appeared nothing more was going to happen, the orb began to spin. With each pass, the orb emitted a low hum—*hum . . . hum . . . hum*—slowly at first, then faster and faster, like a Tilt-a-whirl out of control.

hum hum hum humhumhumhumhumhumhumhumhummhmhmhmhhmhmhm
Spinning madly, the loose snow beneath the obsidian globe began to lift into the air.

☼   ☼   ☼   ☼   ☼

THE COLLISION was like a bad train wreck. As Eddy moved toward the exit of the tent, intent on keeping everyone away from the mysterious cylinder, Brian burst in. The two men collided and sprawled in separate directions. Eddy fell back into Kevin and Eve, knocking them back into the research table, which wobbled, but didn't spill over as Kevin managed to grab its legs and stabilize them. Brian careened forward and fell on the floor without much more incident than a loud "*Oof!*"

Eddy leapt to his feet. His voice boomed with irritation. "What the hell are you doing, Norwood?"

Brian rolled over onto his back, supporting himself on his elbows. He laughed and showed a bright smile. "I did it! We did it! Not only did we get an intact mammoth with enough DNA to clone an army of mammoths, we got a reserve of frozen sperm."

Eddy's eyes squinted, curiosity peaked, but not ready to cheer victory. "What good are frozen sperm?"

"Have you noticed how perfectly preserved the mammoth is?" Brian said with a squeak in his giddy voice. "I was able to remove a single sperm from the mammoth's testes and slowly thawed it out. When it reached room temperature, it became active! Brought back to life! We can do more than clone the mammoth, we can breed them! Modern elephants are simply the distant relatives of the mammoth. Like big cats, their sperm is most likely compatible. It's the most . . . What is that?"

Brian's eyes were glued to an object under the table. He reached under and pulled out the metallic pill-shaped artifact.

Eddy's eyes widened. It had been knocked off the table when Brian barreled into the room. "Put it down," Eddy said, trying not to sound urgent.

"Why? What is it?" Brian asked as he looked the object over.

"It's dangerous," Kevin said. "We think it might be radioactive."

Brian looked confused. "Then why the blazes did you bring it to the site?"

"We didn't," Eve said, looking at the frozen woman, still rigid on the research table. "She did."

A curious expression worked its way across Brian's face as he went from confused to astonished to indignant. "You expect me to believe you found this . . . obviously modern device . . . with her?" Brian motioned to the frozen woman with his head. "You can't be serious?"

Eddy leaned down in front of Brian's face, his expression grim. He held out his hand for the artifact. "Deadly serious."

11

THE FIRST WAVE

Pulling with every sinew his arms could call to battle, Paul pried the bolt loose; the effort sent him toppling backwards. Legs sprawling, Paul tripped over his tool box, spilling its contents and falling to the metal floor. The sound of Paul's body crashing down and the clang of tumbling tools echoed off the metallic walls of what Steve called the "backhoe box." The large steel container was exactly that: a massive box that contained a backhoe which Paul had been fine tuning before its return to Archer Industrial, a heavy equipment rental agency. It was only now that Paul grasped how badly a tune-up was in order.

Paul groaned as he sat up on the cold floor of the backhoe box. "I thought you said Archer rented top of the line equipment? This backhoe hasn't been worked on in years. Most of the bolts are rusted tight."

Steve struggled to remain balanced on the treads of the backhoe while he finished laughing at Paul's calamity. "Hey, man. It got the job done, didn't it?" Steve laughed again and took a long drag from a cigarette.

"You're paid to help fix this stuff, too, you know."

Steve spoke, his voice laced with sarcasm, "No! Really?"

Paul's nose itched with the smell of motor oil and tobacco. It reminded him of his youth, working in his father's shop with all the old timers who had watched their own fathers and grandfathers work on some of the first gasoline powered cars ever built—men who'd seen New York transformed from a horse and buggy town to a skyscraper and taxi cab metropolis. Paul had since been captured by all things mechanical. He drew in a deep breath, and, while his lungs protested, smiled at the memories the odors brought to the forefront of his mind.

Steve hopped down from the backhoe tread and helped Paul return his tools to their proper places in the well-organized toolbox. "See, I help." Steve took a drag, held it in, and let it slide out through his nostrils. "What do you think about all the freakiness, man? We raise a mammoth from the ice, cool, but then this ancient chick falls out . . . I don't get it."

Paul smiled. "That's why you're not a scientist."

"True . . . but we've been with this crew long enough to know some things. And personally, I think something screwy is going on. The way those cables melted and snapped isn't normal. They were wrapped around a hunk of frozen ice and somehow managed to get heated beyond seven-fifty . . . huh, I just told the camera guy, Mark, about that."

"You think he—"

"No . . . not like that. Whatever happened up there would take more brains to pull off than a cameraman has. It just doesn't add up."

Paul arranged his screwdrivers by type and size. "I'm right there with you, pal. But I trust Eddy. He'll fill us in when he knows something."

"Okay, but if you had to guess. What do you think happened?" Steve took a drag of tobacco smoke.

Paul looked up from his refilled toolbox with a smile. "How am I supposed to know? I just drive shit."

A cloud of smoke burst from Steve's mouth as he laughed.

"Am I interrupting?" a soft voice said from the open side of the backhoe box.

"Not at all," Paul said, giving Steve a mischievous glance.

Steve looked at the ceiling with a grimace. "If you're not here to apologize, you can about face right now and go back to leading the frozen armies of the ice queen nation."

Nicole paused, working hard to not react to the insult. "Actually, I did come to apologize."

Steve's head turned so fast that he nearly tore it off. "What?"

"You saved my life. Compared to that, the camera is worthless. We got the footage, anyway."

Steve wasn't quite impressed yet. "And if you hadn't got the footage? Would I still be the world's most hated man?"

"No . . . I didn't mean—of course not. But you should see it! As I grabbed the camera, it panned around toward you and filmed every second, up until the point you dove through the air and tackled us. But you looked very heroic." Nicole smiled.

Steve was happily surprised. "I did?"

Nicole nodded. "And I'm going to make sure that clip makes it into the documentary."

"Great," Paul said. "Give the man another reason to inflate his ego."

Steve's mind barely registered the comment. He had set a goal to save Nicole's life, and he had done it! True, when he saw the ice falling above her, it was pure instinct driving him forward. Saving a life had always been one of Steve's fantasies. But he had fulfilled two goals. Saving a life . . . and it was Nicole's! She was indebted to him! Steve's mind rummaged for the right combination of words that would ensure Nicole answer his request for a date in the affirmative. But the words never made it to his lips.

Steve cocked his head to the side. "You guys feel that?"

"Feel what?" Paul asked.

"Weird. I thought I felt the ground move."

"Ah, must be *amore*!" Paul announced.

Steve glared at Paul, forgetting all about the shaking ice. "One more word out of you, and I'll show you how functional this backhoe can be on your candy ass."

Paul laughed. "Oh, don't tease me, big boy."

Nicole's face reddened. Steve's face was handsome in a rugged kind of way, but his embarrassed, boyish look made him adorable. Maybe she'd thank him again later.

☼   ☼   ☼   ☼   ☼

BRIAN NORWOOD didn't like being ordered around by Eddy Moore. "If it was found with the dig it belongs to me, and I'll be the one who decides what to do with it."

Eddy didn't budge from his position of hovering above Brian, who was still lying on the floor. "This device may present a danger to myself and the rest of this crew, which is still my responsibility. You do not want to come between me and that job."

Brian paused. "Fine . . . but I don't think we should just get rid of it. It could be a find of monumental proportions."

"I agree," Eddy said. "But I don't trust it in your hands."

"And why is that?"

"Because I still don't know what happened to the mammoth."

"Eddy, get off it already. You're staring a stunning success in the eyes and you're still worried about what *almost* happened?"

"Yes," Eddy said. "Give the device to Kevin." Eddy turned to Kevin. "Put it in my backpack. I'll carry the burden."

"You mean you'll steal my artifact," Brian said.

"Norwood, please give me a reason to slug you again."

Brian leaned away from Eddy and handed the device to Kevin, who held it like a newborn baby. Kevin glided it to Eddy's backpack but as he walked, the ice shook with a violent tremor. Kevin's light grip was no match for the vibrations shaking his body. The device slid from his hands and landed on the tent floor. Kevin bent down for the device. As he reached for it, the metallic pill popped open and flashed a red light across his eyes.

Kevin's mind was transported to the surface of another world. The sky was emerald and the water reflected the sky. A massive city sat on the coast of the rolling green ocean and stretched toward the purple clouds above. The beach was a spongy pink and a cool, sweet-smelling breeze, like watermelon, wafted across his senses. With a bright white flash, the world was undone and reorganized. The city was in ruins, burning and billowing clouds of black smoke. A flash tore through Kevin's mind and he came face to face with a creature straight out of one of his comic books, only this was very real, better than any Hollywood special effects guru could create. Its six crimson eyes were stacked from face to forehead in two columns of three. Its teeth were like a great white shark's, and its face was covered in what looked like spires of bone breaking through the skin. It stood on all fours, agile like a cat, but with the cunning purpose of a human. Its muscles rippled beneath its smooth, grey skin. A mane of black hair ran down its back, disappearing along its long tail, reappearing as a tuft at the tail's end. The creature snarled at Kevin and swung its clawed hand toward his midsection.

Kevin fell back and screamed as he slammed back into the real world. Eddy and Eve were leaning over him. "Kevin! Kevin!" Eddy's voice beckoned to him through the haze.

"What happened?" Kevin asked.

"You tell us," Eve said. "The ice shook and you dropped the device. You bent down to get it then froze, like you were in a trance . . . but your eyes were moving like you were seeing something . . . did you see something?"

"Something, yes," Kevin said as the cobwebs began to fade from his mind. He realized that the rumbling ice that had caused him to drop the device, which now lay at his feet, still shook the tent. "What's happening?"

Eddy looked to the tent's entrance, which still flapped open in the wind. "We don't know. Brian went out to check."

"Feels like an earthquake," Kevin said.

Eddy shook his head in the negative, "I lived in Southern California long enough to know what an earthquake feels like. This is something else."

"It's getting louder . . . growing closer . . ." Eve said. "Like a train. Oh, God. Eddy, do you remember Colorado?"

Eddy's eyes locked to Eve's, serious as hell.

"What happened in Colorado?" Kevin asked, eyes wide with a growing fear.

Eddy turned to Kevin, his voice almost a whisper. "Avalanche."

"But we're on a flat plain. That'd be impossible." Kevin looked to Eve, her face frozen in fear. "Wouldn't it?"

A burst of red entered the tent. It was Brian, his lungs burning for more oxygen. He turned and zipped the entrance tight before clinging to one of the titanium support poles. He felt the stares of his comrades and turned to them with wide eyes. "Hold on to something," he said with a shaky voice as the color drained from his face. "And if you believe in God, start praying."

☼   ☼   ☼   ☼   ☼

"OKAY, NOW I know I'm not the only one feeling that," Steve said as a low rumble shook through the backhoe box.

The tool box on the floor began to rattle as the tools shook inside. Paul stared at it. The tool box bounced into the air and spilled over. Paul righted it and started piling the tools back inside. "If this is somebody playing some kind of damn stunt with that crane, I'll kill' em," Paul muttered to himself.

Nicole headed for the open side of the backhoe box, which from the outside looked like a big black cube with one side torn down. Steve followed. They stopped on the open wall of the backhoe box, which shook beneath their feet. To the left was snow and blue sky, the same to the right and straight ahead. Steve and Nicole looked at each other, realizing at the same time where the cacophony of noise was coming from.

Steve broke for one side of the box, Nicole to the other. Approaching the backhoe box, still a half mile away, a wave of white reached high into the sky like a tidal wave of snow. Steve felt his arms grow weak at the sight of it. His legs loosened and he fell to his knees with the realization that they would all be suffocated under a blanket of snow.

Luckily for Steve, Nicole didn't have the same reaction. She grabbed Steve's shoulder and shook him. "Steve! Get up! We have to get inside!"

Steve's body was placid in her hands. His eyes glazed over as his head tilted back, following the icy tsunami into the sky.

Nicole was desperate. "Steve!"

Nothing.

Nicole did the only thing she could think of at the moment, something she knew would get Steve's attention. She grabbed him by the head, pulled him close, and locked her lips to his.

The man was reborn. Steve wrapped his arms around Nicole and returned her kiss. He released her with fire in his eyes.

"Steve . . ." Nicole said.

"What?" Steve was staring into her eyes.

Nicole pointed toward the wave of snow, which was two hundred yards out and four times as high. A shadow loomed over them.

Steve stood with renewed urgency and dove into the backhoe box with Nicole.

"We need to get this thing closed!" Nicole sounded desperate.

"Paul!" Steve shouted as he grabbed a chain connected to the outside of the open wall.

Paul heard the fear in Steve's voice and forgot his mess of tools. He looked up and saw Steve pulling on the chair, trying to pull the large metal door up from the snow. It was a near impossible task, but Steve was tugging. Paul ran to Steve's side and took the chain without being told. They pulled with all their strength and the door budged, free from the ice . . . but they were moving too slow.

"What's happening?" Paul shouted over the rumble, which was monstrously loud now.

Steve's eyes were wide. "Just pull!"

Nicole got in line behind Paul and took the chain in her hands. She thanked God for making her a fitness freak and put her muscles, which were as strong as Steve's, into the chain. The door rose toward them.

The rumble became so loud that their grunts of exertion couldn't be heard. With a sliver of sky still visible through the open panel, everyone gave the chain one last pull. The wall slammed shut and clicked into place. The world went black, but not without sound. A wave of noise surrounded the backhoe box. Steve thought it sounded like being at ground zero during a shuttle launch.

As chaos surrounded them, every noise reverberated off the inside of the dark enclosure. Loud *clunks* echoed like the voice of God as equipment was smashed against the outside of the box. Screams from horrified victims, dozens of the crew who had labored so hard to assist in raising the mammoth shrieked past, carried by the torrent of snow. Other voices were silenced as their bodies smashed into the outside of the box.

"Oh, my God. Oh, my God." Nicole huddled against the backhoe in the dark, listening as shrieking voice after shrieking voice was smashed from existence or drowned by the howling noise.

The rumbling ceased and an eerie silence filled the void. There were no voices outside. No sounds of movement. No signs of life. The only audible sounds were their quick breaths and the pounding of their hearts ready to burst from their ribcages. It occurred to Steve that everyone he knew and loved in the world, other than Paul and Nicole, was dead or dying beneath a solid prison of snow. It then occurred to Steve that they too were sealed in a tomb. If the backhoe box was covered in snow, they would have no way out and no fresh air to breath.

Steve unlatched the wall which they had only moments ago struggled to close. He pushed on it, grunting. The wall, which normally fell open like fresh cut tree, remained upright and solid. They were locked in.

Steve turned and leaned against the door. He slid down onto the floor of the box. The darkness felt oppressive. The smell of oil and gasoline, no longer filtered by fresh air, burned his lungs. He was sure that only three people could have survived the onslaught of snow were now going to die of asphyxiation. Every breath between now and approaching death would be spent breathing this rancid air. He hoped hell wouldn't be this bad.

After reaching into his pocket and pulling out his lighter, Steve lit his cigarette. But he never inhaled the smoke. The orange glow of the lighter lit Paul's face behind the glass of the backhoe.

"Better get out of the way and cover your ears," Paul said. "This is gonna be loud."

SURVIVAL

12

RECOVERY

A sheet of white pocked by blemishes of debris was all that remained of the mammoth dig site, which only minutes ago had been alive with activity. The site had been transformed into a frozen graveyard. The wave of snow had fallen hard and fast, landing like a tidal breaker and burying the site under several feet of packed snow. Some equipment, which was built to withstand immense storms, survived, but the only evidence that humans had once populated the area was the occasional limb protruding from the frozen field like a headstone.

A cone of orange material marked the position of the research tent, its titanium support poles stabbing through the snow. A knife gripped by a strong hand sliced through the tent's skin from the inside and carved a large hole. Eddy peered out through the hole he created and looked up at the blue sky above. "We're okay," he said. "It didn't cover the top."

Eddy turned to Eve. "Ladies first."

"I'm . . . I'm not sure I want to see what's out there," Eve said.

"We'll be okay," Eddy said, doing his best to sound confident.

Eve put her hands on Eddy's shoulders as he wrapped his fingers around her booted foot. He launched Eve up through the roof and she climbed out onto the solid snow. Kevin was next, followed by Eddy, who then pulled Brian out. The work was distracting enough that no one took a look around until Brian was fully extracted and lying on the ice.

Eddy's mind spun as he surveyed the damage. The entire site had been wiped out, and he knew no one else could have survived. The four of them were in the only reinforced tent. Everyone was dead! Falling to his knees, Eddy's hands shook and his throat became tight, his breathing labored and his vision grew blurred. "They're all dead . . ."

After several minutes of shock-induced silence, Eddy said, "We need to get some help out here."

Eve sunk to her knees next to Eddy and held him. "What . . . what about survivors?"

Brian kicked at the ice with his boot. It barely made a dent. "It's too compact. If they weren't killed in the initial storm, they would have asphyxiated by now, not that we could dig them out. We have no tools, no communications . . . and what's worse, the mammoth is back in the ice."

Eddy felt as though he would vomit when Brian expressed concern over an animal that had been dead for thousands of years instead of remorse for the deaths of dozens of people. Their friends. But not everyone had been killed. Eve was at his side and that gave Eddy some comfort. And there was Kevin, too.

With a quick glance, Eddy saw that Kevin was in bad shape. He hadn't said a word and was sitting on the ice, twitching his legs and staring straight ahead, eyes fixated and unblinking. Eddy was sure he was in shock, but rather than feel bad for the man, Eddy was envious. He wished he could shove aside the torment that wracked his mind. He wished he could feel nothing, but Brian's continuing monologue ensured that Eddy continued to at least feel rage.

"We should have reinforced the tent around the mammoth . . . What a loss. Of course, then maybe some of the others might have survived. As it was, the only things that could have withstood that storm was the research tent and the backhoe—"

A roar, like an ancient Gryphon, shrieked from the inside of the backhoe box, which was covered in snow except for a single side. Metal smashing against metal boomed from the box and the exposed wall crashed open at a forty-five degree angle. All eyes turned to the opening.

Eddy stood like a soldier at attention when Steve poked his head out. His eyes grew wide as Nicole climbed out, blocking her eyes from the sun's glare on the snow. Eddy ran toward them like Forrest Gump on a mission when Paul climbed out from the box, amid a flurry of curses. Eve and Brian were on his heels, but Kevin remained sitting, frozen like a statue of Buddha in snow gear.

Steve jumped into the air with a burst of joy as he saw Eddy approaching. "Guys! You're alive!"

After a joyful reunion filled with hugs, tears, and unanswered questions about what had happened, Nicole got her first look around. "Where is everyone?"

Eddy turned to Nicole with glistening eyes. "Nicole . . ."

Nicole spun in every direction, seeing nothing but a mix of white snow and a rainbow of debris. "My crew. Where's my crew?" Her voice shook.

Eddy put his hand on Nicole's shoulder and she looked into his sad eyes. "Nicole, I'm sorry."

"They're dead?" Nicole's eyes widened with the realization. "No!"

Brian stood forward, his mind working. "When the storm hit—"

"That was no storm," Kevin said with a low grumble. He had returned to reality and had approached the group so silently that no one was aware of his presence until he spoke. "We rose that . . . that strange artifact from the ice and it caused this."

Nicole's interest was peeked. "What artifact?"

Sighing, Eddy said, "We found . . . *something* wrapped in the woman's arms."

"What was it?" Steve asked.

Eddy looked into Steve's eyes. "We don't know. It looked modern."

"More than modern," Kevin said. "Futuristic."

"Kevin, c'mon. There's no need to make everyone more afraid." Eddy focused on Kevin's glossed and dilated eyes. "Kev, how are you feeling?"

"I'm fine," Kevin said as he stopped walking and took in every living person. "Why would I not be? I know what happened. I know we're all going to die. We shouldn't have dug it up . . . but we did and now it's going to kill us all."

Eddy held Kevin's arms and looked him in the eyes. "What are you talking about?"

Kevin returned Eddy's stare, his eyes beginning to clear. "I saw them. Just before it hit. I saw them inside the device. I saw them."

Eddy knew he had to change Kevin's train of thought. He was drifting from shock to paranoia. "Kevin, listen. It was a storm, and you have to stay calm. We all have to stay calm or we're not going to make it. The device we found is down there." Eddy motioned to the top of the research tent with his head. "It's back in the ice, okay? It's gone."

Kevin blinked and looked at the top of the bright orange research tent. "It's gone?"

"Yes."

"You wouldn't lie to me?"

"You know I wouldn't."

"Okay." Kevin's arms relaxed and his stance became normal. He took a deep breath and let it out slowly. "I'm okay. Thanks, Eddy."

Eddy nodded and turned to the group. He buried what he was truly thinking in some deep dark hole of his soul and began speaking. "We've encountered some kind of unprecedented atmospheric event. We need to find a communication device and see if we can raise Sam and Mary. If not, we need to salvage what we can and get back to Base Camp ourselves. That means food and transportation for seven. We'll camp nearby tonight and move out in the morning."

"What about . . .?" Nicole looked around the area, her eyes following the carnage of twisted metal and frozen body parts. "We can't just leave them."

Eddy closed his eyes, trying to squeeze every image of death from his mind. "We'll come back for them."

Silence fell over the group. What they now had to do felt colder than the air. Eddy found the small portion of himself that was still willing to fight, even at the brink of death—a parting gift from Jim before he died in Venezuela. "Listen up people," Eddy said with a loud voice as though he were a general about to storm the beaches of Normandy. "This isn't about science anymore. Forget the mammoth. Screw the DNA samples. This is about survival. We need to push our emotions down, stay in control. We'll never get out of this if we all start cracking under the pressure."

Eddy turned his back on the group, surveying the damage and hiding his wet eyes. "Steve, Paul, Nicole, you're on transportation. Find anything that moves and make it work. The rest of us will take care of the food and other supplies. Too many people have died here today, and I'll be damned before I let anything happen to anyone else. We're going to survive this mess, I promise you that."

☼   ☼   ☼   ☼   ☼

AFTER SEVERAL hours of digging through several feet of ice, searching for food and equipment, Eve was exhausted. She was used to digging; they all were, but smashing through a wall of compact snow was jarring to hands and hard on the joints. But the painful labor paid off. They dug up enough supplies to carry them home, with severe rationing of course, but it would keep them alive. But all the concerns and logistics of surviving in the arctic were fading from her mind, replaced by a single concern: where was Eddy?

Eddy had walked away after they had extricated a supply case containing food and water. At first she thought that he was off to oversee some of Steve and Paul's efforts at finding them transportation, but when she looked, they hadn't talked to or even seen him. Eve found Brian and Kevin pulling a snowmobile with a broken windshield from the dense snow, and neither of them knew where Eddy was, either. She spun in all directions, scouring the landscape for movement, and found nothing. Then darkness caught her eyes, the backhoe box, with its open wall looking dim and inviting to anyone not wanting to be found.

Eddy was hiding, and that frightened Eve the most. They needed Eddy now more than ever. She needed Eddy.

The snow beneath her feet crunched as she approached the large, dark opening of the backhoe box. She held still and listened. Wind whistled in her ear, but then grew louder, like a moaning. Eve realized that it wasn't just wind she heard, it was Eddy. He was sobbing like a small child who'd just been scolded. Eve wiped her own tears from her cheeks before they froze. She'd only seen Eddy cry once before and she had hoped she'd never see it again, because tears from Eddy meant that something awful had happened. And it had. Eddy's worst nightmare had been realized ten-fold. The death toll had gone from three in Venezuela to more than thirty in the arctic. She wondered if he would ever be himself again. She prayed he would.

Eve climbed into the backhoe box and was enveloped by darkness. A voice, trying to sound strong, spoke from the black, "Who's there?"

"It's me, Eddy."

"Not now."

"Where are you?"

"Leave me alone."

"Tell me where you are. It's too dark in here." With her last words, Eve's foot caught on something hard and she toppled forward, falling to the floor; the impact echoing off the metal walls.

Before Eve could get to her knees, she felt two strong hands grasping her shoulders. "I have you. Are you okay?"

Eve smiled in the dark, knowing her grin wouldn't be seen. She had tripped on purpose, knowing that if there was an iota of Eddy, the real Eddy, left, he would be by her side in an instant. "I'm not hurt."

"What are you doing here?" Eddy said as he sniffed away some unseen tears.

"Looking for you."

"Is everyone finished?"

"No. I was worried about you."

"Why?"

Eve's mind struggled. The true answer would be so easy to say, but she felt it was the wrong time. They were all emotionally broken and any positive response she might get could turn out to be fueled by a desperate need for love, for comfort. "I know this is hard for you. You're our leader and we need you to survive." She lied.

"Oh," he said with a weak voice.

Was he disappointed?

"Well, don't worry about me. I'll be fine. Just needed to think things through. Wanted to be alone to figure out what to—"

"Eddy."

"What?"

"It's not your fault."

Eddy was silent for a moment, but then a light sniffling noise and sound of shaking snow suit told Eve that he was crying again. Eve reached through the darkness and wrapped her arms around Eddy, pulling him toward her and leaning against the metal wall of the backhoe box. Eddy's head rested on Eve's chest and he held her tight, sobbing into her wool sweater. She ran her fingers through his hair and rocked him like a child. "Eddy," she said, "you know this wasn't your fault. You know there was nothing anyone could have done. You know that what we encountered out here was something no one has ever seen before and there was no way to have prepared for it."

Eddy's breathing evened out and his grip relaxed. He was listening.

"It was a catastrophic accident. But not everyone died. Kevin, Steve, Paul, they still need you. I need you."

Eddy's head grew heavy on her chest; he was asleep. Eve leaned down and placed her face against his. "I love you," she whispered, feeling the warmth of his cheek against hers.

"I love you, too," came a barely audible response.

Eve sat up straight, surprised from the words that escaped Eddy's mouth. "Eddy?"

Nothing.

"Eddy?"

He shifted and mumbled something unintelligible.

Asleep.

Did he know what he had said? Eve sighed and leaned back against the wall. She decided she would ask him, if they survived, but with death all around them, this wasn't the best time to talk about love or start a relationship. She knew they would have to make some tough decisions in the days to come and she didn't want more emotions confusing Eddy or clouding his judgment. She loved Eddy more than anyone else on the planet, but she decided that withholding her affections would be the best thing for him, for all of them . . . just as soon as he woke up.

☼   ☼   ☼   ☼   ☼

EDDY WOKE and found his face in Eve's lap. He sat up straight, feeling renewed strength and a fresh outlook on the world. He remembered Eve coming in, holding him, comforting him, but the words she spoke as he drifted to sleep escaped him now, like a fading dream. Whatever she said, it had worked and he felt prepared to face whatever challenges lay ahead . . . as long as they didn't face another freak storm.

"Eve," he said.

Her eyes blinked open and looked into his. Her vision had adjusted to the darkness and she could see his face clearly. She smiled. "You're awake." Eve looked at her glowing watch. "We've been sleeping for two hours."

Eddy stretched, rolled his neck, and ran his fingers through his hair.

"How are you doing?" she asked.

"Better . . . thanks for helping."

"What are friends for?"

Eddy smiled dully and looked into Eve's eyes. His stomach turned as her deep brown eyes drew him in and held him captive. He knew if he didn't say something, the silent stare would become awkward.

Too late.

"What?" Eve asked with a wrinkled forehead.

Eddy's mind swirled in every direction, searching for an answer that wouldn't make him look like a buffoon.

"Hey, guys! There you are!" A flashlight cut through the darkness and exposed them. The light was annoyingly bright, but Eddy was thankful for the interruption. "Hey, you guys weren't getting frisky or something, cause I can come ba—"

"Steve." It was all Eve needed to say.

"Sorry," Steve said. "Hey, we're all set out here. Come see what we've dug up."

After a quick climb out of the backhoe box and a short walk to the side of a rescued Sno-Cat, Eddy faced the remaining members of his crew. Eve stood to his side while Brian, Nicole, Steve, Kevin, and Paul sat on the treads of the Cat. To the side were two fully functional snowmobiles—enough transportation for them all and any recovered supplies. "Okay, so we have transportation taken care of." Eddy nodded to Steve and Paul. "Good work."

Paul nodded. Steve smiled.

"But communications are still a problem." Eddy reached into a backpack at his feet and pulled out a smashed satellite phone, which looked thick and awkward. "This is the only satellite phone." Eddy handed the radio to Paul. "I need you to fix it."

Paul looked at the broken phone with a raised eyebrow, almost laughing. "The bad news is, there ain't no way in hell this is gonna get fixed. The good news is, we know were we are and can communicate locally." Paul reached into his pockets and pulled out three small devices, which looked like yellow walkie-talkies. "I give you three Garmin Rino GPS Receivers."

Steve said, "They've been preprogrammed with a map of the Canadian Arctic and can show our location within ten feet. But they also serve as two-way communicators. Each has about 20 hours of juice and we should use them sparingly, but they should get us out of here."

Eddy was smiling widely. "How did . . .?"

"Hey, I'm the equipment specialist," Steve said. "And you told me to take every precaution. We could have used Superman, but I thought portable GPS and communication could come in handy. So, ah, there you go. I'm the man."

"You are indeed the man," Eddy said as he took one of the GPS units and looked it over. "Good work." He turned to Brian. "How are we on food?"

"Enough for a week if we ration it right, but we . . . what?"

Eddy's eyes were no longer focused on Brian's. He was staring behind Brian, behind the Sno-Cat. "Behind you," Eddy said.

The group turned at once. Steve twisted with surprise and rolled off the tread and falling to the snow, but no one noticed. All eyes were locked on the five men standing on the other side of the Cat.

"Who the hell are they?" Steve asked.

The oldest of the men, with dark brown skin and marbleized hair hidden beneath a tightly-woven, red winter cap, stepped forward and pushed aside his fur covered cloak to reveal a long, worn spear. "I am an elder of the Inuit people of the North. We are here to help."

13

THE INUIT

The five strange men stood in a line, shoulder to shoulder, staring at Eddy through dark brown eyes. They were dressed in furs from head to toe, looking more like the cavewoman Eddy and crew had extracted from the mammoth than modern men of the twentieth century. What bothered him most was the familiarity of the elder. It wasn't the face or voice that reminded Eddy of someone, it was the man's presence. Eddy couldn't place it, but he was sure he had known this man before . . . maybe long ago.

From left to right, ending at the elder, Eddy recounted their names. "Andari, Hoder, Vayu, Re . . . Reginn? And Marutas. Did I get them all?"

Marutas nodded.

Eddy decided to look past their oddity and get right down to business. If these men were here to help, they sorely needed it, but a few questions nagged at Eddy's mind. He did his best to not sound suspicious. "Let me see if I understand you correctly. You saw the storm from a distance. Correct?"

Marutas, the elder wearing the red winter cap, nodded.

"Okay, so you saw the storm and came to investigate. You have no modern equipment, no snowmobiles, no GPS . . . and no dogs. You came here on foot."

Marutas nodded again.

Eddy squinted his eyes. "We're hundreds of miles from the nearest settlement. How did you get here on foot? It's not that I don't believe you, I just find it amazing."

Marutas looked out over the snow, gesturing towards it with open arms. "Our people have been living this way for thousands years. Survival has always been a priority for my kind and this land holds many secrets that insure our subsistence." The elder lowered his arms and turned towards Eddy. "Tell me, did you unearth anything before the storm?"

Eddy's mind sounded a mental warning. These men knew more than they were leading him to believe. Could the storm that dumped several feet of compact snow and killed their crew and friends have been created by man? Could these men have something to do with it? The notion was too unbelievable. These men wore fur. Manipulating the weather was far beyond their capabilities. Still, Eddy decided it was best to be cautious. "Nothing of interest . . ."

Eddy knew that wouldn't do. His mother had been a gem with small children and he'd watched her redirect them mid-conversation, avoiding conflict at every turn. He had picked up the habit and soon learned it worked just as well on adults, if not better. "Well, hey, I'm glad you came. We could use some help navigating out of here. Can you spare a few days? We'll compensate you for your time."

Marutas nodded.

Eddy smiled. It worked.

"Helping to save your lives is compensation enough," Marutas said. "Thank you."

Eddy was about to turn to his remaining crew, who had been standing by the Cat, listening to the conversation with eager ears. But his voice never had a chance to escape his lungs.

"You will stay here tonight. We will guide you out in the morning."

It wasn't a request. It was an order. Eddy, for one, never enjoyed being told what to do. It's why he was a leader.

Who does he think he is? Eddy thought with irritation.

If this man, this crotchety Inuit, hadn't been a possible means of survival, Eddy would have told him off right there. But he decided a bit of tact would serve them better. "A wise idea, Marutas, but—" was all Eddy got out before the old man looked angry, his brows furrowing into deep lines.

Eddy pressed on. "If you don't mind, many of our friends died beneath the ice we stand on. We would like to camp a short distance from here. Out of respect for the dead."

The elder's face relaxed and he nodded. "Of course," he said. "And we will remain nearby. To ward off the angry spirits of your friends."

The old Inuit turned and walked away. The four others turned and followed him.

Eddy turned to his crew and spoke when he was sure the Inuit men were out of earshot. "What do you think?"

"Give me the creeps," Steve said.

"I agree," Brian added. "There's something off about them. I can't place it."

"We should trust them," Kevin said with urgency. "They might be our best chance of getting out of this mess. And we should try not to insult them."

"We all agree with you," Eddy said, "but being cautious includes scrutinizing everything, even would-be rescuers."

"He's right," Eve said. "We don't know these men. We don't know why they're out here in the first place. I personally find it hard to believe they're this far from civilization without transportation or supplies. I don't care how in tune with nature you are; to survive in the Arctic, you need more than those men have."

"A camp?" Brian asked.

"That would be my guess. And that means they're not being honest with us."

"Well it's not like we're being honest with them." Kevin crossed his arms. "Eddy didn't tell them what we found in the ice when they asked."

"I didn't tell them *because* they asked. Let's say they have a camp. What's the worst case scenario?"

"If they have a camp," Eve started, "they could be after our equipment. They know we've got two snowmobiles and a Sno-Cat. Out here, that's worth a small fortune. They could go back to their camp, get weapons, ammo, maybe more men, and be back by morning to do us in and take the equipment."

"I don't think they'd do that," Kevin said.

"We don't think so either," Eddy said. "But we need to be prepared for anything, right? That's what keeps people alive."

Kevin nodded.

Eddy turned and watched the Inuit men walking further away. "All right, we camp within eyeshot of them, and we'll sleep in shifts."

"If we can sleep at all," Steve said.

"If they do anything strange, we'll leave at first light." Eddy glanced at Paul, whose face was somber and serious. "You've been quiet, Paul; what's your take on this?"

Paul looked up. "I tell you, I've spent a lot of time in the Canadian North. Hunting bear, deer, moose, whatever—it's all good eats. I've known Inuit before. Hell, I have friends who are Inuit . . ."

Eddy waited with wide eyes, suspecting what Paul would say next, but not wanting to hear it.

Paul's eyes rested on the Inuit, who were now fifty yards away. "Those men . . . they're not Inuit."

☼   ☼   ☼   ☼   ☼

NIGHT CAME and with it descended a frightening cold. The only way to breathe outside the tents was with a scarf wrapped over one's nose and mouth so that the air didn't freeze the lungs solid. It was enough to keep everyone inside the tents and out of the night. Or almost everyone.

Steve, Paul, and Nicole had volunteered to tent together. Only a few tents were found, and everyone had to share. They were the first to volunteer. Maybe it was the time spent inside the Sno-Cat on the trip across the ice—they knew they wouldn't kill each other. Or perhaps Steve's rescue of Nicole had warmed her disposition. Steve had hoped so, but he knew it was more likely she felt safer with them, having survived the blast of snow, in part because of her proximity to him and Paul in the backhoe box.

None of them were sleeping. Not one of them had even tried. Nicole had spent the last hour fiddling with her single remaining camera, a new Sony Handicam; not the best in the way of quality, but it got the job done. This hadn't been a complete loss for her. An old habit of keeping duplicates of her most important footage on her person at all times paid off. She had the most important segments of footage from the dig in her coat pocket—another benefit to filming on small digital tapes.

Paul was busy working on the broken CB radio. From the looks of it, Steve knew Paul's efforts were wasted, but he also knew that Paul was just trying to stay occupied. Steve was the only one completely and utterly distracted by the five men who claimed to be Inuit. He could see them through the clear plastic window on the side of the tent, sitting around a fire in the open air without anything more for protection against the elements than some animal furs.

Through the air a light hum, like the whispered prayers of monks wafted into the tent. Steve wasn't sure he was hearing it, but he craned his head like a dog, held his breath and listened. It was there. The men were humming, or mumbling in unison.

After covering the window with a flap of plastic, Steve turned around and faced Paul, his face glowing orange as the electric lantern's light reflected off the orange surface of the tent's interior.

"Anything new?" Paul asked.

"They haven't moved," Steve said, "but they're doing some kind of freaky chant."

Paul nodded slightly. "You see? Not Inuit."

"Well, what are they, then?"

"Damned if I know. I ain't no freakin' linguist."

Nicole picked up her Handicam and turned it on. She pointed it at Paul and hit record. "This is Paul . . ." Nicole looked around the camera at Paul. "What's your last name?"

"Correnti, but I don't want to be filmed." Paul held his hands in front of the camera.

"C'mon," Nicole said. "You're the expert on Inuit people and we have five Inuit—sorry, non-Inuit—men outside. This is interesting. We should get it on film, including the opinions of everyone involved. It will make for good TV."

Steve nudged Paul's shoulder. "Yeah. Then you'd be famous and might stand a chance with the ladies."

"Hey, I ain't got no trouble with the ladies."

"Please?" Nicole flashed her sweetest face, which was unbearably sweet, Steve thought.

Paul sighed. "Okay."

"Make it snappy. I don't want to kill my batteries." Nicole said as Paul moved his hands away from the lens. "Start from the top."

"What's the top?"

"The beginning. Start with your name."

"Okay. Hi, my name is Paul Correnti."

Steve leaned into the picture. "And I'm Steve Riley, equipment specialist."

Paul was unfazed by Steve's intrusion. It was almost as though he expected it, or could at least read Steve's mind. And Steve knew he could. Not in an alien or Professor X way, but in the way someone's next words or actions could be guessed simply by knowing someone so well. Steve knew the right way to describe their relationship was "intimate," but he'd have to be tortured before he'd admit such a thing. They were buddies. Straight buddies. Saying otherwise would get someone punched. That's how it was with him and Paul. They were as close as two straight guys could get.

Paul continued, "After a storm of some sort, which destroyed our dig site . . ."

"And most of the equipment I rented. I'm so dead."

"We were approached by five men claiming to be Inuit. In this region, that would make them Inuit of the Nunavut region."

"Why don't you tell us some more about the Inuit people?" Steve said with a slight sarcastic smile.

"Okay. They're the Arctic version of the Native Americans living in North America, only they lived far enough north that they were spared from the attacks of early European settlers. Unlike the Native Americans in the States, the Inuit continue to thrive and have for well over five thousand years."

"Could that frozen woman be an Inuit?" Steve asked, no longer playing devil's advocate.

"Don't know . . . suppose so, but she was probably around before they had an organized tribal system. So technically, she might not be Inuit. The Inuit people as a whole divide themselves into two main groups; the Yupik live in parts of Russia and Alaska, and the Inupiat live in Northern Alaska, some parts of Russia, but mostly in Canada and Greenland. The men outside are claiming to be Inupiat, but their language is wrong."

"What if they're the Yupik guys?"

"Yupik tribes have no reason to come to Canada. Food is scarce and there are enough tribes in the area to keep competition high. Besides, the Yupik language is very similar to the Inupiat. They're different, but have the same origins. It's like the difference between Spanish and French. They both evolved from Latin, so many of the words are the same or very similar."

"Geez. Let me get your wheelchair for you, Mr. Hawking," Steve said with a grin.

"Stephen Hawking is an astrophysicist or something, you moron, not an expert on Inuit. So shut your trap," Paul returned. "I'm on a roll." He turned back to the camera. "Also, beyond the language problem, there are more discrepancies."

Nicole focused on Paul's face. "Such as . . .?"

"Their clothing is wrong. Inuit people wore fur even up until twenty years ago, but not so much anymore. Of course they still do, but more for decoration."

"Like a rich lady in Manhattan in a mink coat?"

"Sort of, but it's more of a cultural pride thing than a fashion statement. You don't have to be rich to get fur out here, just a good hunter."

"So maybe these guys are trying to tell us they're really good hunters?"

Paul and Steve looked at each other, eyes serious, considering the idea. "I hope not," Paul said. "Modern Inuit are exactly that: modern. They use snowmobiles to travel, dog sleds at the very least, and none of them are stupid enough to set out across the ice without transportation or supplies. They're smart people; the men outside are something else."

"Move to the side," Nicole said as she moved the camera toward the plastic window. "I want to get a shot of them." She lifted the window's covering and aimed the camera out into the night, searching through the view finder for the tangerine glow of the men's fire. She found the fire and focused the lens manually. A figure came into view, sitting by the fire.

Alone.

"Uh, guys, only one of them is there."

"What?"

Steve and Paul crammed around the window and peered out. Nicole stopped recording and put her face between theirs as they looked at the single man sitting by the fire. "Where'd they go?" Steve asked.

"They should be frozen solid by now," Paul said. "No way they could be walking around. This doesn't make sense."

"I don't see the others anywhere."

"It's too dark. They'd have to be near the fire to see them."

"I have an idea," Nicole said as she brought her camera back up. "Night vision."

Steve smiled. "Sweet."

Nicole worked the buttons on the side of the camera and brought the viewfinder to her eye. She pointed it through the plastic window and aimed it at the fire, which glowed white in the otherwise green display.

"Let us see," Steve pleaded like an eager eight year old boy.

Nicole moved the view finder away from her eye and popped open an LCD screen on the camera's left side. Paul stood hunched over behind them and all three were allowed a clear view of the dark night. To the left of the blazing fire was nothing but techno-green snow and pine-green night sky. To the right, there was movement.

Zooming in, they could see that there was something there, perhaps the four missing men, perhaps not. Nicole turned the camera on its side and pushed a few more buttons. She explained without being asked. "Digital zoom."

After pointing the camera back out into the darkness, she relocated the dark figures and zoomed in. The image grew in size but became too shaky to see clearly.

"You have image stabilization on that thing?" Steve asked.

"Good idea." Nicole pushed a button on the side and the image stilled. "How did you know about image stabilization?"

"Spying on hotties at the beach. When you zoom in that much, the picture becomes too blurry and a woman in a bikini looks more like a fat kid."

"I should have guessed," Nicole said as she zoomed in tighter. She took a deep breath and focused manually, clearing the pixilated image as much as possible.

When the picture became clear, Nicole let her breath out and Steve gasped. "They're heading for the dig site," Steve said. "What are they doing there?"

"Remember when the old guy, the one with the red beanie—"

"Beanie?" Steve looked perplexed.

"Beanie. You know, a winter hat."

"Beanie? Ugh . . ." Steve shook his head. "Californians."

"Whatever. When that guy asked Eddy about whether or not we found anything before the storm . . . what if they know about that thing we found? That metal artifact thing. What if they're the ones who buried it in the first place? What if they go over there and find it in that buried tent? What if they get pissed? They have weapons."

"Spears," Paul said.

"Weapons . . . and who knows what else they have hidden in all that fur." Nicole was serious.

Steve looked at Paul. "We should get Eddy." Steve turned toward the tent's zipped entrance and reached out for the zipper.

Ziiiip!

Steve shouted and jumped back, landing in Nicole's lap as the tent entrance was unzipped and flung open from the outside.

"Quiet down!" Brian shouted as he ducked into the tent, fully bundled against the cold. Kevin entered behind him. "It's just us."

"You nearly gave me a heart attack, Buck!" Steve collected himself, but was hit by a thought. "Hey, you guys think something's screwy, too?"

"They're up to something." Brian said.

"We think we should leave while we can. While the other four are gone."

"I second that motion," Steve said. "Where's Eddy?"

"In the third tent," Kevin said. "With Eve."

An uncomfortable silence fell over the group. "Fine," Steve said. "I'll go, but if I find them doing the hibbity-jibbity, you're each buying me a twelve pack of brew when we get back to civilization. Deal?"

"I didn't realize they were an official item," Nicole said.

"They aren't. We all just figure it's a matter of time," Steve said. "Deal?"

Everyone starred at Steve in silence.

"I'm not leaving until everyone of you says 'deal.'"

"Deal," Paul said with a smile.

Kevin moved out of the entrance, giving Steve room to leave. "Deal."

Brian made himself comfortable on the floor of the tent. "If you want to destroy more brain cells with that awful-tasting gruel, fine by me. Deal."

Steve looked at Nicole. She smiled. "Only if you let me help you drink them."

Steve grinned wide. "Deal."

"Deal," Nicole said.

Steve threw on his jacket, pulled on his winter . . . beanie, and wrapped a scarf around his neck, praying to God he would find Eddy and Eve having sex, though he doubted he would. But the prospect of kicking back forty-eight beers with Nicole made him hopeful for the remainder of their ordeal and the future. Steve plunged into the bitter cold darkness and zipped the tent behind him. Steve mumbled beneath his scarf, "Please let them be doing it. Please let them be doing it."

14

ESCAPE

It wasn't unusual for Eve and Eddy to bunk together at night. No one ever joked about it and nothing ever happened. *Ever.* Eddy was always so preoccupied with work that he'd be up at the crack of dawn and work until the sun fell below the horizon and the hum of the generators faded. She was always asleep before him and woke up after he was gone. She was rarely aware that he had been beside her through the night. But to-night was different.

Emotionally exhausted from his earlier breakdown, Eddy was fast asleep in minutes. Eve found sleep impossible. The floor of the tent felt hard and cold. Her hair was wet and matted against her face. Comfort was never part of the plan during an average expedition, but even the small comforts of an expensive trip such as theirs were now buried under the ice. Eve rolled on to her side, facing Eddy. She took in his face, his sculpted jaw rough with stubble, his hair, dark and wavy.

Eve reached out for Eddy's hair and let a ring of it slide between her fingers. "Why are you so impossible to get close to?" Eve whispered.

Then Eve's mind went blank; her brilliant intellect vanished in a wash of emotion. Eve leaned forward and brought her face close to Eddy's.

She pursed her lips and could feel the warmth from his. Eve paused. Would he wake? Would he be angry? Would he—

Ziiiip!

The tent unzipped and the entrance was flung open. Eve rolled away from Eddy just as Steve stepped into the tent, a dim battery powered lantern lighting his path. "Damn," Steve said as he looked down at Eddy and Eve, fully clothed and separate.

"Steve?" Eve asked. "What are you doing?"

Eddy stirred in his sleeping bag and peeled open his eyes. He peered up at Steve. "Steve. It's still dark. Go back to bed."

"Eddy, wake up, man."

Eddy's eyes snapped open a second before he sat upright, fully awake. He'd long since learned what an urgent voice sounded like and had trained himself to react instantly. It had staved off disaster in the past. "What is it?"

"We want to get out of here, like, now," Steve said.

"Who is 'we'?"

"We is everyone."

"Why?"

"The rest of us talked about it. Those guys aren't Inuit, and they've been chanting all night."

"All night?" Eddy asked.

"You couldn't hear them?" Steve asked.

"He was asleep," Eve said. "I heard them, though. Figured it was normal."

"There's nothing normal about those guys. Listen, four of them took off toward the ruins of the dig site. We think they might be looking for that thing we found."

"The metal cylinder?" Eve asked.

"Yeah."

"We left it in the ice," Eddy said. "But why would they want it and how would they know it exists?"

"Questions for another day, my man." Steve handed Eddy his coat. "Right now, it's time to hit the road. We can take that one guy, but if his buddies return and they don't want us to leave . . . Well, that might be a problem."

Eddy looked into Steve's dimly-lit eyes. "What do you want to do?"

"Tie the guy up by the fire and bolt. They got here on their own. They don't need us to get out. I know this sounds dumb, but I got this bad feeling, man. These guys are no good and too much of their story doesn't add up. Leaving on our own might be risky, but staying with these guys is more risky. We know what the Arctic has to offer, but these Inuit . . . they're a complete unknown."

Eddy pursed his lips and nodded. "Let's go."

☼   ☼   ☼   ☼   ☼

EDDY CREPT up behind the remaining Inuit man, who was hunched over, next to the fire, a light mumbled chant still escaping his lips. Steve, Paul, and Brian tip-toed through the snow behind Eddy.

"I don't think this is a good idea," Steve whispered. "We should just jump him."

"They haven't done anything wrong yet," Eddy said, trying to be quiet. "We could be wrong, and if we are, I don't want to hurt him."

"C'mon, man, he doesn't even know we're here. It'd be easy."

"No." To make his point, Eddy started toward the man, stepping hard on the snow.

Steve rolled his eyes and felt them sting with cold.

"Excuse me," Eddy said in a charming, loud voice. "You're Vayu, right?"

The man stood. He towered over Eddy by six inches, and Eddy was six-foot-one. Vayu turn to Eddy and looked down at him, his thick brown skin fully exposed to the thirty below air. The man rolled his neck in one direction, bones popping and cracking, then the other direction, which had a similar effect.

"Sorry to bother you this late at night," Eddy said. "But we've talked it over and we've decided that your help, while generous of you to offer, is unneeded. We'll be leaving now."

The man stared down, expressionless.

"Okay," Eddy said. "See you around." Eddy turned to leave and walked a few steps toward the others. "See that wasn't so hard—*oof!*"

Eddy was pulled back and flung through the air, landing on the ice ten feet away. Brian, Steve and Paul watched as he slid to a stop.

"Holy crap!" Steve shouted.

"You're not leaving this place." Vayu said in the deepest voice any of them had ever heard. "Not now . . ." He took a step forward. "Not ever." He turned his back on them and went to sit back down.

Steve looked at Paul and in a moment of mind reading, they agreed that this was their chance. They charged forward, fists clenched and adrenaline pumping.

Vayu spun as Steve's fist flew down at him. But the punch never made it. Vayu took Steve's arm and used his momentum to fling him through the air. Steve landed next to Eddy, who was only now getting to his feet.

Paul had stopped when Steve was tossed. He watched in horror as Vayu picked his friend up and tossed him as though his one hundred and eighty pounds were no more than a down pillow. Paul reached down into his boot and pulled out a long metal wrench. "Time to show this jerk how we do things in the Big Apple."

After rushing Vayu, carrying himself with an air of confidence that he learned during his schoolyard fighting days, Paul ducked away from Vayu's first swing, which was less of a punch and more of an attempt to slash Paul's throat with his finger nails, which Paul noticed were long and thick. Paul followed up with a swing that should have knocked the man unconscious, or outright killed him, connecting the thick end of the wrench with Vayu's temple.

Shaking off the hit like it was a slap in the face from a three-year-old-girl, Vayu turned toward Paul, who was preparing to swing again, and roared. The sound was like a deep train whistle and it stung Paul's ears. Paul continued with his swing even though his eyes were closed in pain from the shout, but the wrench was caught in Vayu's thick, bare hands. Paul opened his eyes in time to see Vayu lurch forward, take a fist full of his jacket, and lift him into the air.

Paul hung in the air over Vayu's head, sure he was about to be slammed into the frozen ice and made a bloody pulp. But the expected surge of pain never came; he fell straight down, landing on Vayu's back. Eddy had tackled the man at the knees.

"Grab his arms!" Eddy shouted. "Pin him to the ground!"

Brian, who had remained out of the fight, was propelled into action upon seeing victory was near. He jumped on Vayu's left arm, while Paul took the right. Eddy was still wrapped around the man's legs. Vayu began to struggle and it was evident that they could not hold him long.

"He's going to get loose!" Brian shouted.

"Hold on, guys, I'm coming!" Kevin shouted as he ran out of the darkness, wielding a metal pipe. Kevin dove on the man, digging his knee into the man's back.

Vayu grunted with the impact. He looked up and saw Eve and Nicole running toward them with a loop of rope strung out between them. He grunted and pushed down on the ice with his arms, lifting himself and the other four men into the air. Brian was sent sliding across the ice as Vayu tossed him off. Paul was next. Then Vayu reached back and grabbed hold of Kevin, who pounded his knee into Vayu's side over and over, with no effect. Kevin rolled onto the ice, landing with his metal pipe still in hand.

Eddy let go of Vayu and moved away, but not quickly enough. Vayu kicked Eddy in the stomach like a professional soccer player. Eddy curled in pain, vomited, and gasped for air. Vayu stood over him.

Clang!

Kevin smashed the back of Vayu's head with the metal pipe, afraid he would kill the man, but he had no choice. It turned out that murder wasn't something Kevin had to be concerned with. Vayu turned with the speed of a striking cobra, swung his hulking arm out and knocked the pipe from Kevin's hand. Kevin stepped backward, away from the man. Vayu stepped forward, pulling an intricately-designed blade from inside his furry coat.

Vayu's eyes widened and Kevin was sure he would feel his warm blood pour down his neck before he died, but a length of thick rope was flung over Vayu's head from behind and wrapped around the man's waist. Eve and Nicole tried to pull him back using the ropes, but he continued forward, toward Kevin, pulling them across the ice with him.

Kevin's eyes darted back and forth. He'd seen the man's speed and knew he couldn't outrun him. Fighting would be useless. He'd be slashed to bits in seconds. He looked for help. Eddy was still on the ice, though beginning to move. Brian and Paul were just getting to their feet. Eve and Nicole were powerless—they all were. Where was Steve?

The rumble of an engine answered Kevin. All eyes snapped in the direction of the noise. "Out of the way!" Steve shouted from the window of the Sno-Cat. Kevin dove to the side. Eve and Nicole dropped the rope and ran. Vayu had nowhere to go. The metal hull of the Sno-Cat hit him

with immense force and pounded his body into the ice, crushing him under its tank treads.

The Sno-Cat continued forward a few feet until Vayu's crushed body
was revealed, like a human-size road kill. Steve stopped the Cat, opened
the door, and looked back at his handiwork. "Everyone okay?"

But before anyone could answer, Steve saw something he never expected. Vayu's hand reached up and gripped the snow, pulling his torso
up.

"Oh, hell, no," Steve said as he climbed back into the Cat, through it
into reverse and hit the gas. The heavy treads hit Vayu and rolled over his
body, pressing him down. The loud crack was audible even to Steve, in
the loud cockpit of the Sno-Cat. He pulled back a few feet, revealing
Vayu's snapped body, folded over like an omelet.

Steve climbed out of the Cat as the bruised group gathered around the
dead man. Lit by the bright lights of the Sno-Cat, they could see that he
was twisted and broken—definitely dead. Blood soaked the white ice
around his body. Purple blood. It oozed from his body, staining an ever
increasing patch of snow like a giant grape slushie.

"Okay," Eddy said, through labored breaths, as he held his stomach,
"I admit it. They're not Inuit."

"I'm not even sure they're human," Kevin said.

Brian leaned down to the purple snow. "I'd like to take a sample of
this man's blood."

"His strength was amazing . . . super-human," Eve said. "He must be
on some kind of drug, a new type of muscle enhancer."

"Maybe the military has a secret Black Op going on out here?" Steve
said.

Paul rolled his eyes. "Military types don't wear fur."

"Well, I haven't heard you come up with any good ideas since 'They're
not Inuit.'"

"What about a new breed of human?" Eve said. "Some of the northern tribes are still secluded from modern man. They could have evolved
along different paths in the past ten thousand years. Though I'm still
more prone to the drug theory."

"Have any of you ever heard of a drug that turns your blood purple?
It's not right. Really, even dogs bleed red," Kevin said.

The response was blank stares. "I didn't think so," Kevin said. "You can write me off as being a sci-fi wacko if you want and can call me Buck Rogers till the cows come home, but it won't change the fact that this thing is bleeding purple. You might think he's on drugs, or is genetically altered, or even a vampire if you want, but I'm telling you right now: it's not human . . . they're not human, and they know we raised something strange from the ice. If they go to the dig site and find what they're looking for, that thing we left behind in the ice, they won't need us. Human, undead, alien, or otherwise, we need to get the hell out of here. I may enjoy a good run-for-your-life thriller, but I'm not eager to live one."

Kevin had made his point. They raced back to the temporary campsite, tore apart their tents and packed it into the Cat within ten minutes. They crammed into the Cat, mounted the snowmobiles, and were racing into the frozen dark before any of them had a chance to think about the man with mulberry blood.

☼   ☼   ☼   ☼   ☼

AS THE sun rose into the sky, Marutas knelt down next to the flattened body of Vayu. He scanned the area with his old eyes, taking in the footprints, Sno-Cat treads, and other bodily depressions in the snow. "He fought well," Marutas said. "But he underestimated their abilities."

Marutas stood and looked at the remaining Inuit men, Andari, Hoder, and Reginn.

"His life was not at its fullest," Andari said.

"It was his to lose," Reginn added.

Andari nodded. "How could he have been so foolish? After so many years . . . to be slain by whelps. They were unarmed!"

"I have noticed," Marutas said, "that over the years, the resolve of some has faded. The willingness to inflict pain, to seize power, and to influence the wills of others loses power as time passes. The weak have fallen over the years, just as they always do. It is the way of things."

"But we are only four now," Hoder said. "How can we possibly—"

"It is said that there are four corners of the globe and we will each rule a corner. But that is no concern of ours, not until the key is found. It was not with the remains of that contemptible woman from the past, so we must conclude that Dr. Moore did uncover the device."

"Do you think they know its purpose?" Reginn asked with a nervous twitch.

"No. If they knew, we would have sensed their fear."

Hoder looked down at Vayu's frozen blood covered body. "Surely they suspect."

"Agreed, but they will run for safety as all humans do. They will run home like frightened schoolchildren. And we, we will have the joy of the chase, the hunt! After so many years, my heart is pounding, my mind feels the quickening. Too long have we ruled in obscurity. The thrill of danger is ours again."

"We all agree," Andari said. "Killing these humans when they are so close to summoning the Aeros will be a great pleasure, a masterful game indeed. But this whelp . . . You have watched him over time. You know he is smart. You know he is cunning, a true warrior. What if he—"

"Hold your tongue, young Andari," Marutas said with a snarl. "He is cunning for a human, but he will always be just that: human. We are superior in mind and in body. We are Ferox!"

The men cheered, roaring into the frozen air like beasts. After the voices faded, Marutas spoke. "The wisdom of my ages tells me there is some truth to your claim. We will pursue them. We will toy with them like cats with a crippled mouse. But should they discover the truth and seek out the Aeros, we will cut them off at the knees and watch them stain the white snow red with their blood."

<h1 style="text-align: center;">15</h1>

THE ARTIFACT

Three dark specks sped south across the blinding white planes, toward safety. They had traveled through the few remaining hours of darkness, fighting against the pitch black and the numbing cold. Those who were most exposed to the air—Steve, Nicole, and Paul—riding the two snowmobiles, wore extra layers. There wasn't a single sliver of skin exposed to the elements. If there had been, it would have frozen solid.

Inside the elephantine Sno-Cat was Eddy behind the steering wheel and Kevin reading a *Solar Atom* comic book in the passenger's side front seat. Eve and Brian sat in the back, staring out the windows. The cabin shook and rumbled as the metal treads crunched over the ice. The inside of the Cat bounced up and crashed down with creaks from the strained metal. "Sorry about that," Eddy said. "Looks like it gets pretty bumpy ahead. If I had time, I might be able to work around some of this, but as we are now, we have to take what we get."

"No complaints over here," Kevin said.

Eddy had watched Kevin over the past few hours. At first he was quiet, almost vacant—most likely replaying the events of the past few days through his mind: the storm, the Inuit, the purple blood. Over time, as the sun grew bright in the cloudless sky, Kevin grew more relaxed, reading a copy of *Discover* that he left inside the Cat along with a few other magazines and comics. Since then, he had rocketed through a few issues of a science fiction magazine enveloped with the story and images, a few of which Eddy could make out as savage aliens battling a man in red tights. Now Kevin was almost jovial, as though the events of the past twenty-four hours had never happened. Eddy was no psychologist, but he knew Kevin's behavior wasn't normal. Or was it? Maybe he was the only one handling the shock of so many deaths in a normal way. Maybe the rest of them were cold emotionally; they were all cold physically.

Kevin turned the comic like he was looking at pinup girl in an issue of *Playboy*. Eddy leaned over and glanced at the page. It was a two-page spread of a sinister looking creature with large yellow eyes, sharp claws, and two tails. The man in red tights was beaten and bloody at the bottom of the page, secured under the paw of the alien beast. Kevin's hands began to shake. He tossed the comic to the floor.

"Stupid," Kevin said to himself.

No, Eddy thought, Kevin is not reacting in a healthy way to what they've lived through. Eddy was sure he was cracking up, maybe losing his mind, but he wasn't sure. Kevin had a brilliant intellect and Eddy was certain he could make a comeback. He just needed some of mom's good, old fashioned distraction.

"Anything interesting in that issue of *Discover*, Buck?" Eddy asked.

Kevin just stared out the window.

"*Discover* is just a flashy news magazine for the common man who wants to think he's being smart," Brian commented form the back seat.

"Shut up, Brian," Eve said when she saw Kevin's shaking hands. She motioned toward Kevin with her eyes. Brian was seated behind Kevin so he leaned to the right and caught a glimpse of Kevin's now wet face in the right side mirror.

"Don't worry," Brian said. "I don't think he can hear any of us anyway."

Eddy shot Brian an annoyed glance. "Kev, talk to me."

Kevin moved his eyes from the page and up to Eddy's eyes. "It's just a stupid comic book. I'm being stupid."

Eddy waited.

Kevin sighed. "They killed the hero. The hero's not supposed to die."

Aha, Eddy thought, now we're getting down to it. "No one's going to die, Kevin."

Kevin sat still with a blank stare.

"Don't be foolish," Brian said. "It's a comic book. Not reality."

"What do you know?" Kevin shouted as he turned in his seat, facing Brian. "Comics are supposed to be better than life. Idealized people living precarious lives and surviving . . . happily! In real life, my life, all our lives, we've seen how many people die. I know it's not intelligent . . ." Kevin wiped his nose. "I was just trying to escape."

Kevin rolled down his window, letting a blast of frozen air surge into the cabin, and threw the comic out. He rolled up the window again. "I'm done with comics."

Eddy saw that Kevin wasn't cracking up, just making an effort to escape the pains of reality for a while through the adventures of *Solar Atom*. But the creators of *Solar Atom* had let him down, killing the hero and destroying Kevin's escapism. "Didn't they kill Superman a few years back?" Eddy asked.

Kevin looked at Eddy, surprised that he knew the comic trivia. "Yeah."

"Well, is it just me, or are they still selling *Superman* comics at the supermarket?"

"Yeah. He came back to life."

"Is that normal in comic books, for the hero to die and come back to life?"

"Sure," Kevin said, relaxing. "It happens all the time."

"Right . . . And how are *Solar Atom's* sales doing?"

"Down some, but still one of the fan favorites."

"Do you really think they'd kill a fan favorite super hero permanently? Don't you think he'll be back somehow? You, more than anyone, should know that Solar Atom will be back. Sure, his costume might be a little different, or he'll have amnesia for a little while, but he'll be back and that issue where he dies will probably become a collector's item. I'm sure that's why they killed him in the first place—probably some marketing guy's bright idea. So you see? Solar Atom isn't really dead, and we're all going to be fine."

"Oh God," Kevin said with a look of dread on his face.

"What?" Eddy asked.

Kevin looked out the rear window. "I threw it out the window!" Eddy smiled and Kevin began laughing. "Thanks, Eddy."

"At least I'm good for something," Eddy said and yanked the wheel to the left. "Whoa!"

The Cat lurched up and pounded back down, careening over a chunk of ice. Brian clung to his seat and knocked his backpack over. The top of the backpack flew open and a single object slid out, but only a few inches.

"Sorry. Wasn't watching the ice," Eddy said.

Kevin laughed, more relaxed. "Good for pep talks. Not so good at driving. Eddy, you're a—"

Eddy looked at Kevin, whose smile had vanished. He was looking at the back seat wide eyes. Eddy followed Kevin's eyes to Brian's open backpack and saw a metallic silver object poking out. Eddy recognized the object, the futuristic artifact they had raised from the ice, clung to by an ancient women, frozen in the belly of a mammoth.

"What?" Brian said, unaware that the artifact was visible.

"Is that what I think it is?" Kevin said with a shaky voice.

"Is that what you think what is?" Brian was upset. He didn't like not understanding a question.

Kevin thrust his finger out at the open backpack. Brian looked at the pack and closed it. "That's just a thermos."

"Bull!" Kevin grabbed the bag and pulled it to the front seat.

"Hey!" Brian protested and leaned forward in pursuit of the bag. But before he could recover the pack, he was yanked back into his seat by Eve, who was glaring at him.

Kevin open the pack, reached in, and pulled the artifact out, holding it in his hands and staring at it like it was a venomous snake. "You . . . brought this?" Kevin asked, turning toward Brian.

"Of course I recognized that this was a significant find. And since the rest of our expedition has turned out to be a dismal failure, I took this as compensation. For my losses."

"For *your* losses?" Eve was irate. "You sanctimonious, egotistical, bastard!"

"Hey! I invested more than a million dollars in this little expedition! I lost more than anyone!"

The sound of flesh on flesh smacked through the cabin as Eve planted her open palm on Brian's cheek, burning a red handprint onto his flesh. "We lost friends and good people, and you're worrying about money!"

Click!

The artifact popped open, revealing its red flashing light. Kevin shouted and dropped the object between his and Eddy's seat. "Stop the Cat! Stop the Cat, right now!"

☼   ☼   ☼   ☼   ☼

STEVE SAW the Sno-Cat come to a sudden stop as he zipped past with Nicole seated behind him, clinging to his waist. He turned his head and watched the treads on the Cat stop moving.

"Why'd they stop?" Nicole shouted through her thick wrap of scarf, which covered her face and protected her from the cold.

"I don't know." Steve eased up on the throttle and turned the snowmobile around. He noticed Paul turning around as well. They sped back to the Sno-Cat in time to see the doors on both sides swing open.

"What have you done, Brian?" Kevin shouted.

Steve stopped the snowmobile and hopped off with Nicole. They unwrapped their protective face masks from their faces and headed toward the commotion. Paul was right behind them.

Kevin snapped his head toward Eddy. "You told me it was gone. You said it was buried, that we left it in the ice."

"I thought it was!" Eddy yelled.

"What's going on?" Steve said as he approached.

Kevin spun around and held the silver, pill-shaped object in Steve's face. "This is."

Steve raised his hands in the air and stepped back. "Whoa. I don't want anything to do with that."

"You see?" Kevin said. "I'm not the only one who thinks it's dangerous."

"Classic closed-minded imbecile," Brian said. "You of all people, a scientist, should not be afraid of what you don't understand. It's common for people like him—" Brian pointed at Steve.

"Hey," Steve protested.

Brian ignored him. ". . . but *you're* supposed to be a man of science. The unknown is our business. You must see that this object is an amazing discovery. We should be studying it, protecting it, not trying to rebury it in the ice!"

"What about the rest of you?" Kevin asked. "Do you all want to risk your lives for this?"

Eddy stepped forward without a hint of hostility. "Kevin, listen. That artifact might be an incredible find. I wasn't in support of taking it, but we've had it with us for the past six hours without a problem. I don't think it caused the storm, and I don't think it poses any danger."

"What about the Inuit?"

"Non-Inuit," Paul reminded them.

"What about them?" Kevin said. "I know they're looking for it."

Eddy rubbed his chin. "And they, unlike this object, pose a threat."

"Right," Kevin said, nodding. "And they're after it. I know they are."

"We don't know that," Brian said. "And even if they were, they're on foot. We've been traveling at twenty miles an hour for six hours. They're over a hundred miles back by now."

"You thought they had a camp," Kevin said to Eve. "What if they're only a few miles back, tracking us on snowmobiles? They could have guns, more men . . . I don't want to die because of this thing."

"No one's going to die," Eddy said as he took another slow step forward.

Kevin took a step back. "Let's put it to a vote. Who wants to leave this thing behind?"

Kevin looked at Eve. She stared at the snow.

"You know how I feel," Brian said.

"It's safe," Eddy added. "If it were dangerous, or emitting radiation, or something else harmful, we'd know by now."

Kevin looked at Paul. "Hey, don't look at me. Eddy tells me where to go and I go," Paul said.

"Yeah, man," Steve said. "Eddy wouldn't put us in danger. He thinks it's safe. Good enough for me."

"And it will make a perfect ending to my documentary," Nicole said. "We went to raise a mammoth, but got so much more. I say we keep it and find out what it is the first chance we get."

"You heard them," Eddy said as he reached out his hand, waiting for Kevin to hand him the artifact. "Give it to me and I'll make sure it stays out of sight for the remainder of the trip. Kevin . . . you know you can trust me." Eddy moved forward, his hand only inches from the device.

Kevin snapped back, reeling away from Eddy. He raised the artifact over his head. "Fine! If you don't have the clarity of mind to see what's necessary, I'll destroy it myself!" Kevin threw the cylinder down on the ice and stomped on it with his thick boot. But the ice was solid and slippery. The device slid out from beneath his foot and sent him flying backwards. He landed hard on the ice, hitting his head.

Eve was by his side, checking his head for injuries, and Kevin began to sob. "Kevin," she said, "You okay?"

"We're all going to die out here! Can't you see that? They're coming for us. They're coming for that thing and when they find it, they're going to kill us all! I saw them! I saw them . . ."

All eyes were on Kevin. Eddy knelt by his side. "Try to calm down, Buck. You hit your head pretty hard."

"I think we should ice it," Eve said.

"Just lay him back down in the snow," Steve said.

Kevin shoved Eve away and shouted, "Why aren't you listening to me? I know—"

An unfamiliar voice interrupted. It spoke a language that reminded Steve of the subtitled Japanimation cartoons he watched in high school, but there were no subtitles to translate the sentence. Steve turned toward the voice and stepped back, as did everyone else. Standing before them was a tall figure, dressed in a cloak that looked like Obi Wan Kenobi's. The man's face was covered in darkness provided by the hood of the cloak. He stood still and silent until he spoke again, "*Pode entender me?*"

And again, "*Können Sie mich verstehen?*"

And again, "*Lei me può capire?*"

16

MESSAGE IN A BOTTLE

"*Kunn De forstår meg?*" the cloaked man said again.

Eddy noticed that the man was standing behind the artifact. Other than the brown hooded cloak, he couldn't see any other of the man's features. The only way he knew the cloaked figure was a man was by the deep gravely voice. He couldn't see the man's hands, feet, or face, which was obscured by the hood of cloak.

It was obvious to Eddy that this man was trying to communicate, asking a question in various languages, but what? He felt the cloaked figure posed little threat but took a defensive position between the man and the rest of his crew.

"*Vous pouvez me comprendre?*"

"That was French," Eve said. "He said something about understanding . . . but I don't know what."

"Lei me può capire?"

"Holy mother of God. That was Italian," Paul said as he did the sign of the cross. "Sounded like my grandmother."

"¿Me puede entender usted?"

"Spanish," Eddy said. "Do you . . . do you understand . . ."

"Do you understand me?" the cloaked figure asked in perfect English.

"Yes," Eddy said. "We understand you."

"Forgive the confusion," the cloaked figure said. "There are many un-known languages on this world now, and this device has limited capabilities. My name is Artuke."

"Incredible," Kevin said as he got to his feet, his panic completely subsided.

"Who are you?" Eddy asked.

"Can't you see what he is?" Kevin said.

Eddy glanced at Kevin but kept his mouth shut. Kevin wasn't himself and Eddy didn't want to upset him again.

"I am a recorded messenger, able to adapt and learn. Please listen to me. You are much different than the last human this key came in contact with. I fear too much time has already passed. It won't be long before you, too, are found."

"You . . . you're a recording?" Eddy said.

"Yes," Artuke said. "I believe the best way to describe what I am in a way you could understand would be a hologram."

"I knew it," Kevin said.

"This is messed up," Steve said.

"Who was the last human you came into contact with?" Brian asked as he stepped forward, next to Eddy. He looked at Eddy with a smile. "Contact with a being from the past!"

"Her name was Haphnee of the Jetush. A skillful warrior, though judging from the numerous transmissions I am detecting in your atmosphere, I imagine she is long since dead. Perhaps you found her?"

Eddy nodded. "She was holding that device." Eddy pointed to the artifact.

"Yes," Artuke said. "The key. She would have guarded it with her life."

Eddy was shaken by what they were witnessing. He had so many questions, but one kept resurfacing, again and again, refusing to be snuffed out. "You said it wouldn't be long before we were found. Found by who?"

"The Ferox."

The answer came so quickly and so bluntly that Eddy was sure the hologram wasn't joking. "Who are they?"

"Ask the one called Kevin. I revealed the Ferox to him when we interfaced."

All eyes turned to Kevin, who was stunned. "That was real?" Kevin said. "Those creatures are real?"

"Yes," Artuke said. "And at present, I detect their numbers worldwide to be only four. This is not good."

Eddy wanted to apologize to Kevin for doubting him, for not believing him, but it would have to wait. "Why?"

"The Ferox abandon a planet only before they are certain its destruction is assured. With their numbers so low and no fleet detected in orbit, your race must be nearing self-destruction."

"They're from space," Kevin said. "Aliens. I was right."

"Preposterous," Brian said. "The chances of life on other worlds are—"

"Better than you might think," Artuke said. "We have found that undeveloped races such as yours surmise that all life in the universe evolves along similar lines. That oxygen and water are required elements for life. You assume that life can only have five senses and can detect only three dimensions. Such assumptions are wrong and misguided. They are evidence of the Ferox corruption."

"If these Ferox guys came all the way to Earth from some other galaxy," Steve said, "then why are they trying to destroy us, and how can four of them pull it off?"

"The Ferox are evil in ways you cannot begin to comprehend. They are the corruptors of worlds, whose motivations go beyond even my understanding."

"This is nuts," Steve said.

"I second that," Paul added.

"You're alien to this planet as well, aren't you?" Kevin asked, as excitement filled his voice.

"Yes."

"And the Ferox . . . they came to your planet and tried to corrupt you as well." Kevin was smiling.

"Indeed. My race is called the Aeros. We first encountered the Ferox before your race had even appeared on this world. They thrive on chaos and create it by infiltrating a civilization and rotting it out from the inside, like a cancer. The Ferox brought our race to the edge of annihilation. But their plot was discovered and stopped. We now travel the cosmos cleansing worlds of the Ferox infection, rooting them out wherever they hide. We came to Earth ten thousand years ago and no Ferox presence was found. We left behind a beacon transmitter and a key to activate it. Haphnee must have been on her way to the transmitter when they found her."

"You keep referring to this key." Eve said. "Where is it?"

Artuke looked down at his feet. "The key is the object you raised from the ice. It is the object which is now transmitting my image."

Kevin rubbed his chin and thought aloud. "If Haphnee died before making it to the transmitter, then no signal was ever sent and the Aeros don't know the Ferox are here." Kevin looked up at Artuke. "Is the transmitter still functional?"

"It should be, yes."

"Then we will finish in her place," Kevin said.

"Wait a minute," Brian said. "We're going to take the word of a . . . a hologram? What if this is an elaborate hoax? There are some people who would like to see me lose my fortune over something like this. We're just supposed to believe all this? That aliens are infecting our planet with no other goal than to see us kill each other? That—"

"Yes," Artuke's voice boomed. "You will believe me, or your race will be blotted out from beneath the stars."

"Was that some kind of veiled threat?" Brain asked Artuke, then said to Eddy, "Was that a threat?"

Eddy gripped Brian's shoulder and pulled him back. "Our planet seems fine to us. How do we know the Ferox are even here?"

"The Ferox have the ability to alter their visual appearance and are masters of cultural blending. Do not bother speculating about how these things are possible. The answers are beyond your minds. But evidence of their presence can be seen in every facet of your civilization. Evil organizations on Earth, past and present, are almost certainly led by Ferox. The Nazis, the Khmer Rouge, the slave trade, the Inquisition, the Taliban, all possess the calling card of the Ferox. Your crime, your weapons of mass destruction, your—"

"Okay, okay, we understand," Eddy said. "But we have suffered tremendous losses. Our crew and supplies were destroyed."

"By a storm?" Artuke asked.

"Yes," Eddy said, squinting. "How did you know?"

"The Ferox, while savage in nature, are also technologically advanced."

"As advanced as you?" Kevin asked.

"Yes. They have developed machines that can manipulate planetary weather. I imagine that several of your planets 'natural disasters' have, in fact, been Ferox attacks. I will give you the same advice I gave Haphnee. If you see a small black orb floating above or resting on the ground, hide or take cover. Your life will be surely lost if you do not."

"Another threat," Brian said.

"A warning," Artuke corrected.

Artuke raised his arms into the air and a three dimensional map of the Arctic rose out of the snow around them. "Time is short, humans; take the key to these coordinates and raise the citadel." Numbers appeared in the snow, longitude and latitude. "Activate the beacon from inside and the Aeros will return to purge Earth of the Ferox and help guard it against future infection. We will bring you to an age of enlightenment and peace."

Artuke's body became fuzzy, translucent. "The key's power cells are draining. Please hurry. You are being tracked. The Ferox's weakness is their willingness to take risks. They will allow you to get close to the citadel before confronting you, but they will find you. Exploiting this weakness may be your only chance. I will not be able to contact you again. Good luck, my friends."

Silence fell over the group, but Steve could only take it for a few seconds. "Shit, man. Intergalactic war. This blows."

☼   ☼   ☼   ☼   ☼

THE TEAM stood next to the Sno-Cat like Greek statues, frozen in time. Eddy spoke. "I need to break this down. If I make a mistake along the way, correct me. Okay?"

Nods all around.

"We found this 'key' frozen in the ice, clutched in the hands of an ancient woman named Haphnee. Somehow, Kevin activated the device and a hologram of an alien, Artuke, who appeared to be human but whose true identity is still a mystery, tells us that the human race for thousands of years has been influenced by a second alien race, the Ferox, who are leading all of humanity down a path of self-destruction."

"Maybe they're like angels and demons," Eve said. "The Ferox came down to Earth at a time when men, *Homo sapiens,* I mean, were still relatively new to the planet, like fallen angels. The Aeros have been fighting them the entire time—angels."

"You don't mean to suggest that these folks are in fact angels and demons?" Brian huffed. "The idea is preposterous."

"Everything is preposterous to you, man," Steve said.

"Of course not," Eve said. "But what if their presence gave rise to the idea, that something beyond our understanding was controlling us, leading us to evil, to sin."

"The concept of sin is relative and outdated," Brian stated.

"Let the lady talk," Paul said. "And one more crack about religion will earn you a crack to the skull."

Brian furrowed his brow and pursed his lips.

Eve continued. "If these Ferox brought corruption—sin—to our world, then by definition they are demons."

"Alien, techo-demons," Kevin said. "That can change form and influence nations . . . Has it occurred to anyone that Artuke talked about the Ferox like the ones who were present thousands of years ago, are the same bunch on Earth today? These things, they're old, really old."

"Great," Nicole said. "Now we have geriatric techno-demons chasing us. Can we go now?"

"In a minute," Eddy said. "First we need to figure out where we're going."

"What do you mean?" Steve asked, and the looks from the others said that they wanted to know, too.

"Well," Eddy laughed, "if we agree that this is all . . . real, and not some elaborate hoax—"

"No way this is a hoax," Kevin said.

"Then we need to decide whether or not we try to take this key . . ." Eddy bent down and picked up the key. It snapped closed in his hand, concealing the red light. ". . . and finish what Haphnee started. Should we take the key to the transmitter?"

Everyone was silent.

"If we do this, I want everyone in. One hundred percent. If any one of you don't want to, we head home as fast as we can. If we all agree, we head north, to the transmitter. Kevin?"

Kevin looked at Eddy, surprised to be asked first. He fidgeted for a moment then looked resolute. "Listen, I know I freaked out back there, but you have to understand. I saw all this. I saw their planet, the Ferox . . . I . . . I know what they look like. What they really look like, and none of you believed me. I thought I was going crazy and I panicked. I'm sorry."

Eve placed her hand on Kevin's shoulder. "Any one of us would have had the same reaction. There's nothing to apologize for."

Eddy said, "Tell us what you think."

"I think," Kevin started, "that this is the chance of a lifetime. Here we are, a bunch of nobodies in the overall scheme of things, nothing more than microscopic specs that appear and disappear in a relative nanosecond. But we have the chance to alter the fate of our planet, which could alter the fate of our solar system, and eventually or galaxy—if the human race survives another hundred thousand years or so."

"Buck is on a roll," Steve said with a smile.

"I'll be the first to admit, this is a dream come true for me. Aliens, the fate of the planet, this is the stuff I read about every day and now I have the chance to live it. I was wrong about one thing before: I said I wasn't eager to live through a thriller. I was wrong. This is the best thing to happen to me since I married Salina."

Kevin paused. The muscles in his face fell and pulled his cheeks down in a deep frown.

"What is it?" Eddy asked.

"Salina, Bruce, and Peter . . . if something happens to me out here, they'll never know what happened to me. They won't even know if I really died or not."

"Think logically," Brian said. "Should we choose to believe all this rubbish about global moral decay being caused by shape shifting aliens, our lives and the lives of everyone we know are moot, an illusion."

"That's cold," Steve said.

"No, he's right," Eddy said. "The only way our lives and the lives of everyone else on the planet will matter, really matter, is if they are free of evil influence. Everything up until now has been molded to fit a particular desire—destruction. What we see on TV, our wars, terrorism, plagues, all of it could be a result of Ferox influence."

"Imagine what the world might become without them," Eve said.

"I've decided," Kevin said. "I'm going. If the rest of you decide not to go, I'll take a snowmobile and do it alone. Either way, I'm going."

"Hold on, Kevin, let the rest of us decide before you wage a one-man war."

"An appropriate analogy," Kevin said. "Because when you stop and think about it, that's what this is—a war. I don't know about you all, but the idea that we seven could change the course of history, literally save the human race and change the balance of power from evil to good, is very exciting."

Eddy turned to Brian. "Kevin's in. What about you?"

"We've made so many discoveries in the past few days, some of the most important discoveries of all time. But it needs to be studied thoroughly and scrutinized carefully. Since you're all so prone to charge in headlong without giving a passing thought to science . . . or profit, I will most definitely be coming along, though I'll admit, more from scientific curiosity than some foolish notion that removing four alien creatures from the planet will stop the downward moral spiral of the human race. My answer is yes, most definitely."

"Well that was a long-winded waste of time no one wanted to hear," Paul said. "Try this next time: I'm in." Paul crossed his arms and looked at Steve.

"Hell," Steve said, "someone's got to protect Paul's ass. I'm good. I'm in."

Steve looked at Nicole.

"I've still got a camera. I go where the action is. I'm totally in."

Eve turned to Eddy and smiled. "I go where you go."

Eddy sighed, feeling the weight of this decision on his shoulders. He wasn't sure who to trust. The Inuit they had encountered obviously had ill intentions, but to trust an alien hologram thousands of year old . . . The idea was ridiculous. "I'm not so sure."

"What?" Kevin looked confused for a moment, then resolute. "Eddy, I know you changed in Venezuela. I know it hurt you. But we can't just let this go."

"How do you know the hologram is telling the truth? How do you know we won't all die for nothing?"

"I know I won't be able to live with myself if I don't try. Just the chance that this is all real, that our lives are influenced by these things, makes the attempt worthwhile." Kevin crossed his arms. "And like I said, I'm going with or without you."

Eddy looked into the eyes of each and every one of them. All were giving him the same look. They were going without him . . . but they needed him. "We're both in," he said, speaking for himself and Eve as one. The sentence felt strange at first, but then comforting.

"Same seating and we'll double time the speed. From what I understand, these Ferox are more dangerous than the Arctic, so environmental concerns are out the window. Stay close and move fast." Eddy turned to Paul and pointed to the numbers carved into the snow, "Plug those coordinates in the GPS and set a course. Let's go."

The group broke up. Paul, Steve, and Nicole hopped back onto the snowmobiles, while Kevin and Brian climbed into the Sno-Cat. Eddy and Eve lingered behind a bit.

"You're doing a good job," Eve said.

"Thanks."

"You afraid?"

"Terrified."

"Good. Just making sure."

"You know, your analogy—angels and demons. At this point, my world view has been shaken so much I'm about willing to believe anything."

"Get to the point," Eve said with a smile.

"The point is, if you were right and these creatures were demons, or at least the evil force that inspired humans to create the concept of demons, that would make their leader the Devil."

Eve stopped and thought about the comment. She closed her eyes, raised her eyebrows and shook her head. "Ugh, then let's hope we don't meet up with him."

"You don't understand," Eddy said. "We've already met the Devil."

Eve looked at Eddy, her brown eyes stunned and wide, so huge they were almost comical. She enunciated every syllable. "Marutas."

17

FORWARD

Miles of endless ice and snow passed without event. Kevin and Eve had fallen asleep in the rear of the Sno-Cat, while Brian drove and Eddy rode shotgun. All remained silent as they plowed north, toward the unknown, toward the Aeros citadel.

Eddy was lost in thought, debating their current action. He knew they were in real danger, perhaps more danger then ever before; but if what the holographic man, Artuke, said was true, then all of humanity was in peril. The idea that aliens, beings from another planet, maybe even another galaxy, had arrived on Earth thousands of years ago with the singular task of corrupting mankind, was preposterous. A day ago he would have rolled on the Arctic ice, laughing, if someone had tried to convince him that E.T. had landed, peacefully or otherwise.

Eddy glanced to his left. Brian was adjusting the rearview . . . again. His pondering of the existence of alien life faded, replaced by a jealous suspicion, though he did not know why. There was nothing in front of them, nothing behind—just a smooth white carpet from horizon to horizon. There were no roads, and the only other moving vehicles were driving twenty feet to their left—the snowmobiles. Eddy peered at the mirror without moving his head and imagined the angle from Brian's eyes and how his vision would reflect off the mirror. He followed the imaginary line back, moving his head casually, as though he were bored. His eyes came to rest on Eve's breasts, which were accentuated by the tight, black sweater she wore. Earlier, she had removed her coat; the Cat often grew quite warm from the excellent heating system and four warm bodies. Brian took her exposure as permission to grope her mentally.

It occurred to Eddy that he was overreacting, like a teenage boyfriend wanting to punch out any guy who glanced Eve's way. But then he decided he wasn't overreacting. Eve was his friend, one of his best friends, and he had the duty to protect her from the thoughts he knew must be swarming through Brian's mind. Of course, Eddy knew he had similar thoughts about Eve from time to time, but they had an understanding between them, didn't they? The attraction between them had always been palpable, but they were both mature adults and work had to be done. It came first. Work always came first. But there was no reason he couldn't defend Eve against the lustful thoughts of a man she'd want nothing to do with.

Of course she'd want nothing to do with him. Even as he thought it, Eddy doubted. *Maybe they have a secret romance. Maybe Brian has reason to look at her that way? Maybe Eve is tired of waiting?*

Eddy cursed himself for being an idiot and decided not to believe the thoughts rolling through his mind—the lies. Eve was special to Eddy and he was her protector, whether she knew it or liked it didn't matter. His mind was made up.

Brian's hand reached for the mirror, gripped it and adjusted it, moving it down.

Lips pursed and eyebrows low, Eddy gripped the mirror and turned it up. "Eyes on the road, Brian" he said in a deep voice that said much more.

"What road? Brian said. "There's nothing out there but snow and ice."

Eddy knew he was right and couldn't argue without giving his intentions away. His intentions were transparent.

Brian smiled. "Besides, I'm just enjoying the view." Brian adjusted the mirror again, making no effort to hide where he was pointing it and what he was looking at. He took in Eve's form, closed his eyes, and shook his head with a big grin.

Eddy was sure that if he could read minds, he might beat Norwood to a pulp for what he was thinking.

Brian opened his eyes. "You know, Eddy. With your track record, what is it now . . . thirty-five deaths in two expeditions? I think in the future, you'll be taking orders from me. Not to mention that I already pay your bills. You might want to be nicer to me."

A tight grin on Eddy's face showed his clenched teeth. His unblinking eyes made Brian nervous.

Eddy turned to Brian. "Another word from you and I'll happily make it thirty-six."

Pfft. Brian chuckled. He was about to say something, but Eddy cut him off. "You don't think anyone here would miss you, do you? I may have a bad track record. I may be responsible for the deaths of *three* people. But you forget that every one of the people left alive would give their life for me and I for them. Do you think they'd do the same for you? Do you really think they would argue about leaving you behind?"

Brian looked nervous, but his defensive nature pushed him forward. "What about getting paid? Hm? If I don't survive, who's going to write your checks?"

Eddy stifled a laugh. "Some things supersede money, Brian. Someday you might learn that."

Now Brian laughed. "Nothing is more important than money."

Eddy leaned back in his seat. "Has it occurred to you yet, that the way you think, the darker desires of your heart might be caused by the creatures we now seek to defeat? If this all turns out to be real, what will become of you when the Ferox are gone? People like you will be exposed for who you really are—followers of the Ferox."

Pfft. Brian laughed again. "You sound like some religious fanatic now. How you ever become a respected scientist is beyond me."

"A lot is beyond you."

Brian looked in the rearview, taking in Eve's form. "You think she's beyond me?"

"Point that mirror at yourself and take a good long look. Try and find something worth loving."

"You don't think she could love me for my money?"

Eddy shook his head with a smile. "Now you're just trying to make me angry."

"How do you know she hasn't already? I think you'd be surprised what she would do for the right amount of currency. Everyone is greedy, Eddy. Even your little angel." Brian looked in the rearview again.

"You know what?" Eddy said. "You're right."

Brian cocked his head to the right, surprised.

"There is no road," Eddy said. "The rearview is useless." Eddy snatched the rearview and yanked down, snapping it away from the windshield. He rolled down his window and tossed the rearview out into the snow.

The blast of cold air from the open window roused Kevin and Eve from their naps. "What's going on?" Eve asked, half asleep.

Eddy glared at Brian, who glanced at Eddy in fear. "Not a word," Eddy said with a strong whisper.

"Who opened the window?" Kevin asked as he pulled his jacket over his chest. "It's freezing in here."

"The heat was on the fritz," Eddy said. "But I fixed it. Go back to sleep. Everything's fine."

Too dazed to argue or think clearly, both Eve and Kevin nodded back off to their dreams.

Eddy glared at Brian one last time before turning away to look at the side view mirror, which gave him a perfect view of Eve's sleeping face.

☼　　☼　　☼　　☼　　☼

AFTER ANOTHER half hour of silent driving, the radio crackled inside the Sno-Cat. "Hey guys," Paul's voice said over the radio. "Can we make a stop soon? I gotta take a wicked piss."

Eddy picked up the CB and held the button down, "Copy that, Paul. We could all use a good stretch. How about we—" Eddy looked out the windshield, eyes locked on something in the distance. "What is that?"

"What is what?" Paul's voice questioned.

"I don't see anything," Brian said, looking out the windshield.

"Over there," Eddy said, pointing. "Looks like a bunch of poles sticking out of the snow." Eddy pushed the CB button again. "Two o'clock, guys. Head for that structure. We'll take a break when we get there."

"Copy that," Paul said.

"I'm on it," Steve added as he rocketed forward on his snowmobile, Nicole clinging to his waist. "Whooo!"

As they grew nearer to the structure, Eddy was impressed by how large it was. And there were others, several others. From one hundred yards out, Eddy felt a chill run up his back, climbing over his skin like a horde of army ants. It was like nothing he had ever seen before, morbid and scientifically wonderful at the same time.

Brian stopped the Sno-Cat near one of the largest skeletons and they climbed out, one at a time, mouths agape. Before them was a graveyard of gargantuan proportions. Tall ice heaves served as headstones for the skeletal remains of what looked like giants. Rib cages fifteen feet tall shot into the air, built like jail cells. Giant skulls lay still, mouths open in perpetual screams and vertebrae, they were scattered everywhere, like short stools, big enough for a man to sit on comfortably.

Steve summed up what most of them were thinking. "What the hell is all this?"

"Whale carcasses," Eve said as she examined some gouges on the exterior of a rib, which was as thick as her legs. "Several different species, but most are blue whales. Big ones."

"But how did they get here?" Steve asked.

"Probably hunters," Eve said. "They must have stripped off the meat and left the bones on the ice. Perhaps even on a yearly basis. During the summer, this area is probably very close to the water."

"That would account for so many skeletons," Eddy said.

"I don't like it," Kevin added.

"Could have been the Inuit," Paul said.

"Inuit?" Steve asked. "As in *our* Inuit? The evil dudes chasing us?"

Paul gripped a tall rib and leaned back, letting the bone hold his weight. It was strong as steel. "No, the real Inuit. Hunting blue whales was made illegal a long time ago."

"The International Whaling Commission declared them to be a protected species in 1966 because their population had dramatically decreased over several years of over-hunting," Brian said with an arrogant smile.

"Right," Paul said. "But the Inuit have continued hunting whales."

"So these Inuit guys break the law?"

"Sort of," Paul said. "But the law doesn't apply to them. They hunt the whales because there isn't a whole lot else to eat. They get food, oil, and weapons from the whales. They kill only what they need and make very little impact on whale populations. And they do it by hand."

"But why would they leave so many whale carcasses behind?" Eve asked.

"I don't know," Paul said. "Maybe there's something defective about these."

"Maybe they were left as a warning?" Kevin said.

"I noticed that several of these skeletons have scratches in them, and puncture holes, like they've been bitten by something huge," Nicole said.

"Killer whale?" Eddy asked.

Eve inspected a tooth mark. "Could be. Packs of killer whales have been known to attack and kill blue whales. It's not unheard of, but the bite radius and puncture depth would suggest something smaller."

"Polar bear," Paul said. "They probably feed on these remains when they're left. Now that I think about it, I've heard that if a polar bear defeats the men hunting it, the bear is seen as being godly—Nanuk, the great lonely hunter."

Brian raised an eyebrow to a lofty position on his forehead. "You're saying that these Inuit fellows killed all these whales and left them here for a godly polar bear to eat?"

"Just that it's a possibility," Paul said.

"If you're right," Eve said. "It's been a while since the Inuit believed in bear gods. If any of these skeletons were left here in the last few days, the snow would be covered in blood. There hasn't been a fresh snow in a month. If there ever was a bear here it's probably long gone now, or it starved to death, waiting for its next meal."

"This is all interesting," Paul said as he walked toward a mound of ice heaves, "but nature is calling." He disappeared behind the wall of ice.

"Yeah, enough about the stupid bears," Steve said, growing bored. "Let's get a move on."

Eve laughed. "You won't think they're stupid if you see one."

Steve crossed his arms. "I don't need a lecture."

"Polar bears are the largest land predators on the planet," Eve said.

Steve rolled his eyes. "Here comes the lecture."

Eve continued. "They're stronger than lions, as fast as a jaguar, and larger than the Siberian tiger. They can weigh up to fifteen hundred pounds."

"That's like all of us combined," Steve said, starting to look impressed.

"What's most impressive is that studies have shown that they are nearly as smart, if not as smart as apes; meaning they use tools and have a significant memory."

"Meaning?"

"Meaning, don't slap one in the face only to go back a year later and expect to shake hands. It'll remember you."

"How the heck do you know so much about polar bears, anyway?" Steve said.

"Evolution, my dear. Studying animals that disappear also means studying animals that have become something new. Some species don't die out completely, some become specialized. They change."

"Like fish growing legs."

"Yes, or like brown bears growing in size, developing webbed feet, and adapting white fur during the last ice age."

"Like people evolving from Neanderthals."

"Exactly."

"Only our evolution has been altered by an outside force," Eddy said. "Who's to say what we would have become without the Ferox?"

"Maybe we'd still be running around in loin cloths."

Eddy felt a knot twisting in his stomach. Artuke had told them that every despicable act on Earth had been performed by the Ferox or under the direct influence of the Ferox. But that would include technological advances. If the Ferox made men evil, then they also made mankind technologically advanced. It was true, that the more advanced humans became, the greater evils they dealt each other. The atom bomb. Chemical and biological warfare. Even planes had been flown into buildings. But if ridding the world of the Ferox slowed development, hindered wars, and weakened nations, would humanity be so glad to see them go? At this stage of development, would humanity be better off without the Ferox?

Eddy remembered Artuke's promise that the Aeros would return to Earth, that they would weed out the Ferox influence. He felt comforted knowing a greater intelligence would aid in their recovery from evil influence. But what would the human race become? What was the future of their planet? Eddy's thoughts were interrupted by Steve.

"Where's Paul? He's been gone longer than it takes to drain the lizard."

Eddy scanned the area, his view blocked by massive skeletons and tall towers of ice. He vaguely remembered which way Paul had gone, but couldn't place it exactly. One thing Eddy did know was that Steve was right. Paul had been gone too long, and in the Arctic, that was never a good thing. It usually meant you were dead.

18

THE BEAR

The maze of ice heaves closed in around Paul. He looked in every direction, scouring for a view of the crew or Sno-Cat. He relaxed when he didn't see them. Feeling safe and secluded, Paul began to undo his layers of pants and long johns. After many years of living with a large Italian family who never knocked on the bathroom door, Paul had become a very private bathroom user. His other family members saw no problem taking showers, brushing teeth, and urinating simultaneously while talking about the Yankees.

After getting a paper route and earning some money, Paul bought and installed a new doorknob on the bathroom door—one with a lock. It was the first thing he had used a screwdriver on and since that day, he'd been hooked on fixing things. No one had ever walked in on him again. Installing the door lock started Paul on the road that led him to become proficient at fixing everything from game systems to airplanes. And in all the years since his childhood, his penchant for privacy had not waned.

Paul took advantage of the walls provided by the ice heaves and massive skeletons to work his way back into a private area. Even if the crew came looking it would take them ten minutes to find him—easily enough time to take a leak. Paul lowered his shoulders, rolled his head from side to side and began to relieve himself. He laughed as he began to write his name in the snow, steam rising with each letter, only there was something wrong with the "l." The snow wasn't melting. Paul squinted at the white snow, wondering how it was resisting the heat of his urine.

The snow moved.

Paul gasped, stepped back, and put his pants together too quickly, soaking the front. The snow continued to move, spinning, growing taller. A single black object, the size of a clenched fist, caught Paul's attention. It was hard to see, as snow fell from the rising object. He saw two round black objects floating above the first and they disappeared momentarily, returning to a full circle a moment later—they blinked. Paul realized then that he was staring into the eyes of a beast.

The polar bear stood over nine feet tall, but its frame was thin, almost emaciated. It hadn't eaten in some time had no compunction about eating human flesh. It slammed down onto its front paws and snorted as it began to charge.

Before thought could enter Paul's mind, his body reacted on instinct. He turned and ran, fleeing from the bear, but in his confusion he ran left instead of right, deeper into the maze of ice and bone.

☼   ☼   ☼   ☼   ☼

EDDY STOOD at the ribcage of a blue whale and peered through, looking for any movement. He had ordered everyone to stay still. They couldn't split up, not here. He called for Paul several times, but knew his voice wouldn't carry far through the walls of frost and skulls. He put his hands in his pockets and felt something hard. He grasped the object and felt a flash of hope. Eddy held the GPS communicator up to his lips. Eddy had one. Steve had another, and Paul had the last. "Paul, come in, can you hear me?"

Static.

Then a voice. "Paul, man, speak to us, buddy? Where the hell are you?" It was Steve.

Eddy thought Steve was doing an admirable job of covering his concerns, but he knew Steve was as worried as the rest of them.

Still static.

"I—don't . . . where—you?" It was Paul, through breaks of static. He sounded winded, like he was running, like he was . . .

Eddy looked back to the Cat and locked eyes with Steve, who even from thirty feet looked terrified. Steve's voice came over the communicator. "Say again, Paul. Where are you? Say again!"

Static, almost thirty seconds of it. The waiting was excruciating. Then it was shattered. "Help me! Oh God, help me!" Paul's voice was torn with sheer terror, but Eddy noticed something: the voice hadn't come from the GPS communicator, it had shouted over the static, not through it.

Eddy searched in every direction with his eyes and his ears. His ears found him first, a shuffling of snow and ice, a desperate scramble. *What the hell is happening?* Eddy turned toward the sound and saw the top half of Paul, crawling out from behind an ice heave twenty feet away. He had only been twenty feet away! "Paul!" Eddy shouted as he made a mad dash. He could hear the rest of the crew sprinting up behind him.

"Paul! Paul, man! This isn't funny!" Steve was shouting. "Paul!"

Paul's face contorted with pain for an instant and his body fell slack. Eddy slowed; something was not right. An instant later, Paul's body was pulled out of view. Something had just pulled a full grown man across the ice as effortlessly as a child yanking the sheets off a bed. Eddy stopped running and held out his hands for the rest to stop.

Everyone, save Steve, slowed to a stop. Eddy had to tackle him to the ice.

"Let me go, man!" Steve screamed as he struggled to get free. "Paul's in trouble!"

"Paul's gone!" Eddy shouted, surprised that he had said it. But he knew there were only two things that could have done that to Paul. "Think about it! What could have done that?"

Steve looked into Eddy's eyes, afraid to answer.

"That was either one of the Ferox," Eddy said.

"Or a bear," Steve finished.

"Oh God," Eve said. "The bear is still here."

The sound of cracking bones and tearing flesh froze everyone colder than the ten degree air. All eyes locked on the edge of the ice wall where their friend, where Paul, had been dragged and was now being torn to pieces. Tears streamed down Steve's face and he began to whimper, but even his heaving chest stopped moving as a large, blood-covered muzzle appeared from behind the ice.

The bear emerged, starving, but still massive. At nine hundred pounds it was half its former weight, a gargantuan creature, raised on an endless supply of whale meat. But now this king of the north was starving and one human would not satiate his appetite. The bear roared and charged.

Eddy lept to his feet and pulled Steve up with him. "Back to the Cat!" Eddy commanded. "Everyone!"

The group ran for the Cat, pounding the snow as fast as they could, but Eddy remained standing. He knew the bear could outrun them, and at least one of them, if not two, would never make it to the Cat. This bear needed to be distracted.

"Eddy! What are you doing?" Eve screamed, her voice tormented.

"Get to the Cat!" Eddy shouted, furious at her for stopping. "Now, damn it!"

Eve continued forward and Eddy ran for the ice maze. His legs burned from the cold and exposure, but Eddy knew his only chance of escape lay in the ninety degree turns of the maze; not that it had helped Paul any. Eddy glanced over his shoulder but didn't feel the presence of the hulking bear. He stopped and turned around.

The bear had pursued the others! This bear was unlike other predators. It was indeed smart. Eddy surmised that the bear realized how much food it would need, so instead of taking the easy prey, the lone prey, it was going for the big kill, the herd. It wasn't trying to kill a single meal. It was trying to survive the winter—and that meant more meat than Eddy and Paul combined.

Eddy grasped a large chunk of ice as the bear came within ten feet of Eve.

Why did you stop?

He took aim.

Five feet.

Please, God, let this work!

Eddy's arm surged forward and released the chunk of ice. It spun through the air and shattered on impact with the bear's skull. The beast grunted and slid to a stop, turning toward Eddy. However, the blunt impact was only enough to cause a momentary distraction. Eddy smiled. It was enough. The doors to the Sno-Cat slammed shut as Eve dove inside, pulling the bear's attention back to the group. The bear inspected the Cat and realized its prey had escaped.

Swirling emotions unlike any he had felt before consumed Eddy as the bear turned to face him. Forty feet separated Eddy from the bear and twenty feet from the wall. He knew the bear could run twice as fast as he, and maybe even faster in the snow. Eddy had half the distance to run, but even if the bear only doubled Eddy's speed, it would catch him at the entrance to the maze. Eddy decided that a head start was a wise choice. He broke into a flat out run, straight for a portion of ice and bone that was open and wrapped around to the right. He hoped that it didn't wrap around to a dead end, or it would become one, literally—Eddy's dead end.

The grunting breath of the running bear was loud behind Eddy and it pushed his faster. From the moment Eddy started running, he knew the bear would catch him in an all-out race. He began unzipping his jacket. As he took it off, ten feet from the maze entrance, the cold hit his chest and took what little breath he had away. Eddy looked back and saw a moving hulk of white. The bear was upon him.

The jacket flew over Eddy's head and the polar bear pounced on it a second later, shredding it with its claws. The beast must have realized the jacket held no value, because it pounded forward. Eddy had gained a second from the ploy.

But it was enough. He reached the vertical bars of whale ribs and grasped hold to the nearest one, taking the ninety degree turn at full speed. The bear, however, was not so agile. Its formidable mass, while convenient for killing, was a hindrance when it came to maneuvering . . . and stopping. The bear dug into the snow with its claws, but the effort was useless. He slid forward and crashed into a wall of ice. The impact shook the bear but it regained its composure and scrambled into the maze, growling.

The bear came to a crossroads created by a spine the size of a telephone pole, a twelve foot skull and towering spires of ice. It looked in either direction and sniffed the air with its crimson-stained snout. The bear looked left, narrowed its eyes and headed deeper into the maze, moving with confidence.

☼   ☼   ☼   ☼   ☼

THE SOUND of boots crushing snow was barely audible as Eddy's heart surged blood past his ear. His chest rose and fell like the waves of an incoming tide, sucking in oxygen and freezing air. He felt his body growing cold, his muscles growing weary. But the knowledge he possessed pushed him forward. If he stopped moving, stopped fighting, he would become a meal for a polar bear the size of Volkswagen Bug.

Exhausted, Eddy stopped and gripped a five inch thick bone projecting from the ice. He held his weight on the bone and attempted to slow his breathing, taking deeper, longer breaths in an attempt to clear the swirls of color that danced before his eyes. He scanned the area and found three choices. One, to the right, looked dangerous, filled with sharp spines of shattered bone, not to mention it headed away from the Sno-Cat—of course, that was his guess. Another, straight ahead, looked like smooth sailing; a straight path for fifty feet . . . a straight path would do no good. It would allow the bear to see him and give it room to pick up speed. That wouldn't work, either.

Looking to the left, Eddy eyed the third path, a tangled web of ribs and vertebrate, like a ghastly obstacle course. It looked like the most physically challenging of the three choices, but it went in the right direction—still a guess—and it would slow the bear down. Eddy lurched to the left and entered the congested path, squeezing between a pair of ribs. Not a second too soon.

A sound like knives scraping across a washboard sent Eddy falling back onto the ice. The bear had just swiped at him! He didn't even hear it coming. It weighed as much as five men and could travel as silently as an ant on a sand dune. The bear had taken hold of the ribs and shook the cage, frustrated that its prey was just out of reach. Eddy pushed away, gasping for air.

He realized that exhaustion was making him careless, that he had taken too long to decide on a path. It had almost cost him his life. It was a mistake he could not afford to make again. Eddy dug his gloved hands into the snow and pulled up two handfuls, rubbing it onto his already cold face. The freezing cold stung his lips and shot pain into his eyeballs, but his mind cleared and his thoughts became sharp again.

Eddy slid over a spine and climbed through two massive eye sockets. He looked back. The bear paced, watching him. Eddy moved further down into the cluttered path, pulling himself along next to a spine, half frozen in the ice. He glanced back again, just in time to see the bear tear off down the straightaway that he had decided against. Eddy remembered Eve's words about the bear. It was smart. It lived here. What did it know that he didn't?

A wall of ice, frozen around a ribcage, floated a foot and a half off the icy ground like a miniature arch. Eddy tried to climb it, but its surface was slick and didn't offer any stable handholds. He lay on his stomach and began sliding underneath the six foot, thousand pound block of ice, which hung precariously in the air. Eddy's heart pounded as he slid through the small space. He felt the cold pressing on him from above and below. If the bear were to jump on top of the block, he would be crushed beneath.

Breathing harder, Eddy began to struggle through the enclosure; his hands and feet scrambling like a panicked salamander. Then he was free. His head slid out first, then reaching out with his arms, he dug in to the snow and pulled himself from under the block, onto an open path with compact snow. Eddy caught his breath and looked in either direction. The path was clear and stretched straight to the left and the right. Eddy looked down at the snow beneath his face and his vision focused on what he realized was a paw print. He took in the area around him. It was covered in paw prints. He realized that this path was so clean cut because the bear walked it often. If this bear was as smart at Eve suggested . . .

Oh, hell!

Eddy jumped to his feet and began running to the left, just as the bear rounded the corner to his right. He looked forward and saw twenty feet of straight away, which ended at a jagged chunk of ice. A dead end.

Glancing back, Eddy saw that the bear was not running at full steam. It knew he was cornered. It knew he was defenseless. It was taking its time. Eddy reached the frozen wall and looked up: eight feet of ice. Eddy looked at the bear. It was close enough now that he could see the stands of drool dripping from its jowls. Eddy reached up onto the wall, found a handhold and pulled up. It held.

To hell with you, Eddy thought, you may know these paths, but you've never chased prey with opposable thumbs! Eddy jumped up and pulled. He rose higher and dug his foot into the ice, pushing hard. He heard the bear grunt as it began running again. Eddy bent his knees, held on tight with his left hand, then leapt up with the force of all three appendages and grabbed on to the top of the ice. He pulled with his right arm, feeling the sinews of his muscles snapping from the strain, but in seconds, he was sliding onto the top of the ice wall. Safe. For now.

Eddy breathed rapidly, in and out, lying on the eight foot wall. He turned his head to see the bear, which he thought would be pacing angrily below, but instead he came face-to-face with the Arctic giant. He cursed himself for forgetting how tall the bear was on its hind legs. It snapped at his face, just missing. It roared at Eddy and he could smell and feel its warm bloody breath waft across his face. The bear swiped at Eddy and caught his chest, tearing open the outer layers of his clothes, creating a wound, which, if his clothing had been any thinner, would have sliced open his stomach like a ripe watermelon.

Eddy rolled away from the bear without thinking and fell off the other side of the wall, descending eight feet to the snow below. Eddy hit the frozen ground hard, landing on his back. The impact knocked the breath from his chest and made him feel as though his lungs had been removed from his body. He sucked air, but felt as though he got nothing got in. He sucked again and again, but his lungs were not satisfied.

I can't die like this! Air! I need air!

Eddy tried to get to his feet, but the best he could manage was a toddler-like crawl. He turned and gasped again, but this time, not for air. He lurched backward and slammed against the ice wall, knocking any air that had reached his lungs back out. But he forgot all about his depleted lungs as he stared straight forward with a blank expression.

Lying on the ice, twisted and deformed, was a body half dressed in snow gear, half eviscerated. Paul's eyes were glassy, almost frozen, staring up at the sky; his mouth open, trapped in mid-scream. The snow around his body was frozen red, like a Satanic Sno-cone, a torture for the damned. Eddy leaned forward and saw Paul's crucifix hanging from his neck. He knew removing the body would be impossible, but he felt he needed to bring something back to bury. Eddy moved forward, still seeing stars and gasping for air. His fingers protested as he gripped Paul's cross in his hand and pulled. He fell back and began crawling for what he believed was the way out. It took him thirty seconds to crawl twenty feet. Air came quickly now, but his muscles had been pushed too far. He felt his body crushing his bones. A stabbing pain shot through his right calf.

He flinched and shouted, thinking the bear had caught him. But nothing was there. It was just a muscle spasm. Eddy inched forward, sliding on his stomach, determined to find freedom.

His arms gave up and for a moment he lay motionless.

Get up, damnit!

He was frozen.

Move your arm!

Eddy's finger twitched.

A pressure around Eddy's shoulder's made him fearful, but he didn't flinch or scream, he was too tired, too depleted. But the movement was smooth, painless. He opened his eyes for a moment and glanced to the left. Steve. He glanced to the right. Kevin. Looking forward, through closing eyes, Eddy saw Eve standing in front of the Sno-Cat's open door, waving them on, her face stretched with fear.

As Eddy's eyes closed and his world descended into darkness he heard Eve's voice. "Eddy, my God. He's bleeding."

Then other voices.

"Look out!"

"Here it comes!"

"Close the door!"

Then a loud *whump* and a *roar*.

Then nothing.

19

BREAKING

Pain stabbed at Eddy's eyes as glowing white light filled his vision. Eddy squinted against the light while his hand hovered in front of his eyes. He sat up and felt a dull ache inside his head, pulsing with each beat of his heart. His body was sore all over, like waking up the day after running a marathon. The discomfort he felt reminded him he was still alive, and for that he was glad. He looked down and saw that he was lying down on the back seat of the Sno-Cat. The front seat was empty. He was alone.

Then it all came back to him. The bear. Paul. Every gory detail of what he had seen . . . the smell of Paul's dead body. The pain in Eddy's head grew worse with every thread of memory, weaving through his skull, pulled by a dull needle. His thoughts raced as he held his head in his hands, trying to squeeze out the pain. Had the bear gotten to the others? Maybe it was out there right now, eating one of them, eating Eve.

Eddy pushed the pain aside in an instant and reached under the front seat. His hands found something hard and cold. He pulled out a large wrench and burst out of the door with a grunt, ready to beat the bear to death if need be.

Steve fell backward and screamed as Eddy flung himself from the Sno-Cat. "Dude! What the hell!"

Nicole gasped and rolled away, fearing that Eddy might fall on her, or worse, club her with that wrench in blind rage. She jumped up and stood behind Steve.

Eddy took every breath like it might be his last. His eyes darted in every direction, looking for trouble, looking for the bear. But all he saw was the Sno-Cat, the snowmobile, and his crew, all but Paul. Eddy lowered the wrench in his right hand and held his head with his left. "Sorry, I thought . . ."

Eddy dropped the wrench as bright colored dots swirled in his vision. He stumbled, but was caught by Kevin. "Whoa, there . . . Here, sit down." Eve took Eddy by his other arm and helped support his weight.

Kevin eased Eddy onto the Sno-Cat's tread. "What happened?" Eddy asked. "Where's the bear?"

"We left that son-of-a-bitch behind," Steve said. His eyes were red and bloodshot. Eddy thought Steve looked as though he hadn't slept in days. Paul.

"Steve. I'm sorry. Paul was—"

"I know, man," Steve said. "He was a friend to all of us. Don't give me any special treatment. Okay? Paul wouldn't want us pissing and moaning over him, anyway."

Eddy could see that Steve had mourned Paul's death all he could in one day.

Steve crossed his arms. "Just promise me that if we survive the next few days, you and I will come back out here and hunt that bear down. To the ends of the Earth if we have to."

Eddy nodded and said, "To the ends of the Earth."

Kevin put his hand on Steve's shoulder. "To the ends of the Earth. We'll find that bear."

Steve cracked a smile. "Thanks, Buck."

"Don't forget me," Nicole said. "I'm in, too . . . ends of the Earth, and all that."

Steve smiled at Nicole and she put her arm around him, rubbing his shoulder.

Eddy stretched from side to side, feeling his muscles easing out, relaxing. "How long was I unconscious?"

"Three hours. We only stopped a few minutes ago to stretch our legs and relieve ourselves," Brian said as he looked down from the top of the Sno-Cat. "A combination of exhaustion and mental trauma put you into a fairly deep sleep. You had us thinking you might be in a coma for a short time."

"How did you know I wasn't?"

"You were snoring," Eve said with a smile. "And you were talking in your sleep."

Eddy looked mildly surprised. "I was talking in my sleep? What did I say?"

Kevin smiled and looked away, Eve pursed her lips, and Brian went back to gazing at the frozen expanse through a pair of binoculars. Eddy could see that whatever he had said was embarrassing. He decided he didn't want to know.

"Sorry to interrupt your jovial interlude," Brian said from behind the binoculars, "but we have trouble, incoming at three o'clock."

Everyone jumped to their feet at once and rushed around to the other side of the Cat, staring out in the direction Brian pointed. Straight ahead was a wash of white that undulated lightly. To the east was more of the same: flat, white nothing. To the west was a choppy field of ice spires, jutting toward the empty expanse of blue sky.

"There's nothing out there," Nicole said.

"I don't see anything," Eddy said, glancing up at Brian.

Brian thrust his hand down. "Step on the snowmobile and climb up," he said.

Eddy took Brian's hand after climbing onto the snowmobile and was hoisted onto the metal roof of the Cat. After placing the binoculars to his eyes, Eddy focused and scanned the horizon. "Nothing's there."

"They're still a good ten miles out. Check the horizon."

Eddy rotated from right to left, taking in every ounce of ice and sky. Then he saw them, four specks of black against a white background. "Found them."

"What is it?" Eve asked.

"Our friends from the dig site," Eddy said.

Steve's face twisted with confusion. "The Inuit?"

Eddy nodded.

"But they were on foot," Steve said. "There's no way they caught up with us."

"Maybe they have transportation hidden somewhere?" Eve said.

"I doubt it," Eddy added. "There's no place to hide anything out here, and from the looks of it, they're still on foot."

"Let me look again," Brian said as he raised the binoculars to his eyes. "We must be missing something."

"You are missing something," Kevin said.

All eyes turned to Kevin.

"You're operating under the assumption that the men chasing us are bound by human laws. We need sleep, food, shelter, and transportation to survive the cold. These men are not human. They're Ferox. What applies to us doesn't apply to them."

Eddy looked into Kevin's serious eyes. "He's right."

"We need to do something," Nicole said with a nervous twang in her voice.

"Yeah, man," Steve said. "These guys are going to catch us in no time. We gotta get out of here, like, now."

"We need a strategy," Kevin said. "If they can out power us, maybe we can outwit them."

"What do you suggest?" Eddy asked with raised eyebrows.

"Easy," Kevin said with a smile. "Oldest trick in the book."

☼ ☼ ☼ ☼ ☼

"NO WAY," Eddy said with a stern look in Kevin's direction. "I'm not going to let you go out there alone."

"But it will work, Eddy. It always works."

"Kev, you learned that trick playing a game."

"I used that trick playing a game. I learned that trick from history. The military does it all the time. It's called a diversionary tactic. They'll be so focused on all of you in the Cat that they'll forget all about me." Kevin took in a deep breath and let it out slowly. "How far are we from the co-ordinates Artuke gave us?"

Brian looked at the screen of the portable GPS. "Three miles due north. We're almost there."

"You see. They don't know where we're going. I'll head out on foot, following the coordinates. You travel, heading for the same coordinates, but in a wide arc. They'll follow you, not me. I'm alone. Defenseless. And they'll assume the cold will get me."

"And what if it does?" Eddy asked as he paced in the snow.

"It won't. It's only a few miles, and we have three hours of light left. I can do it. They'll never think that the one guy alone has the key. It doesn't make sense."

Eddy crossed his arms. "No way."

Steve looked down from his post on top of the Sno-Cat, where he stood with Nicole, watching the horizon. Nicole looked out through the binoculars as Steve spoke. "Guys, listen, these jerks are moving like bats out of hell. They just gained a mile on us in two minutes. They'll be here in a couple of minutes. If we don't start moving, and I mean at like top speed, they'll catch us before we get there."

Eddy clenched his fists. "All right. This is what we're doing, and I don't want to hear a word of argument from anyone . . ."

Eddy scrolled across everyone's eyes, making sure they were listening.

"I'm going out alone, just like Buck said."

"Eddy, no," Eve said, but before she could get out another word, Eddy continued in a louder voice.

"I'm in better shape than anyone here. I can jog the three miles flat out without stopping. If they do follow me, I'll stand the best chance at outrunning them."

Steve hopped down from the Cat. "I see no one did the math. They just ran, on foot, a mile in two minutes. Eddy, these guys are moving at thirty miles an hour. That's like Olympic sprinters, only they're not slowing down after one hundred meters. You can't outrun them."

"But I can put the most distance between me and them. No more arguing. Get in the Cat and start moving. Now."

Every one stood frozen, like human popsicles buried in the snow.

"Now!" Eddy's voice was filled with anger.

Steve and Nicole headed for the snowmobile and got ready to head out. Brian climbed into the Sno-Cat and started the engine. At least some of them were listening. Eve strode up to Eddy, eyes locked on his.

"If I don't see you again? If this is how you say goodbye to me, I'll hate you for it." Eve turned around and headed back to the Cat.

Kevin stood next to Eddy. "She loves you, you know."

Eddy turned to Kevin. "I know."

"Better not die, huh?"

"I'll try not to."

Eddy stood closer to Kevin. "Kevin, listen. These aliens. These Ferox. They've been here on Earth, studying us, molding us. Could it be true that the very tactic we're attempting here could have been conceived of by these guys?"

Kevin looked surprised. "I hadn't thought of that."

"You're an experienced game player, right? You use strategy like that all the time." Eddy turned his whole body toward Kevin as if to emphasize his next words. "When you see the lone man coming . . . who do you take out?"

Kevin's eyes widened. "The lone man. Every time."

"Why?"

"Experience tells me that he's the real threat."

"I don't think we can beat these guys on an experience level."

"Then why are you going?"

"Because I'm counting on them chasing me."

"That's crazy. Why?"

"The oldest trick in the book is about to be re-written."

Kevin's forehead became crisscrossed with wrinkles. Then he gasped and his anxiety disappeared. "That might just work," he said with a smile. "But only once."

"Once is all I'll need."

☼   ☼   ☼   ☼   ☼

THE FOUR men reached a crossroads of sorts. To the north was a single set of footprints. They could see by the depth of the depressions that whoever had gone in that direction, on foot, was running. With good reason, Marutas thought, smiling. This prey was turning out to be just what he needed to satiate his innate desire to hunt. But this was no simulated hunt. They hadn't thrown people into a jungle and hunted them down like dogs to a fox. No, this was much better. This was real. The danger was real. And it spun through his mind like an intoxicating drug.

Marutas's grin widened. The bedraggled group of scientists had not just beaten Vayu, they had killed him with a brutality that Marutas respected. Vayu was a strong warrior and had fought in hundreds of wars over the past ten thousand years. Not only had he fought, but he had instigated them as well. Vayu had been one of the elite, one of the last five chosen to stay on Earth and finish the job.

But Vayu had ultimately failed his station. A pity. These humans, who now had the key and thought to undo everything they had worked so hard to achieve, had killed him. They had dared to kill a Ferox. Vayu's spilled blood would not go un-avenged. Marutas would eat their hearts before the day was through. But he would not underestimate his prey. He would learn from Vayu's mistake. He looked at the boot-crushed snow and turned his gaze northwest, taking in the two sets of tracks. One wide, the other narrow—the Sno-Cat and snowmobile no doubt. The snow beneath the tracks was torn up and flung. They were moving fast, dangerously so.

Interesting.

On one hand there was the obvious choice. Safety in numbers. Rapid transportation. Supplies. The crew left in the Sno-Cat would make better time and survive the night, if it came in time. They were the obvious choice to carry something as important as the key. But then they had left him with a second choice. The footprints.

Their leader would never let one of his crew strike off alone. So he had done it himself. But he was a resourceful man, and overconfident. He would never trust one of his crew to do as good a job as he could. So he would take the key, hoping that his pursuers would follow the obvious choice.

Oh, but the Ferox are much wiser than you. We are your masters.

Marutas turned towards the footprints again, ignoring the bitter cold stinging his face. The lone man had gone north with the key. He would be their prey. Let the orbs take care of the others.

Before giving the order to head out, Marutas smelled the snow where the human group had stopped. So many footprints were pushed into the snow. He could see them now, arguing over what to do; crying over their fallen comrades—that fool in the maze of ice and bones. They had found him, by following the scent of blood, nearly picked clean, just like the whales. But the bear had been nowhere in sight. He sniffed the air again, more deeply, and caught a whiff of it—fear. They were afraid, and with good reason; they would all be dead soon.

But what they didn't know. Oh, how glorious it will be to see their faces when they learn the truth, just as the last of their blood escaped their bodies. He would tell them then about the mighty Aeros. How much greater would it be to see them dying without hope, only then to realize that humanity, their blessed humanity, was going to be destroyed—one way or another.

Marutas barked the order and all four men began running north, following the single line of footprints.

20

THE SPLIT

In the cold vacuum of space, biological life ceased to exist. But this cold expanse between worlds, separating spheres of gravity, was home to another kind of life—electronic. The black sphere, which had spun in Earth's orbit for thousands and thousands of years undetected by man, blinked to life. A solitary light blinked red as the black orb floated noiselessly over the white crust of ice, hundreds of miles below.

Spinning, the orb turned the red light toward the ice covered ocean, taking it in like a cycloptic, bodiless monster. It sensed an energy signature, a presence that it had waited for since its creation and placement in the freezing void. While scientists might call this basketball-size device a simple machine, its creators would argue that it was very much alive and capable of great emotion; not the complex range sentient beings might take for granted, but a single emotion, burned into its sensors and data chips—hate, loathing, animosity—for one single object: the key, and even more, for the biological units within its proximity.

With a blast of blue flame, the sphere broke orbit and pushed into Earth's atmosphere. It couldn't feel the heat created by the friction of Earth's atmosphere on its thick outer skin. Even if it could, the pain

wouldn't compare to the rage its artificial intelligence felt for the five beings it had been ordered to destroy. It would strike the humans down,
using the environment against them as it was designed to do. And for its
glorious attack it would be rewarded with death. Like a stinging bee, it
would fulfill its single purpose in life, defense of the clan. After so many
years waiting, searching, it would be free to cease functioning.

A burst of cold air extinguished the flames as the black orb entered
the lower atmosphere. Its speed increased as it descended from far
above, dropping down on its unaware prey. The circuits buzzed with
electric excitement, the orb's hatred burning, overloading every system in
preparation for its final deadly service.

☼   ☼   ☼   ☼   ☼

A THICK haze of luminous snow spun through the air behind the
snowmobile, which Steve had gunned, full throttle. The bitter wind stung
his face through the thick scarf he had wrapped around his nose and
mouth. Nicole's arms, tight around his waist, gave him warmth, enough
to give him hope. Paul was gone. In the blink of an eye.

Steve felt his eyes grow wet and his vision blur as tears began to well
up again. Unable to wipe the freezing wetness away, Steve mentally
changed the subject. He focused on the task at hand. Eddy had taken off,
by himself—a desperate gamble to throw off the creatures pursuing
them. Steve tried to imagine what they might look like, aliens from another planet. His mind rattled through the possibilities.

He knew they had a physical presence. He'd seen enough science fiction in his lifetime and Buck was always talking about aliens, so he knew
that some believed they might just be energy, conscious energy. Steve
didn't like that idea, but unless conscious energy could become physical,
breathing, speaking humanoids, these Ferox were not them. Then there
was the realm of the microscopic. Who was to say that microorganisms
couldn't evolve into intelligent beings? Steve knew that if this were the
case, the human race would be doomed. He'd seen a television special
that showed how our best efforts over the years had wiped out several
microscopic terrors, but then how new ones rose from the primordial
stew every day, and the ones humans didn't eradicate, mutated or grew
resistant to even the toughest antibiotics. It struck Steve that in a way, the

human race was already under attack from the microscopic realm. The tiny invaders had been waging war for thousands of years. He wondered how long the current stalemate would last.

But what the team now faced was the stuff of nightmares. Physical creatures that were stronger, smarter, and capable of amazing physical feats had invaded the Earth thousands of years ago, plotting the demise of the human race. Steve's mind raced with the ramifications of such information. Since the beginning of time, people had a sense that the evil they were capable of was not how they were meant to be. Steve would never tell anyone, but he grew up going to church and even spent a good deal of time going to Sunday school. He knew all about Noah, Adam and Eve, and Jesus. But he had also been acutely aware of the presence of evil in the world. But unlike some people, evil just seemed so normal to Steve. He watched the news without feeling angry about the car bombings, fires, and murders. They were bad things that happened to other people—not part of his life. And humanity brought these things on themselves, he thought. We made the atom bomb, we created biological weapons, and bullets, and hand grenades, and landmines filled with seven hundred metal balls so that when it exploded anyone within a certain radius would be turned into hamburger. *We* did all that. The human race did that, and what right do we have to whine about it all the time?

But now he knew better. What they taught him in church was true. There was an evil in the world of men that influenced us. True, left to our own devices, we probably would have succumbed to evil . . . but maybe not. And the thought that all the wars, all the death and suffering that swarmed across the planet on a daily basis might have never been. It was the Ferox who promoted evil in the world. It was the Ferox who inspired man to hate, to kill, and to create weapons that made people afraid. The Ferox were to blame for it all. And ultimately, the bastard beasts from another planet were responsible for Paul's death.

"Slow down!" Nicole's voice broke through Steve's flurry of thoughts.

Steve eased up on the throttle and looked back. The Sno-Cat was small in the distance. Steve slowed down even more and turned to face Nicole. "Sorry about that. I was just lost in thought."

"You want me to drive?"

"Maybe."

"Cause, you know, I'm not ready to die yet. Especially on a snowmobile."

Steve could see Nicole's smiling eyes behind her goggles. "I'll be more careful."

Steve was locked on her eyes, the only part of her flesh he could see, but so beautiful, so captivating.

"Time to start being more careful!" Nicole shouted.

Steve turned around, facing forward, and swerved to the right, narrowly avoiding a chunk of ice that would have flipped them over. "Sorry," Steve said, feeling very stupid. But if he had to die looking into those eyes, so be it. He gazed ahead, checked the ice for obstructions and saw none. He slowed the snowmobile so that it was crawling along. If they hit anything now they would either climb over it or jolt to a halt. Either case was acceptable—he had to see those eyes one more time. They gave him hope.

Steve turned around, his heartbeat quickening—then he felt the frustration of something calling his attention away from Nicole's eyes, and at the same time, the uneasy twist of nerves that came with seeing an object in the sky.

Steve looked up, away from Nicole's face, not wanting to believe what he was seeing.

"What?" Nicole asked. "Did we lose the others?"

Steve stopped the snowmobile without moving his eyes away from the distant object.

"What is it?" Nicole asked as she began to turn around, following Steve's eyes into the distance.

"In the sky," Steve said.

Nicole's eyes locked on the object and she let out a small gasp. A single black object was descending behind the Sno-Cat. But it was impossible to tell if it was close and small or far away and large. Nicole slung her backpack off and placed it on the ground. She pulled her camcorder out, flipped on the power and opened the LCD viewfinder. Steve peered over her shoulder and watched as she found the black speck, zoomed in and focused. They could see a single black sphere rocketing down from above.

"Oh . . . no," Steve said.

"Didn't that guy, Artuke or whatever, tell us about these things?"

Steve dug into his pocket and removed the portable GPS communicator. He took in their position and realized that with the current route of travel, they were still two miles out from their objective. Steve cursed under his breath as he pushed the button on the side of the communicator.

"Guys, this is Steve. You better start hauling ass back there. We got company."

☼   ☼   ☼   ☼   ☼

EVE FLINCHED as Steve's voice broke the silence. No one had said a word. She was sure that each of them was thinking the same things. What was going to happen next? Would Eddy survive alone? Would any of them survive? The tone in Steve's voice told her they might receive an answer to one of those questions very soon.

She took the communicator, which was resting between the two front seats and pushed the button. "Say again, Steve. Did you say we had company?"

"Hell, yes!" Steve's voice came back. "Turn around and take a look for yourself."

Eve turned to Kevin, who was in the backseat. He spun around and looked out the back window. Nothing but snow. "I don't see anything back there."

Eve spoke in the communicator. "We don't see anything."

"Look up!" Steve shot back.

Kevin looked out the back again, but this time let his eyes wander up, towards the deep blue sky, which was empty except for one small aberration. Kevin jumped back away from the window. "Speed up!" He shouted at Brian, who was beginning to sweat.

"This thing can't go any faster!" he shouted back.

"What is it?" Eve asked.

"A black sphere," Kevin said, as his mind tumbling through the myriad of scenarios that now faced them. These things had the power to alter nature. Artuke claimed that just one of these things had created the wave of snow that decimated the dig site and killed dozens of people.

Eve was coming to the same conclusion. "This is going to be bad." She held the communicator as she looked out the front window. They were approaching Steve and Nicole now, who were still stopped on the ice. "Steve, get the hell out of here, now!"

Through the windshield she could see Steve and Nicole climbing on the snowmobile. She heard the rev of the snowmobile's throttle as they passed Steve and Nicole in the Cat.

"Here it comes!" Kevin shouted from the back.

"What's it doing?"

"Nothing. Just flying towards us. It looks like it's going to hit the ice."

Maybe it's malfunctioning," Brian added as he watched the sphere approaching in the side view mirror.

Kevin shuffled from one side of the backseat to the other, hoping for a better view. He gasped as the sphere dove into the ice, sending up a plume of snow. "It's in the ice. What's it doing in the—" Kevin froze, unsure if what he was seeing was real. The ice opened up behind them. A giant fissure, like the parting of the Red Sea, split directly behind them.

"It's opening the ice. It's opening the ice and coming straight up behind us! Turn right! Brian, turn right!"

"I hear you!" Brian yelled as he yanked the wheel to the right.

Kevin rolled across the seat, slamming against the inner wall of the Cat. Eve was pulled hard by the turn held tight by her seatbelt. She raised the communicator to her lips as the air was pushed from her lungs. "Steve! Make a hard right! Now! Turn right!"

As the centrifugal force of the violent turn wore off, Eve was able to straighten herself enough to take a look out the driver's side window. What she saw made her insides churn with fear. The crack in the ice, now far to the side, was neck and neck with Steve and Nicole. Even worse was something she hadn't noticed before—the ocean. Off to the left, maybe four hundred yards out, was a sparkling blue expanse of water, the Arctic Ocean. Eve realized at once that if Steve and Nicole were on the left side of the crevice, by the time it was done, they would be stuck adrift on a massive iceberg created by the sphere. There would be no way for them to escape.

☼　　☼　　☼　　☼　　☼

STEVE EYED the black sphere with steely resolve. Nicole was screaming something in his ear, but he was so focused on getting ahead of the obsidian orb carving the ice up like a Thanksgiving Day turkey that he didn't hear a word of it. Steve pushed the snowmobile for all it was worth and began making ground. He knew he had to get on the other side of it. He'd been watching the ocean growing larger out to their left but never saw any significance in it until now. As though a gust of wind had pushed them forward, the sphere fell behind. Or had it slowed on purpose? There wasn't time to think about it and Steve took the one chance he knew he'd get.

With a quick jerk of the handle bars, Steve and Nicole lunged to the right. But as they crossed in front of the orb, it sped up with incredible energy and ate away the ice beneath their tread. The ice opened up beneath them and Steve felt his stomach rise like he had just dropped into a rollercoaster ride. As they toppled downward, Steve was able to twist around. He wanted to look death in the eye. He thought it would be a bone jarring experience, a quick snap of the spine or crush of the skull. But what he saw below made him shiver. This would be no ordinary death, no quick release. He was going to freeze to death and drown at the same time.

Steve and Nicole hit the water at the same time. The snowmobile landed five feet away, but Steve wished it had landed on his head and killed him faster. Steve's breath shot out of his lungs as the cutting cold tore through his clothes and attacked his skin. He felt the weight of his waterlogged jacket and pants pulling him down. He saw the shimmering ceiling of water fading away as he was pulled into the freezing deep.

So this is how it's going to end, then?

Movement to Steve's right caught his attention. Nicole was thrashing as she sank beside him. Nicole! Steve discarded his clothing, shedding his jacket and boots faster than a schoolboy who needed to pee. When he felt buoyant enough, he reached out and grasped Nicole's hand. She turned to him. Her beautiful eyes looked sick. He pulled at her clothes and was able to get her jacket off. Then he hammered at the water, heading for the surface.

Water sprayed into the air as Steve and Nicole burst onto the surface, gasping for air, screaming in agony and shaking with cold. Steve knew they'd be dead in under two minutes now. If only—

Whack! A rope landed in the water between him and Nicole, followed by a voice. "Grab the rope!" It was Brian. "I'm going to start the Cat and pull you out!" Brian's head disappeared from the top of the icy crevice.

Steve allowed himself the briefest smile before his teeth started to chatter. They were going to be all right; really cold, but they would survive. "Grab the rope," Steve said to Nicole as she struggled to stay above the water.

A surge of adrenaline filled Steve's blood vessels and he felt warmth course through his body. He took hold of the rope and pulled himself out of the water. He dug his feet into the frozen ice wall, held onto the rope with one hand and extended his shaking free hand to Nicole. "Take my hand. I'll pull you out."

Nicole reached for Steve's hand but came up short. As soon as she stopped using it to tread water, she began to sink. "I can't do it!"

"Kick hard with your legs!" Steve shouted. "And use one hand on the rope!"

"I can't!" Nicole broke into tears. "Just leave me here."

"I'm not going to do that!"

As Steve stretched his body out, extending his hand to Nicole, he ignored the shouts form above. He assumed they were shouting encouraging things to Nicole. But he was struck by a single word. He wasn't sure who yelled it. Could have been Kevin. Could have been Eve. It was almost as though the word were suddenly implanted in his mind—*killer*. His chilled mind filled in the blanks as the water rose to his left.

At first he thought it might be a submarine, rising out of the ocean depths to save them. But the gleaming white spot, which always looked like an enormous eye to him, told him that this black missile wasn't man-made.

The massive orca surged out of the water, mouth wide, teeth gleaming. It descended on Nicole and clamped its jaw over her head. The water sloshed for a moment then became still. The whale was gone as quick as it had come, and Nicole with it. She was dead before she even knew there was a threat.

Steve's body trembled with fright and cold. His feet loosened on the ice and he slid back into the water. He wanted to die. First Paul . . . now Nicole . . .

Please, God, take me, too.

Steve couldn't feel the cold anymore. He couldn't feel his body. And his mind was numb, too, almost beyond reason. The water began to creep up around his neck, squeezing the breath from his throat, stinging his skin. As he prepared to embrace his fate, his body stopped moving.

With all his strength, Steve looked up to see what had snagged his hand. He squinted up at the bright sky and focused his vision on a face. Kevin was hanging from the rope, just above him. He saw Kevin slide down into the water and thought he felt something wrap around his waist. He wasn't sure, though. Maybe the killer whale had come back and bitten him in half.

Steve became aware of Kevin's presence again, only much closer—face-to-face. Steve smiled dumbly as his mind began to cloud over. "Hey Buck . . . what are you doing here?"

"Saving your life," Kevin said.

Steve was struck by how strong Kevin seemed. It was a new side to the man he'd never seen before, aside from the digital battlefield. Steve smiled. "Cool."

Then someone turned out the lights in Steve's mind and everything turned dark.

21

THE ICE CAVE

The fire kept the living room of the strong cabin at a toasty seventy degrees, but other rooms in the multifunctional dwelling could chilled Mary to the bone if she stayed put too long, such as the communications room. She shivered as she held the CB to her mouth. "Mammoth dig site, this is Base Camp Alpha. Do you copy? Over."

Mary sat still, listening to nothing but static. She put the CB down and rubbed her hands together. With no response forthcoming, Mary picked up the CB again. "Dig site, this is Mary. Will someone pick up the damn line. Over."

No response. Just the static hiss of dead air.

Mary put the CB down, stood, and stretched. She entered a long hallway, still cold, but not as chilled as the communications room. Every step forward brought the warmth of the living room as she neared it. She could smell the sweet smell of warm pine. Her hand grasped the door handle—it was gloriously warm.

The door slammed behind Mary as she flung herself into the living room and bounded toward the fire, over which hung a massive moose head. Reclining in a brown leather chair, Sam moved a book away from his eyes and looked at Mary over his spectacles. "Any word?"

"Not yet," Mary said as she held her hands out toward the flames, feeling the pinpricks of thawing flesh stinging her open palms. "I think they might be in some sort of trouble."

Sam raised an eyebrow. "Now what makes you think that?"

"I've been trying to reach them for two days, just now for a half hour straight. They're not just refusing to pick up; they're not there."

Sam smiled. "Now, Mary, you know how Eddy can get. Work is everything to him. If they've made some kind of discovery, you can bet you won't hear from him for another two days."

"That's just the problem," Mary said with a straight face. "Eddy isn't in charge of communications."

Sam closed the book, but left his finger wedged between the pages to save his place. He leaned forward. "Who is?"

"Eve."

Sam's face sank and his eyebrows furrowed, creasing his tan forehead. "How's the weather been up there?"

"Radar shows everything is clear."

"Maybe a mechanical problem? Atmospheric events?"

Mary shook her head. "No sunspots, and they have Paul and Steve up there with them. I'm not sure what could have happened, but they must be in some sort of trouble."

The leather chair creaked as Sam leaned back and bit his lower lip. "Weather permitting, we can go check on them tomorrow. They've handled bad situations before. I'm sure they're fine."

"But better safe than sorry," Mary added.

Sam pursed his lips and rubbed his eyebrows. "They could just be distracted."

"I can't think of anything that would keep Eve away for so long."

"Maybe she and Eddy finally . . ."

"Except that. Let's hope you're right."

Sam nodded. "In the meantime, you might want to keep trying to reach them."

"Unless you plan on sleeping in that chair tonight, I suggest you take a turn in the freeze box."

Sam stood and let his head bob back and forth to show his aggravation at being disturbed. He handed the book to Mary.

"Where are we?" She asked.

"Chapter ten," he said. "And you better give me the details tonight."

Mary settled into the chair and picked up reading where Sam left off. It had been a tradition of theirs for years. While one worked, the other read, and that night, over supper or lying in bed, they filled in the holes for each other, telling the story in their own words and adding personal thoughts. They were planning to grow old together, and neither one wanted to run out of things to say.

But as Mary scanned the words on the page, she realized her side of the story would be lacking in details tonight. Though she saw every word, most of the text faded to the back of her mind, which was occupied by worry for her friends. They could already be dead and frozen solid and she wouldn't be the wiser. The Arctic was unforgiving like that. Mary knew that better than most people, but then again, so did Eddy.

☼　　☼　　☼　　☼　　☼

WALKING IN a straight line was all Eddy could think about. His legs were sore, burning with cold. His arms were wrapped tight to his chest and had not moved in an hour. The pulling pain on his back and shoulders was due to the backpack he carried, but it was necessary, the key to their success. Doing his best to move quickly, Eddy had become exhausted but maintained his pace, spurred on by Eve's last words. He wanted to save the world. Who wouldn't? But he was more concerned about seeing Eve again, and telling her the truth.

Eddy moved his right arm for the first time in a long time and felt a stab of pain in his wrist. He knew he should move his arms, shake them around to keep the blood circulating, but the effort it took seemed extreme. He reached into his pocket and looked at the GPS screen. He was only a half mile from his objective. Almost there.

The thought spurred him on. His feet quickened across the snow with the hope that Eve and the others would be waiting with the warm Sno-Cat, ready to heat his frozen bones. He hadn't taken in his surroundings in some time. Moving in a straight line was easier if he didn't look around. He glanced to his left. Snow. He glanced to his right. Ice. Then, with a groan from his muscles, he turned around and stopped.

Eddy's arms fell to his sides as he looked back through his tinted goggles. Perhaps a football field away, four objects moved—running straight at him like linebackers from hell.

Running was the only thing Eddy could think to do. But if Steve's calculations had been correct and these Inuit, Ferox, could run at thirty miles per hour, Eddy was in trouble. In his current quasi-frozen state, Eddy would be lucky to outrun an Arctic seal. But he had to try.

One foot hit the ice, then another and another. In moments, Eddy was up to speed and—*whump!* His foot caught the pant leg of his other leg and sent him sprawling toward the ice. But when he hit, the ice was soft, just a few inches of snow covering a round hole. At first, Eddy feared he'd landed in a breathing hole created by seals, but the icy cold water never hit. He began to slide, headfirst, through a glowing tube of blue ice.

Eddy was too tired to resist the pull of gravity, which pulled him ever faster through the tunnel that nature had constructed like a water slide, twisting and turning. He felt the walls of the slide disappear and air on all sides and nothing below . . . until he hit the rock solid ice floor, which was polished smooth like an ice rink.

The air was knocked from Eddy's lungs, but he felt nothing break; all the padding provided by his many layers had spared him from a snapped rib or two. He slid across the surface of the ice cave and stopped when he slammed into a pillar of ice which connected both ceiling and floor.

Eddy crawled to his hands and knees and worked his way onto his feet. He was battered, confused, and now lost, but he was still very aware that the Ferox were bearing down on him. Whether or not they would pursue him into the cave was a mystery to Eddy, but he didn't want to find out the hard way. He took in the massive cave. Around him were tunnels in the ice, as though they had been carved by some ancient civilization. The cave was lit dimly from above and bright sunlight filtered through the ice roof. Eddy held onto the ice pillar as he looked at the GPS screen, which glowed in the dark cave. He found his bearings and headed in the direction that the GPS indicated. He might be lost under the Arctic ice, but he wasn't going to stop. If there was a way out of this cave system, he was going to find it.

Eddy skittered across the smooth ice, working just as hard to keep from falling over as he did to move forward. His progress was slow but continuous. As he delved deeper into the cave system, the light from above began to fade some and he used the GPS screen as a kind of flashlight, holding it out in front of him to light his path.

A sound behind Eddy made him jump and spin. It was far away, deep in the cave behind him, but still in the cave. Eddy lost his balance and fell to the ice, doing his best not to alert the Ferox to his position. The cave had been a blessing in disguise. Eddy realized that he should have been dead. If not for this maze of ice which hid him from his pursuers and sheltered him from all the elements save the cold, he would have died at the hands of the Ferox. Eddy slid onto his hands and knees, inching across the floor. He found crawling to not only be more quiet, but also much faster. His balance was much better on his hands and knees and, except for the pain in his kneecaps, easier on the body.

Eddy crawled his way through the cave, stopping every few feet to listen. Then he heard something new, not from behind, in front of him—water. He slid forward, rounded a spire of ice and came into a clearing where the roof was thin and the cavern well lit. A hole in the ice floor gave way to ocean water, but what struck Eddy even more was the proliferation of life in the room.

Walruses of every shape and size lounged around the open pool of ocean water. Some were male, with large tusks, like legless saber-tooth tigers. Others were females lounging in groups of five or ten. All had thick folds of brown skin, like fat, very tan, wrinkled old women. But standing taller than the rest was a massive male bull, with tusks the size of Eddy's arms and a body that looked to weigh nearly four thousand pounds—the walrus in charge. Eddy smiled as he realized he was seeing something spectacular, an ice cave ooglit, were the massive creatures were known to haul themselves out of the water for rest and copulation.

Eddy had just come one hundred feet through a long winding cave and didn't want to back track. The walrus herd was between him and the next cave, which he hoped headed in the right direction. But the only way through was past the seagoing behemoths and the gigantic king walrus. Eddy didn't know much about walruses; he'd seen enough *National Geographic* specials to know that they didn't eat people, although he imagined the big one was fully capable. Sliding on to his stomach, Eddy started out across the outer fringes of the cavern, doing his best to fit in and not stand out too much. He moved the backpack higher, onto his head, to give him a more authentic shape. He was sure that the first walrus to spot him would either laugh in a walrus way or sound the alarm.

The stench in the room was penetrating, filling Eddy's nostrils. It was a putrid smell, which he knew was a mixture of walrus dung and urine. While disgusting, he thought it best if he slid his way through some of the muck. Smelling like a walrus might come in handy.

Fighting back the bile in his throat, Eddy squirmed through a chilled puddle of urine and feces. A second later, he feared he had suffered the stink for no reason. He felt the ice shake and a sound like a deformed trumpet reverberated through the ice cavern. Eddy looked up to see the large bull sliding across the ice toward him. Droves of smaller males and females scurried out of the way, diving into the freezing water. Eddy knew fighting would do no good. It could crush him in seconds or impale him with its massive tusks.

Eddy did the only thing he could, curled up in a ball, held his backpack over his face and waited to be crushed. But the attack never came. His heart continued to beat and his lungs continued to breathe the rancid air. A bark, like that of a very large dog filled his ears, drowning out the sound of his own screaming voice. Eddy peered over the top of the backpack and saw a smaller female, perhaps one thousand pounds, between him and the bull. She barked violently at the giant and held her head high.

The bull paused as the female sniffed Eddy from top to bottom. When it reached Eddy's face, it looked into his eyes. Eddy knew he better think of something. He made his eyes as wide and pitiful looking as possible and lowered his head. He whimpered like any small animal did when it was in danger. The message was clear: "save me!" The female turned to the bull and gave one last loud bark. The bull snorted, lowered its threatening stance, and backed away. The female turned back to Eddy and nudged him. Eddy got the message. "Get out of here before he changes his mind."

Eddy slithered across the remainder of ice, keen to keep his head low and his stance unthreatening. He was aware of the bull's massive head following his progress. Relief struck as Eddy entered a tunnel on the opposite side of the cavern. The bull let out one last bark, warning against any return trips. Eddy leaned his head on his arms and took deliberate breaths. The work of sliding across the room wasn't difficult, but the threat of the beast looming over his head took his breath away.

Then the smell struck again. Eddy, sure he wasn't about to head back into the Walrus ooglit, shed his outer layers, which were moist with feces and growing colder by the moment. Lighter and energized by surviving one of the most extraordinary encounters of his life, Eddy struck out again, crawling through the cave system.

Progress was quick. Now accustomed to sliding across the ice, Eddy was making quicker time than he had on the outside, and so far, there had been no sign of pursuit. The GPS screen showed that he was a mere two hundred yards away from his goal. Were the others there waiting for him? Would he be able to find a way through the ice? It occurred to Eddy then that both he and the others were carrying the GPS communicators. They should be able to speak to each other, if they were in range and if the ice didn't block the signal. Eddy held the communicator to his mouth and his lips began to form the first syllable of his words when a sound echoed through the cave system.

He recognized it right away, having heard it only minutes ago. The walrus herd was barking all at once. He could hear the splashing water as they dove into the ooglit pool. Then came the roar of the king. Like a dinosaur, it let out a thundering shout as it charged across the ice. Eddy could swear he felt the ice shake. He'd put an impressive distance between him and the walrus herd since he saw them, but he knew that the large bull was no ordinary walrus and its weight was incredible.

It occurred to Eddy then that the Ferox must still be behind him. Working their way through the ice caves, they must have stumbled into the ooglit. But he knew they wouldn't crawl through waste to cross the expanse, nor would they cower before the walruses. And there were four Ferox. He imagined that the response garnered from the large bull was even more ferocious than it had been with Eddy.

Perhaps the bull would kill the Ferox for him. They were much smaller and had to be weaker than the beast. Eddy smiled at his good fortune, having made friends with the herd. The bull called out again, sounding furious. Then it was silenced with a loud squeal, the likes of which Eddy had never heard. It tore at his heart, knowing that the king, countless years old and the brave protector of his herd, had just been killed. The four thousand pound, sword-tusked creature hadn't even slowed them down.

Eddy wanted to cry for the beast, but now he knew how close the Ferox were and that they were still chasing him. He was nearly to his destination, but feared he would not make it. The Ferox were relentless pursuers, and if they could kill the walrus bull, they would make short work of him. Eddy cursed the Ferox in his mind. They had destroyed his life and the lives of countless others.

Scrambling on hands and knees, Eddy began to make good time across the ice . . . then stopped when he heard a sound that stabbed a pain in his chest—breathing. Large lungs sucked in air from the cavern just behind him. The Ferox had found him.

22

HAIL

A cacophony of screaming voices behind a static hum burned at Steve's ears. He couldn't see anything, or feel anything. He felt as though someone was standing behind him, laughing over the voices, but he was unable to turn around. Then he felt the voice had a body and the body was holding a knife . . . no, knives. Maybe ten of them, or hundreds, but they were about to cut into his back. He tried to run but his legs were frozen in the water. Frozen. A black man with white eyes opened his mouth full of knifes and bit Steve in half.

Steve's eyes popped open wide and he could feel his body. He knew this was real and not a dream as the black man with white eyes had been, because his body hurt all over. But he felt warm and that was a welcome change from the freezing he experienced in his dreams. It then occurred to him that he didn't know what he was looking at. In front of him was a brownish blob: hair. Steve became aware that he was in very tight quarters, sandwiched between two very warm objects.

Squinting with suspicion, Steve took the blanket that was draped over him and lifted it up. He peered into the darkness and as his eyes adjusted, his fears were confirmed. "Ah!"

Steve sat up straight as Kevin jolted and fell off the back seat of the Cat and landed on the floor. "What the hell is going on?"

Eve twisted around from the front seat, where she sat behind the steering wheel. "Relax, Steve, you're still a virgin."

"That's not funny," Steve said with wide eyes. "I can't believe you just said that."

Brian was crushed against the back of the seat, where Steve was pushing on him. "Well, I gather it worked."

Steve was irate. "What the hell worked?"

"We had to get you warm," Kevin said as he pulled a shirt over his head, covering his naked body.

"So you molested me?"

Brian sat up behind Steve. He was naked, too. "You would have gotten hypothermia and died within minutes. We had to warm you up fast and the hot air from the Cat's heating system wouldn't have done the job. Body heat saved your life."

"Okay, fine. But why couldn't Eve have done it? I didn't need to wake up to two men feeling me up!"

"If I had done it," Eve started with a smirk, "you would have woken up feeling me up."

Steve smiled. "Okay, you got a point there, but . . . where's Nicole?"

Smiles faded throughout the Cat.

"What?"

Kevin looked up, his long johns half way on. "You don't remember?"

"Remember what?"

"Why you had hypothermia? Why you were wet to begin with?"

Steve rubbed his temples with both hands. "All I remember was this awful dream I just had. This guy, all black, with big white eyes and knives for teeth. It was . . . It wasn't a dream."

Kevin shook his head, no, in agreement.

"She's gone?"

Kevin nodded, yes. "Sorry."

"Oh."

Steve stared straight ahead, looking at nothing. "Do you think she felt much pain?"

"Doubtful," Brian said. "Her body would have been numbed by the water and she was already suffering from shock. She didn't feel a thing."

"Good," Steve said. He looked out the windshield. "Where are we?"

Eve looked back at Steve with a worried expression, concerned for his emotional health.

"Don't look at me like I'm a wounded freakin' puppy. Just tell me where the hell we are."

Eve sighed. "Closing in on the coordinates. We're about a quarter mile from our goal and moving fast. We should be there in about ten minutes."

Steve nodded. "Where are my clothes?"

"They were too wet to wear. We left them behind."

"You expect me to go around the Artic with my ass in the wind?"

Kevin let out a light chuckle.

"I'm glad you think this is funny."

Eve turned around from the front. "We divided up our clothes and found some extras. You might look like a patchwork from the Salvation Army, but at least you'll be warm." She handed Steve a pile of clothes and he began to dress.

Steve turned to Brian. "Put your damn clothes on, man. This ain't no social club."

Brian smiled and began to dress. He looked up as he fastened his pants around his waist. Something wasn't right. They were slowing down. "Why are you stopping?"

"Gas," Eve said. "We're out."

"There's a spare in the back," Steve said. "Should be enough to get us there."

Eve turned to Steve. "That's great, but how are we going to get back to civilization?"

Steve shrugged.

Kevin poked his head through the top of his second shirt. "If the Ferox don't catch us, you mean."

"I hate to be the first to realize this," Eve said. "But we're on a one-way trip."

"Perhaps the Aeros have transportation inside the citadel," Brian said.

"If there's a citadel."

Eve grimaced at the suggestion. "Do you really think we're going to be able to use alien transportation that's thousands of years old?"

"You're probably right," Brian said. "But there's supposed to be some kind of interstellar communications device. Most likely high powered, too. I'm sure we can attract someone's attention and find shelter from the cold."

Kevin looked at Steve, who was just finishing putting on his hodge-podge of winter clothes. "Maybe you could get the GPS communicators to work with the transmitter."

"Sure," Steve said with an air of confidence. "I'll just break out my universal guide to alien/human technological amalgamation. Oh, wait. Phooey, I left it at home."

"It was just an idea," Kevin said.

"Look, maybe if Paul were still around, sure. But I just rent the stuff and can fix basic problems. I change the oil, tighten the screws, plug stuff in . . . Paul's the one who fixed the hard stuff. Okay? I can't fill his shoes so please don't act like I can."

Kevin looked down at the floor. "Sorry."

Steve sighed and patted Kevin on the shoulder. "Don't sweat it, Buck. You're my main man now. Brian's got a massive bug up his ass—"

"Hey," Brian said.

Steve ignored him. "And Eve, well, she's a chick."

"Thank you for noticing," Eve said.

"So unless Eddy gets back here in one piece," Steve looked at Eve, "which he will," Steve looked back at Kevin, "it's just you and me, mi amigo. *Comprende?*"

Kevin smiled. "Si. Muchas gracias."

"De nada," Steve said. "Now let's go fill this beast up and save the freakin' world."

Everyone wore slight smiles as Eve pushed open the door. Their smiles faded as the bitter cold swept through the cabin. Eve stepped out into the frigid air and shook with cold and fright.

☼   ☼   ☼   ☼   ☼

KEVIN FELT the sting of cold air on his bare face as he stood by while Steve drained the last of their gasoline, four gallons, into the Sno-Cat's gas tank. The last few days were a blur to him. It felt like years ago that they had survived the tidal wave of snow and met the alien stranger who sent them on a quest to rescue humanity. It was his worst nightmare and favorite fantasy rolled up into one. Initially, all Kevin had felt was embarrassment about the way he handled the original situation. He couldn't remember many of his thoughts, but he recalled feeling an anxiety that squeezed his chest and throat. But he'd improved since then.

Now he had saved Steve's life. With Eddy gone on his own, someone had to be the rescuer, the strong one. Kevin was as surprised as the rest of them that it had been him; Buck Rogers, indeed. Kevin had become the hero he always wanted to be. True, occasionally he had the opportunity to drive an injured bicyclist to the hospital or save a neighborhood kid's fish from a broken tank, but now he had saved a man's life. He was a hero. Of course, all the heroes he knew of said things like, "Just doing my job," or, "Anyone would have done it." That's what made them truly heroic, that what they had done was no bigger than an everyday, casual event. That's how he'd have to act, too. If anyone knew how excited he was about being a hero, his heroic stature would be sullied.

"There we go," Steve said, breaking Kevin's thoughts of heroism. "Should get us where we're going, but once we get there, we're stuck."

"We'll be fine," Kevin said with confidence—that's what heroes did, instill confidence . . . and figure out the rest later.

"What makes you so sure?" Steve asked.

"Just a feeling," Kevin replied.

"Illogical," Brian said. "Feelings are irrelevant. In survival situations, it's better to be emotionless and do what needs to be done."

"Okay, Spock. This coming from the man who can't score with women without flashing his fat wallet," Steve said with a smirk.

"You don't think emotion helps overcome fears?" Kevin said. "If I wasn't so scared that Steve might die in that water, I wouldn't have been able to climb down and save him."

"And you risked getting yourself killed, too," Brian said. "You could have just as easily fallen in, or been eaten by the orca. Then we would have lost three people."

"You're one cold bastard," Steve said. "If you fall in, you can bet I won't be risking my life to pull your butt out."

"And I wouldn't advise you to do so," Brian said.

Steve shook his head as Eve leaned out of the Cat. "All right boys, enough with the tough stuff. Let's get—"

Kevin saw Eve's eyes widen. "What?"

Eve pointed above their heads. All three looked up.

Steve jumped back. "Whoa!"

Brian backed away.

"Get in the Cat!" Kevin shouted as the black orb hovering above them began to spin, emitting a low *hum*.

The three dove into the Cat and slammed the doors shut.

"Go! Go! Go!" Steve shouted.

Eve grabbed the key and was about to turn the ignition when she stopped. "What's that?"

A light tapping began to sound on the roof of the Sno-Cat. Kevin looked out the windshield and saw tiny balls of ice bouncing off the hood. "I think it's hail."

"But it looks tiny," Steve said. "We'll be fine in the Cat."

"I don't know," Brian started.

"What now, Mr. Negativity?" Steve said. "You going to tell us how hail is actually very deadly? How if you get stuck in a hailstorm, it's better to run and hide instead of saving your friends?"

"Something like that, yes."

"Well, you can kiss my ass. We don't need to hear anymore of your bullshit."

The light ping of hail grew louder as more and more of the tiny balls bounced off the metal hull of the Sno-Cat. "Actually," Kevin said. "I think this time we might want to listen to him."

"Glad to see you've decided to become the voice of reason, Kevin," Brian said.

Kevin feigned a smile. "Bout time, right?"

Brian nodded. Kevin clenched his teeth.

It was a rhetorical question, you jerk.

"Regardless of your distain for my opinions, I do know a few facts to which you all might pay attention."

Steve waved his hands in the air. "Okay, you big bag of hot air. We're waiting. The hail is falling and we're all waiting."

"Hail can become considerably large. While the Cat may provide some protection, hail has been known to smash windshields." As Brian spoke, the hail grew in size. The sound became a loud roar as the golf ball-size balls of ice bounced off the Cat.

"You see?" Brian said. "They're growing in size already."

Crash! The windshield became a spider web of cracked glass. A hole in the center was the size of a man's fist. Steve reached between the seats and pulled out a baseball-size ball of ice. "This is bad."

"I hate being right," Brian said.

Crash! A second orb of ice plowed through the window, which was now letting smaller bits of hail fall through the holes. The front seat became covered with white balls of ice.

"Get in the back," Kevin said as he moved to the back seat. Eve followed him.

Eve looked at Brian as all four were squished in the back. "Does hail ever get bigger than a softball?"

"I don't think so," Brian said.

"Oh, sure, now that we're getting pelted you suddenly aren't Mr. Know-it-all any more."

"Look, I never said I was an expert on hail, just that—"

Crunk! The metal roof caved in above them as a basketball-size depression pushed down into the ceiling.

"This . . . is not good." Steve said.

"I guess that solves the hail size debate," Eve said. "What should we do?"

Crunk! The ceiling was pounded again, but this time it was followed by the sound of twisting metal. Hail was building up above them.
Kevin looked up at the ceiling. "That's not going to hold. We need to get out of here."

"Where would we go?" Brian asked as he looked out the window, seeing hail landing in the snow to all sides.

Whack! The roof lurched down as something massive landed on it. "Under the Cat!" Kevin shouted. "Hurry! Before the doors are wedged shut."

Kevin flung open a door and leapt out, diving under the large vehicle with Eve close behind. Then Brian hopped out and scrambled for the protection of the Cat's body. Kevin saw Steve's feet hit the hail-covered ice as he jumped from the Cat, but then Steve fell forward like a cut tree. A stain of red could be seen on the back of his head where a chunk of ice had hit him. Kevin knew he wouldn't last long under the constant barrage of ice; if one of these big ones hit him, he'd been dead in an instant.

He knew Brian and his cold logic wouldn't risk saving Steve. It was up to—

Before Kevin could react, Eve flung herself out into the barrage of hail, grabbed Steve's pant legs, and yanked him back under the Cat. The clanging of ice on metal grew louder and faster by the second. It sounded like the finale at the largest fireworks display in history. Then, with a massive boom, the entire Sno-Cat shook and sank down above them. Laying flat on their stomachs, they barely had room left to move.

Then it stopped. The hail disappeared from the sky and the loud static of falling ice ceased to tap on the Sno-Cat's exterior.

"I think it's over," Eve said as she pulled herself out into the open. She stood precariously on the carpet of ice balls and turned around to see the Cat. "Oh, God."

The Cat was destroyed. A ball of ice the size of a mini-Cooper was lodged inside, crushing the front and back seats. Brian and Kevin stood next to her.

"I think it's safe to say that we're on foot from here," Kevin said.

Steve groaned from under the Cat. "Can someone get me out of here?"

Kevin reached down and took Steve's hands. With a grunt, he slid Steve out from under the Cat. Steve lay on the icy field and held the back of his head. He looked up at the crushed Cat, shook his head and said, "You know, I'm getting sick and tired of being unconscious."

"At least you didn't wake up naked this time," Kevin said.

Steve smiled. "True, but I think I'd prefer that to walking a quarter mile with a concussion." Steve climbed to his feet and held onto Kevin's shoulder. "Anyone have some Ibuprofen?"

"I think we're all going to need some," Kevin said. He wasn't in too much pain at the moment. So far he'd been one of the lucky ones. He'd avoided injury thus far, but he had a feeling that wouldn't last. As they neared the end of their journey, he knew the stakes would be higher. He was sure that if they survived the next few hours, they'd all be in more pain than a few aspirin would help.

23

UNDER THE ICE

With numb fingers, Eddy pulled himself forward across the ice. He had made it down another three tunnels without being caught or torn to pieces, so he was thankful for that, but the thick, raspy breathing continued behind him. The ice in this portion of the cave seemed thinner, clearer. A few times Eddy swore he could see creatures moving beneath the ice, maybe the fleeing walrus herd. Eddy imagined that if he were any heavier he might have fallen through. He made sure to keep three pressure points in contact with the ice at all times to keep his weight distributed.

Then something caught his eyes—a slice of color which differed from the blues and whites that glowed from the diffused sunlight shining through the snowy ceiling. A crimson colored wall rose out of the ice, all the way to the ceiling. Eddy crawled to the object and saw that it was grooved with wavy lines, reaching the surface. A speck of blue sky greeted him as his eyes turned up. This was his way out!

Eddy dug his fingers into the grooved area; a perfect fit. But before he could pull himself up, a voice broke his concentration.

"You've done well," Marutas said.

The old Inuit stood ten feet from Eddy, still wearing his furs and red winter cap. Eddy glanced from side to side. "Didn't lose your friends, did you?"

"Oh no, they're around here somewhere . . . perhaps feasting on the entrails of your friends." Marutas walked a few feet closer and stopped. He knelt down to Eddy's height. "It's fitting in a way. I let you live, once; now I am the one to take your life."

"What are you talking about?" Eddy demanded.

"You don't remember me? A pity."

"I'd remember your ugly face."

"Sticks and stones."

"Go to hell."

"I've already been there. But then, so have you. You remember Venezuela, don't you Eddy?" Marutas was all smiles.

Eddy said nothing, but his mind raced with ideas of how to survive this mess, though he was also curious as to what the old man knew about Venezuela. Perhaps the Ferox had done some research since their first encounter?

"I remember it like it was yesterday, don't you? The screams. The blood. It was a pleasure to kill your friends that day. If not for your ferocity, I would have killed you as well. But you inspired me! That day you became what we hope all men will become."

"How do you know what happened?"

Marutas turned his back on Eddy and walked a few feet away. "You mean to tell me you can't remember the face of the man who spared your life?"

"I remember his face, and I'll kill him when I see him again, but it wasn't your face."

"Look again."

Marutas spun around. Eddy gasped and pushed against the red wall, feeling warmth emanating from its surface. The face was the same! The winter hat had become a red bandana. It was the man! He had killed Harry and Kat!

"You bastard!" Eddy shouted as he lunged for Marutas's throat. But Marutas was too quick. He grabbed Eddy's outstretched arms and spun, throwing Eddy back against the red wall with a thud. Eddy slumped to the floor.

Marutas stood over Eddy, looking down at him. He squatted down and looked Eddy in the eyes. "Better warriors than you have tried and failed to kill me. How's your shoulder?"

Eddy's layers of sleeve were torn away before he knew Marutas had even grabbed hold. His scarred shoulder was revealed underneath. "You really should have had a better doctor take care of that." Marutas smiled. "The scar could have been hidden better. It must have served as an awful reminder these past few years."

"I didn't want to forget."

Marutas grinned and held his hand in front of Eddy's rosy red face. The hand began to change. The fingers grew longer and grey. The tips became like the talons of a bird of prey, curved and exquisitely sharp. Eddy's eyes widened. "You have yet to see our true form. Perhaps I will show it to you before you die. But first, some business."

Eddy held his breath. What business? he thought. Just kill me and get it over with!

"The key, please. I believe it is in your pack."

Eddy held his breath. The key.

Sitting up straight, Eddy removed the backpack from his shoulders and brought it around to his lap. He reached inside and grabbed hold of a hard, metal object. "If I give you this, will you let the others live?"

"You assume they're still alive."

"Fine. If they're still alive."

"No."

"Why not?"

Squinting, Marutas said, "You're wasting my time . . ." Marutas's eyes opened. "No. You're stalling. Why?"

Marutas reached for the backpack and Eddy pulled out his hand. He brought a wrench around and smashed it into Marutas's skull. The man fell to the ice and Eddy jumped to his feet. Eddy decided to press the attack and swung the wrench at Marutas's head again, hoping to end this fight once and for all. But Marutas saw the blow coming and dodged it, rolling to the side and using the momentum to flip back onto his feet.

Marutas growled, though he still looked dazed. Eddy wasted no time maintaining his advantage. He charged with the wrench, swung it again and caught Marutas on the cheek. He heard the clang of metal on bone, but no crack. Marutas howled and Eddy tackled him to the ice. As they slid across the floor Eddy heard a terrifying sound. A light cracking noise filled the air. The thin ice was giving way.

With speed Eddy could only dream of, Marutas jumped to his feet and stood. He smiled. "Eddy Moore. You please me every time I encounter you . . . but I'm afraid this will be the last time." Marutas backed against the ice wall and dug his fingers into it, then his feet. He crawled up the wall and hovered near the ceiling.

The wrench dropped to the ice as Eddy moved out into the center of the room. He clenched his fists, preparing for a fight he knew he'd lose. "C'mon then, coward. Stop hiding out of my reach and fight!"

A roar the likes of which Eddy had never heard, not from a lion or any other earthly beast, escaped Marutas's lungs as he swooped down from the ceiling. Eddy dove to the side and rolled toward the red wall. He managed to jab his fingers into one of the wavy crevices before Marutas struck the floor.

Eddy turned around to see Marutas standing on the shattered floor, which had somehow remained intact. Marutas lowered like a cat about to pounce. Eddy had only one chance. He raised his leg into the air and brought his boot down hard on the ice. The cracking noise grew louder, and Marutas looked down.

The ice shattered beneath Marutas as he attempted to leap away. The force of his jump sent the ice crumbling beneath his feet and he plunged into the frozen water. He thrashed and yelled, clawing at the ice with his sharpened gray fingers. But the ice was fragile and every time he grabbed the edge, it crumbled in his hands.

Wasting no time, Eddy threw his backpack on and began to scale the red wall. His fingers burned from his weight but he held tight, moving up toward the dot of blue sky. He could hear Marutas splashing in the water, but it was clear he would free himself from the freezing ocean; and when he did, Eddy was sure he would waste no time in spilling his guts.

Smashing through the ice with one hand and gripping the grooved wall with the other proved to be harder than Eddy hoped. He swung at the ceiling with his fist several times, feeling the skin over his knuckles grow raw, but freeing very little ice. Eddy looked down and saw the pool of ice empty. Marutas was free.

A growl shook the cavern below and Eddy realized it was not human. Marutas had talked about his true form earlier. He wondered if that was the form he now took. A shadow below raised the hair on his exposed arm. It was huge and non-human. Eddy shouted as he swung hard at the ceiling of ice.

The force of his blow shook the ceiling and a portion caved in, tumbling down into the pool of ocean water. A bright swath of blue sky was exposed over Eddy's head. He heaved himself onto the ice and rolled onto his back, panting from the effort and ignoring the burning snow on his sleeveless arm. Marutas had disappeared, though Eddy was sure he was still on the hunt. Or was he? Eddy wondered if it was the saltwater that bothered him. No, the Earth was covered with saltwater . . . Perhaps the cold, then? Maybe. There had to be some reason the Aeros built their citadel so far north, beneath the frozen ocean. Of course, Marutas could just be prolonging the inevitable. Eddy had put up a valiant fight, again, and Marutas seemed to respect such outbursts of violence.

Eddy rolled onto his stomach, praying that the ice below him, which he now knew was the ceiling over a vast system of ice caves, would hold his weight. While every bone in his body gave protest to the effort, Eddy got to his feet and was happy to feel the easy grip of rough ice and snow beneath his boots.

The GPS communicator was warm in Eddy's hand. He looked at the screen, which seemed dimmer than before, but could still make out his position and that of his final destination, which was unbelievably close. Eddy turned in the direction indicated on the map. His eyes opened wide.

In the distance was a single red object, jutting out of the ice and reaching for the sky. It looked to be the same color as the grooved wall he had only just climbed. Eddy smiled and held the communicator to his lips. "Hey, guys. This is Eddy. You out there? Over."

Eddy took his lips away from the communicator and held it to his ear. Nothing. Eddy's forehead scrunched as he took it away from his ear and gazed at the LCD screen. It was blank.

"Damn."

The batteries were dead. Eddy pocketed the device and struck out for the gleaming beacon of hope. His legs pounded with sharp stabs of pain brought by each footfall, like someone was throwing golf balls at his shins. He knew if he survived this mess, he'd be in serious pain for at least a few weeks. He hoped he'd be spending those weeks with Eve.

As thoughts of Eve's face swirled in his mind like a light speed slide show, Eddy's pace began to pick up and the pain seemed distant, unimportant. He resolved to expose his heart to Eve when they returned to civilization. He only hoped that after all this time, she'd receive him.

He thought back to when they had first met, that summer at the tyrannosaur dig site. She'd crept into his heart back then, but after their budding romance nearly destroyed his future career, he'd forced himself to keep an emotional distance—all because of a single test.

And now he was here, being tested like never before, and there weren't any other students to steal the answers from. The red streak of vertical material placed in the ice by an alien civilization came into clear view. His pace slowed and he looked from east to west. Nothing. The others were nowhere in sight. They were either stuck somewhere on the ice . . . or dead. Eddy dropped to his knees. He might be able to save the planet, but he'd failed to save Eve. In that moment he knew he should have clung to Eve, regardless of the effect she had on his career. The effect she had on his heart suddenly seemed much more important. He turned and looked back the way he came.

Climbing out from the ice were four figures. Eddy realized that Marutas had probably just gone to collect the others before finishing him off; now all four would have the pleasure of dicing his body with their inhuman claws. They walked toward Eddy with a calm, confident stride. Eddy shuffled away from them, but his energy was sapped. He was defeated. His legs stopped pushing against the ice and he waited for death.

24

THE CHASM

Brian estimated the crevice to be fifteen feet across, a hundred feet deep, and perhaps miles long. They had come all this way, survived such hardships, and for what? To be stuck here, stopped by the split ice. He could hear his father, screaming at him in his head.

That's just like you, taking something important and screwing it up! You're worthless and you'll never amount to anything, no matter how much money you have.

Brian squeezed his fists. That bastard was always right. Even from his grave he found ways to torment Brian. "Well, this is just perfect," Brian said.

Kevin sat on the ice and crossed his legs. "Looks like we're done."

"There's got to be a way around," Eve said. "We're only a hundred yards out. It's got to be just over that rise."

Brian looked across the gorge where the ice rose up about ten feet, just enough to keep them from seeing the other side and feeling a stab of hope. If they could contact Eddy, maybe they would have a chance. Brian's eyes widened. "Eddy."

"What?" Steve asked as he paced near the chasm's edge, peering down to its sharp, icy bottom.

"The GPS communicator. Give it to me."

Steve paused, then pulled the communicator from his pocket and tossed it to Brian. Brian switched it on and pushed the button. "Eddy, Eddy. This is Brian. Do you copy? Over."

Static.

"Eddy, if you can hear me, answer, damn it! We're stuck!"

"You didn't say over," Steve said.

Brian glared at him. "Eddy, answer me, now!"

"If Eddy could answer he would have," Eve said.

"Yeah, man. He could be running for his life. Or maybe buried in snow. Or frozen."

Eve shot Steve a harsh glance.

"Sorry. Look, he's probably just out of range or his batteries died. Just forget it, okay?"

Brian looked at the GPS screen and saw the markers for their current position and the coordinates given to them by Artuke. They overlapped. "We're so close."

"We have to start going around," Eve said.

"It could take days to circumvent the entire gorge," Brian said. "We'll freeze to death as soon as night falls."

"Would you prefer we just sit here and freeze to death without trying? Is that it, Brian? Are you giving up?"

Brian glared at her.

"That's just like you, quitting when we're so close."

Brian's eyebrows sunk on his forehead. "What did you just say?"

"You're quitting . . . you're always the first to give up." Eve threw her hands in the air. "If it wasn't for Eddy's persistence, we'd never get anything done. Thank God we brought him, or you'd have us all dead by now."

"That's it!" Brian lunged at Eve, reaching for her throat.

"Whoa!" Steve shouted as he jumped in between the two. "Calm down, Bri. No reason to go *Lord of the Flies* on us. All right?"

Brian huffed with every breath. "Don't call me a quitter! Don't you ever do it again."

"I'm only saying what I see," Eve said as she crossed her arms.

"You're just like my father," Brian said, his face twisted with anger.

"Sounds like your father was a smart man," Eve said, knowing she was goading him on, but with Steve between them and Kevin coming up behind, she didn't have much to worry about.

"My father is . . . was . . . I hate my father, and you're just like him!" Brian ran forward, attempting to round Steve, but Steve had him by the waist and they rolled to the ice.

Brian landed on top of Steve and raised his fist back to punch him. But Kevin was quick and caught Brian's fist, holding it back. Brian raised his other fist to swing at Steve, and Kevin caught that one, too.

"Let me go!" Brian roared. "You're all just like my father! Let me go!"

Steve was white with fear. "Calm down, man! We're not your father!"

"You're just like him! Always judging me! Making me small! I hate you! I hate—" Brian's eyes locked on an area just to the right of Steve's left ear.

Steve moved his eyes to the side, but didn't move his head. "What?"

"What's that?" Brian asked, his voice shaky but calm.

Steve turned his head and saw what Brian was looking at; a loop of rope had fallen out of Steve's backpack when they toppled to the ice. "Oh, a rope."

"What do you mean, 'Oh, a rope'?" Kevin asked as he let go of Brian's wrists.

"I kept it from the Cat. It's the rope you used to pull me out of the water with. Why?"

Eve stood over Steve and thrust both hands out toward the gorge. Steve looked at the gorge then back to the rope. "Oh . . . Hey, I've been hit on the head a few times today and I nearly died, like, twice, so cut me some slack. At least I thought of bringing it in the first place. Now get off me, you big oaf."

Brian climbed to his feet and Steve sat up. Eve reached into the backpack on Steve's back and pulled out the length of rope, which was thin, strong, and very long. She smiled as she began to tie a loop around one end. "Now if you boys are done rolling around in the snow and throwing temper tantrums, I'd like to find Eddy and be done with this mess. Any problems with that?"

They all just stared at her.

"Good," she said.

Brian inched towards Eve. She watched him with a wary eye. "Sorry about that. I've been seeing a shrink since my dad died . . . He thought something like that might happen some day. Can you believe he wanted me to make paintings to express my rage?" Brian laughed. "Look, anyway, it wasn't really me, so I'm sorry."

"You're trying to deny responsibility for it?"

"What?"

"If it wasn't really you, who was it?"

Brian stood still.

"You, or not you, next time you threaten me or anyone else on this crew, that makes you as bad as these Ferox jerks. Got it?"

Brian looked at the ice. "Right. Sorry."

Brian hated his father more than the idea of evil aliens. He decided that Eve was right. He had attacked his crew, people he respected. From then on, the Ferox would become the living embodiment of his father. He was sure that if his psychologist knew what his situation was that he would agree; transplanting his hatred for his father onto world-corrupting beasts from another planet would be a very healthy choice.

☼   ☼   ☼   ☼   ☼

IT TOOK Eve several tries before she was able to lasso a tall spire of ice on the other side of the cavernous chasm. She tied off the rope on a solid chunk of ice she felt sure would hold them, as long as they went one at a time. Still, she couldn't make any promises. Steve argued that the ice might not hold their weight, and Eve volunteered to cross the expanse first. The rope was hard to grip, but having her feet wrapped around took some of the weight off her fingers. She managed to shimmy across the rope in a minute and a half. The hardest and most precarious portion of the journey was getting off the rope. She had to spin around and grasp the slippery edge of the gorge and pull herself over the edge. Her fingers dug in deep and she was able to slide onto the ice, like an Arctic snake. She stood on the far side and waved back. "Piece of cake, boys. Who's next?"

Steve threw himself onto the rope and pulled himself across like a well-trained marine. He was exhausted by the time he reached her and she had to drag him onto the ice, but he kept his manhood intact.

Steve lay on the ice and looked up at Eve with a smile. "Ever see a 'boy' do that?"

So predictable.

Eve smiled. "Boys *and* girls, actually, but when they were done, they weren't panting for air like my father's overweight basset hound. You'd think that for a dairy farm, the man would have invested in a sheep dog or something. Old Walter didn't to much more than eat and pass gas. You two would have got along fantastically."

Steve fell back down on the ice and continued panting. "Harsh, man."

Kevin was next on the rope. He was moved slowly but steadily. It was apparent his weight was taxing his muscles. Kevin's pudge was catching up with him.

"C'mon, Buck," Steve yelled. "Get a move on!"

Kevin stopped moving about three quarters of the way across. "Give me, ugh, a break," he said, upside down. "It's not like . . . I hang . . . from a rope . . . like a damn monkey on a daily basis!"

As Kevin spoke his last word, his boots slipped off the rope and his lower body began to descend into the pit. Kevin cried out like a frightened animal, but his fingers held tight. He swung by his hands, hanging above certain death. "I can't make it," he said.

"Put your legs back on the rope!" Eve shouted.

Brian was biting his fingers from the other side, watching with rapt attention.

"Kevin, listen to me," Eve said. "Swing your legs up one at a time and wrap them around the rope. Your legs can hold the weight and your hands can pull you across."

Kevin swung a leg up and missed the rope by a foot. "Ugh, I can't!"

Eve saw that Kevin's backpack was weighing him down. "Lose the backpack," Eve said.

"I—I can't!" Kevin shouted. "Ugh, we need it!"

"Don't be ridiculous, Kevin," Eve said. "Whatever's in there isn't worth your life."

Kevin made no move to lose his backpack. His arms were shaking, wiggling the rope like a freshly twanged guitar string. Sweat poured down his forehead, stung his eyes, and froze to his cheeks, cracking his skin.

Eve was about to shout again when Steve put a hand on her shoulder. "I'll handle this," he said with a smile.

"Hey, Buck. You know you suck as a gamer," Steve said with a biting tone.

Kevin did his best to look at Steve. "Ugh. What?"

"You suck. At every game you've ever played. Even I could wipe the floor with you. I never wanted to say it before, but you're a lamer, a camper, and a spawn killer."

Eve gripped Steve's shoulder and gave him an incredulous stare.

Steve whispered into her ear, "Don't sweat it. It's gamer lingo. Very insulting." Steve stood at the edge of the chasm and shouted again. "Admit it, Buck. You could never beat me in a RTS . . . a FPS or a RPQ."

"RPG," Kevin shot back.

"Whatever. You suck at them all."

"Please," Kevin said, forgetting his situation. "You're, ugh . . . You're a newbie."

"Prove it," Steve said. "You check out now, and I'll tell everyone that I smoked you in a mano-e-mano death match using only the handguns."

Kevin's response was instant. He swung both legs up onto the rope with a burst of energy and began to pull himself across, grunting with exertion the entire way. When he reached the edge, Eve and Steve pulled him onto the ice. Their grip loosened and both fell back, landing on the ice. But Kevin was safe on the frozen surface. He rolled over onto his stomach, catching his breath, but still managed to speak between gulps of air. "You are . . . a . . . dead man . . . when we . . . get back . . . to civiliza-tion!"

Steve smiled. "How about, 'Thanks for inspiring my pudgy ass, Steve. I am forever in your debt and will let you win the next game, pro gratis.'"

Kevin smiled. "Thanks."

"You're welcome."

Eve sat up and looked across the ice. To her amazement, Brian was already half way across. She smacked Steve on the arm. "Get ready to pull Brian up. He's on his way across."

Steve's eyebrows furrowed and he sat up, looking at Brian on the rope. "I'll be damned."

Kevin sat up. "He's making us look like Girl Scouts."

"Speak for yourself," Steve said.

As Brian reached the halfway point, the loop of rope slipped up on the chunk of ice, pulled by Brian's weight. Brian paused. "What was that?"

"Nothing," Eve said. "Just keep moving."

Brian pulled himself twice more and the rope slipped again, hanging on near the top. Brian dropped a few more inches. "What's going on?"

"The rope's slipping off," Kevin said.

Eve saw that the rope was sliding at a steady pace. In seconds it would fall from the top of the ice and Brian would fall into the chasm. "Hold on tight, Brian. It's going to—"

The rope snapped from the ice, flinging small chunks into the air. Brian shouted out as he began falling straight down. As the rope slackened and became loose in his hands, Brian swung the rope around his wrist and tightened the loop just as the rope became taut again and his descent was transformed into a speedy arc, swinging towards the frozen wall.

Brian cried out in pain as he slammed into the frozen wall, which was as hard and unforgiving as concrete. His thigh throbbed with pain but the rope remained secure and his hands held tight, aided by the loop which was tight around his wrist. Brian dangled over the expanse kicking his feet, trying to spin and place his boots on the ice surface.

Eve's head poked over the top. "Can you climb up?"

"In gym class, I was one of the kids who never reached the top . . . I certainly can't do it now." Brian thumped against the wall, hitting the same bruised thigh he had just crushed. He cried out in pain and felt his grip loosen. "Just leave me be," Brian said. "I'm done."

"Shut up, Brian," Eve said over the edge in a similar voice that she had used to chew him out earlier. Brian closed his mouth and attempted to breathe through his nose and out through his mouth. A moment later he felt his body surge up, stop, the surge again. They were pulling him up!

Steve's hand reached over the top, grabbed onto Brian's fur-lined hood and yanked him up onto the ice. This time all four lay on the ice, panting, sucking in air like it was the last oxygen on the planet.

"I think we all deserve Christmas bonuses for that little trick," Steve said.

Brian smiled. "At least time and a half."

"Cheapskate."

Brian laughed, but then held his leg in pain, clenching his eyes shut. When he opened them again, his laughter stopped. It was a dramatic enough change to gain everyone's attention.

"What?" Eve said without moving.

"Above the gorge," Brian said.

Eve raised her head and looked up. Floating above the open crack in the ice, three feet up and four feet out was a solid black sphere with a single, red blinking light. She gasped.

"Oh, hell no," Steve said.

All four got to their feet. Eve took in the area. In front of them were the gorge and an alien black sphere that could manipulate weather. To the left and right was nothing but flat ice and behind them was a small rise, which they hoped would lead to the end of their journey—and Eddy. But even finding Eddy on the other side of the rise would not solve the current predicament; if anything it meant that he would die with them. But they had no choice. They had to run. They had to—

Before Eve could say a word, Steve began speaking. "All right you mechanical piece of crap. It's go time and you're going down."

Eve looked back at Steve. He had gathered the length of the rope, which was still looped around their side of the ice, and had tied the other end around his waist. "What are you doing?" Eve asked.

"Time for a little payback," Steve said. "For Paul and Nicole. I'm not gonna let this thing hurt anyone." Steve reached into his pocket and pulled out a large flathead screwdriver. Before anyone could say another word, Steve ran toward the edge and launched himself out over the gorge and tackled the black sphere like Superman stopping a locomotive. The black orb fell down below the edge of the gorge, but recovered, hovering a few feet below.

Eve peered over the edge and saw Steve clinging to the sphere with both legs and one hand, while his free hand was pounding the shell of the orb with the tip of the screw driver. Eve turned to Kevin and Brian. "Hold the rope! If that thing falls, we're going to need to pull him back up!"

Kevin, Eve, and Brian grabbed the rope and pulled up the slack, holding some of Steve's weight so he wouldn't have to. From inside the crevice they could here Steve spewing a slew of curses that would make some people faint.

Inside the gorge, Steve clung to the orb like a tree frog to a leaf. He wasn't letting go and he wasn't going down without a fight.

The sphere began to spin, slowly at first, but with each turn it began to gain speed. Steve continued his assault but had only managed to dull the screwdriver and scratch the surface of the sphere. Then he noticed an anomaly on the sphere's surface: the red light.

He swung at the light, realizing it was the only apparent weakness on the surface of the sphere. He swung once and missed. He swung again and the screwdriver glanced off the side. He raised his hand back and brought the screwdriver down with a ferocious roar. The tip of the screwdriver shattered the red light, plunged deep into the sphere's innards, and stuck there.

The sphere spun madly and whipped Steve out, away from the wall, causing him to lose his grip on the screwdriver. Steve was able to bring himself around, putting his feet out before slamming into the ice wall. His knees protested at the impact, but held strong and absorbed most of the shock. Below, the orb continued to spin, but it was falling. The sphere crackled and sparks flew from inside as its spinning slowed to a stop.

Steve reached the top in just under two minutes, but lay on the ice for five before lifting his head. Kevin and Brian were lying with him, catching their breath, but Eve was gone. Steve looked from side to side and didn't see her anywhere. Then he heard a voice from above. He couldn't make out the words, but recognized her voice.

"Where are you, Eve?" he shouted.

"Up here!" he heard her respond.

Steve looked up and saw Eve standing on top of the snowy rise. He held his hand over his eyes, blocking out the bright sun as it began its descent toward the horizon. "What are you doing?" he said.

"Get up here!" Eve said, but her voice conveyed more urgency than the words. Steve, Brian and Kevin all sat up and looked at Eve.

"What's up?" Steve said as he climbed to his feet.

"I see Eddy," Eve shouted back. "He's not alone."

CITADEL

25

THE OBELISK

Hobbling as best he could on weary legs, Eddy narrowed the distance between himself and a ruby obelisk, ten feet tall and two feet wide. He could see its surface gleaming like a polished gemstone in the sun; a treasure hunter's dream. He couldn't understand how it had never been seen before, or how it had managed to stay above the ice and snow for all these years; a question for another day at another time, which in the grand scheme of things was really only an insignificant distraction. Life and death hung in the balance now. Eddy refocused.

The four Ferox had appeared from the ice behind him and were now giving chase and closing the gap. Eddy had no recourse other than running. He kept his course straight, making a beeline for the obelisk, but what he'd do when he got there he had no idea. It seemed his gamble would not pay off. The others were nowhere in sight.

Maybe they had fallen victim to the elements. Or perhaps there were more than four Ferox after all. Or those black spheres, like the one that caused the storm back at the mammoth dig . . . maybe one of those—

Eddy pushed the images from his mind. They wouldn't help now. Eddy was twenty feet from the obelisk when his exhausted body gave up.

He fell to his knees and balanced on his hands, catching ragged breaths of air as best he could. The snow crunched behind him as the four Ferox, who still maintained their Inuit form, approached from behind.

"You've won," Eddy said.

Marutas stopped five feet from Eddy. He stood with confidence, while Reginn, Hoder, and Andari stood behind him, sporting maniacal grins.

"Was there ever really any doubt?" Marutas said. "But do not push my patience further. Give me your backpack now."

Eddy turned to Marutas and stood to his feet. He slid the backpack off his shoulders and held it in his hands. "All this . . . for one insignificant object."

"You have no idea the power of the insignificant object in your hands."

Eddy squinted. "It's just a key."

"While the object itself does little more than give one access to the Aeros transmitter placed on this planet thousands of years ago, as has been done to hundreds of planets across the cosmos, if that signal were to be sent . . . oh, the power. I would like to see your face when your Aeros 'saviors' returned to cleanse this planet of our presence. I wonder how long it would take you to realize how awful a mistake it was, calling for the Aeros to return."

Eddy smiled. "I understand the way you think. Your manipulations won't work on me."

"Indeed," Marutas said. "Your will is too strong. Truly, you are an adversary to be respected."

The other Ferox chuckled, finding amusement in Marutas's words.

Eddy realized he was little more than the butt of a Ferox joke. He held the backpack over his head. "You want it?"

Eddy turned and threw the backpack with all his strength. It soared through the air and disappeared into a deep crevice. "Go get it."

Marutas smiled wider. "The actions of a desperate man, attempting to cling to the last pitiful moments of his life." Marutas turned to Reginn. "Go get it."

Reginn strode toward the crevice and peered down. "It's deep," he said with a rough, monotone voice.

"Change for our friend, then," Marutas said.

Reginn nodded.

What Eddy saw next would alter the way he saw the world and universe forever. Reginn fell to his knees, but they were no longer knees; they transformed into massive two-toed feet equipped with raptor-like claws. His hands changed as well. His middle finger and ring fingers merged into one, while the index and pinky grew out, each wielding a razor sharp claw. His skin turned thick and gray and his clothing of furs pulled back, lining the top of his growing body. Reginn's torso became like that of a predatory cat, but twice the size of even a Siberian tiger. The furs retracted even further, becoming a flowing tuft of hair growing along the creature's spine. As the hair pulled away, it revealed powerful limbs, twitching with muscle, which were still humanoid in form, in that the musculature and fingered hands were similar . . . but it was not human, not in the least.

Reginn turned toward Eddy with a snarl, revealing row after row of gleaming white, razor-like teeth. On the sides of his face were lines of bony protrusions, piercing his skin from the inside and tearing out as they grew longer, like horns. But what were most striking were the three sets of red eyes, starting with a larger primary set and tapering up the long forehead. That each set moved independently of the others only added to the freakishness of the Reginn's new form. Wriggling behind the beast was a long tail, upon which a bundle of hair grew out like the tip of a painter's brush. The tail snapped back and forth like an agitated cat. In a blur, Reginn dove down into the crevice, using his sharp claws to scale the wall like some kind of awful spider.

Eddy's mouth was wide. "You *are* demons."

That got a laugh from Marutas. "You'd like to hope so, wouldn't you? Then dispatching us would be as easy as calling upon God to extricate us from your planet. But there is no global priest here to save you, and since we are beings of the physical world, even God himself cannot stop us."

Marutas held out a finger, which grew barbed and grey. He stepped toward Eddy, who made no effort to back away. "Now tilt your head back like a good boy and let me slit your throat. I'm thirsty."

"Stop!" a voice from behind Eddy called out.

Eddy spun around so quickly that it hurt his neck. He recognized the voice, though he couldn't believe it—Eve. His eyes widened as he saw Eve, Kevin, Brian, and Steve standing next to the obelisk. Nicole was missing and they all looked badly beaten, but they were alive, and Eddy felt regret for the fact that he was about to die.

"Ah," Marutas said as though he were welcoming more friends to a party. "You survived the spheres. Impressive. Futile, of course, but impressive."

"Get away from him," Eve said as she took a step forward.

Hoder and Andari moved out in either direction in an apparent effort to surround the newcomers.

"I'm afraid that your journey has come to an end," Marutas said.

A surge of motion caught everyone's attention as Reginn leapt out of the crevice in full Ferox form. He soared ten feet over the ice and landed on all fours next to Marutas, clutching Eddy's backpack in his dagger-teeth.

Eve stopped with a gasp and stepped back.

Brian held his hand over his lips.

Steve's eyes went wide.

While it was apparent that their situation was far worse than any of them had feared, Reginn's sudden appearance made Hoder and Andari pause in their advance. Reginn spat out the pack and transformed back into his Inuit form. The group was silent.

Marutas picked the backpack up off the ground and opened the top. He looked at Eddy. "You provided us with some much needed sport and for that, I thank you. But all good things must come to and end. And this is yours." Marutas shook the content of the pack out and it spilled out onto the ice: a wrench, lantern, canteen and some spare clothes. Marutas stared at the items on the ice, searching the pile over with his eyes.   He snarled and turned his head toward Eddy. "Where did you hide it, human?"

"I never had it," Eddy said, the beginning of a smirk on his face. "You've been outsmarted, Marutas."

"Where is the key? Tell me now or watch your friends die by my hand."

"Okay! Okay . . . I'll tell you where it is . . ."

Eve's forehead crinkled with concern. "Eddy, don't. It's our only leverage."

". . . But you're not going to like what I tell you."

Marutas looked confused.

Eddy turned to Kevin. "Kevin. Show him."

Kevin held the key up above his head, smiling wide. "Oldest trick in the book," he said. "Re-written by Eddy."

Marutas hissed, but Kevin was already placing the key in a depression which was identical in size and shape to the key. He slammed the key home and a loud *hum* filled the air. Then . . . nothing.

Marutas laughed. "You have done nothing more than power the citadel and open a door that has long since been buried. No signal will be sent and you will die just the same."

Eddy feared that this time Marutas was right. Nothing was happening. Nothing at all! Eddy rolled away from Marutas, fearing that his attack would come quick. When he turned around to face Marutas, he found himself facing four fully changed Ferox, bearing their fangs and extending their claws. This was going to be a bloodbath.

Steve and Kevin yanked Eddy to his feet as they backed away from the savage aliens whose purpose was clear. They were stopped by the cold surface of the obelisk against their backs. The Ferox advance was slowed as the ice began to shake, worse than any earthquake the coast of California had ever experienced. The ice began to split all around them. Hoder was the first to fall in, then Reginn. Andari scurried away, then jumped through the air like a wild gazelle. The ice he was meaning to land on fell away and Andari disappeared into the newly-formed gorge.

Marutas pushed forward. The unyielding resolve could be seen in all six of his ruby eyes, glowing like the embers of Hell. As he pushed down on the ice with his hind legs and lunged into the air, the ice beneath Eddy and the others lurched up into the sky. Marutas collided with a solid red wall, which was curved. As he fell down with the crumbling ice, he saw his prey being carried away atop a round platform, which was at the top of a tall tower. Marutas growled as he fell.

The Citadel was rising.

Eddy held on to the obelisk with every ounce of strength he had left. He couldn't see what was happening, but he felt his stomach twist as the tower defied gravity, rising high into the sky. The air became more biting as they shot higher and the wind pulled at his clothes. His bare arm was covered with goose bumps and his teeth began to chatter. Then the rumbling stopped and all he could hear was the whistle of cold air passing by his ears.

Eddy opened his eyes and loosed his grip on the obelisk. He did a quick check of his immediate surroundings, taking in every member of the team. Steve and Kevin were on either side. Brian was off to his left and beginning to dust snow from his chest. And Eve . . . where was Eve? Eddy stood and almost fell right back over. He had been in tall buildings before and was always amazed at how dizzy looking down made him feel, but now he was standing on top of something very tall, perhaps twenty stories, with no windows separating him from the air.

With wobbling hands, Eddy reached out and grasped the obelisk again, holding it tight. He took in the platform they were standing on. It was very small, perhaps six feet in diameter of flat space around the obelisk, which was a square foot the bottom and tapered toward the top, coming to a point like a classic Egyptian obelisk. Steve and Kevin clambered closer to the obelisk, afraid of what would happen should they lose their grip. Eddy looked at Brian, who was closer to the one side of the obelisk that was hidden from Eddy's view. "Brian, is Eve with you?"

Brian looked to his right. "No."

Eddy felt a lump grow in his throat. Eve was gone.

"Eve?" Eddy said and followed with a loud shout. "Eve!"

"I'm right here, Eddy," Eve's voice said from below. "No need to shout."

Eddy turned and saw Eve standing a few feet below the small platform. She stood on a wire mesh walkway which rounded the entire tower. If Eve weren't standing on it, he would never have seen it. "Eve, thank God. I thought you were dead."

Eddy lowered himself onto the wire mesh, which he found to be surprisingly firm beneath his feet. He looked into Eve's eyes and smiled. "I'm . . . I—" Eddy put his hand on her face and caressed her cheek. "I'm glad you're not dead."

Eve smiled. "Me, too."

What Eddy saw next took all his attention away from Eve. His mouth dropped open and he turned his face away from Eve's. Spread out before them was a massive structure, a ruby red city. There were several buildings within the citadel, all connected by a series of halls. Everything was red, except for the windows reflecting the sky, snow, and other buildings within the city. It looked as though it should be bustling with activity but was barren of life. The red material was unlike anything Eddy had seen before. It was hard like metal but not as cold, and its contours seemed stone-like, different than anything else on Earth. Several of the walls had grooved, wave-like designs along the bottom. Eddy recognized the patterned walls. He had scaled one not too long ago beneath the ice.

At the center of the massive city was a flat expanse. At the center of the expanse was a widening gap, as two flat doors opened and exposed their insides to the sky. Inside, Eddy saw what looked like a radio telescope. It looked different, fancier, like the Lamborghini of radio telescopes, but the basic design was the same. The doors clunked to a stop, but nothing else happened. The transmitter was dormant, waiting to be activated. Eddy was sure that was where they needed to go. They just need to find a way there.

"Hey, guys . . ."

Eddy turned toward Steve's voice. He was standing with Kevin and Brian on the mesh walkway. All three were looking at some sort of device imbedded in the tower wall.

"I think this is a door," Steve said.

Eddy walked behind Steve and saw a faint line in the wall, like the scratch of a razor blade. It was in the general shape of a door. The device next to the door looked like an inverted sculpture of a human face. The material inside glowed like sea-glass.

"I don't see a door handle," Brian said.

"Try pushing it in," Eve said.

Brian, Eddy, and Steve set to pushing at the door, while Kevin inspected the strange device off to the side.

Steve grunted with effort. "Don't just stand there, Buck, give us a hand."

Kevin waved him off and continued inspecting the inverted face.

Eve looked down and her face went slack. She rammed the door and pushed with the men. They all looked at her with questioning eyes.

"Our friends are back," she said.

Everyone looked down to see all four Ferox, in full bestial form, bounding up the side of the tower like rabid mutant squirrels. Everyone pushed harder, but the door did not budge.

Kevin looked at the pushing group. It was apparent that even with his help, the door was going nowhere. It occurred to him that the door had no hinges. It must slide open, he thought, like the doors in *Star Trek*. But how to open them? He looked down and saw the Ferox approaching. He could hear their breath, their growls of bloodlust. The team was running out of time.

Without another thought, Kevin placed his face into the depression and felt warm energy tickle his face. Through his closed eyes, he could saw bright white light move up and down, from forehead to chin and back again. The door whooshed open and Eddy, Eve, Brian, and Steve fell inside. Kevin stood in the doorway with a smile.

Steve was flustered. "How the hell did that happen?"

"Every door has a lock," Kevin said. "I just figured that in this case, the most logical choice for a key would be the human body."

Steve stood up and looked down, out the door. The Ferox were within twenty feet and closing fast. "That's great, Buck, really it is, but can you figure out some way to close the door?"

"Stand away from the door," Kevin said.

Everyone moved back as Kevin placed his face into a device just like the one outside which had unlocked and opened the door. *Whoosh!* The door slammed shut.

Steve walked to the door, sighing with relief. "I think this should hold them off." Steve tapped on the door twice with his knuckle.

Tink. Tink.

Whum!

The door was hammered from the outside. Steve fell back with a shout. The door was hit again and again, followed by muffled roars from the outside. The group backed away from the door and found themselves confined in a small cylindrical room, like the inside of a soda can. The only light came from a glowing golden circle on the wall opposite the door.

Steve turned to Kevin. "Okay, Buck. You're the sci-fi genius here. You got the door open. How do we get out of this room?"

"I have no idea," Kevin said with a shrug.

"How about we push the yellow button with an arrow pointing down?" Eddy said. Without waiting for an answer, Eddy pushed the button, which was at waist level directly across from the doorway.

Like a theme park ride, the floor beneath them shot down so fast that their feet left its surface for a moment. But soon they were safe, rocketing down the dark tunnel into an alien citadel. Eddy's stomach twisted as the descent continued. At least they were moving away from the Ferox, who continued their assault on the outer door. A roar, muffled by the door, echoed off the obsidian walls that surrounded them; Eddy felt like he was being swallowed by a fiery dragon. He only hoped the belly of the beast they were descending into would be more hospitable than the frozen wasteland outside.

26

THE CITADEL

The ceiling rose fifty feet above them to an arched point. Columns ran from floor to ceiling every ten feet like ribs, and in between each column was a window forty feet tall, which let the bright blue sky fill the hallway with daylight. The floor was tiled in varying shades of red and the walls and ceiling were constructed from a deep maroon metal. Eddy felt as though he were walking through the veins and sinews of some massive creature.

They had been walking for almost ten minutes, passing from hallway to hallway. They came across a series of compartments that looked like barracks, with row after row of enormous metal beds, ten feet tall and thirty feet long,—the beds of giants. Pressing forward, they continued on a course that Eddy hoped might take them toward the transmitter he saw from the top of the tower.

At the end of the hallway, which Eddy believed was at least the twentieth of its kind they had tried, was something they hadn't yet seen within the confines of the massive citadel: double doors with actual handles. But these were no ordinary doors; they spanned the entire distance between floor and ceiling, fifty feet tall. The handles, if that's what they were, looked to be six feet wide. The doors were a deep yellow and played in beautiful contrast to the ruddy walls. Eddy found it curious that a structure he believed served as a transmitting station was as massive and elaborately designed as a royal palace. The team stopped ten feet from the tall doors.

"Anybody got a ladder?" Steve asked. "I don't think we can reach those handles."

Everyone looked up at the large handles floating ten feet above their heads.

"I'm starting to think," Eve said, "that this place wasn't designed with just humans in mind."

"I would have to concur," Brian added. "It's possible that this structure is a kind of prefab dwelling created with a myriad of different corporeal species in mind. It could accommodate humans and a variety of other species."

"I have a different theory," Kevin said. "But you're not going to like it."

Everyone turned to Kevin. He stood next to another inverted face key, frequent among the many doorways.

"Let's hear it," Eddy said.

"Did you happen to notice what surrounded this structure?"

Everyone glanced at each other like clueless kids in a history class. Steve raised his hand.

"You don't need to raise your hand, Steve," Eve said with a snicker.

"Just being polite . . . Ah, walls. There was a pretty tall and thick wall that ran around the entire city."

"Bingo."

Steve stuck his tongue out at Eve.

"The only things out of place are these key mechanisms shaped like human faces. They look like they were installed after this structure was built. Their coloration is off and the materials they're built from are different from the walls. This structure wasn't built for human occupation; it's been modified so that human beings could open doors. The rooms full of gigantic beds and these enormous doors . . . it all leads to two conclusions."

Kevin looked into everyone's eyes, one at a time, making sure he had their attention. "This is a base, built for creatures much larger than human beings."

"And?"

"A base implies occupation," Kevin said then paused, letting the implications sink in. "If the Aeros return to rid our world of the Ferox, which I believe such an advanced race could accomplish from orbit, why do they have a heavily fortified base of operations placed in a region of the globe that is 100 percent inhospitable to human beings?"

Kevin scanned their eyes. "They don't plan on leaving."

Brian scratched his head.

"So you're saying the Aeros are just as bad as the Ferox?" Eddy said.

"No. I'm just saying it's a possibility . . . that the layout of this structure implies certain things that I find unsettling."

"What do you think we should do?" Eddy asked.

"At this point, I don't see that we have much choice. We know the Ferox are attempting to infiltrate the citadel. Maybe they have already. If we don't get help soon, we're all going to die in here. We should keep moving."

The men jumped as the doors rumbled to life. They stepped back as the golden door swung in, revealing a massive domed amphitheater. Eve took her face from the facial-key. "Let's stop jabbering then, and get a move on." Eve walked through the doors backward, without looking where she was headed. "And people think women talk a—"

Eve had turned around enough to see the new room and take in its massive size. She stopped walking and looked up at the ceiling, hundreds of feet above. "Oh . . . my . . . God."

☼   ☼   ☼   ☼   ☼

STANDING AT five hundred feet tall and more than three football fields in diameter, the alien amphitheater was a marvel of engineering and staggering ingenuity. Eve imagined that architects could spend a lifetime studying the internal support structures for such a creation. But the size of the place wasn't what was most striking. It was the domed ceiling which was separated into six sections, each a massive, arced triangle. And within each section was a magnificent mural which put the Sistine Chapel to shame. It would have taken Michelangelo and his assistants a thousand years to complete the images on the roof of the dome.

Eve couldn't make out the medium. It held the brilliance of fresh paint, but it was not paint. The images were so vivid that they were almost three dimensional, as though she could reach out and touch an alien civilization. Knowing they were still being pursued by creatures who'd like nothing better than to feast on their entrails, Eve lingered on each image for only a short period of time.

She saw images of a civilization. In the background was a city that looked much like the citadel they were now making their way through. Lounging around the city were thousands of creatures, whose true form she couldn't make out from the mass of individuals. She skipped ahead. The next image was much the same, only it had a darkness to it that she couldn't quite capture. The next image showed one creature becoming two: one she had never seen before, large and flowing . . . but she couldn't keep her eyes on that creature because the second held her attention so close—a Ferox.

She scanned the next images which depicted a war, an end to a war and a single image of the new alien creatures standing on top of what looked like planets. Eve was about to further scrutinize the images when her train of thought was interrupted.

"You guys getting any bad vibes about this place?" Steve asked.

Eve blinked and looked away from the ceiling. "It's beautiful."

"Depends on your definition of beauty," Steve said.

Eve raised her eyebrow and looked at Steve.

He smiled. "C'mon, Eve, use that feminine intuition and tell me what you see, aside from the pretty pictures."

Kevin, Brian, and Eddy had been listening to the conversation and at Steve's insistence to Eve that she look at something other than the ceiling, all looked down. Kevin's eyes went wide. "Whoa."

Eve looked out at the amphitheater and took it in, looking for whatever it was Steve had found. At the center was a large flat surface, like marble. Its single varying features were what looked like drainage grates in the floor. Surrounding the oval floor were a series of massive barred gates built into massive walls, three smaller gates on each of the long sides and two very tall doors, perhaps fifty feet tall on the ends. Above the walls were row after row of seats like oversized bleachers, though plush and more comfortable looking. Then she noticed something else—the place smelled new, sterile, as though it had never been used—as though it were waiting to be filled by an expectant audience ready to watch some kind of spectacle taking place in the arena below.

Steve grew impatient as Eve looked the amphitheater over. "Let me give you a hint," Steve said as he held out a clenched fist. He held his fist out and extended his thumb, which he then turned down.

Eve's eyes locked on Steve's fist. "Gladiators?"

"Or something like it," Kevin said. "Those grates in the floor suggest that some kind of liquid is being drained from the floor and those barred gates don't look very friendly."

"But this is an advanced civilization," Eve said.

"People said the same thing about the Romans," Brian added.

"I think it's safe to say," Eddy started, "that there is more to the Aeros than we expected. But these are alien creatures. We can't make any judgments based on assumptions. This whole place could be a giant swimming pool where they hold synchronized swimming matches, for all we know. The one thing we do know for sure is that the Ferox want us dead. I suggest we speculate later, if we live."

Eddy started the long trek around the alien coliseum and Eve walked with him. Everyone else followed close behind. "Eddy," she said. "What if Steve's right?"

"Sporting events similar to gladiatorial battles still happen today," Eddy said. "Even in our modern society. Bullfights in Spain, cowboy rodeos in the south, even cock fighting in Mexico are basically the same as the original gladiator matches. Animal versus animal. Man versus beast. Most societies on Earth have their own form of entertainment where life and death hangs in the balance."

"Even still," Eve said, "you can't deny that what we've seen since entering this . . . fortress is slighting disconcerting."

Eddy looked into Eve's eyes. "Actually, I find everything that's happened in the last three days extremely disconcerting. But I have yet to see an alternative. If the Aeros hold gladiatorial matches where one of them battles an animal, or maybe even a Ferox, fine. Far be it from me to judge an alien civilization."

"Could it be that the amazing Eddy Moore is missing the obvious?" Eve smiled at Eddy.

Eddy returned the smile and put his arm around Eve, pulling her close to him and squeezing her tight. "When this is all over, remind me to ask you on a date."

Eve's face flushed red, but she staved off the urge to act like a giddy little girl. He was probably joking, anyway. She was sure of it. Eddy had said that before, using it as a defensive weapon whenever she brought up a difficult subject. Eve pushed him away. "That's not going to work this time."

"What?"

"You're trying to get my hopes up, thinking it will distract me."

Eddy glanced at Eve. She caught the nervousness in his voice. "Get your hopes up?"

"Yes. You say that, thinking I'll get all giddy and stupid because the man I love has finally asked me out, then you shut me out again."

Eddy stopped in his tracks. His face fell flat. He looked sick, like he might throw up. "Say that one more time."

Eve ran through the sentence, looking for what had made Eddy react so strongly. When she heard the words inside her own head, she reacted just as strongly. But this wasn't the right time. This wasn't the right place. Standing on the cusp of some kind of alien coliseum while running from savage creatures was not how Eve had envisioned telling him how she felt. She decided to play it cool.

"See?" Eve said. "Two can play the distraction game."

Eddy face relaxed.

Was he relieved?

Eve pushed on. This was a subject for another time and place. "Tell me what you're afraid to say out loud," Eve said, knowing it would put Eddy in an awkward situation. Was she talking about love or aliens? Even she wasn't sure.

Eddy rolled his neck on his shoulders and ran his fingers through his wavy black hair. Steve, Brian, and Kevin stopped next to Eddy. "What's up?" Steve said.

"Eve was just making a valid point," Eddy said.

"I did?"

"You are right about everything."

"I was?"

Eddy nodded. "About what I didn't want to say . . ."

Eve felt a knot in her stomach; twisting, tightening. Having this nerv-ousness right now is ridiculous, Eve thought. This whole thing was silly. She had forced Eddy's hand, and now she would regret it. She'd be em-barrassed in front of the others and would be reduced to a blubbering emotional woman in their eyes. Still, she waited to hear his voice.

"What if the combatants of this arena are human?" Eddy asked. He raised an eyebrow at Eve, smiled, and walked on. The others followed him, discussing the possibilities of human combat in an alien arena, but she ignored most of it. She replayed Eddy's words in her mind.

Valid point . . .

Right about everything . . .

Everything including what? Eve's mind demanded to know.

Everything!

Eddy knew what she was really talking about. She had said the word.

Love.

Everything included love.

Eve ran to catch up with the others as they neared a new set of doors with an inverted human face next to it, but somehow her feet felt lighter and the concerns of the past few days seemed less painful. She had found love, and it was the most precious discovery of her career. Maybe.

27

STRATEGY

After leaving the coliseum, they stumbled upon a room which was different than all the rest for two reasons: First, its door was human-size, and second, the door was open. At the center of the room was a circular console built from emerald-colored steel. The only lighting in the room shone red from the floor along the curved walls. Eddy crept towards the console as the rest of the crew followed him into the room.

The surface of the green console was etched with intricate designs of wavy lines, just like the outer walls of the citadel buildings. Eddy searched the console for a screen or some kind of interface, but all he found was an imprint of a human hand. It was much like the inverted human faces they had used along the way, illuminated green glass; but the light from within was pulsating, beckoning.

Eddy held his hand out over the imprint and felt warmth from within every time it glowed. He lowered his hand so that it hovered inches above the imprint.

"Are we sure that's a good idea?" Brian asked.

Eddy turned his head toward Brian. "After all this, you want me to stop?"

"I'm just saying that we're all in this together and that it would be nice if you consulted us before making any more potentially life-threatening choices."

Eddy pulled his hand away and cocked his head to the side. "Life-threatening? We don't even know what this is going to do."

"Exactly my point," Brian said. "We don't know if this thing triggers a self destruct device . . . or—"

"Or it could just be an alien trash compactor," Eddy said. "You're right, we don't know, but there's only one way to find out."

"We've just begun to search this room."

"We don't have time to search."

"I thought you'd given up making rash decisions, Eddy."

"Would you like to be in charge?"

"Technically, I have been since the mammoth was raised from the ice."

"This isn't a mission to raise a mammoth! We're trying to stay alive!"

"If I recall correctly, that's what we were trying to do in Venezuela: stay alive. We all remember how that turned out."

Eddy stared into Brian's eyes as though to burrow a path straight through his skull. "You might be interested to know, Dr. Norwood, that the man who killed our team members in Venezuela was a Ferox."

Brian's forehead wrinkled. "Now you're just being preposterous."

"The man who killed our friends is now trying to finish the job." Eddy looked into everyone's eyes. They were listening. "I fought with Marutas before I reached the obelisk. He remembered me, knew my name. He changed his face and I'll never forget what he showed me. The man who killed our friends and spared my life was Marutas . . . a Ferox."

The others were stunned. Brian was unfazed. "Eddy, don't you think that's just a little too—"

"Brian," Eddy interrupted, his voice booming like a king's, "go to hell."

Eddy jammed his palm into the human hand imprint. A circle of light burst from the center of the console then faded. Eddy took his hand away and for a moment, nothing happened.

"You're lucky that didn't—"

"Welcome, friends," came a voice which was familiar but chilling to the bone.

Everyone turned toward the voice and took a step back. Eddy's vision was held by a shimmering object which floated in space. He'd seen it once before and knew exactly what it was: Artuke.

The holographic image of Artuke, still just a cloaked figure, continued, "I see your ranks have diminished since last we spoke. I am truly sorry for your loss, but the time to act is at hand."

"Artuke," Eddy said, stepping forward. "We are in your debt for providing this fortress for our protection and for calling the aid of the Aeros . . ."

Artuke's hooded head nodded.

"But we have some questions."

"Questions?" Artuke's voice was tinged with impatience.

"Yes. We've seen some things . . . A stadium, the large doors, a barracks . . . that suggest you have not told us everything there is to know about this structure and its purpose."

"You speak the truth, human."

Eddy didn't like the way Artuke used the word, human, as though it were somehow a demeaning insult. But perhaps it was simply a way of communicating to whom he was speaking. Eddy knew that sometimes body language or certain words that were used in early contact with certain tribes in the Amazon had resulted in unwelcome differences, and some people were killed as a result. Eddy was determined to be better then that.

"This citadel was built for many purposes. When it was left on your world, it was unknown if the Ferox would plague your civilization or not. Many scenarios are anticipated. At the height of Ferox occupation, a war would have been waged on your soil and the citadel would have served as our fortress while the Ferox were routed from your world. As for the size and scope of this citadel, the projected figure you see before you is merely a transmission of an image used to convey information. The Aeros are, in fact, much larger than human beings."

Eddy was still uncomfortable but the explanation made sense. "So the citadel won't be used by you now? There are four Ferox left on Earth. Destroying them should be an easy task for creatures of your advanced technology and stature." Eddy was making a play at the alien intelligence's ego, hoping it would garner him more information.

"This is true. Upon our arrival, the Ferox's physical threat would be neutralized . . . but you must understand; they have infected your society. The Aeros will remain on Earth until your species has been . . . cleansed."

"Cleansed?" Eddy said.

Before Artuke could speak another word, an alarm sounded, wailing through the structure.

"What's that?" Steve insisted.

"The outer perimeter has been breached. Internal sensors are detecting three . . . four Ferox entities."

"How did they get in?" Eve asked.

"The Ferox are infinitely crafty. They can find the chink in even the strongest armor. But we must not discuss this any longer. With you so close to reaching your goal, the Ferox will waste no time seeking you out and dispatching you."

A single drawer slid out of the console. Inserted in two depressions were two sets of rods which were attached in the middle. "Quickly, humans, remove the maps."

Eddy took one set of rods. Steve took the other. "These are maps?" Steve said.

"Pull the two rods apart," Artuke instructed.

Eddy pulled at the two rods and a thin mesh of clear material stretched out between the two rods. On the clear sheet was a very detailed internal map of the citadel. It was labeled in English.

"I have programmed the maps in your language so that they will be easily understood. We have stocked an armory with weapons suitable for human use. Follow the maps to the armory and prepare yourselves. Then you must activate the transmitter manually."

"Why can't we go straight to the transmitter?" Steve asked.

"You will be dead in three minutes," Artuke said with confidence. "The Ferox have undoubtedly picked up your scent. They have been heading for this location since entering the citadel."

"Now he tells us!" Steve said as he hustled toward the door, holding the map out in front of him.

Kevin, Brian, and Eve followed Steve to the door. Eddy took two steps toward the door and turned around to the image of Artuke. "If anything you have told us turns out to be a lie, I'll make sure this citadel is wiped off the face of the Earth."

"Understood, human. Do not fear. You are on the side of right, as are we."

Eddy headed out the door and turned left, following after the others. The image of Artuke faded away and the room was consumed by darkness.

☼   ☼   ☼   ☼   ☼

STANDING TALL on the roof of a short supply building, which was all but buried in snow, Sam gazed out at the white plains of snow, wondering what danger might lurk beneath and above the ice. The blue sky, that only an hour ago was thick with dark clouds spewing hordes of white flakes like an invading army, was now vacant. He hoped it was a sign of things to come.

After years of Arctic living, Sam had grown accustomed to the stinging air as it froze the skin, but the chill he now felt wasn't brought on by a drop in temperature; it was fear. Enough time had passed that mere technical malfunction could be ruled out. Eddy and his team hadn't checked in, and that usually meant people were dead. Mary had prepped the chopper and the weather was beginning to clear. They'd be flying north in just a few minutes, most likely to uncover the frozen remains of their friends.

This wouldn't be the first expedition lost to the Arctic, nor would it be the first Sam and Mary had the ominous pleasure of extricating from the ice. But this felt different to Sam. If it could happen to Eddy and his team, with all their experience and all their fancy equipment, than it could happen to anyone—even himself.

He had long felt that he and Mary were invulnerable to the bitter cold; that the land held a mutual respect with them . . . and he had seen that in Eddy, too. But now . . .

Sam's face contorted as a new thought slammed into his mind. It hadn't occurred to him before. Maybe the lack of communications had little to do with the Arctic or the weather. Sam realized that the scope of their excavation was expansive and the amount of money spent was extravagant within the field of science. They must have been expecting massive returns on the investment. Sam knew that Brian Norwood was a shrewd character and that spending money wasn't just fun, it was a means to a profit. Whatever they were after out there, in the ice, must be worth a fortune.

And where there was money to be had, thieves were never far behind; it was one of the reasons he and Mary hated going to the city. Sam held a cigar to his dry lips and sucked the smoke into his mouth, tasting the sweet burning flavors. Crime had finally reached the Arctic, but he knew it wouldn't linger, not under his watch. Sam flung a rifle over his shoulder and walked down the snow-covered roof.

The chopper sliced through the air above his head and came to a stop on what should have been a cleared helipad, but was merely a snow covered square. Sam held his hand in front of his eyes, protecting his face from the loose snow being whipped up by the chopper blades. The thrown snow felt like bullets against his cold skin and he remembered what it like dropping into the jungles of Vietnam. He only hoped he wouldn't find as many bodies on the other end.

Sam climbed into the chopper, gave Mary a quick peck on the cheek, and a thumbs up. Mary smiled and pulled the chopper up into the air. As the chopper turned north and rose into the sky, Sam felt the rifle firm in his hands and prayed he wouldn't have to use it.

☼   ☼   ☼   ☼   ☼

THE MATTE surface of the map displayed a crystal clear image of the citadel's layout, drawn out in glowing green lines like an architect's blueprint. It took them through three hallways which were all very short and slimly decorated, but the grand hall they had just entered was something different.

On one side was a series of tall doors; on the other side was a series of windows that looked out over the conglomeration of red buildings, the brilliant outer wall and the stark whiteness of the Artic ice.

Eddy took in the walls and ceilings. From the floor to about five feet up was the standard wavy pattern that seemed to be a prevalent Aeros design, like shutters on human houses. Between the windows were the same rib-like columns that led to the ceiling. But it was the coloration of the walls and columns that caught the eye most. They were textured, almost like marble, with varying shades of red, mixed with streaks of white, like a perfectly marbleized cut of steak. They were descending deeper into the beast, and Eddy wondered if they would live long enough to find their way out again.

Remembering the map, Eddy looked down and saw that it indicated an armory at the end of the massive hallway, which was cast in dramatic shadow. Where the light came through the windows, a perfect luminous window-shape cut through the darkness on the floor and opposite wall, but where there was no window, the hall was pitch black, as though the reflected light was being absorbed by the red surfaces. Eddy could see the end of the hallway now and saw a human-size pair of doors, next to which was an inverted human face lock and key system. Eddy's pace quickened.

"You'd think they would have put this stuff closer together," Steve said as he shuffled along, doing his best to keep up with the others. Even Brian, who was limping, seemed to have more speed than Steve, who'd been complaining of a brutal headache.

"The armory is just ahead," Eddy said.

"Good, cause I'm going to—"

A low growl echoed from the rear of the hallway and rippled past them, bouncing off the walls and growing in volume. The group turned around toward the noise and looked back, searching the light and dark portions of the lengthy hallway. Three hundred feet back, a figure emerged from the darkness, running into the light. Eddy recognized Hoder, still in his human form.

Hoder entered another portion of darkness and disappeared from view. Out of the darkness came another roar, this one filled with bloodlust and anger. Eddy began to back away, towards the armory and everyone followed. As Hoder spilled out into the light again, he was transformed into his true bestial self. He ran on all fours. His hair swung wildly down his back and from the tip of his thrashing tail. His jaw was set open, revealing his dagger-like teeth, and his six eyes were honed on them like heat-seeking missiles.

Steve shouted and made for the armory doors like an Olympic sprinter. He reached the lock first and thrust his face in. The doors whooshed open and Kevin ran in, followed by Eve, Brian, and Eddy. Steve ran to the door and was pulled in by Eddy. They fell back to the floor and looked up. Hoder had launched himself into the air and was about to cross the threshold into the room, where Eddy was sure he would tear them all limb from limb. The doors slammed shut just before Hoder reached it. The impact of Hoder hitting the outer doors was deafening, but the doors held tight. The door was struck again, but with less force. Hoder wouldn't be getting through. A third impact never came.

Eddy sighed and sat up with Steve lying in his lap. He looked down at Steve. "I thought you had a headache."

"My head hurts, but I like it attached," Steve said with a smile as he looked around the room. His eyes went wide. "Wow . . ."

Eddy looked around the room, which was rectangular and filled with rack after rack of weaponry. Towards the front of the room were weapons suitable to early man: spears, swords shields and axes; but looking deeper into the room, Eddy saw what he thought must be projectile weapons. The Aeros, ever the planners, had an armory full of weapons that spanned the entire evolution of mankind. Had the cavewoman, Haphnee, made it this far, she would have found weapons that made sense to her. He wasn't the only one who noticed.

"The range of weaponry spans the entire history of humankind," Brian said. "How could they possibly know that we would develop gun powder and projectile weapons based on a hand held, index finger trigger? We could have just as easily developed shoulder mounted laser cannons that are triggered by winking."

"I don't think so," Eddy said.

Brian looked at Eddy, waiting for his opinion.

Kevin spoke for him. "If everything we've learned is true, then what we know of modern warfare, from swords to ICBMs, are really the creations of the Ferox. The Aeros must have known how our weapons would develop because they've seen it all before. So they created an armory filled with weapons that would make sense to any stage of human development. They said that we're in the final stages of Ferox infection, on the road to self destruction . . . I imagine that there won't be much in here we don't recognize."

"Couldn't have said it better myself," Eddy said as he picked up a sheathed sword with an ornate handle. He drew it and held it in front of his eye. The metal reflected the yellow light which streamed from the floor at the edges of the room. The blade was slightly curved and razor sharp, like an ancient Japanese Katana blade. The metal was etched from base to tip with the familiar wavy line decoration.

"It's light," Eddy said, "And probably stronger than anything we know how to forge." He smiled. "Find whatever you're comfortable using and arm yourself. We need to get moving before the other Ferox arrive."

The group spread out around the room, picking up weapons, carefully selecting what they thought would provide them with the most protection. Eddy slung the sword over his back and found some light armor which reminded him of the ancient samurai, though he was sure that this armor could stop bullets if need be. He found two projectile weapons and attached one to each hip. He wasn't sure what they did and was afraid to try them out in such an enclosed space, but he was confident they were designed to kill Ferox and with the typical handgun design, he was hopeful that he could figure out how to fire them.

Eddy turned to the others, who had armed themselves similarly. "Everyone ready?"

Steve laughed as he looked at the group, dressed in various styles of armor and wielding strange and unusual weapons. "We look like the fricken' Lost Boys from *Peter Pan*."

Wham! The door shook with an impact from the outside.

"And there's Captain Hook," Kevin said. "Just in time."

The door was hit again, this time with a startling force. The doors were hit again and the seam in the middle was separated slightly. Eddy stepped back as a single claw wriggled its way in between the doors and pushed, opening a cavity large enough for the rest of Hoder's hand. The door protested as the grey clawed hand pushed, but it was now evident that the beast would soon be through the door, and the team was trapped inside.

28

DEVELOPMENTS

Eddy stretched the map out between his hands and scanned it with his eyes.

"What are we gonna do?" Steve said.

Kevin leaned over Eddy's shoulder. "He's almost in, Eddy. I don't think we have time to plan an escape route."

"This doesn't make sense," Eddy said as he looked at the armory layout. "This shows a back door to the armory, but—" Eddy looked at the back wall, where on the schematic, a door that led to a long narrow tunnel was shown. "I don't see anything there."

The door creaked as the metal began to give way. Hoder pulled his claws out of the newly formed hole, peered in with two red eyes and roared so loud that Eddy had to stifle the urge to cover his ears.

Eddy pounded toward the back of the room, where there were two racks of weapons. The first rack contained modern projectile weapons, like amalgams of crossbows and handguns. The other shelf contained weapons that Eddy couldn't begin to understand. Between the two racks was a seamless wall.

"Eddy, what are you doing?" Eve said, her voice overflowing with anxiety. "That thing is almost in. We need to fight it."

Eddy didn't hear a word she said. His mind was focused on the task at hand. "There's got to be a lever or some other kind of key. I don't see any seams for a door . . ."

Wham! Hoder hammered the door from the outside and the hole grew larger, bending inward. Hoder stuck his entire head through the hole and hissed at Steve, who backed away from the door, holding out a weapon, which he had no idea how to use or what it did.

Eve stood between Eddy and the wall. "Eddy, wake up. We need to make a stand and staring at this wall is not going to help."

"The schematic shows a door."

"There *is* no door," Eve said as she turned to the wall. "Look!"

Eve leaned back toward the wall, but kept on going. She fell straight through the wall like it wasn't even there.

"Whoa!" Steve said.

Wasting no time, Eddy ordered the others through. The group rushed through the door and into a tight hallway, which was more like an over-sized ventilation duct. Kevin stopped at the entrance next to Eddy. "You know where this goes?"

Eddy smiled. "I will when we get there."

They heard the metal doors being wrenched apart from the front of the room. They couldn't see what was happening, but it was evident that Hoder was moments away from infiltrating the room and discovering their escape route.

Kevin walked through the wall and Eddy followed close behind. The tiny hall was cramped and Eddy soon found himself crawling on his hands and knees, because running while being perpetually bent over became quickly uncomfortable and his weary body was close to calling it quits.

☼ ☼ ☼ ☼ ☼

THE ARMORY door gave way and buckled inward. Hoder burst into the room, roared, and whipped his head from side to side. His six eyes squinted when no attack came and no prey was seen fleeing. His sensitive nose took in the fragrant smells of human flesh; four men and one woman. They were so close . . . but where had they run?

Upon seeing the inside of the room, Hoder realized that he was lucky to be alive. He had barged in on a fully stocked armory. If the humans had any guts in them, Hoder thought, they would have made a stand here . . . and they might have succeeded. But they were cowards and they were running.

Hoder felt his mouth water. The chase was on. He knew that Marutas would want to be notified of their location, but he was so close, and what a victory it would be if he took them all alone! Marutas had failed to stop their leader when he had the chance. Hoder would not be so forgiving when he caught him. He imagined how delectable it would be as he cut open their midsections, spilling their guts. He would hold their flesh in his hands while they watched, and he would eat them alive.

Following the human scent to the back of the room, Hoder became puzzled. There was no other door, no escape. Where had the humans gone, and what kind of Aeros trick aided their escape? The Aeros were known for their trickery, and he knew there was more here than his eyes could tell him. Hoder closed his six eyes and breathed in the human scents, letting them tickle his nose. The scents entered his mind and transformed into an image, a haze of human stench that led . . . into the wall.

Hoder opened his eyes and reached out his massive arm toward the wall. His hand passed straight through the wall and he paused. Interesting. Hoder stuck his head through the opaque illusion of a wall, wary of a sneak attack. He took in the dimly lit corridor and saw no threat. He squeezed his body in and realized that if a sneak attack where to come, he would be hard-pressed to maneuver.

A shifting of light fifty feet ahead, where the tunnel made a sharp right, caught his attention. He focused his all of eyes on the location and saw through the darkness. His prey was still well within reach! They must have escaped the armory just as he had entered. Hoder transformed into his human Inuit form, bent down and surged into the tunnel. He was more vulnerable to attack, but he could catch his prey more quickly. He crawled down the tunnel, heartbeat quickening; he would soon be drinking the blood of his enemies.

☼   ☼   ☼   ☼   ☼

INKY BLACK swirled before his eyes.

He was awake.

The interface caught him up on thousands of years of history, jamming his mind full of information which may be pertinent to his mission. His head pounded with pain as the frigid waters supplied by the Arctic Ocean swirled away from around his body. He was weak; his consciousness was a swirl of chaotic thoughts, trying to separate new information from millions of dreams.

The tube of glass six feet thick slid open and he fell to the floor like a freshly cut evergreen. The room shook as his body struck the hard floor. Laying still, he let his mind wrap itself around the new situation, the one he had spent an eternity frozen to act out. He, like many others, had been left to wait for the inevitable, when the time would come to purge a land like an antibiotic waiting for the germ to show itself.

As the events of the past few days and the interactions the holographic unit had with the humans surfaced to the forefront of his mind, it became clear that his job might be one of the hardest yet. He pushed himself up, fighting gravity with his tree trunk-size arms. He got to his feet and was across the stasis lab in four steps. In his weakened state he wouldn't make it too far, but he had to be updated on the current situation. If he was awakened from his slumber, it was because any number of events happened, none of them good.

The internal sensors relayed the information to his cortex: Five humans had entered the complex. They had communications with the holo-unit and began to ask disturbing questions. The influence of the Ferox could be heard in their questions, and the system, designed for a single purpose, used a tactic that worked on nearly every race infected by the Ferox: fear. The doors had been opened and four Ferox had entered.

Acting as planned, the humans had sprung back into action and were making their way through the complex. But the Ferox had other plans. While some were indeed chasing down the human threat, others were headed elsewhere, which was why the system had been set off and the stasis chamber deactivated.

And so Artuke of the Aeros had been roused from his slumber.

Artuke stood and stretched his arms toward the ceiling, nearly touching it. It had been too long since he last did battle, but now the Ferox would again taste his might, and these humans, who he so graciously had attempted to save so many years ago, would be cleansed. Artuke took two steps and easily covered the distance to the tall door. He ducked under the door frame and headed out into the hallway.

☼   ☼   ☼   ☼   ☼

THE FLOOR of the tunnel became loose and noisy as the group pushed forward. Eddy imagined that they must be in a duct that ran over an empty space. The metal buckled every time Eddy placed a hand or knee down, and popped loudly back up as he moved forward. With five of them moving through the tunnel it was bound to attract attention, but there was no going back.

Eddy noticed something changing in the past few minutes. The noise had grown louder and the hairs on the back of his neck rose up. "Everybody stop!" Eddy whispered.

Everyone froze, but the noise continued.

"What's that?" Eve asked.

Eddy didn't have to look back to have his fears confirmed, and he didn't have time to answer. He knew Hoder was close. "Move!"

The group bounded through the tunnel like scrambling rats. The noise became almost unbearably loud, but the tunnel grew larger and allowed them to move more rapidly. Of course, this would allow Hoder to move faster as well. Eddy glanced over his shoulder and saw Hoder in his Inuit form enter the larger portion of the tunnel. As soon as Hoder had room, he transformed in one fluid motion without stopping into his Ferox form.

Eddy shouted and ran forward, bumping into Kevin, who toppled forward into Brian and so on until Eve was knocked forward, landing on the floor of the tunnel with a thud. The tunnel swayed back and forth, confirming Eddy's thoughts about it being suspended over an open area. A hiss brought Eddy's attention back to the creature approaching from behind. Hoder was only feet away and reaching out with his claws.

The sound of snapping metal stabbed through the air. Eddy felt the sudden pull of gravity and began sliding away from Hoder. The tunnel had snapped where Eve had fallen and bent to an angle leading down to a flat surface. The group slid down the smooth metal like it was a giant slide and spilled out of the other end.

Eddy was the last to scramble out of the metal tube, kicking his legs out like they were covered with hundreds of invisible insects. Eddy turned and looked back up the tunnel. Hoder was there, his eyes glowing red in the darkness of the tunnel. But he wasn't advancing. He was holding his distance, wary of an ambush at the end of the tunnel.

"Is he up there?" Steve said.

Eddy nodded. "But he's not budging."

"He's going to wait for us to leave," Kevin said. "We're armed with weapons he's obviously afraid of. If he tried to come down after us, he'd be at our mercy."

"What do you suggest?" Brian said. "That we go back up there after him? We can't very well just wait for him to grow impatient and come down so we can kill him."

"I don't know," Kevin said. "I just thought it might be important for you to know what he's thinking. Once he gets out in the open, he has us. In there, he doesn't have much of a defense."

"Which puts us nowhere," Brian said.

"That's it," Eve said with a huff. She pushed Eddy aside and looked up the vent shaft. Hoder hissed at her from the top. Eve sat up and removed a weapon from where she had attached it to the belt around her waist.

"What are you doing?" Eddy said.

Brian stepped back. "Do you even know what that thing does?"

"I will in a second." Eve leaned back down to the tunnel, aimed the weapon straight up and pulled the trigger. A crackle like thunder filled the air and shook the room. Eve squinted as a bolt of electricity shot out of the tip of her weapon, made contact with the metal vent and rocketed up towards Hoder.

She heard him shriek in agony as the glowing blue energy struck his body. He convulsed and pounded the sides of the shaft with his massive fists. The vent shook back and forth, swaying above their heads. Then it was over. Hoder slumped down and let out a slow sigh. He was dead.

Eve sat up and held the weapon up. "Lightning gun," she said, as though it were no big deal. The men stared at her in stunned silence.

"You realize that was very reckless," Brian said.

Eve ignored him, got to her feet, and looked around. "Looks like we're the main course."

"What?"

"We're in a dining room," Eve said.

Steve saw nothing but a flat surface. Above was a tall ceiling to which the ventilation shaft was attached, minus the portion which now descended to the floor at a forty-five degree angle. "Looks like a big empty room to me."

"And what do you think it is you're standing on?" Eve asked as she walked away.

"The floor," Steve said.

Eddy paused as he noticed an aberration in the floors surface, like part of the floor was missing. Eddy looked in the other direction. It was the same. "I think she's right."

Eve turned around and faced the men. "This isn't the floor, gentlemen. This is a table top."

Steve spun as he took in the size of the table and the view in either direction became clear. They were in an immense room and were standing on the surface of a table he imagined was the size of an aircraft carrier. Brian put his hand over his mouth. "Unbelievable."

"Anyone else get the feeling that these Aeros guys are huge?" Steve asked.

"If no one has any complaints about it," Kevin said, "I'd like to leave now. I don't feel very safe sitting on an alien dining room table after having been almost eaten by one. It just doesn't seem like a smart thing to do."

Bursting metal boomed from above and a body fell from a hole in the vent. Steve dove out of the way as Hoder's body fell the distance and landed on the table. As his body hit, the sounds of cracking bones and tearing flesh filled the air.

Steve stood, sucking air. "These bastards scare the crap out of me even when they're dead!" Steve kicked Hoder's chest, which triggered a release of air and a slight groan to escape his mouth, which was frozen open. Steve jumped back and tripped. Eve caught him and straightened him out.

Steve yanked his arms away from Eve. "Can we go now?"

Eddy nodded and walked toward the edge of the immense table, looking for a safe way down. It was twenty feet from the table top to the floor and jumping wasn't an option. The group fell in line behind Eddy, and Steve brought up the rear.

Steve rubbed his temples. "Damn, my head hurts. That better be the last time I need to run for my life today or I'm gonna lose my mind." Even as Steve said the words, he knew it wouldn't be the last time he'd be running for his life, not today. He knew there were three Ferox left and they wouldn't stop until they were all dead. Steve rubbed his temples harder and tried to wipe away the image of the six eyed creatures with the jaws of great white sharks. Steve chuckled and his head pounded. Well, he thought, it'd be a hell of a way to go.

29

ALONE

Following the map was an easy enough task, but covering the enormous distance and navigating over and around some monumental obstacles plagued their progress. Getting down from the giant table had been a trick, jumping eight feet to a chair top and scaling down the remaining twelve feet on a grooved portion of table leg had proven complicated, time consuming, and exhausting. Steve grew slower at every new cavernous room. Brian was limping and in obvious pain. The others were exhausted.

Eddy had been pushing them hard in an attempt to outrun the Ferox, even though he knew they could just as easily already be ahead of the team, just around the next corner, waiting to eviscerate their bodies. The thought kept him moving forward at a steady pace, but what motivated him slowed the others down. He noticed how wary they were of dark spaces and how slowly they moved through shady corridors.

Looking at his map, Eddy saw an opportunity to do something he knew would be met with resistance, especially from Eve, but was necessary nonetheless. He had to leave them behind. Eddy led them to the large room which was labeled "Staging Area" and was positioned on the opposite side of the giant coliseum through which they had originally entered. Eddy followed the distance between the staging area and the transmitter and imagined he could cover the distance in ten minutes, but with the group dragging on the way they were, it might take them another half hour, and that was far too long.

Eddy used the inverted human face lock and entered the staging area. The others followed. "Take a few minutes to rest," he said.

Steve plopped down on a human-size bench and held his head. Brian sat next to him and stretched his injured leg, grimacing in pain. Kevin rolled his neck and arched his back with a yawn. No one noticed the size or contents of the room. They were all too preoccupied with their discomfort to notice. Eddy headed for the door.

"Where are you going?" Eve asked.

Eddy stopped and turned around. Eve had her arms crossed defiantly, as though she knew what Eddy's next words were going to be.

"I just want to take a look around," he said.

Eve raised an unbelieving eyebrow.

Eddy sighed. "No offense, but you're slowing me down."

Eve's eyebrow rose even higher.

"Ugh, Eve, you know I don't mean you personally. Look, I can make better time on my own. You know I can. This is a secure room and we're not being followed. If the Ferox were to catch all of us out in the open, we'd be dead. Those of us who could run, wouldn't, because we'd want to help the others . . . right now, if we get caught, we die. Alone, I might stand a chance. We all might. I've already faced these guys by myself and I lived to tell about it. I'm going to—"

"You're right," Eve said.

"What?"

"That makes sense . . . but . . . just go." Eve turned towards the others. "I'll take care of the guys."

Eddy placed his hand on Eve's shoulder, spun her around, and looked into her deep brown eyes. "I'm going to come back. I promise."

Eve showed a slight smile, though Eddy thought it looked forced, fake. "I know you will."

Eddy's forehead wrinkled as he attempted to decipher what Eve was saying or thinking. He'd read somewhere that men and women communicate differently. When men said something, it was exactly what they meant. But with women it was a different story. If a man were asked, "Are you hungry?" it didn't necessarily mean that the woman was concerned whether or not he was actually hungry; they very well could be saying, "I'm hungry." It had never made sense to Eddy, how a question could really be a statement and vice versa, but he now wished he'd finished the book.

"We can talk about this when I get back."

Eve smiled the fake smile again and Eddy lost his patience.

"Dammit, Eve. If you've got something to say, then say it."

Eve placed her hand on Eddy's cheek. "Sorry." She kissed his other cheek. "I'm just worried . . . and we will talk about it when you get back."

Eddy stepped back into the hallway and the doors began to close.

"Be careful," Eve said with an honest smile.

Eddy smiled back and the doors closed.

"Where's he going?" Kevin asked.

"The transmitter."

Kevin's voice raised and octave and he grumbled, "Without us?"

Brian scratched the back of his head and let out a chuckle. "Just typical Eddy, hogging all the glory."

Eve snapped her attention to Brian and shot invisible laser beams through his head. "He's trying to save our lives. If we had stayed with him, all of us might have died. You're not moving very fast, Brian. He could've taken you with him so that when the Ferox are chasing you down, they'll catch the slow guy first. You ever stop to think that if they had found us again, you'd be the next to go? He's trying to save your life."

Brian pursed his lips and offered no defense. Eve looked away from Brian and squinted her eyes. She turned to Steve, "You still have a map?" Steve nodded, careful not to shake his head too hard, and pulled the map from his pocket and stretched it open. The map glowed to life, displaying glowing green lines and text in English.

"Where are we?" Eve asked.

With darting eyes, Steve took in the entire map, retraced some steps, then pointed to the map. "Staging area."

"For what?" Eve asked.

Steve shrugged. "Don't know. But the other end of this room looks to be connected to the arena floor at the base of the coliseum.

Eve shook her head as though in disbelief. "Well, that's not very comforting."

Kevin looked Eve in the eyes. "Why?"

Eve nodded with her head, motioning for them to look back into the room in which they sat. The staging area was full of racks similar to those of the armory, only the weapons that lined the walls of this room were more primitive. Swords, spears, shields, netting, and even tridents lined the walls. Mixed in with the mash of weaponry was an array of armors, from solid metal to wire mesh, and several ornate helmets. What Eve found most disturbing was that while the majority of this citadel was constructed for creatures of enormous size, this staging area was built for human beings.

Walking to the back of the room, Eve felt her legs growing weak with fear for what she might see. Then she saw what she had hoped wouldn't be there—a barred gate. They were standing in a room where human beings would be dressed and armed before entering the coliseum to do battle. Eve looked through the bars and saw the giant arena stretched out before her. It looked even bigger than before. She could only imagine the absolute terror someone might feel, looking through these bars at a race of giant aliens, preparing to do battle for their pleasure.

"This is not good," Kevin said as he stood next to her. "The implications of this room are ominous at best."

Eve nodded.

Kevin turned his gaze toward Eve and said, "We should find Eddy."

"No."

"Why the hell not?"

Eve turned to Kevin. "We don't know which way he went, and if the Ferox catch us out in the open, we'll never make it. The only way for all of us to survive is for us to stay put."

"Like kids lost in a grocery store?" Kevin asked.

Eve nodded.

"I hated being a kid . . . helpless."

Eve motioned to Steve and Brian, who tended to their wounds on the harsh bench. "We can't leave them behind. If the Ferox found them here, they wouldn't stand a chance. They need us."

Kevin nodded and looked back out at the arena. "I'll tell you, though; I seriously hope I never have to see this view from this perspective again."

Eve smiled the same fake smile she'd offered Eddy earlier. She felt a pain in her chest as a surge of anxiety rose up her spine and threatened to burst her mind. Come back, Eddy. Come back soon.

☼   ☼   ☼   ☼   ☼

FIVE MINUTES had passed and Eddy was halfway to his goal. He was moving quicker than he had with the group and was glad to be making good time, but his legs were beginning to burn. He had forgotten his earlier several-mile trek through the frozen wasteland outside and was beginning to feel a weight in his legs that had been masked by adrenaline and fear. But now he was just running, moving down endlessly long hallways of enormous scope. No one was chasing him. The fear of an excruciating death faded, and he felt like a marathon runner with no crowd to cheer him on.

He was beginning to sweat profusely and felt his thighs chafing beneath his layers of pants and thick thermals. It was much warmer inside the citadel. Not like the dry forced hot air of a house in the winter; more like the natural heat of a rain forest, though less humid. Then a strange thought struck him. His legs showed signs of wear and tear brought on by running against the will of gravity, but his lungs were fine. The burning that usually filled his chest while running long distance wasn't there and his thoughts were inexorably clear. The air . . . it was thick with oxygen. The atmosphere was being filled with oxygen, well beyond the needs of humans.

Eddy thought back to his summer internship when he'd met Eve and almost ended his career. That last question on the pop quiz. The easy question he knew the answer to and still knew the answer to: "What is one possible atmospheric change that could have theoretically wiped out the dinosaurs?" There were, in fact, several different answers but the one that made most sense to Eddy was lack of oxygen. Larger creatures such as dinosaurs required larger amounts of oxygen to support their massive bodies. For some reason, whether it was an asteroid impact that filled the atmosphere with carbon dioxide or the Ice Age that killed off much of the oxygen-producing plants, the dinosaurs ran out of oxygen to support their massive bodies. It was one of the reasons smaller mammals flourished in the wake of the thunder lizard's rule of the Earth.

An atmosphere this dense with oxygen told Eddy that the Aeros were indeed massive creatures. They'd need more oxygen to keep themselves alive. Without it, they'd asphyxiate; in theory, of course. They could breathe sulfuric acid just as easily. But he believed it was most likely that oxygen was a common denominator for life. Hopeful scientists had protested the idea for years, expecting to find life in the most inhospitable environments, but they weren't being practical. None of that mattered now, anyway. It was apparent that life in the universe was flourishing, oxygen dependant or not.

Eddy's feet slowed as he came to a dizzying revelation. The atmosphere was being modified. When they first entered the citadel he hadn't noticed the air. It felt normal. But in the past minutes it had grown thick, and Eddy had felt his energy level rise. But if the atmosphere was being adapted for Aeros anatomy . . . that would mean that the Aeros were there now; unless they were preparedness overachievers, believing that Eddy would be successful and the citadel would be prepped for their imminent return.

A noise in the atrium ahead made Eddy's slowing legs stop. It was a voice . . . feminine. Human. Eve.

Eddy picked up his pace and ran into the circular atrium which was the meeting place of four long red hallways. At the center of the room was a pool of water so deep that Eddy imagined it must be a direct opening to the ocean, a thought that was reinforced by the cool air swirling through the room. Eddy stopped at the entrance of the room and saw Eve standing on the other side of the pool of water.

She turned and faced Eddy when he entered. "Oh, Eddy!" Eve started around the wide pool, looking very concerned and frightened.

Eddy didn't budge. "What are you doing here?"

"It was awful . . ."

"Where are the others?"

Eve came around the bend, hobbling towards Eddy with a visible limp. It made Eddy cringe to see her injured and he wanted to do nothing but run to her and hold her tight, but his legs protested and remained glued to the floor.

"Eve, stop," Eddy said as he held out his hand. She slowed and looked at Eddy with a painfully twisted face. "Where are the others?"

Eve sobbed. "They're dead! The Ferox ate them alive. I couldn't watch! I ran . . . I'm so ashamed."

"How did you get in front of me?"

Eve looked confused. "I—I've been running this entire time . . . Have you noticed the change in oxygen? I could run for hours."

"You weren't followed?"

"I don't know! I didn't check! Oh, Eddy, hold me . . . please."

Eve held her arms out to Eddy, desperate for him to embrace her. Eddy stifled the urge to weep for his dead friends and hold Eve in his arms, but there were a few things he couldn't shake. He knew Eve. She would have died fighting with their friends. He would have, too. But she ran . . . It didn't make sense. Eddy gasped as he looked into Eve's crystal blue eyes. Blue eyes!

Eddy pulled what he knew was a lightning gun from its holster on his hip and got off a single shot that sent "Eve" jumping through the air like a gymnast on steroids. The lightning cracked through the air and struck a barren wall. Eve landed like a cat, twenty feet back. She brushed a clump of smoldering hair from her shoulder and casually clapped her hands. "Well played. I can see why she's so taken with you."

"You don't know anything about us," Eddy said with a sneer, offended that this beast would take Eve's form. It felt blasphemous.

"Ahh, but I do. You see, we've been following you, monitoring your progress. Really quite impressive."

"So you keep saying, but now there are only three of you left. I can't help but wonder why you continue missing the target."

"Ever the antagonist. Attempting to force my hand, draw me closer so you can use the weapons of our enemies against me."

"*Your* enemies," Eddy corrected.

Eve's form changed and became Marutas, the Inuit. Then he laughed. "Ignorance is bliss. You know, it was a Ferox who coined that phrase. You see, from our perspective, it is very humorous."

"I'm still not impressed."

"You will be."

Marutas strolled towards Eddy, who kept his weapon trained in Marutas's general direction. Eddy backed away, attempting to put himself on the side of the room he needed to be headed. If he needed to make a run for it, better it be in the right direction.

"You have noticed the atmosphere, haven't you?"

"It's thick with oxygen," Eddy said. "No doubt in preparation to support the large size of the Aeros."

Marutas smiled. "Your deductions are correct. The Aeros, while lacking in numbers, are massive creatures who use their size to impose their will on the universe."

"Just as you use savagery to impose yours."

"A technicality."

"You're wasting your time," Eddy said as he aimed the weapon. "You've shown yourselves to be a deceiver of worlds. What makes you think I would take your word?"

"A valid point," Marutas said, dropping his shoulders.

Marutas jumped into the air with incredible speed. Eddy paused as he witnessed Marutas human body disappear and reemerge as a hellborne beast. As Marutas's six red eyes zeroed in on Eddy's body and his body shifted to grab hold, Eddy dove forward, rolling beneath the razor claws and barrel chest. Eddy squeezed the trigger and a streak of electricity shot up, for a moment passing through Marutas's torso then streaking toward the roof.

The weapon malfunctioned with a burst of sparks and grew too hot in Eddy's hand to hold. He dropped the weapon to the floor and it shattered just as Marutas's giant form crashed down and slid into the wall. Wasting no time, Eddy pulled the sword from its sheath on his back and held it in his right hand. With his left hand, he drew the weapon holstered on his left side.

Marutas flipped over onto his feet and shook his body like a wet dog. A cloud of burnt hair fluttered to the floor and filled the room with an incredible stench. He hissed at Eddy and charged forward, ignoring any threat that Eddy's raised weapons might pose. Eddy pulled the trigger of the handgun and the force of the projectile that rocketed out from its muzzle threw Eddy's hand back. The weapon flew through the air and splashed into the pool of ocean water.

The thick netting caught Marutas in mid-air and yanked him back, tangling his limbs and pinning him to the floor. He ferociously clawed at the wires and began snapping through them. Eddy could see that Marutas would be free in mere moments and he was still wary of doing battle with the beast at close quarters, even while he was tangled up.

Eddy headed for the exit, running in the direction he knew the transmitter was located. He turned as he entered the hallway and shouted, "I can't see how your species has lasted so long. If the rest of the Ferox fight like you, it's a wonder you're not extinct!"

The roar that Marutas unleashed billowed down the hallways and made the hair on Eddy's neck stand on end, even though the fear he felt was subsiding. He had faced Marutas three times now and had escaped twice, relatively unscathed. Though with no ice to crack beneath Marutas's feet and no projectile weapons to fend the beast off at a safe distance, Eddy wasn't sure how their next encounter would turn out. He knew taunting Marutas would only enrage him more and perhaps even inspire him to escape from the netting sooner, but he felt the more Marutas gave into his feral side, the more Eddy might be able to outwit him. Eddy knew he needed every advantage. This was an uphill battle that began at the base of Mount Everest, and he still had a long way to climb before reaching the summit.

30

GLADIATORS

Twenty minutes. That's all it had been since Eddy left them in the Aeros staging area. Eve thought about how the Romans used their coliseum; humans battled beasts to the death in the early days, but the Roman populace soon became desensitized to human goring and animal slaughters. Men began to battle men; often, criminals or Christians were forced to square off against each other. She wondered who would be persecuted in this arena. Ferox sympathizers? Would they have to battle Ferox? Aeros? Or some other kind of alien creature they have yet to encounter? The prospects of the giant arena made her arms shake.

Eve squeezed her arms around her kneecaps in an effort to ease her twitching muscles. She was much warmer now, even after shedding her snow gear. The temperature had risen and the atmosphere had become thicker. It made their thick clothing uncomfortable and sticky. The four of them had stripped down to pants, T-shirts, and long john tops. All had taken their alien armor off as well.

"I feel like a kid who got locked in a department store over night," Steve said as he leaned against the wall next to the set of doors that led to the outer hallway. "Like I should be having fun, playing with all this stuff, but not able to shake the feeling that I'm going to get in trouble for being here."

Kevin nodded as he strode towards the back of the room, looking over the racks of weapons. "Or like someone is watching you?"

"Right, like through those little black domes that stick out of department store ceilings and you can't tell if there's a camera inside or not. I hate those things."

Brian grunted as he stretched his legs, standing next to the bench that had supported his weight for the last twenty minutes. "Though I prefer them to the hovering black death orbs."

Steve smirked. "Death orbs? It lacks your usual wordy descriptiveness, but I like it. You guys think someone is watching us now?"

Eve shook her head. "Being watched implies that someone is around to watch, and I haven't seen any Aeros around . . . and the Ferox, well, this place wasn't designed for them, so if there is a security system, I doubt they'd be able to access it."

A sound that reminded Eve of childhood came from the other side of the staging areas doors. It sounded like her first dog, Argus, sniffing at her bedroom door in the morning. She had always found the sound to be a pleasant greeting in the morning, but this time it caused her heart to slam in her chest, pumping blood audibly past her ears. She froze.

"What's wrong?" Steve asked in a hushed, very tense voice.

Eve stepped away from the doors and spoke, "Something's outside the door."

Everyone fell silent and listened.

"I don't hear anything," Steve said.

It came again, a light sniffing that ran up the center of the door along the seam where the two sides came together in the center. The sniffing was followed by a gentle scratching at the door.

"What if it's Eddy?" Steve said.

"Eddy wouldn't sniff the door!" Eve said with a look of frustration.

"He could be hurt," Steve added. "Just cause it sounds like sniffing doesn't make it sniffing. What if he's just sliding against the door? What if he's sniffling? Like, crying or something?"

"Steve," Eve said in an authoritative voice, "that is not Eddy. That is sniffing."

Steve's looked concerned. "What are we going to do?"

Kevin walked to the front of the room. "It may not know we're in here, but it can probably smell us," he whispered. "I think it will figure out that we're in here sooner or later. Right now we have the element of surprise on our side. I say we open the doors and hit it with everything we have."

"Sounds foolhardy to me," Brian said. "A plan almost worthy of Eddy."

Eve, Kevin, and Steve glared at Brian.

"If it wasn't for Eddy, we'd all be dead," Kevin said. "The only reason we've had any success is because we're not thinking the way we're pro-grammed to think. They're the most God awful things any of us has ever seen, and they scare the crap out of me. They know this and expect us to respond like any normal person should: with fear. Opening this door our-selves is the best chance we have. Whether Eddy is successful or not, we need to kill these Ferox before leaving this place, or we'll never be leav-ing at all."

Brian sighed and walked toward the door, drawing one of his alien weapons. "Fine."

The group gathered in front of the doors, each wielding a weapon they weren't sure how to operate. Steve walked to the imprint of a hu-man face and prepared to unlock the door by placing his face inside. "Ready?"

Eve nodded.

Kevin gave a thumbs up.

"Open it," Brian said. "Let's get this over with."

Steve thrust his face into the lock and when he heard the sound of the doors whooshing open, he jumped back and took aim through the open doors.

Eve gasped as the doors opened and the enormous Ferox spun around toward them, surprised. This creature, if given a chance, could kill them all with little effort. She was sure of it.

Kevin squeezed off the first shot and a net exploded from his gun, entangling the shocked Ferox. The beast fell to the floor and growled as it fought to untangle itself. Brian fired next and a spray of projectiles fired out and tore through the Ferox's thick hide. It howled in pain but continued to struggle. It wasn't enough.

Eve knew what her weapon did. She'd used it once before, quite successfully. She aimed her lightning gun and pulled the trigger. A blast of
energy ripped through the air and hit the floor next to the Ferox. Eve
kept the trigger pinned and adjusted her aim. The bolt struck the Ferox
and it writhed on the floor, but Eve felt the weapon growing hot. Her
instincts kicked in and her hands let go of the weapon. "It's too hot!"

The Ferox began to rise. Though it was still tangled in the mesh of
netting, it was apparent that it would soon attempt to kill them all once it
was free. Steve stood in the doorway, pulling the trigger on an oddly
shaped weapon. He was pointing it at the Ferox and pulling the trigger
over and over again.

"Look for a safety!" Kevin said.

"I did," Steve said as he continued pulling the trigger. "There's nothing on this thing but a little display screen with little things that keep
changing."

Kevin ran to Steve's side and looked at the weapon's display screen.
His eyes widened. "It's a countdown!" Kevin ran away from Steve,
deeper into the room. "Get rid of it!"

Steve tossed the weapon out into the hallway and it landed next to the
stunned Ferox. The group ran deeper into the room, hiding behind a row
of helmets and armor. Steve was the last to arrive and dove to the floor
just as the explosion ripped through the air.

The loud boom was followed by a shriek and a clatter of noise created
as the shockwave pounded into the staging area and threw dozens of
weapons in the air. Swords stabbed into the walls, spears chopped
through benches. A sword pierced a breastplate behind Eve and sliced
open her shoulder. She grunted, rolled forward, and held her arm in pain.

When the dust settled, the room resembled a pincushion. Eve looked
up and noticed that the gates to the arena had been blown open. A door
to the right that they had never seen before lay open. She felt a hand on
her shoulder and looked up to see Steve, looking very concerned.

"You okay?" he asked.

Eve grunted as she stood, still holding her shoulder. Her tan long-
john shirt became stained with blood. "I'll live," she said. "Though a few
stitches wouldn't hurt."

Eve noticed that Kevin was exploring the contents of the newly
opened room, and Brian was already in the hallway inspecting a purple

stain on the floor. Steve and Eve entered the hallway and looked down at the mass of violet blood mixed with bone fragments and tubules of what Eve thought must be Ferox intestine.

Steve chuckled, out of breath. "He definitely . . . didn't see . . . that coming."

"No," Brian said with an ominous tone, "but I think *he* will."

Eve turned to where Brian was looking and saw another Ferox charging towards them, perhaps fifty feet away. She realized then that it might be only seconds before she died.

☼   ☼   ☼   ☼   ☼

STEVE STARED at the doors in disbelief. When they had first entered the room, the doors had shut on their own, like a supermarket entrance; but this time after they had all run back inside, the doors remained unmoving and wide open. "Why aren't they closing?" he shouted.

"Move further back!" Brian said. "There must be some kind of sensor system that we're still tripping."

Steve and Brian moved back, but the doors remained fully ajar. Steve looked to his left as Eve walked between them, brandishing a sword. "Grab a weapon, guys. If we make a stand together we might be able to do this."

Steve frantically looked for a weapon and pulled a spear out of the wall. Brian returned with a club.

Steve returned to Eve's side, bracing for the impact he knew would round the corner any second now and take his head clean off his shoulders. "Where's Kevin?"

"No time! Just get—"

The roar came from behind them and they all turned in time to see a hulking object bearing down on them from the back of the room. They dove to the sides, avoiding the massive metal machine. "Look out!" Kevin's voice came, as the four wheeled vehicle built like a hummer and race car combined sped past and rammed the Ferox as it entered the doorway.

The Ferox was flung back out into the hall and slid against the wall on the other side. Kevin backed the vehicle up and stopped next to Steve. "Climb in! He's getting up!"

Steve jumped in the passenger's seat of the vehicle while Brian and Eve piled in the back where some kind of weapon had been mounted. Kevin eased what Steve concluded was the throttle and the vehicle moved back, away from the Ferox, who was now rousing itself from the floor, and straight out into the arena. Once in the open, Kevin slowed the vehicle, pushed a button and moved the throttle forward again. They zipped off forward, headed for the opposite end of the capacious arena.

Steve smiled. "Buck Rogers to the rescue!"

Kevin grinned, thoroughly pleased with himself.

"How did you figure out how to operate this thing so fast?"

"I've discovered that being an avid video gamer can come in handy. Sometimes I like to challenge myself by playing games without ever reading the instructions. Figuring out how to drive this isn't much different. Of course, all I know how to do is go forward, backward and stop. There are a lot of other buttons here—I have no clue what most of them do."

"Well let's figure that out later!" Steve said with a worried expression. "Right now, we need to haul ass!" Steve grabbed the throttle and pushed it forward. He was pinned back in his seat for a moment as the vehicle accelerated.

"What are you doing? I just figured out how to steer this thing!"

Steve jabbed over his head with his thumb, indicating that Kevin should look behind them. Kevin turned his head and glanced back. His eyes went wide and his hand eased the throttle further forward.

The Ferox still gaining on them, its hair swinging violently as it pursued them on all fours, its red eyes gleaming with sour hatred.

Steve took in the vehicle and their surroundings. It was obvious to him that the unfolding spectacle they were now a part of might be found entertaining to the civilization that built this monstrosity. He heard the crowd cheering as the puny humans ran for their lives, pursued by a creature that was sure to deliver a bloody death and bold spectacle. Steve felt that there was no escape for humanity now. It was becoming clearer and clearer that they might just be trading in one evil for another, like a smoker who starts drinking to make quitting easier. It was self-defeating. Either way, he ended up dead.

But Steve wasn't ready to die yet. He climbed into the back with Eve and Brian, who were busy holding on for dear life. Steve grabbed the handles on either side of the strange weapon and realized that this, too, was built for human hands. His index fingers reached out and felt two triggers. He pulled them.

Nothing.

Steve searched the cannon for some kind of power switch or safety and found none. He looked up and saw that the Ferox was still close behind, though not gaining as rapidly. Steve turned to Kevin, whose white knuckled fingers were clenched around the butterfly-shaped steering wheel. "Start hitting buttons!" Steve shouted over the thick wind stinging his cheeks. "One of them must activate this thing!"

Kevin looked back and saw Steve's hands on the cannon. He nodded and moved his right hand to a console covered in buttons which were marked in a language foreign to him. He pushed the first button and the vehicle started slowing down. He hit the button again and the car jolted forward. He pushed the next button and the car burst forward with the speed of a dragster. Kevin was squished in his seat and Steve gripped the cannon to keep from spilling out the back. Brian and Eve lurched toward the back, but being on the floor were in no danger of spilling out.

Glancing back, Steve saw that they were leaving the Ferox in the dust. He looked forward and saw the tall wall on the other side of the arena speeding towards them. "Turn!"

"I can't! We're moving too fast!"

"Then slow down!"

Kevin pushed the button again and the vehicle began to slow, but not fast enough.

"Hang on!" Kevin shouted as they approached the wall.

Brian and Eve braced themselves on the floor and Steve clung to the cannon like a baby baboon to its mother. Kevin yanked the wheel to the left and the vehicle turned. The metal body of the vehicle protested under the stress of the turn and its two left wheels lifted off the solid floor. The tires squealed almost loud enough to mask Steve's shout as his fingers loosened and he was tossed from the vehicle.

Feeling a rib crack as he hit the floor, Steve grunted in pain, but as he slid to a stop, he knew it was the least of his worries. The others had made the turn and were speeding off to his left, while directly ahead of him was the Ferox, bearing down on his position like a charging bull. Steve felt his hips. His weapons were gone. He reached into his pocket and pulled out a small jack-knife. He knew it wouldn't stop the Ferox, but he might get in a few good shots before dying—maybe even blind an eye or three.

Steve held the knife out in front of his body and braced for impact. It then occurred to him that the charging Ferox was moving at incredible speed, headed in a straight line. Steve felt the impervious wall behind him and caught his breath. When the Ferox came within fifteen feet, Steve dove to the side. He saw the Ferox bear down on the solid floor of the arena, attempting to stop, but the floor could not be pierced by its claws. A loud screech, like fingers on a chalkboard, echoed through the arena.

Steve clenched his teeth at the sound as he crawled further from the beast. He heard a loud *whump* and knew the creature had struck the wall. He looked back and saw the others, speeding toward the Ferox, who was already getting its bearings. The vehicle hit the Ferox and pounded it against the wall. It howled in pain and Steve heard some of its bones snap like branches. Steve was limping toward the vehicle when he saw the Ferox attempt to push the vehicle away. Kevin stepped on the gas and the Ferox howled again.

As Steve climbed into the back of the vehicle, smoke from the tires began to swirl in the air around him. He coughed at the acrid smell, but did his best to focus on what he knew he had to do. He grabbed the cannon and swiveled it around toward the wall, aiming it at the upper torso of the massive alien. "Push some more buttons!"

Kevin did, one after another, while keeping the throttle at full. Steve pulled the triggers after each consecutive button push.

Once. *Click, click.*

Twice. *Click, click.*

Thrice. *Click, click. Paft! Paft! Paft!*

Six darts like huge arrows fired from the cannon in rapid succession, each finding its way through the thick hide and sinews of the Ferox. It howled but was silenced as the fourth stake pierced its throat.

Kevin eased the vehicle back and they stared at the limp body of the Ferox as it hung on the wall, pinned by the six large arrows. Kevin, sucking in air, turned to Steve with a smile. "Nice shooting."

"See . . . Not everyone . . . has to play . . . video games . . . to be good at killing aliens," Steve sighed and caught his breath. Before he could relax, the ground shook. Steve paused, holding his breath, as did everyone else.

"Was that an explosion?" Brian asked.

"Maybe," Eve said.

Then the ground shook again, but not violently.

The shaking grew more intense and came in series. *Boom. Boom. Boom.*

Steve turned in the direction he thought the vibrations were originating and his eyes widened as he saw two large tentacle-like appendages grip the bars of the tall barred gate, one hundred yards to their right.

"Can someone please tell me what the hell that is?"

31

OPPOSITION

Eddy was sure that evil was lurking just behind him. As he ran, he glanced back over his shoulder with almost every step, almost tasting the stench of Marutas as he closed the distance. Realizing he couldn't outrun the monster, Eddy found a dark nook to hide in, drew his sword, and prepared to surprise the beast. He was sure that the Ferox would have perfected the art of the ambush, but he was also confident that Marutas wouldn't expect one puny human to be a problem. Of course, small forces defeating large armies by ambush had long been a successful tactic, and Marutas was most likely aware of that . . . perhaps had even led several himself over the years.

Eddy shook, realizing that he would soon be pitted in mortal battle with a creature as old as human civilization. Marutas was no doubt stronger, faster, and smarter than Eddy and every other human being on the planet. But Eddy remembered how far they had come. Perhaps the Ferox had become careless over the years. Without a challenge to keep their wits about them, maybe their instincts had dulled. Eddy hoped so. He was sure it was the only thing that had kept him alive thus far.

The sound of claws clacking on the solid floor drove Eddy's breath into his lungs where he held it. Eddy pushed his back into the cool wall, almost a relief from the thick, warm air. Sword at the ready, Eddy tensed his muscles and prepared to lunge forward. But before Eddy had his chance, the clacking claws slowed their advance and were replaced by an audible sniffing. Then the clacks stopped all together. There was a snort, then a laugh.

The clacks were replaced by the sound of clumping boots on the floor.

Marutas had retaken a human form only seconds before the alien fiend began to speak. "You continually astound me, Eddy. Really. Good for you. Making a stand here. Now. When you're so close to your goal."

Marutas paused.

Eddy imagined he was checking some of the other hiding places along the dimly lit hallway. His keen sense of smell told him that Eddy had stopped, but not exactly where he was hiding. Eddy's chest burned as he still held his breath. He knew he'd have to expose himself sooner or later, and hiding like a child wouldn't save him. He was best off showing no fear.

Eddy padded silently into the hallway and saw Marutas in his Inuit form, checking a darkened portion of the wall that was inset a few feet, like a park bench. Surprised at how slow the Ferox's reactions were, Eddy felt more prepared to fight this creature. "Over here," Eddy said, concealing his anxiety behind a calm voice.

Marutas turned to Eddy, hardly looking surprised by his sudden appearance or by the fact that Eddy held his sword out to his side, ready to do battle. Marutas opened his mouth to say something but the words were never uttered.

"No more talk," Eddy said.

Marutas nodded and started to morph into his alien form, growing in girth and bulging with gray, skin covered musculature. When his human eyes disappeared and his six fiery eyes began to emerge, Eddy raised his sword and bolted forward. He swung the sword down just as Marutas jumped away. The sword hit the floor with a clang and vibrated painfully in Eddy's hand. He wasn't so upset that he'd missed the mark as he was relieved he hadn't broken the blade.

Marutas leapt twenty feet and clung to a wall at the side of hallway. He turned his six eyes toward Eddy and hissed.

Eddy knelt down to one knee, keeping an eye on Marutas, and picked up a clump of newly cut hair. He held it up for Marutas to see. "Looks like you're getting slow." It was then Eddy noticed Marutas's labored breathing. Could it be that the thick atmosphere—necessary for the Aeros—hindered Marutas? In the frigid arctic air Marutas had been quicker and more powerful than any mountain cat, but inside the citadel he moved at almost human speeds, though his strength was still far superior. Eddy felt hopeful as he stood to his feet and raised his sword.

Soaring down from the wall, Marutas landed on the floor, took two leaps toward Eddy and began swinging with both hands full of razor sharp claws. Eddy felt like he was fighting eight men but was shocked to see that as he parried and blocked Marutas's incoming claws, he sustained no injuries. Eddy was sure that those claws were as strong as steel and that if they struck his flesh, he'd be torn open like a gutted fish . . . but they never made contact with his skin.

Marutas moved with a blur of attacks. Eddy blocked the first five swings, but six and seven made it past his defenses. His upper left thigh throbbed with bolts of pain as three claws tore open his thick pants and into his flesh. The sting was intense but not as bad as the shockwave of agony that pulsed through his body when one of Marutas's claws stabbed into his left bicep, rendering his arm all but useless.

On the defensive, Eddy backed away, heading in what he thought was the right direction. In desperation, Eddy thrust forward with the sword, a move that Marutas had not seen coming. Eddy had meant to push Marutas back but managed to slice the beast's right shoulder, and deep. Marutas reeled back and growled, staring at the wound and sucking in the thick air.

Leg hammering with pain as his feet hit the hard floor, Eddy ran for the end of the hallway, which turned to the right, and, Eddy hoped, straight to the Aeros transmitter. It was only seconds before Eddy heard the clacking of claws on floor and he knew he was being chased. But Marutas had slowed down, too. He could hear each footfall and could sense that Marutas wasn't moving anywhere near top speed. Eddy prayed it would be enough.

☼   ☼   ☼   ☼   ☼

KEVIN HAD dreamed of seeing things like this. In fact, this entire nightmare had been close to something more like a dream come true. Remove the human death toll, and this might very well be the most exciting time of his life. He saw the two large fingers grip the bars of the massive gate, just as Steve had. They where stark white, but had a kind of pinkish undertone. Their texture looked soft but Kevin imagined they'd be clammy to the touch. But the sensation that overwhelmed all others in Kevin's mind was the sheer size of the appendages . . . if that's what they turned out to be.

"I, um, I think we should get out of here," Steve said.

"He's right," Brian said. "Let's get the hell out of here. Now."

Kevin almost laughed to hear Brian lose his cover of intellectual snobbery and speak like a normal person. The size of this new creature frightened him more than even the Ferox. Couldn't he see how incredible this was? Couldn't any of them? This was an alien creature, never before seen by mankind. This was great!

"I don't think we're in any danger," Kevin said. "It's trapped behind that gate."

"Buck, you've been heroic n' everything, but now it's time to listen to Steve-O. Full throttle, out the way we came. Pronto."

Kevin smiled as he swung the vehicle in a long arc around the arena, putting some distance between them and the gated creature but allowing them a better view of it . . . and it of them. "You can't seriously mean you're not curious."

"Yes, I can," Steve said. "Everything we've discovered on this little trip has wanted to bury us in snow, eat us alive, or spill our guts onto the floor. I'm in no mood to find out what this thing wants."

"Look, it's obviously some kind of animal kept here for the games," Kevin said.

Eve raised an eyebrow. "And it's managed to survive ten thousand years? I'd hate to think that God created every other form of alien creature immortal."

Kevin sunk into his seat. "Good point." But he didn't turn towards the end of the arena they had come from, where the gates still lay blasted open. He stopped the car at the center of the arena and turned his head toward the gate. "C'mon," he said under his breath. "Give us just one look."

As though the creature had heard Kevin, it stepped forward into the light of the area. Kevin gasped as he saw its full body come into view behind the thick bars of the gate. It was massive, maybe forty-five feet tall. Its hands had three digits each but were built like elephant's trunks, perhaps even with the opposable grabbers at the ends. But it was the creature's face that was most amazing. It had two large black eyes that denoted intelligence and captured his attention. Below the eyes were three appendages, like the prickly fingers of a starfish, dangling over where he imagined a massive mouth must be. The creature loomed tall but stood with a hunch. Kevin scanned the creature's white, naked body, past what he thought must be genitals. What captured his gaze most were the giant's legs, which were built like tree trunks, broadening toward the bottom until they merged with gargantuan feet, each the size of a Buick.

The creature grabbed hold of the bars with both trunk-like hands and began to push. The gates gave way and spilled open.

Eve gripped Kevin's shoulder like a striking anaconda. "Kevin. We need to leave now."

"Why?" Kevin asked, even as he moved the throttle forward and spun around towards the blown out gates, which seemed to be very far away now.

"That creature must be Aeros," Brian said.

Kevin looked back at Eve with wide eyes. Steve looked petrified.

"My God," Kevin said as he looked back as the creature stepping into the arena, shaking the floor. "You're right."

Steve gripped Kevin's shoulder on top of Eve's hand. "Kev . . . in the future, you need to listen to me when I say it's time to go."

Kevin nodded.

"Umm," Brian started from the back, "I think now would be a good time to accelerate . . . he's coming up fast."

Kevin didn't bother to look back. He could tell by the frequency of the vibrations he felt in his seat that the creature was indeed moving quickly. He stomped the acceleration and made a beeline for the exit.

The shaking grew more violent as what they believed was an Aeros, one of the builders of this arena where men would be fighting for their lives, closed the gap. Kevin shouted as they plowed into the staging area at near full speed. They crashed through the room, running over weaponry and armor and slammed into the hallway. Kevin pulled back on the throttle and the vehicle slowed to a stop.

"What are you doing?" Steve asked as he looked back into the staging area.

"It can't fit through there," Kevin said with confidence. "We need to figure out where Eddy went."

"I still have the other map!" Steve said as he pulled it from his pocket. He opened it up and looked at the glowing green layout. "Take a right!"

Kevin twisted the steering wheel and slammed the throttle forward. They peeled out on the puddle of purple Ferox blood that remained smeared on the floor and disappeared down into a long dark hallway.

As the hum of their vehicle faded into the distance, it was replaced by the heavy sound of giant footsteps. A large white foot fell, splattering the Ferox blood. Moments later a second foot fell, twenty feet away, following the fleeing team.

☼　☼　☼　☼　☼

THE IMPACT came without warning. Eddy was tackled from the rear like a line backer had just caught him unaware behind the line of scrimmage. The hard floor slammed against his body and immense weight held him down. Eddy could smell the pungent vinegary odor of the beast as its crushing weight threatened to smother him. His sword was pinned between him and what he knew as Marutas.

Eddy exhaled and, as he attempted to suck in a breath, and found that his chest didn't have the strength to lift the crushing weight above. He felt his head fill with a painful pressure as his heartbeat pulsed rapidly, searching his bloodstream for more oxygen. What a cruel fate, Eddy thought, to die of lack of oxygen when the atmosphere was so thick with it. With his body melting into the solid floor, Eddy had one recourse. His right hand, which still had a firm grip on the sword's handle, was free and able to move.

Twist the sword so that the blade was up, then draw it out as far and as quick as he could sounded like a great plan, in theory. It would slice open his attacker and free him from the massive weight that pushed the air from his lungs. But there was one major flaw. Eddy had no idea which way to twist the sword; if he guessed wrong, he would slice open his own stomach and make his own death that much more excruciating. But he had no other choice.

Eddy twisted the weapon and felt the metal of the blade pressing down on him. He then realized that with this weight on the blade, even if the dull side was against his body, it still might cut him open. But as glimmering points of light began to dance in Eddy's vision, he knew it was now or never. Eddy squeezed the sword hand and yanked it out. He felt the metal slide across his stomach but felt only a slight sting. He wasn't sure if he had cut himself open that he'd even feel it at the moment, but a loud shriek told him that he had turned the blade in the right direction.

The weight lifted from Eddy's body and he sucked in one desperate breath after another. Eddy looked up to see Marutas clutch his chest and lurch away. He moved his large arm and hissed at Eddy after seeing a large gaping wound which chugged purple blood.

Eddy smiled. His plan had worked, but he was still too weak to escape. He looked at his stomach and saw a raw red line where the dull blade had rubbed away a few layers of skin, but that and a light-headed feeling was all the damage Eddy had sustained during the attack. His left arm pounded with pain but he was still alive and fighting. This alien savage had met its match!

Eddy regretted thinking the thought as soon as it entered his mind.

Marutas was on up on all fours, breathing heavily but headed straight for Eddy with death glowing in all six of his ruby eyes. Too winded and tired to move, Eddy did his best to hold the sword in front of his body—a mild threat at best. If only he had time to catch his breath.

Marutas, chest heaving, raised his razor talons, preparing to strike Eddy down. He paused and tilted his head. Eddy couldn't hear anything over the pulse of blood rushing through his mind, but the Ferox's superior ears heard something. Then Eddy heard it, too, a hum like an engine, growing louder.

Marutas turned toward the sound and Eddy used the distraction to scuttle away, moving as far from the Ferox leader as he could. The sound grew louder and Eddy knew it was an engine of some kind . . . but an engine to what? He could tell it was some type of vehicle, coming this way, but friend or foe he had no idea.

After climbing to his feet, Eddy took a peek over the crest of Marutas massive form and saw something that made a smile spread across his face. Charging towards him and Marutas was a vehicle, like a futuristic dune buggy, and in it were Eve, Kevin, Steve, and Brian! Eddy almost laughed out loud as Steve, manning some kind of cannon, unleashed a cloud of large darts which whistled through the air and stabbed the floor around Marutas. But the beast, though wounded, was still quick. Marutas jumped to the wall and scurried up, ducking into a carved out crevice which featured some kind of alien statue.

The vehicle screeched to a halt next to Eddy and Eve bounded out, grabbing Eddy's right arm. "Eddy! You're hurt!"

Eddy took Eve and squeezed her close to him, balancing his weight but enveloping her more than was necessary. "I'll live."

Eddy climbed into the back, aided by Steve and Brian.

"What is this thing?" Eddy asked.

Kevin looked back from the passenger's seat. "Long story. We'll tell you later."

"Fair enough," Eddy said.

"Which way?" Kevin asked.

"Straight ahead then right, maybe thirty yards . . . we're almost done with this mess."

Eve looked into Eddy's eyes with a look of disappointment. "I'm afraid it might not be that easy."

Eddy sat up straight. "Why not?"

Eve pointed back down the long, tall hallway. At the far end Eddy saw something that filled half the width and three quarters of the height of the open space. Eddy made no attempt to take in the rest of the hulking form. "What is it?"

"An Aeros," Brian said. "We think."

"Aeros?" Eddy looked confused. "Isn't that a good thing?" Even as he asked it, his heart told him it wasn't.

"No time to explain now," Eve said and turned to Kevin. "Just get us out of here."

The vehicle surged forward under Kevin's control and they rocketed down the hallway. A dark blur followed them close behind, clinging to the wall and moving fast. And even as they rounded the corner, the thrumming of colossal feet on the dense floor grew louder.

THE TRUTH

32

SHALL SET YOU FREE

The turn came so suddenly that no one even had time to brace for the impact. Kevin veered to the right, but the alien vehicle was moving so quickly that it slid sideways for thirty feet before careening into the solid red wall. The tires on the left side snapped free, and as the vehicle spun, the torn metal caught on the floor and spilled the vehicle on its side. Eddy and the others tumbled out like fish from a bucket.

Eddy struggled to his feet and scanned the area for any immediate danger. Finding none, he searched for a direction, a path to guide their way. A large set of double doors, sixty feet tall, loomed before him. Like a speck on the wall, one of the lock units shaped like a human face sat to the side of the doors. Eddy glanced at his crew; all were climbing to their feet—alive, for the moment.

After plunging his face into the lock mechanism, Eddy heard the giant locks clunk open and the doors began to slide to the sides, disappearing into the walls. Eddy ran to Eve, who was sitting on the floor, and helped her to her feet. "Let's go," Eddy said.

No one replied, but they all heard the message. The group hobbled through the doors and entered the new, cavernous room. Eddy paused as he gazed from side to side then looked up, following a massive structure which was built like a telescoping tube. At the top of the tall tube rested a gigantic dish, like a radio telescope. The room was several hundred feet in diameter, round and domed at the top. It was devoid of equipment, save the dish and a human-size console at its base. A rhythmic yellow glow caught Eddy's attention and he headed for the console, the others close behind.

When he reached the console, Eddy saw that the glow emanated from an imprint of a human hand, much like the one from the round room where Artuke had provided them with maps. This was it! This was the single moment for which so many of their friends had lost their lives. The Ferox evil was over and the Aeros would rule over a new era of peace on Earth. Eddy caught his breath when he heard his own internal monologue.

The Aeros would *rule*.

Knowing time was short, Eddy forced his doubts away and raised his palm over the hand shaped imprint. He began to lower it.

"Eddy, wait." It was Brian.

Eddy turned to Brian and waited for an explanation.

"I'm not so sure that's a good idea."

"You haven't been sure about a lot of things that have worked out," Eddy said.

"Yes, but this time we all agree with him," Eve said as she placed her hand on Eddy's and pulled it away from the imprint.

"I don't understand."

"I don't have all the answers," Eve said. "But I know that there is more to these Aeros than we've been told."

"You're right," said a human voice that was both familiar and shocking.

Eddy spun to see the hologram of the hooded figure, Artuke, standing among them like he was really there. But this time he removed his hood and smiled at them with kind eyes. His hair was short and his face clean shaven. His teeth were brilliant and his cobalt eyes were bright. He was a supermodel and five star general rolled into one. Eddy instantly distrusted him.

"There is much you haven't been told because it would only confuse you. But please, there is little time. You must activate the transmitter."

"I'd like some answers first," Eddy said.

"The remaining Ferox is closing in on this position."

Eddy crossed his arms. "I'm afraid I'm going to have to insist."

Artuke remained silent.

"Let's start with the coliseum," Eddy said.

The hologram of Artuke paced as he said, "You must understand that your people have been infected by the Ferox for almost a full term. You are corrupted, some beyond salvation. Many are so corrupted that they will fight against us in defense of the Ferox way of life."

"Which is what, exactly?"

Artuke paused and turned to Eddy. "Chaos."

Eddy nodded. "I have seen the Ferox for what they are and I know that they are evil. But I don't know anything about you. The coliseum looks as though it was designed to house human combatants."

"That's because it was," the voice of Marutas sounded out from twenty feet away as he approached in his Inuit form.

Eddy clustered with his crew and held his hand over the yellow hand print. "Move another inch and I'll activate this thing."

Marutas paused then smiled. "You may find the goals of my people to be evil, human, but what we have given the human race is a gift."

"Do not listen to his lies," Artuke said with a loud voice. "He will corrupt you further."

Eddy's mind spun with the possible scenarios that played out in his head. Marutas would kill them once Eddy was clear of the transmitter, but he was beginning to trust the Aeros as much as he trusted Marutas. Then Eddy realized the truth. With his hand hovering over the button, so to speak, he held all the control. He could sway the battle in either direction by putting his hand down or pulling it up. There was only one thing he wanted to do with that power: get some answers.

"Let him speak," Eddy said to Artuke, but the tone of his voice revealed it was more of a command than a request.

Marutas smiled. "What the Aeros don't want you to know is that we, the Ferox, and they, the Aeros, were once one and the same. Millions of years ago our single race divided into two. Those of us who chose free will were cast out, banished to the far reaches of our galaxy. We evolved in new and hostile environments, while they evolved on our oxygen-rich home world. Our single crime was choosing free will over collective thinking and they damned us for it. The Aeros created the Ferox, but we still share the same blood."

"You corrupted our civilization!" Artuke blurted out.

"*Our* civilization," Marutas returned with a cold glare.

"History lessons aside, your past gives you no right to bring your twisted version of free will to our planet," Eddy said.

Marutas sighed. "Can't you see the truth yet, Eddy Moore? A species such as yours cannot be taught the ways of war in an instant. You must learn over time."

Eddy furrowed his eyebrows and opened his mouth to speak, but Kevin had put together the pieces first.

"You're raising the human race to be soldiers," Kevin said with a blank stare.

"Indeed."

Artuke stood between Eddy and Marutas. "They are corrupting your species, and the Ferox influence must be routed out of you before they can culminate their plans. Listen to me. Your planet *will* be destroyed."

"But not by the Ferox," Eve said, stepping forward. "The Aeros will destroy our planet."

"If you join the ranks of the Ferox military," Artuke said. "You will have left us no choice. Please understand, your people need to begin anew."

Steve leaned against the console and spoke, "And now, if we call the Aeros back . . . you're going to take over, enslave the human race, and kill everyone you feel is 'corrupt.' And some you'll even make fight for your entertainment . . . battling Ferox, maybe even other corrupted species. You guys are pricks."

"Watch how you address me, human!" Artuke's outburst caught everyone off guard.

"Eddy," Marutas said. "I have given you the truth. We are using your race, we are corrupting you, but it is to strike back at our own oppressors! If we have taught you anything, it is that creatures like the Aeros are the most evil of all! My people have been chased throughout the universe for millennia and have suffered greatly in the wake of their genetic cleansing."

"There must have been another way for you to fight back!" Eddy said angrily.

"Every emotion you have coursing through your veins comes from the Ferox. What they wish to cleanse from this planet is inside every one of you! The free will to choose freedom! To fight, no matter what the cost, against those that oppress you! We have molded this world to take offense at what the Aeros are doing!" Marutas stated, as though giving a rousing state of the union address, which Eddy was sure he had done in the past.

"But you've killed millions upon millions of human beings!" As Eddy spoke he felt the floor vibrate.

"A necessary evil . . . that is what my race has become, for without our influence, our absolute corruptive nature, your race and others like you would never learn to feel our plight—to understand."

Eddy's mind was a cauldron of chaos. He felt dirty as he began to understand what Marutas was saying. If it was all true—and he was beginning to believe it was, because Artuke was no longer arguing—then was Marutas in the right? If humanity was given the choice to be exterminated, or, through the corruption of others, survive and perhaps even win, would they choose to corrupt? Eddy believed they would . . . but that was only because humans were evolved to think so. What would the human race have been without Ferox intervention? Peace loving, simpleminded creatures who still lived off the land, or more like the Aeros? The possibilities were mind boggling, but Eddy's loyalty was to the human race as it was, whether human evolution had been influenced or not.

The Ferox were using humanity and other races in an attempt to fight the Aeros, who were oppressing them, killing them, simply for thinking for themselves—free will. Throughout time, humanity had considered free will the ultimate gift. When God wanted to show Adam and Eve that he loved them, he granted them free will, the ultimate gift, because it gave those first humans the choice to love or not love God. Forced love was no love at all. Could the same be applied to the Ferox? Were the Ferox the creatures who gave mankind an understanding of the gift of free will? Did the Ferox love humanity?

Eddy was shaken from his thoughts as the floor shuddered beneath his feet. He was surprised by the silence that followed.

"Activate the transmitter, human." Artuke stood in front of Eddy, glaring. "Activate it now."

Eddy shook his head. "I choose not to."

"You have made a foolish mistake to ally yourself with the Ferox threat. When the Aeros return it will not be to cleanse you but to destroy your species. You are corrupt beyond redemption."

"I think that's for us to decide," Eddy said. "You're not going to be our judge, jury, and executioner."

"On the contrary, human . . . I will be." Artuke looked up towards the door and smiled. "It is time that we meet face to face." Artuke raised his hand toward the door.

Eddy followed Artuke's human hand toward the door and looked into the large black eyes of the hulking creature he had only glimpsed back in the hallway. Its shadow fell over the group like a black cloud. Eddy knew they were in real trouble. The Ferox were one thing; at least they could be fought in a conventional sense, but this thing was enormous. One step and the entire group could be rendered nothing more than a stain on the floor.

The hologram continued to speak. "I give you my true form, which has remained in stasis for thousands of years, chilled by the Artic waters, waiting to awaken to the day when I might aid humanity in the glorious duty of purging the Ferox. But I have discovered humanity to be a lost cause. I will begin the cleansing immediately. Starting with you."

33

WAGING WAR

"Move!" Eddy's voice cracked as he screamed the order.

The group scattered as Artuke's gigantic, white, two-toed foot slammed down on the hard floor. Eddy toppled forward, knocked off his feet by the earthquake-like explosion of energy. His thoughts were not on his own mortality but the lives of the others. Eddy spun around and found Eve heading for the opposite wall, and Kevin and Steve hobbling away together toward the massive doors.

Brian was missing. He was nowhere to be seen. Eddy's eyes searched the massive room frantically but found nothing. A slurping sound struck Eddy's ears as he looked back toward Artuke, lifting his foot, preparing for another attack. There on the floor was a limp and flattened body. Eddy saw what was left of Brian's crushed face and felt a sour taste rise in his throat. The soft innards of Brian's pulverized body were a mass of twisted and crushed flesh, indiscernible as individual organs.

A shadow fell over Eddy and he looked up. A large white heel descended toward his head. Eddy closed his eyes and accepted his fate, which would be the same as Brian's. The power of the impact was immense, but far less than Eddy had imagined it would be. Then, as Eddy expected death would come, followed by some kind of afterlife experience, he felt the wind. He heard the whoosh of air past his ears. Heaven was a windy place. He opened his eyes for a better look and screamed with horror upon seeing three luminous red eyes glaring back at him. He was in hell!

Eddy felt foolish as he realized he was being carried by Marutas in his Ferox form. He'd fought this creature so fiercely only minutes ago and was now screaming like a frightened monkey staring down a tiger. But what was most amazing about this new development was that Marutas, who had been fiendishly and unrelentingly trying to kill Eddy, had saved his life!

Eddy felt the floor sink away as he was pulled up the wall. He turned and saw the three-fingered, squid-like hand of Artuke reaching out for them as they climbed higher on the wall. He was yanked up as Artuke's tendrils pounded the wall just below his dangling feet.

Then he was hauled to the side and into darkness. He saw the light of the room fade away as he was dragged down a lightless tunnel. The dark eye of Artuke peered at him from the hole, but then moved away. The walls vibrated as his massive form pounded the floor, probably pursuing the others.

All motion stopped and Eddy was alone with the six red eyes. The eyes faded away and Eddy was greeted by a human voice. "Are you alive?"

"Yes," Eddy said. "Thank you." There was no reply as he sat up. "Why did you save me?"

"I saw in your eyes . . . understanding. The human race is nearing a time when the Ferox will reveal ourselves, our plight, and ask for the aid of the human race."

"Conveniently leaving out the part about how you've evolved us into people sympathetic to the Ferox war."

"You speak the truth, but I saw in your eyes that you understand. Your heart, at its core, beats to the Ferox drum."

"You're forgetting something," Eddy said in the darkness. "Free will. What if the human race turns you down?"

"That . . . has never happened," Marutas said.

"You've succeeded on so many levels. I do understand the horrors of genetic cleansing. What the Aeros have done and are doing enrages me, as it will most people on Earth. But, given the choice, given true free will, I would choose to take no part in your war. You have corrupted our race. You have committed unspeakable crimes against humanity. You are no better than the Aeros."

Silence enveloped the dark tube. Eddy held his breath, expecting to see the red eyes reemerge before his head was bit off. But nothing happened. Eddy listened; he couldn't even hear Marutas's breath. It was then that Eddy realized he was alone. Marutas was gone.

☼   ☼   ☼   ☼   ☼

IT TOOK Eddy five minutes to crawl back to the opening where he and Marutas had entered the tunnel. It was a circular hole five feet in diameter, most likely for ventilation, Eddy thought. He looked down and saw that he was thirty feet above the floor. A pattern of wavy lines were carved into the wall as they were in most rooms and Eddy felt a wave of relief. He'd used these markings to scale a wall before, fleeing from Marutas in the ice cave. He knew he could get down if he had to, but he wasn't so sure that was a good idea at the moment.

Standing tall on the other side of the room was Artuke, bending over what Eddy thought must be Brian's remains. But what was he doing? Eddy could see that Artuke was probing the area with his trunk-like fingers, but what could he be after? Eddy saw something that made him gasp. From such a distance it was hard to be sure, but he thought he saw Artuke's gigantic fingers pick up a human hand. Brian's hand.

Artuke took two steps and was at the console where the imprint of a human hand still glowed yellow. The severed hand was placed on the imprint, and the room came to life. The roof clacked loudly as it split in the middle and began to peel away in either direction. The telescopic pole which held the massive dish began to slide up toward the ceiling. Eddy felt a lump solidify in his throat and he climbed down the wall, acting on pure instinct, knowing he had to stop a message from being sent but not sure how to do so.

As Eddy reached the bottom, the roof made a resounding clunk as it finished opening. The dish neared the opening as Eddy made a dash for the transmitter's massive base. The giant Aeros, with his back turned to Eddy, stiffened as if sensing a presence. Eddy froze in his tracks.

With a speed impressive for such a grand creature, Artuke spun around and glared at Eddy. They were a hundred feet apart, but Eddy knew Artuke could cover the distance in just a few steps. His only chance was to find cover or outmaneuver the massive and hopefully clumsy behemoth. With all the speed Eddy could muster, he bolted around the outer circumference of the transmitter's base. Artuke was close on his heels, but, as Eddy had hoped, could not take the turn at high speed.

Rounding the base of the transmitter, Eddy took the chance to inspect its inner workings. He saw tubes and wires, the function of which he could only guess. He was sure the telescoping arm worked on a hydraulic system but wasn't sure how he could disrupt its rising. A sound above his head caused him to look up. He saw that the dish was now high above the roof and turning toward a point in the sky. Eddy knew the signal would be sent at any moment.

The floor beneath Eddy's feet shook like an erupting volcano, tossing Eddy forward. He hit the floor hard on his elbows and grunted. He rolled over and saw Artuke lumbering his way, a look of pure hatred in his glossy black eyes. A noise like bursts of compressed air sounded in the distance, followed by a light grunt from the massive Artuke. The low sound vibrated through Eddy's body and he was glad that the giant hadn't screamed; it might have liquidated his body. Artuke reached for his shoulder and pulled out two small arrows; though Eddy knew they were only pin pricks to the beast, they had at least bought him some time.

"Eddy! Run!" The voice was far away, but he recognized it as Eve's. He glanced toward the massive open doorway, and saw Eve, Kevin, and Steve standing on the back side of the broken down alien vehicle. They'd been clever enough to right the thing, wheel it all the way into the room, and shoot Artuke in the shoulder just in time. Thank God for them, Eddy thought as he got to his feet.

But Eddy stopped short as Marutas landed in front of him in Ferox form then morphed into his Inuit self. He was wielding a sword and what Eddy recognized as one of the lightning guns. Marutas held the sword out to Eddy. "See what you can do about that," Marutas said as he glanced up at the large dish, which was still rotating.

Before Eddy could respond, Marutas changed back into his Ferox form, leapt over Eddy's head, and charged towards Artuke. But the giant saw him coming and raised a fist to crush Marutas.

Paft!

A blur shot across the room and a booming wail reverberated through the room as Artuke shouted in pain. Eddy looked up as he covered his ears, which would be ringing for weeks, and saw Artuke clutching his left eye.

Good shot, guys!

Eddy climbed into the network of metal and wires of the transmitter and watched in amazement as Marutas lunged onto Artuke's back, dug in his claws and scaled the giant's spine. Artuke thrashed as he attempted to reach back and tear Marutas from his skin, but he couldn't reach. It was the last thing Eddy saw as he entered the maze of pipes.

The network of wires and metal was confusing to Eddy. He'd never seen alien technology in action before! How was he supposed to disable it? Of course, he knew he had a better chance at this than he did with Artuke. Eddy decided that the best strategy was to just start hacking. He swung his sword in a rage, sometimes severing wires and sometimes clanging against solid metal.

Through a space in the network of piping, Eddy caught a glimpse of the action outside. Marutas was at the base of Artuke's neck and almost in range of the giant's massive hands, which he was sure could squeeze the life from Marutas like a massive constrictor. Marutas slashed at Artuke's neck, causing him to shout in pain. Eddy covered his ears as he watched Marutas dig into the base of Artuke's skull, take aim with the lightning gun, and pull the trigger.

Blue energy crackled through the air and jolted into Artuke's skull. His humongous body shook as the energy tore through him. Muscles twitching from head to foot, Artuke looked done for. It was then that Eddy noticed Marutas was convulsing as well. He was shocking them both to death.

Remembering his own mission, Eddy continued hacking until one set of wires spewed sparks. Eddy looked up and saw that the dish was no longer moving. Did he stop it, or had it already stopped? Eddy wasn't sure. He looked back at the wire he had just cut and saw that he was only half way through the bunch. He swung again and severed the cable clean through. The wires exploded with sparks and the entire base of the transmitter began to shake.

That did it, Eddy thought as he worked his way out from the network of pipes and cables. Once free, he saw that the electricity had ceased and that Artuke was dumbly stumbling back and forth. Marutas still clung to Artuke's neck, but was hanging limp.

A shriek echoed through the colossal room and drew Eddy's attention to the ceiling. He saw the dish fall back toward the room, the telescoping arm sucking in segment after segment of metal, but then it caught. With a wrenching groan, the huge pole, pulled by gravity, began to bend. It fell like a tree cut half way up and swung down in an arc.

The dish fell like a razor sharp sickle and connected with the side of Artuke's skull, slicing, chopping the top of his cranium off like a ripe can-taloupe. His knees collapsed and his body lurched to the side and crashed to the floor.

Running as fast as he could, Eddy dove for cover behind the damaged vehicle, ducking with the others who had survived. A cacophony of twisting metal, falling flesh, and sparking wires filled the air like some kind of evil orchestra warming up. Then it was over.

Silence.

Eddy was the first to stand and inspect the damage. The transmitter was destroyed—a pile of rubble. Artuke's dead body lay still, his exposed brain, the size and shape of a Volkswagen Bug, was spilled out on the floor, slathered in the same purple blood that flowed through the Ferox. Next to the brain was a still, dark figure—Marutas.

His feet began moving even before Eddy knew what he was doing. He heard the others raise protest, but he ignored them. He broke out into a run and found himself kneeling down over Marutas's still form. The beast began to change and the old Inuit they had met a few days ago stared back at Eddy.

Marutas smiled and gazed at Eddy through human eyes. "You have inspired me, Eddy Moore . . . revealing to me that I have become what I loathe . . . and in return I give you a gift . . . free will. The choice to join in our war or abstain from it is now yours to make. The human race is now on its own . . . I hope when the choice comes . . . that you will choose . . . wisely."

Marutas's eyes closed and his body fell limp.

Eddy stood and for some reason he couldn't fathom, he began to cry. It could have been the relief that their ordeal was almost over. It could have been that he now feared the future, what would become of the human race without its secret society of leaders. But what worried Eddy the most was that he was sad to see Marutas die. This beast had tried to kill him and his friends, but his ideas, his goals, were understandable. If the war that waged through the cosmos ever reached Earth, he was sure humanity would become involved; but which side they would choose . . . that, at least, would be their choice.

☼　☼　☼　☼　☼

AFTER TWO hours of searching for an exit, the group found a ventilation shaft that ran to the outside. Stripped of their outer layers, the cold hit them like a spray of painful bullets, tearing at their skin. Steve shook. "This is stupid, guys. We sh-should go back inside. My nutage is shrinking back up inside my b-body!"

Eddy smiled, glad to see that Steve hadn't lost his sense of humor.

"He's right," Kevin said. "We're going to freeze to death out here. There might be food inside. We can try to find a way to contact the outside world."

Eve crossed her arms, half in defiance, half in an attempt to warm herself against the biting air that grew colder as every minute passed and the sun descended toward the horizon. "I, for one, would prefer to never set foot in there again."

"Okay, okay. I'm sorry," Eddy said as he looked into Eve's eyes. "But we need to go back inside. We're going to die of hypothermia if we stay out here for the night."

Eddy took a deep breath and let it slide out between his lips. "Here's what we're going to do. We'll spend a few days here, maybe two, collecting supplies and transportation if we can find it. Then we'll make a beeline south and see if we can hook up with civilization. Any problems with that?"

Eddy looked into everyone's eyes as he ran his fingers through his hair.

"You're the boss," Steve said.

Kevin gave a mock salute and a wide smile. "Aye, aye, captain."

Eddy met Eve's eyes and they stared at each other in silence for a moment. "I go where you go," she said.

Eddy smiled. "Have I told you I love you yet?"

Eve blinked twice and caught her breath. "W-what?"

Eddy's smiled widened. "I love you."

Eve threw herself into Eddy's arms and planted her freezing lips against his. The cold disappeared and a new hope filled them both.

Before Steve could say any of the several anecdotes that had entered his mind when Eve and Eddy kissed, a loud chopping sound fluttered through the frozen air.

Eddy looked up as he turned away from Eve's lips and he laughed out loud as he saw a helicopter floating sideways toward them. He could see Sam sitting in the open side and Mary in the pilot's seat.

Eddy turned to Eve. "Looks like you get to go home now."

"Will you be coming with me?" Eve asked.

"I go where you go."

Eve kissed Eddy again, pressing herself against him and forgetting the horrors of the past few days.

Steve waved his arms in the air. "Hey! Hey guys! Over here!"

"I think they see us," Kevin said, his face brimming with joy.

Steve squinted at Sam as he hung out the side. "What's he doing?"

Kevin looked, too. "I think that's a rifle . . ."

"Why's he aiming it at us?"

Kevin turned around and saw a white blur headed straight for Eddy and Eve. "Get down!" he shouted as he tackled Eddy and Eve to the ice.

A loud crack rang through the air and was followed by a loud thud. Kevin stood, sucking in air, eyes wide. "What the hell?"

Eddy turned his head to the side and looked into the dark, dead eyes of the same polar bear that had killed and eaten Paul. He pushed himself away and stood to his feet, pulling Eve up with him. As the helicopter landed on the flat ice in a tornado of snow, Steve walked up to the polar bear and kicked it as hard as he could. "That's for Paul." He finished by spiting on the bear and kicking it one more time.

Steve turned and headed for the chopper where Sam and Mary waited to deliver them from harm and grant them warm baths and hot food. Kevin followed Steve to the chopper and Eve followed, too. She turned back to Eddy, who was looking up at the glorious red towers of the

Aeros citadel. "The universe is an evil place," he said as he turned away from the citadel.

Eve placed her arm around Eddy and they walked toward the chopper together. "Do you think the entire universe is filled with evil creatures?"

"I'd like to think that the human race, left to our own devices, would have turned out okay. But we were given free will and it was our choice to follow the Ferox. With them gone, the evil we do will still be our choice." Eddy looked at Eve. "But when I look into your eyes, I'm convinced of the alternative. Evil isn't everywhere. We just need to choose what's good."

Eve looked up at Eddy, just before they entered the torrent of snow kicked up by the helicopter blades. "And what's your choice?"

Eddy smiled wide, feeling his heart beat relax for the first time in days. "I choose you."

EPILOGUE

DISTRESS

In the pitch black of space, a sphere of charcoal sat silhouetted against the bright blue of the Pacific Ocean, hundreds of miles below. One of the last of its kind, this orb had been waiting for thousands of years, like the others, but waiting for something different. While the other spherical satellites remained hidden like predatory cats, waiting to pounce on prey and wreak havoc, this one had been designed differently. The electronics that made the others lethal, weather-manipulating killing machines could not be found within the hard shell of this sphere.

This sphere was created for a single purpose of utmost importance: to intercept any Aeros signals that might leave the planet and report them directly to the Ferox leadership.

Its long wait was over.

The signal came in a quick burst. It was only ten seconds long and cut off abruptly, as though something at the source had disrupted the transmission. The escaped message came and went with the speed of light, originating from the Arctic north and heading toward the Aeros home world. The message was simple but clear—Earth belonged to the Ferox.

A single red light began to blink on the outer rim of the sphere's surface. The orb silently began spinning. Its red light soon became a blurry red line that streaked around the outer surface of the sphere.

Then in a blink, the sphere rocketed forward, but not toward Earth. The powerful bullet ripped through space, incinerating space dust and feeding itself on solar radiation. It was past the moon in ten seconds, through the elliptic path of Mars five minutes later. As it plowed through the asteroid belt and neared the swirling clouds of Jupiter, a bright flash opened up a hole in space. In an instant, quicker than the human eye could perceive, the sphere was gone from the solar system.

A blue circle of light glowed for an instant and was replaced by a yellow flash. The orb spilled out of space and slowed down as it entered a vast network of tubing. It moved forward at great speed, up and down, spinning around corners, like a rollercoaster devoid of passengers. It shot out of a perfectly carved exit and lazily lulled to a stop, dropping into a round depression, which held the sphere in place. A shadow fell over the sphere as a figure gazed down at it through six crimson eyes. The broad mouth filled with razor teeth turned down in a frown—good news was in short order these days.

The Aeros had been called to Earth.

ABOUT THE AUTHOR

Photograph by Tom Mungovan

JEREMY ROBINSON was born in Beverly, Massachusetts in 1974. He stayed in Beverly through college, attending Gordon College and Montserrat College of Art. His writing career began in 1995 and includes stints on comic books, and thirteen completed screenplays, several of which have been produced, optioned or have gone into development. He is also the author of two non-fiction books: *The Screenplay Workbook* and *POD People – Beating the Print-On-Demand Stigma* as well as the Barnes&Noble.com bestselling novel, *The Didymus Contingency.*

He currently resides in New Hampshire with his wife, Hilaree, daughter, Aquila and son, Solomon.

He can be reached via the web at www.jeremyrobinsononline.com or directly at info@jeremyrobinsononline.com.

ALSO AVAILABLE FROM
BREAKNECK BOOKS

THE LAST KNIGHT

By Eric Fogle

"...one of my top ten reads of the year and I would recommend that this book makes everyone's 'To Read' list..." –Fantasybookspot.

www.breakneckbooks.com/fog.html

By James Somers

"...a nice read of battle, honor, and spirituality... that left me wanting more." -- Fantasybookspot

www.breakneckbooks.com/soone.html

HEIR TO THE KING

SOME FREEDOMS ARE WORTH DYING FOR

By Sean Young

"...captures the imagination and transports you to another time, another way of life and makes it real." -- Jeremy Robinson, author of Raising the Past and The Didymus Contingency

www.breakneckbooks.com/sands.html

BREAKNECK BOOKS
PUBLISHING COMPANY

Printed in the United Kingdom
by Lightning Source UK Ltd.
121141UK00001B/157-159